Following the
Wrong God Home

CATHERINE LIM

ORION

An Orion paperback

First published in Great Britain in 2001
by Orion
This paperback edition published in 2002
by Orion Books Ltd,
Orion House, 5 Upper St Martin's Lane,
London WC2H 9EA

A CIP catalogue record for this book
is available from the British Library.

ISBN 0 75284 474 1

Typeset by Deltatype Ltd, Birkenhead
Printed and bound in Great Britain by
Clays Ltd, St Ives plc.

Critical acclaim for Catherine Lim

Catherine Lim grew up in Malaysia but lives and works in Singapore where she lectured in Applied Linguistics before turning to writing full time. She has published seven collections of short stories (two of which have been used as GCSE texts by Cambridge University), five novels, a book of poems and hundreds of articles.

By Catherine Lim

THE BONDMAID

THE TEARDROP STORY WOMAN

FOLLOWING THE WRONG GOD HOME

To Jean and Peter
with love

Part One

One

From the sky, a tiny blob of something fell and made a small whitish splatter on the front of the gleaming silver Mercedes, narrowly missing the bride and groom dolls perched on the nose amidst a froth of white and pink tulle. The chauffeur, Arasu, who had been patiently waiting for the last half-hour, got out and looked up to see a wildly fluttering dove in clumsy flight. Doves were lucky for weddings, shit was not. The luck and the shit cancelled each other out on the bridal car. The bride was beautiful, so much so that Arasu wanted to compliment her, being almost part of the family. But he held back. Later, he was to reveal to close friends, in a whisper, 'She looked sad.'

On her wedding day, on her way to church in the gleaming silver Mercedes 350 that drew admiring looks all the way down Pek Kiew Street and up MacGregor Road, Yin Ling felt an overwhelming sadness. It threatened to spill over in tears and spoil the meticulous makeup that had taken the beautician a full three hours that morning, at a cost of a cool five hundred dollars. The tears rose dangerously; in alarm, she beat them down and the expensive mascara and rouged cheeks were saved.

But only for a while. The sadness would not go away. It had come many times in her life, but not as stubbornly. It swirled inside her, a turgid stream seeking release. She had to do something quickly, or it would rise again, flood her eyes, splatter her cheeks, melt the five-hundred-dollar makeup, reduce the glory of the bridal ensemble of chiffon veil, duchesse satin gown, satin shoes, lace gloves and lilies that had cost three thousand dollars to a grey shambles of crushed dreams.

Concentration always did the trick. She focused her attention on the first object before her eyes: the bald patch at the back of the chauffeur's head. Smooth and gleaming, like polished brass, it had at its centre a few very fine almost invisible hairs, which she now studied intently, noting how, paler and softer than baby down, they trembled in a current of air coming from somewhere. She watched them sway and dance. The tears receded. She was saved – for now.

Her mother-in-law, who had insisted on accompanying her to church, had not noticed anything, fortunately. She was preoccupied with a full surveillance of the bridal gown. A perfectionist, she had efficiently divided the map of surveillance into precise grids for exhaustive checking, so that her sharp eyes, proceeding systematically from one square inch to the next, were able instantly to detect the smallest faults and her expert hands to effect the necessary correction. Thus, in quick succession, she saw a loose thread on the left sleeve, which she snipped off with the miniature scissors she always carried in her handbag, some specks of talcum powder near the neckline, which she deftly dusted off with her handkerchief, a hair caught in the fine lacework of the bridal glove, which she extricated.

Her mother-in-law, who seldom paid compliments, said, 'You are very beautiful today. I am not saying this because you are my daughter-in-law. Everyone knows Mrs Chee always speaks from the heart.' She had picked up from somewhere the magisterial habit of referring to herself in the third person.

She leant forward to speak impatiently to the chauffeur, who had turned on the car radio to catch a pre-election speech by some politician. 'Arasu, turn that off,' she said, and none other than the Founder of Modern Singapore, the great MTC, Mah Tiong Chin, known only by the awesome initials, was cut off in the middle of a sonorous denunciation of all those who would seek to harm the city-state: the Communists, the trade-union activists, the religious ultras, the racists, the subversives, the leader of the opposition, V. S. Ponnusamy.

The cheek of the man. Turning on the radio for his own entertainment, in a bridal car. She would have to complain to her son, Vincent.

A slave to her perfectionism, Mrs Chee had not slept all night, worrying about the smallest details of the wedding. At one point, she had got up to check that the *longan* tea, which was to be used for the tea ceremony after the church service, had been brewed properly by the maid. It was of the best quality, imported from Taiwan.

And would Luan remember to use the red satin pouch for the receiving of the *ang pows* from the guests at the wedding dinner, instead of some ugly cash-box with a slit in the centre? Her sister tended to be forgetful. Really, the bride's side should have offered to help in the preparations. But one could expect nothing from Yin Ling's cold, uncommunicative mother. Oh, oh, not the ordinary red satin pouch but the one with the dragon embossed in gold thread. She must remember to tell Luan.

Mrs Chee's memory, ever efficient, stacked up this extra reminder. She took out of her handbag a small bottle of Tiger Balm, which she rubbed delicately on each temple. Then, with eyes tightly closed, she inhaled its soothing pungency. It was a small interruption only; soon she was back at her work of inspection.

5

Only vaguely aware of the fussily adjusting fingers moving all over her, Yin Ling submitted meekly to the next stage of the checking process, which concerned the bridal jewels. She had no idea what had been put into her ear-lobes, round her neck, at her chest, wrists and on her fingers by her mother-in-law that morning; she had only a faint recollection of a tingling sensation as enormous, blindingly sparkling diamonds were snapped, clipped, clasped, pinned, slipped and hung on her. Someone had stood her in front of the mirror to see the overall effect. She remembered thinking, I look like a Christmas tree, but of course said nothing, not wanting to sound ungrateful. The jewels had been taken out of her mother-in-law's deposit box in the bank vault only the day before, and would be duly returned, presumably after the gala wedding dinner at the Grand Winchester Hotel. For other occasions there were exact duplicates in paste, which could be worn freely and without fear, even on holiday.

'You want a robber to rip off your ear-lobes or chop off your fingers for paste?' Vincent had teased.

'At least the real things will still be safe in the bank for posterity.' She had laughed. It was a practice universal among the rich and bejewelled in Singapore. Mrs Chee, who had the pleasure of seeing her prized collection on display only rarely, maintained a dignified restraint, adjusting the huge dangling ear-rings only once, the enormous star-shaped pendant twice.

If Yin Ling were to carry out her own surveillance of her wedding apparel, she might find something secretly sewn into the hem of the skirt – an amulet blessed by the priests of the Kek Lok Thong Temple, or a tiny roll of prayer paper conferring luck, health, prosperity, progeny, long life on the wedding couple. On her way to the Cathedral of the Divine Saviour for her wedding, she wore, hidden in her dress, the powers of ancient, pagan gods.

'Oh, it's nothing,' her mother-in-law would be sure to say, with a quick laugh and a wave of the hand, if discovered and confronted, as had happened years ago when her son had located and ripped out a tiny jade amulet sewn into the seam of his trousers, on the day of his final-year university exams. Once powerful, Mrs Chee's gods were now made to work in stealth, stitched into the clothes of the unsuspecting, ungrateful young. Her son, now waiting for them in the cathedral with Father da Costa, basking in the warm glow of joyous Christian hymns, might be pretending not to notice the small, hard lump in a corner of his suit pocket, the ancient gods' promise of many sons. A god's tear-drop. It did not matter, as the amulet, blessed by the temple priests, was prized by its intimate association with divinity.

'My mother's usual nonsense,' was Vincent's usual explanation. He spoke with the highest filial regard of his mother's nonsense, for he was able to separate the pure gold of mother love from the dross of absurd traditions.

False gods, true gods – Yin Ling would concentrate on anything to keep back those tears. For she discovered, to her dismay, that Arasu's bald patch was losing its hold – and one by one, each alternative subject that came into her mind, soon fell away from it.

Oh, Ben, Ben.

In desperation, she looked away from her mother-in-law and out of the window. She saw a succession of images, increasingly blurred, for the tears were filling her eyes now – the Cathay cinema advertising some John Travolta movie, a McDonald's restaurant crowded with boys and girls in white and brown school uniforms, a lifesize cut-out of the celebrated 'Singapore Girl', advertising Kodak films, with her radiant smile and demure *batek* sarong-and-blouse, a skinny, sunburnt trishawman trying to coax an oversized tourist in

Hawaiian floral shirt and bermudas into his vehicle, a newly opened noodle bar, its front adorned by a row of congratulatory bouquets ostentatiously mounted on tripods, a shop sign in awful English – 'Sale! Best bargain! Customer not satisfy, money will return!' – a young woman in a black power suit and high heels, carrying a black leather briefcase, hurriedly crossing the road, a huge signboard with a picture of a lung in the last stages of cancer, a warning to smokers.

The Mercedes glided past three young motorcyclists, each with a female pillion rider, all wearing identical glittery crash helmets, all with the air of excited expectancy at the start of a race. One of the happy pairs was likely to end up smashed on the road – the accident statistics were high for reckless motorcyclists. One of the pairs looked up, saw her peering through the car window, smiled, waved and shouted something – probably 'Good luck!' or 'Congrats!'

Now her mother-in-law saw. She said, frowning, 'What's the matter?' A young girl about to marry Vincent Chee Wen Siong, who had been included among Singapore's Fifty Most Eligible Bachelors by *Lifestyle* magazine and singled out for grooming in public service by the Minister for National Development – who was probably among the waiting guests in the cathedral – this young girl, who came from a family of low status, whose deceased father, a known gambler, once went to jail for his debts, whose mother was unfriendly and sour-faced, who had nothing to recommend her beyond a university degree and moderate beauty and who stood to inherit all those jewels now on loan, had no right to look unhappy on her wedding day. With a snort of pure pique, the future mother-in-law might even have been provoked to say, 'It's my Vincent who should be crying!' or 'It's Mrs Chee who should look unhappy, I tell you!'

Mrs Chee had known only a little about Yin Ling's troubles

of the preceding months, for as she often complained, 'My son never tells me anything.' But she knew enough to decide now, on their way to church, to deliver a bright, sharp little lecture to this new member of her family. 'We have a good family name. When Vincent's father was alive, he was one of the most respected members of the Chee clan. He was a personal friend of the late Sultan of Johor. His sister married the late Attorney-General. You are marrying into our family. Vincent has chosen you. I don't know what happened, and I don't want to know.'

Of course she knew what had happened. She knew of the *ang moh* involved, for Mrs Chee kept her eyes and ears open at all times. If she had had her way, any girl who got involved with any of those white foreigners, with their drinking and womanising, would have been instantly eliminated as a potential daughter-in-law.

'I leave it to my son to tell me what he wants,' she said. 'You young people have your problems, I have mine. All I want is for you to remember that, as Vincent's wife, you have to preserve the good name of our family.' She broke off and said irritably to the chauffeur, 'Arasu, why are you taking this route?' It had occurred to Arasu to take a different road to avoid the traffic jam that always formed along Orchard Road at this time of day and he had to take part of the blame for what happened next.

The Mercedes was negotiating a narrow road called Hin Ngiap Lane that skirted one of the oldest housing estates in Singapore, soon to be redeveloped in a major upgrade of government property. The multi-storey block of flats stood in its present dereliction in the desolation of a children's playground vandalised beyond all repair. Its inhabitants were mainly old and retired or young and embittered. There was an old metal rubbish skip, painted green, next to the playground, and near it a crowd had gathered, forming a circle to look at something on the ground. Their serious expressions, the quiet whispering among them, suggested a discovery of tragedy, their inaction that there was nothing to do but wait for the police to come. Meanwhile, they gazed with undisguised fascination at the dead body on the ground. A woman came running up to pull away a man, presumably her husband, clearly fearing messy involvement once the police arrived and started questioning witnesses.

Mrs Chee said sharply, 'Arasu, drive faster.' Even the faintest glimpse of death was bad on a wedding day. When she had got married, thirty years ago, the car taking her and her husband to the photo studio for their bridal photograph had had to make a detour to avoid a funeral procession. She had heard the clashing of cymbals, the wail of trumpets, had caught sight of the huge, flower-and-banner-bedecked lorry carrying the coffin, but, fortunately, not of the coffin itself. Still, her mother had afterwards made her wash her face in water purified by prayers and flower petals.

Mrs Chee said, 'Arasu, I told you to drive faster.'

Yin Ling leant forward and said, in a voice shaking with urgency, 'Stop!'

Arasu said, turning slightly, 'Eh, madam? What?'

Yin Ling made the puzzled Arasu stop.

'What are you doing?' gasped her mother-in-law, but Yin Ling was already out of the car making her way towards the crowd near the rubbish dump, holding up her long wedding dress with both gloved hands.

An elderly man and a woman next to him were the first to notice her. They stared; the woman nudged her neighbour who also looked up. She was joined by two others, one of whom pointed and said something excitedly. In a short while, everyone in the crowd had shifted their attention from the body to the beautiful bride in their midst. A stunned silence fell as they fixed their eyes on her.

Men in rough T-shirts, shorts and sandals, women in cotton blouses and trousers, an old man in a white singlet and faded pyjama bottoms, carrying his lunch in a brown paper packet tied with string and looped around two fingers, a child with a dribbling nose and a Mickey Mouse cap on his head all stared at her, in her bridal gown, her jewels sparkling, a visitor from the other side, who had succeeded in moving out of the dank, dismal flats into a gleaming new house with a garden. She merited more stares than the dead body on the ground. Half expecting to see a camera-toting television crew emerge, set up their equipment and bark instructions to the bride-model, they began to realise that this intrusion was real, not make-believe.

Ignoring them, Yin Ling stood over the victim laid on a spread of newspapers. It was a tiny newborn baby, still with its umbilical cord attached, its face blue, its little naked body remarkably well formed. It lay peacefully in its crumpled nest of old newspapers, its head blocking out the smiling faces of George and Barbara Bush, its bottom a fiery speech by MTC to the Workers' Union, its tiny toes touching the beautiful face of a young model in a Triumph bra. An abandoned newborn, one of a number regularly left alive on doorsteps, at bus-stops, outside hospitals, or thrown down rubbish chutes or into garbage dumps, probably still alive at this point but not likely to survive cold, hunger, the impact of flung bottles, cans and boxes, the attack of scavenging cats and rats. Somebody must have found the baby, raised the alarm then laid it on the ground, afraid to do anything further while waiting for the police. A still alive baby would have been wrapped immediately in a warm towel and taken to hospital for compassionate

11

attention; a dead baby merited only curious, pitying stares before being taken away by the police.

Yin Ling stooped down and picked up the body. She held it in her arms, moving aside the enormous, star-shaped pendant to let it nestle, unobstructed, on her chest. A fly buzzed on its left eyelid, and she brushed it off. The crowd watched silently. If she had looked up then and asked questions – who found the baby, when, where, how? – they would have fidgeted, looked down, remained silent or slunk away.

Yin Ling never looked up. She continued to hold the baby and look at it. She thought its mother was probably a frightened teenager, one of the hundreds of students or factory girls who had been made pregnant by boyfriends, strangers, fathers. She thought of sex: she had a vivid image of the precise moment of the baby's conception, a moment of raw, brutal passion when a man, in the stealth of night, broke through his daughter's resistance and small, fragile body, then got up, zipped his trousers, warned her not to tell anyone, and left the room. Reports of such brutality sometimes surfaced in the *National Times*. She saw the girl getting up, pulling her clothes tightly around her, going to the bathroom to wash out the red, searing pain. More sex – the man, meeting no resistance, came the night after and the night after that.

Yin Ling held the baby, aware now that her overwhelming sadness was in some way connected with it and its desperate mother, its savage father. Suffer the little children: ironic use of the word. The dead baby in her arms proliferated into a hundred dead babies and living children who might have been better off dead, away from the crushing weight of pain and deprivation on their young years. She remembered a visit to a neighbouring country with Vincent and his mother only the year before, where dirty, skinny children with matted hair

12

followed them everywhere. She remembered a hungry-looking little girl carrying a naked baby on her thin hip, both covered with sores. One of Vincent's mother's rings could convert into several years' freedom from hunger for her and her baby brother. The arithmetic of guilt must have hit all three of them at once, for together they had flung handfuls of coins into the crowd before fleeing back to their hotel. She was the worst of them all because she had been the first to flee from the horror and the pity. Better off dead? She had seen the small son of one of Vincent's cousins, replete with toys, cry miserably for a special fire engine that happened to be out of stock, and she had seen a magazine picture of a group of children in a war-torn neighbouring country all horribly maimed by landmines, happily kicking a football and smiling for the camera.

She looked up for the first time at the circle of faces watching her and was aware that the sadness was connected with them too. The men in the rough T-shirts and dirty sandals – what sort of lives did they lead? The old man with his lunch dangling from his fingers – could he be the man she had read about in the newspapers some time ago, who had gone eagerly to China to find a young wife, and had come back, sad and bitter, cleaned out of his entire life's savings? The old man would probably be dead in a few years, dragging his dream with him to the grave.

She looked beyond the crowd, fixing her eyes on the decaying flats in the background, where men and women would continue to have sex, have children, have their children fulfil their dreams of moving out into the promised land of bright houses and condominiums and swimming-pools, have children who would turn out cold and callous, dashing their dreams, hurrying them towards that moment of fatal decision by the railings, that desperate plunge down ten storeys to the ground below. Those tall Housing Development Board buildings – what hadn't they seen in their time? In her own block of flats, there had been two suicides: an old woman, suffering from cancer, had lit a last joss-stick to honour her gods before leaping from the twelfth floor; a fruit-seller whose wife had left him and their two small children threw down one child, then the second, before plunging to his own death, from the eighteenth.

Birth, sex, life, death, betrayal, pain, hope. The gods brooding in the darkness of their shrines, temples, churches stopped their ears against the cries and said, 'Don't blame us.' No longer an abstraction, no longer a topic for cosy discussion in a café or for the writing of clever poems in Yin Ling's elegant, gold-embossed black notebook, the suffering poor came together in a shrieking coalescence and hit her hard, so that she had to steady herself and make sure she did not drop the baby.

She heard shouts and turned to see her mother-in-law running towards her, panting and gasping, holding one shoe in her hand and waving it wildly so that the crowd moved out of range of its menacing power. But there was no menace, only fear. Mrs Chee had scrambled out of the car, broken into a run and tripped on the high heels newly bought for the wedding. One shoe had fallen off and she had picked it up and continued her run to reach her future daughter-in-law. Her fear centred on the Chee jewels: she had to prevent them being snatched off by the hostile crowd in the slummy area to which the girl – insanity of insanities – had exposed herself. All those diamonds from her safe-deposit box, in the midst of a hungry, rapacious, thieving crowd.

Seeing the dead baby cradled against bridal white, Mrs Chee let out a scream. The fear, this time, was a greater one, rooted in the deepest core of a thousand-year-old tradition that required the living to respect the dead, but to avoid, at all cost, the taint of death's touch, especially upon a bridal day.

Mrs Chee dropped the shoe and rushed forward to prise bride from dead baby. Within a few inches of them, she stopped and backed off: she, too, must be protected from harm. She turned to face the parked Mercedes and shouted to Arasu to come and help. Only vaguely aware of the faces crowding in upon her, she screamed at her daughter-in-law to put the baby back where she had found it and get back to the car. Watching the girl lay the dead baby gently back on the newspapers, the long diamond ear-rings shaking with her movements, Mrs Chee was seized by a return of the first fear and started screaming again, for a quick return to the car to save the jewels. Overcome by both fears, she burst into tears.

By that time, Arasu had come up. With admirable calm and cool efficiency, he waved away the still staring crowd and guided the two women back to the Mercedes, only pausing to pick up the shoe, which Mrs Chee had dropped in her confusion.

Back in the car, Mrs Chee stopped crying, struck by the urgency of a need even greater than that of getting to the church in time and not keeping the Minister for National Development waiting. She would remember that day, the wedding day of her son, for the incredible demands made on her quick thinking to avert disaster. 'You would never, never believe it,' she was later to tell her friends. For she had seen the stain on the bridal gown, a small, pale smudge under the left breast. The blood of a dead child. 'Arasu, drive straight to the Kek Lok Thong Temple. Tank Road. Quick.' The temple was at least half an hour's drive away.

Arasu said, 'But, madam—' and was screamed down.

Yin Ling, noticing the stain, began cleaning it off with saliva.

Her mother-in-law said tersely, 'It's no use.' These would be the only words she would speak to her daughter-in-law for the rest of the day. As for her son, she would wait for the wedding to be over to tell him of the day's madness.

Yin Ling had only a vague sensation of being driven along an unfamiliar route. She found herself thinking, in a calm, detached manner, of the anxiously waiting congregation in the cathedral, of Vincent looking repeatedly at his watch and apologising to the Minister for National Development, of her mother, in neat, prim *cheongsam* sitting in the front row, staring impassively ahead. She looked out of the window and read calmly the names of the roads they passed: Ransome Road, Yusuf Road, Ban Tong Avenue, Mulberry Lane, Empire Road. The ubiquitous Singapore Girl in her lovely sarong. A florist's shop, embracing European chic by calling itself 'De Flower Shop'. A row of grimy old pre-war shop-houses, about to be pulled down, one already reduced by fire to a skeleton of charred timbers. Old and new Singapore glided by, as she sat watching in her bridal car.

A little girl with elaborate corn-row braids decorated with multi-coloured beads sitting in the back of a passing car, her nose pressed to the window, saw her and turned excitedly to tell a woman by her side. The woman held up the child's arm in a friendly wave. Yin Ling waved back. She suddenly thought of Ah Heng Cheh, her faithful old servant, who was not allowed to attend the wedding in case her senility, more troublesome than a child's restive naughtiness at a public ceremony, caused her to say or do strange things in front of guests. Ah Heng Cheh was probably asleep in her room at home, or praying to her god on his altar. Or she might simply be talking to him, as she had recently become accustomed to do.

At the Kek Lok Thong Temple, her mother-in-law led her quickly to an altar, found a bowl of holy water and began to

16

sprinkle her with it. She stood quietly, aware of a few staring faces, of a woman making deep bows before a black-faced deity, clasping in both hands an enormous bunch of lit joss-sticks that sent up clouds of acrid-smelling smoke. She felt a few drops of cold holy water touch her face, neck and arms. The evil emanations from the little corpse had been dispelled.

She was ready once more to be driven to the Cathedral of the Divine Saviour for her wedding to Vincent.

Oh, Ben, Ben.

Two

If, years later, after he had left Singapore and returned to his job as a lecturer at Berkeley, Ben Gallagher had been asked where he and Yin Ling had first noticed each other, he might have got both the place and the date wrong. She would remember precise details – a Sunday evening in February 1984, exactly a year before her wedding, at the Monckton Food Park, in the seafood section. Exactly three seafood stalls – 'Ah Meng Lobster', 'Monckton Best Seafood' and 'Best Good Luck Hairy Crab' – had stood between them. The Monckton food-sellers were renowned for harassing customers, overcharging, making rude remarks: that Sunday a durian seller and his assistants had formed a menacing ring round a couple who had smelt and prodded the fruit without intending to buy it, and the steamed-crayfish-seller had presented such an enormous bill to a group of Japanese tourists that they overcame both shock and innate politeness to question and argue.

When the government's courtesy campaign moved on to target rude shopkeepers and hawkers – surveys had shown that tourists invariably ranked courteous service among the top three things they looked for – the Monckton Food Park was at the top of the list. Yet the place unfailingly drew tourists and locals alike, its celebrated steamed lobster and chilli crab, satay, oyster omelette and *roti prata* known as far away as New York, Amsterdam and Tokyo.

Vincent was cutting up roasted pork for old Ah Heng Cheh, whose few remaining teeth could no longer manage meat but who rebelled, like a child, against her regular diet of rice porridge. His mother was sitting opposite them, and he directed her attention, without looking up from the pork, to a table some distance away, where a young, tanned, long-haired girl in daring blouse and daring tight trousers stood smiling and talking to a blue-eyed, brown-haired, bearded man, presumably a tourist, in a loud Hawaiian shirt and shorts, who was eating chilli crab with his hands.

Monckton Food Park discouraged soliciting but could do nothing about it. As soon as the city lights went up, the girls poured out from nobody knew where and hung around in the open-air eating places and bars where tourists and expatriates would be found. They were young, mobile and fluent in English, and displayed a fine selectivity: they had no time for the local men, thank you very much, with their gauche ways, their pretentious Rolex watches, massive jade rings and toothpicks dangling vulgarly from their lips, and whose rough Hokkien accent reduced the English language to a mish-mash of unintelligible sounds. The girls, young, pretty, sophisticated, wearing mini-skirts and tank tops and carrying Gucci bags, disdained to be even remotely associated with the tired, jaded, non-English-speaking women in the famous Desker Road, Little India and Geylang districts, who received, alike, businessmen coming in stealth in their Mercedes-Benzes, and construction workers with the grime still on their clothes and in their fingernails. There were two distinct classes of working females in Singapore, each with its own distinctive clientele.

'Look,' said Vincent, as slips of paper, bearing phone numbers, passed between the long-haired girl and the bearded man. But, still laughing, she was already leaving the table and he had resumed eating.

19

Mrs Chee said severely, 'That's why we're having more and more of it in Singapore.' Herpes. Gonorrhoea. And now Aids. The government issued warning statistics, warning posters flashed on TV and movie screens. But Mrs Chee spoke with the detachment of one whose world was far removed from that of disease-carrying girls and easy tourists. She watched her son meticulously cutting up the roasted pork for old Ah Heng Cheh. His solicitousness for any other would have aroused maternal jealousy, but for an old servant who belonged to another family it merited rebuke. Mrs Chee said, with a sharp little laugh, 'Vincent, you never do that for your mother.'

'You have all your teeth intact, Mother,' said Vincent, and proceeded to shake some sauce and pepper on to the cut pieces, exactly as the Old One liked it. Yin Ling thought, If I could love him for nothing else, I would love him for this. Not even her own family had shown this kind of attention to a much-loved servant, long past her years of service. Yin Ling's mother and brother had already said, 'After your marriage, we should think of putting her in a home.' Ah Heng Cheh had begun to give a lot of trouble in her old age. As each year came round, everyone expressed surprise that she was still alive.

Vincent turned to Yin Ling and said, 'Watch,' the object this time being much more respectable. The Minister for National Development in a casual *batek* shirt was leaving the food park with his wife and two daughters after a meal. He turned, saw Vincent and actually came over, his family following. He was a gracious man.

'You were the president of the Students' Union, some years ago, weren't you?' he said, shaking Vincent's hand. 'I saw you on TV. I recognised you at once.' Vincent told him he was at present doing a Ph.D.

'Good! Good!' said the Minister affably.

'This is Yin Ling, my fiancée,' said Vincent proudly, putting an arm around her shoulder. 'She's doing a master's course in linguistics.' A couple at a nearby table heard and looked up, impressed.

'Good! Good!' said the Minister again.

He included Mrs Chee, Ah Heng Cheh and Yin Ling in his broad smile, also the admiring couple at the nearby table who had recognised him, and then he was gone. Yin Ling saw the flush of pleasure on Vincent's face. His mother said, 'What a nice man. Not arrogant like some of them,' thinking of MTC who was the most arrogant of all. The flush spread to Vincent's neck and ears. Others reddened with embarrassment, Vincent with joy.

Slim and trim, he expressed joy in eating and seeing others eat. He ordered liberally, and soon the table was crowded with plates, bowls, tureens of hot, steaming, delicious-smelling food.

'Too much, too much,' complained his mother, but he continued to summon the stall attendants with more orders. Every time they went out to eat, she brought home packets of left-over food.

The chilli crab was a must. It came in a huge platter, the crab claws thoughtfully pre-broken so that one just had to use one's fingers to pull out the luscious meat, then clean them in small bowls of hot water freshened with cut lime. The crab came in a generous smothering of the famous chilli-garlic-egg-white sauce, and was so tasty that every bit was soaked up by small squares of white bread provided for that purpose.

Monckton Food Park had managed to get its chilli crab into the brochures that the Tourist Promotion Board disseminated worldwide. 'Monckton Food Park,' said the American tourists invariably to their tour guides, pointing to the brochures. 'And what's a hairy crab? Four Organs Soup?'

Vincent said, still flushed with pleasure, 'Ling, shall I order some to take back to your mother?' Yin Ling's mother steadfastly but politely turned down all invitations to join in the happy food outings, disliking the very sight of Mrs Chee, the very sound of her voice.

Vincent ordered chilli crab for his future mother-in-law. His love for his fiancée overflowed in generosity towards everyone connected with her. Women could love, truly and deeply, from gratitude alone. She thought, How good he is to me, his generosity the greater for his daring to defy his formidable mother, who was already compressing and twisting her lips, and looking this way and that, a sure sign of her displeasure.

He left to get Yin Ling's favourite *popiah*, at the far end of the food park, before it sold out. When he returned, his mother said, 'You will have no time for your own dinner if you keep looking after other people.' But there was one more person to see to – herself. Vincent practically quarrelled with the *laksa* seller for forgetting to put in the mint leaves without which she could never eat *laksa*.

Beaming with contentment, Vincent surveyed the three women in his life, whom he had so conscientiously looked after – his mother, his fiancée and his fiancée's old servant, whom he had promised to take care of after their marriage. He gave his fiancée's hand an affectionate, surreptitious squeeze under the table. She smiled at him.

A child of about eight or nine, with a serious adult face, came to their table. Hovering in the background, looking on nervously, was a thin, sickly-looking woman, probably his mother. The boy had some small sheets of paper in his hand. No, he was not selling lottery tickets. No, he was not selling anything. Vincent, who invariably shook his head in vigorous dismissal at any approaching vendor, was prepared to hear what the serious-faced child had to say. In a monotone, the boy proposed a game and explained the rules, probably for the tenth time that evening, for the hundredth time in his self-appointed role of family breadwinner, extracting money from rich Singaporeans and tourists to support his sickly mother and possibly a brood of younger siblings. The sheet of paper showed crudely drawn lines for the game of noughts and crosses. If Vincent won, he would get two dollars. If he lost, he would have to pay only one. The boy, his thin, sharp little face devoid of expression, waited for an answer.

'Think of the psychological ingenuity,' said Vincent, highly impressed, to Yin Ling. 'Who would want to win money off an urchin like this? He must be making tons of money every night.' He surveyed the urchin's shorts, skilfully tattered for the occasion, the T-shirt cleverly oversized, falling over one shoulder. 'With even half that ingenuity he would do excellently at school.' He turned back to the boy and said, 'Are you at school? What's your name? Do your parents know what you're doing?'

The boy who, all this while, had been holding out his hand with the noughts and crosses sheet, abruptly withdrew it and shot off, nimble as a monkey. They next saw him at the table of two elderly ladies still in their tourist sunhats. One of the ladies had obligingly begun the game. The boy stood beside her, watching intently.

'It's outrageous,' said Vincent, 'that we do not have compulsory education in Singapore. Our MPs should be debating this in Parliament. One of these days, if . . .' He always expressed his ambition modestly, with a conditional, in an unfinished sentence. A hundred issues of national interest, particularly those related to education and caring of the elderly, buzzed around in his head, but they could wait.

A woman with matted hair and smelly clothes came up. Begging was not allowed. The woman asked for a dollar for her son who, she said, had just had an operation. Mrs Chee said, 'One can't eat in peace here.'

Vincent said, not looking at the woman, who was boldly thrusting forward an upward-facing palm, 'Begging is not allowed.' When he was president of the Singapore University Students' Union some years ago, he had regularly organised fund-raising events for at least a dozen charities, one of which picked up such vagrants and took care of them. He added to Yin Ling, 'Don't. It will only encourage begging,' but was too late to prevent her slipping some money to the woman. Despite her bleary eyes, Ah Heng Cheh saw, said something incomprehensible and chuckled. 'You could write a poem about her, you know,' said Vincent smiling. Yin Ling hid her poems from him but, as her fiancé, claiming entitlement to her body, mind and soul, he searched out the precious notebook of her most private thoughts, and when caught leafing through it, assumed a casual air and continued reading for a calculated few more seconds before tossing the book aside with studied ease. Yin Ling looked down, pained. He saw, and was contrite. 'Sorry,' he said, and gave her hand another affectionate squeeze.

It was Mrs Chee's turn to say, 'Look.' There was a commotion going on at a table some distance away. The occupants seemed to be quarrelling, waving angry fists, shouting at each other. At a closer look, the scene resolved into two confronting parties, unmatched in numbers: on one side was a crowd, comprising a man and woman, their three young sons and an elderly woman, and on the other, the single adversary, a dark-skinned girl, in T-shirt and sandals, clearly the Filipino maid. The couple and the maid were shouting at each other, standing over what appeared to be an

24

abruptly terminated meal of rice and noodles. The man raised his hand and the maid screamed. Later, in court, the man would say that he never touched her, he was only threatening her because she was shouting abuse at him in front of so many people. Suddenly the girl broke away and the man dashed after her, followed by his wife, while the rest of the family stood huddled together, watching tensely.

An empty Coca-Cola bottle fell to the floor and smashed, causing someone to give a little scream, and it was at this point that some of the onlookers, fearing trouble, hurriedly gathered up their things and left, while others decided to stay to watch what promised to be a tantalising after-dinner diversion.

The girl, screaming, dashed hither and thither, chased by the man. She ran to a table where two couples sat, and sobbed out to them, 'Help me!' Sensing trouble, the two men and two women looked away, intensely uncomfortable. The men gestured to the women to get away first, which they did, gathering up their handbags and shopping, looking away from the pleading maid. They were joined by more people hurrying away. The tables around the maid were soon emptied of their occupants.

Vincent said, 'Let's go,' and helped Ah Heng Cheh up. The old servant protested that she had not finished eating. 'Let's go,' he repeated, for Yin Ling was staring at the girl, now on her knees, clinging to the leg of the bearded foreigner in the Hawaiian shirt. Vincent said, 'What are you looking at? Let's leave,' but Yin Ling would not move.

The girl's accusations against her employer came out in sobbing fragments – 'Sir . . . slapped me . . . Mam hit me . . . iron . . . the dog . . .'

By this time, the pursuing man had caught up with her. His face taut with fury, his fists clenched, he said, 'You come home this minute,' at which she let out a shriek and clung more tightly to the bearded man's leg.

The bearded man raised her to her feet. 'What on earth—' he said.

The employer, ignoring him and livid with rage, said to the girl, 'I'm taking you to the police station now. You can say whatever you like. I'm making a report. Then I'm putting you on the next flight home. You can collect your salary from your agency at Wellington Street. You are a thief, and an immoral woman.' He said this loudly, for the benefit of those looking on. By this time his wife had come up, and said, 'She stole my mother-in-law's gold bracelet!' She felt it incumbent on herself to explain further and turned to address the onlookers. 'We even took her out with us to eat in restaurants—'

'I didn't . . . They beat me, locked me in,' howled the maid, pressing herself against the bearded man, like a frightened child. Then she bent her head, her long thick hair covering her face like a black curtain, and stood very still. 'Sir, I don't want to go. Don't let them, sir . . . please.'

'What's going on?' said the bearded man. 'The girl's clearly in distress—'

'You stay out of this,' said the employer belligerently, addressing him for the first time. 'You foreigners think you're so high and mighty!'

His wife repeated, 'You foreigners!'

'Wait a minute!' said the bearded man.

'Ling, I said to go,' said Vincent and pulled her away. Yin Ling continued to stare. She saw the employer and the bearded man now facing each other and shouting.

'You foreigners think you can interfere!'

'You're a bully and a bastard!'

'You foreigners are shit!'

'What's the matter with you?' This time Vincent showed his

annoyance. His good mood was gone. As she walked away with him, she turned quickly to have a last look, and saw, with a start, the bearded man looking at her. Perhaps it was the intensity of her gaze that had drawn his: right in the midst of a brewing storm, when all his energies should have been mobilised for fight or flight, the man had suddenly turned to stare at her. She had a glimpse, as Vincent hurried her away, of his return to the fight. He had a protective arm around the frightened girl and was saying loudly, 'I'm prepared to testify in court.'

There had been moments in her life when a secret thought became a fervent wish that became desperate longing. Inexplicably, she longed to see this man again.

Inside the car, on the way home, Vincent began to talk about the encounter with the Minister for National Development, in a return of good spirits. His mother chose to talk about troublesome maids and foreign visitors.

If only, Yin Ling thought. The longing had become almost palpable and that night would enlarge the moment at which their eyes had met.

Years later, she remembered to ask him if he had testified. For she did not remember reading about the case in the papers.

But he was not interested in talking about the maid. Turning to face her and drawing up her hands to lay them against the prickliest part of his beard, a peculiar prelude to tenderness, he said, 'Let's talk about you.'

She said, 'There's nothing to say about me. Let's talk about Ah Heng Cheh.' He was not interested in Ah Heng Cheh either. By now his face was pressed on hers, his arms strongly, warmly wrapping her. She remonstrated, half laughing, aware of the impending danger but loving him. 'Ben, she's kept herself alive so far. She may not last much longer.' Her love for this man, overpowering, perilous, needed to steady itself against some noble purpose: 'We have to help Ah Heng Cheh fulfil her dream.'

Three

Ah Heng Cheh had a dream. In it, as usual, she was on a long journey, walking along one deserted track after another in unknown country. Her feet were blistered and one track continued to lead to another with no end in sight. No houses, no people. A child in the distance, a stray dog, even a bird in the sky would have been comforting. It was truly forsaken country. A wind arose, causing her blouse to flap around her. It even loosened the neat knot of hair at the back of her head, so that she had to pause to redo it. On and on she trudged, cradling in her arms the small statue of her beloved god, wrapped respectfully in a piece of soft red satin.

Finally, she saw something that made her heart beat with gladness. It was a gate at the end of a track. The gatekeeper, an old man with a long white beard and very bushy white eyebrows, asked, 'Old Mother, where are you going?'

She said, 'To find the home of my god-with-no-home. I've been trying to do this for fifty years. Can you help me?'

The old man said, 'Have you any money?'

She brought some out of a deep pocket inside her blouse, but it was the wrong money, being that of living people. The old man, looking at the small pile of notes and coins lying on her palm, shook his head. 'You'll have to go back, Old Mother.'

'But I have come such a long way!'

'There's nothing I can do, Old Mother.'

She turned sadly to begin the long journey back. She had failed her god again. He would continue to pine to go home. Disappointed gods, like children, broke into tears. She gently lifted a corner of the satin wrapping and saw a large one rolling down his face. It made her want to cry too. 'Don't cry,' she said. 'I always keep my promises. You have served me so well in your time. This is the least I can do for you.'

Ah Heng Cheh told her dreams only to Yin Ling, for no one else would listen. She told stories of her little god, of his many acts of kindness, but of where he came from, she knew nothing. In her old age, she asked urgently, 'Who will help me return my god to his home?'

In her old age, her tales of her god became more and more outrageous. As a young girl in China, she had gone one day to get some firewood from a forest, and was returning when a bolt of lightning appeared in the sky and chased her, until it was beaten back by her god. On another occasion, a demon from the First Court of Hell appeared and terrorised their village. 'Help us,' she said to her god, and he instantly vanquished the demon. Again and again, the grinning, snub-nosed god, with no power but kindness in his heart, saved them from evil. But now he was getting old and tired, and wanted to go home.

Yin Ling, studying late into the night, going through her lecture notes, working on course assignments, would see Ah Heng Cheh standing by the door, unable to sleep and, like a fretful child, needing the comfort of attention. The young whispered among themselves about the smells emanating from old bodies, intimations of mortality, ineradicable by soap or shampoo; Ah Heng Cheh, sleepless at night and wandering around, smelt. Yin Ling's mother had said several times to her, 'Do something about it. You're the only one she listens to.'

Her brother Kwan had said, 'It's the joss-sticks. A dry and musky smell. Not too unpleasant once you get used to it.'

Tales, tales! How ardently Ah Heng Cheh told them. Yin Ling's favourite story concerned herself as a child, not the strange gods that inhabited Ah Heng Cheh's world. When she and Kwan were young children – she must have been six, Kwan nine – their grandfather died. At his funeral when all the members of his family, even down to little children, had to shed tears as a sign of respect, she and Kwan, in deep mourning black, were engaged in a private game that made them giggle softly. There they were, two disrespectful children, delving into each other's pockets, pressing their hands on their mouths in a delicious conspiracy of secret merriment. Ah Heng Cheh's sharp eyes saw their inappropriately happy faces, her sharp ears caught the obscene sounds of the suppressed laughter. She descended on them with fury, pinching their arms and legs with such energy that they began howling. 'That's better,' she said grimly.

Ah Heng Cheh remembered the incident well. 'You and your brother were black and blue all over,' she chuckled. In primary school, at the Convent of St Elizabeth, at the age of eight, Yin Ling wrote about the incident and titled her composition 'Real Tears at a Funeral'. Her teacher, Sister Josephine, was so delighted that she made her read it out loud to the whole class.

Kwan said, 'I remember. I don't think it was funny at all.' He, too, had been taken care of from birth by Ah Heng Cheh. Although he did not care for Ah Heng Cheh's tales, he had become puzzled by her obsession with her god, and had come up with several theories concerning the origin of the statue. Its slightly deformed body – one shoulder higher than the other, one arm shorter than the other – its bulging forehead, snub nose and friendly grin demonstrated that it was not the statue of a high-ranking god. Ah Heng Cheh's god did not belong to the pantheon of exalted, ferocious warrior and emperor gods who were regularly worshipped in the major temples amidst giant joss-sticks in golden urns, and whose feasts were celebrated with great pomp and devotion. These gods rode across the skies and threw lightning bolts. Ah Heng Cheh's god of no status and no home probably came low in the divine hierarchy and claimed no temple, shrine or festival of his own. Another possibility, of course, was that he was not a god at all. A monk, perhaps, a philosopher, a historical character, even a minor player – a clown? the village idiot? – in some long-ago opera in Ah Heng Cheh's ancestral village in China, whom she had promoted to a god.

'Look,' said Kwan. 'Just look at these pictures.'

Out of curiosity, he had gone to the National Library to look for books on Chinese gods and deities. His Christianity forbade any contact with the dark world of ancestors that should have been renounced long ago, but his curiosity prevailed. Upon his marriage to a devout Christian, he had duly converted, and now retained only an occasional academic interest in the religion of his forebears. The most exhaustively researched tome yielded picture after picture of angry-faced, powerful gods, serenely smiling gods, gods who took on the likenesses of animals, gods with severely distorted features such as enormous barrel bellies or massively domed foreheads, gods decked out in the most magnificent costumes, gods who wore only simple rough robes and sandals, gods with bushes for beards, gods with the round, smooth, pure faces of children. There was no picture even remotely resembling Ah Heng Cheh's god. Kwan said, 'I don't remember ever seeing the statue, as a child. And we used to open Ah Heng Cheh's trunk, to rummage among her things, just to annoy her. Do you remember anything?'

There was an occasion, Yin Ling vaguely recollected, when she had seen the statue, wrapped in white paper, in a corner of Ah Heng Cheh's cupboard, among her clothes. She had been about to touch it when Ah Heng Cheh slapped her hand.

Kwan said, 'What a laugh. Our lives turned upside down by an old servant's obsession with a god that isn't.' He meant his mother's life, for he was living a convenient distance away in an apartment in a new condominium, worlds removed from the small, cramped, government-subsidised HDB flat that he had shared with his mother and sister before his marriage. It would always be the greatest source of pleasure to him that through hard work, shrewd investments and a good marriage to a woman from a wealthy family, in roughly that order of importance, he had bought at the age of thirty-one an apartment in a condominium that could only increase in value. From the comfort of his new home, Kwan felt great pity for his mother, burdened with an old servant who had crazy dreams and who had lived too long.

Now and again, he brought up the possibility of Ah Heng Cheh following Yin Ling to that big bungalow in Rochester Park upon her marriage to Vincent. Vincent's love for her might prevail over any aversion that his mother – spoilt, arrogant, fastidious – would most certainly have to Ah Heng Cheh. After all, the big house in Rochester Park had many rooms. That, thought Kwan wistfully, would end his poor mother's agony. For agony it had become. Their mother, who had reverted to her maiden name of Alice Fong when their father's death had forced her to take a job as a clerk in a small company, could have borne, with patience, both the forgetfulness and the touchiness as that measure of gratitude due to an old servant who had served the family faithfully for generations. Ah Heng Cheh, as a young woman, had assisted the midwife at Alice Fong's birth, had brought her up because her mother was always ill, seen her get married and then gone on to bring up her two children when she had to go to work.

'You are very good to an old servant,' her neighbours said to Alice Fong. The grateful employed servants to look after their old servants; the ungrateful put them in squalid old people's homes.

'She served us well so we will do our duty towards her,' said Alice Fong, with cold precision. In the same tone, she might have said, 'I married. It was my duty to have children so I bore a son and a daughter.' Her form of Christianity, different from her son's, emphasised the sacrosanct quality of sacrifice and duty. She brought to it her own special brand of joylessness, which would see the coming marriage of her daughter to Vincent Chee Wen Siong, already stirring excitement and envy in both her daughter's friends and their mothers, as one more duty discharged.

When Kwan's son was born, she made the correct, dutiful hospital visit and gave a generous *ang pow* on the occasion of the child's First Month celebration, then shrank back into the quiet, dull world of her work as a clerk and as a devoted helper in her church's activities. It was the same for Kwan's second child. Alice Fong shrank from small children's rough touch and noisy laughter. Her two grandchildren had learnt to tiptoe quietly around her, to say, 'Thank you,' politely for her *ang pows*, then pass them on to their mother as useless gifts not worth keeping. They would look around timidly to make sure their grandmother had not seen.

'You have gone beyond your duty in your patience,' her neighbours said, for everybody could see that Ah Heng Cheh was giving a lot of trouble in her old age. For instance, on the evening after their return home from the Monckton Food Park, after Vincent had so kindly cut up the roasted pork for her, she complained, as soon as she sat down on her bed and began to fan herself, that she was hungry because nobody had given her anything to eat.

Alice Fong said, with weary exasperation, 'You've just come back from your dinner.' She might have saved herself the trouble of a response. The Old One's forgetfulness made her ask whether lunch or dinner was ready only minutes after her bowl, spoon and chopsticks had been cleared away, and about when she would be taken to the Buan Ki Temple only half an hour after she had been brought back, with the smell of the afternoon heat and joss-stick smoke still on her clothes.

It was pitiful – a frightened old woman trying to negotiate the gaping holes, left by memory's collapse, along the road of each day's existence. Sometimes she fell in and had to be pulled up from danger, as when the Filipino maid Romualda – kindly employed by Vincent at his own expense – saw her shaking into her palm some pills from a bottle that the doctor had prescribed for a stomach ailment only minutes after she had been given the daily dose. The maid uttered a little scream of alarm, dashed forward and was in time to prevent an overdose. Thereafter Alice Fong placed the bottle on the topmost shelf of the kitchen cabinet, well out of the Old One's reach. A restive child was less troublesome because it could be scolded and punished.

Ah Heng Cheh liked to go out on her own – her legs were still strong and her eyesight good – but either she forgot where the lift was or, having taken it to go down the twelve floors, forgot the correct turning to reach the market and the stall that sold her favourite bean-paste buns. Romualda's chief duty was to accompany her each time, but the strong-willed, independent old woman had eluded her many times and slipped out on her own.

'Mam,' Romualda had said, in tears, 'she was right in the middle of the road. I tried to drag her away. She refused.' Two cars had screeched to an angry halt; only the deference due to grey hair had prevented the drivers shouting abuse. But one had vented his anger on Romualda, shaking a fist at her as she led the Old One away.

'Don't tell me anything,' said Alice Fong quietly. 'Tell Yin Ling. Or Vincent. He pays your salary.'

Once Ah Heng Cheh managed to find her way home on her own, carrying a paper bag stuffed with steaming hot, bean-paste buns, a present for everyone, and beaming like a child about to be praised for a good deed. 'Look!' she said happily, and brought out the buns, one by one, to hand around.

Kwan, who happened to be visiting with his wife and two small children, had leapt up and made a fuss of her. 'Cute,' he said. 'She can be cute and likeable when she wants to be.'

Kwan's two small children liked to see her laugh, to observe closely the sole tooth wobbling precariously on her lower gum. But she could swing from laughter to suspicion in a moment, disconcerting everyone. Her eyes, bright and glittering in her seamed face, her tongue swift to beat back a perceived insult, Ah Heng Cheh pulled tightly around her, like a cloak against a chill wind, the remnants of respect still owing to her to carry her through the bleakness of her remaining years. She banged doors, flung things to the ground, pushed away the food Romualda set in front of her, spat, made loud sarcastic remarks to the cat, a passing fly, a framed photograph on the wall, anything in her immediate line of vision, if she thought people were showing disrespect. In her old age, the crudest terms of abuse surfaced to disgust those around her. 'Ah Heng Cheh, you must never use such language again,' said Alice Fong severely.

A troublesome old parent might be tolerated or even humoured, but tradition's sacred decree of filial piety did not extend to aged servants, regardless of their long years of service. But Ah Heng Cheh would never starve, she would always have a roof over her head, she would have proper medical care and finally a decent funeral, her wishes meticulously observed as to how her material possessions (a pitiful amount of jewellery comprising two pairs of jade ear-rings, a jade bangle and a gold ring, and a tiny, useless plot of land somebody had enticed her into buying more than fifty years ago) would be disposed of, and which temple she would like to have her ashes kept in.

'I would like to be buried in the land of my ancestors.' Preposterous request! She would be cremated, like everybody else, in Singapore. Once a year, on the Feast of the Hungry Ghosts, or more suitably on the anniversary of her death, her ashes would be visited. But no joss-sticks could be held in the Christian hands clasped together in respect.

Kwan had spelt out precisely the measure of the family gratitude owing to a servant of sixty years. Out of Yin Ling's hearing, he grumbled to his mother who, being a woman of few words, was glad to leave to him any discharging of annoyance. Why couldn't the Old One be like any of those old men and women one saw everywhere in the HDB housing estates in Singapore? Senior Citizens – a title newly created by the government to replace the offensive 'aged' or 'elderly' – took good care of their health, exercised, found useful things to do and were not a nuisance to the young. We are a young and driven society, screamed Singapore, but we must always show respect for the old.

Old Ah Leong Chek, aged eighty-eight, two years older than Ah Heng Cheh, got up early every morning to do *tai chi*, then went to the market to have his favourite breakfast of fish porridge, stayed around to chat with other senior citizens, came home for a nap and was out again in the afternoon, keeping himself happily occupied. His three children provided him with a monthly allowance, which he managed so well that he could afford substantial *ang pows* for his seven great-grandchildren during the Chinese New Year.

Ah Sim Cheh was even better: at eighty-seven, she helped out in her son's vegetable stall in the market, sorting out the produce every morning, sprinkling water on it to keep it fresh, pinching off the brown, thread-like tails of huge mounds of bean sprouts because, thus cleaned, they could be sold for more money.

Ah Sim Cheh's neighbour, Ah Wong Chek, was becoming forgetful and unkempt, but he never bothered anyone or was petty or peevish. He spent all his time taking care of his two *merboks* in their cages. He sometimes took the cages to the void deck in one part of the housing estate to join the other old men there with their singing pets. They hung up the cages, then sat or squatted on the ground, smoking, drinking black coffee from tin mugs, and listened for the singing to begin, solace for lonely hours. As soon as one *merbok* raised its head in song, the others followed. In the past, only a few old men had straggled in with their birds. Then, over the years, as more men and birds assembled, the government thoughtfully provided stone benches for the old men to sit on and proper metal poles across the void deck ceiling for them to hang up their cages. It proved a boost for the tourist industry as well, for when the number of bird-cages swelled to become an overhead forest of bamboo, delicately latticed, sometimes covered with fluttering good-luck red thread, the air filled with the pure notes of a hundred competing birds, some tourist guide had the clever idea of including the *merbok* corner as a place to visit. The tourists got down from their buses, followed their guide and were enchanted by the scene in front of them. Their cameras clicked furiously, taking in the singing birds and listening men, or zooming in on a particularly interesting old face, seamed more deeply by solitude than years, or a bird, its little throat throbbing, singing as if its life depended on it. Some of the old men smiled and waved at the tourists; the rest ignored them to concentrate on the magic of their *merboks*.

Senior citizenship in gentle, peaceful, contented preparation for sundown, this was what the young wanted, not the agitation of mind and spirit that was so inconvenient. To be fair to her, Ah Heng Cheh's restiveness was not as bad as that of those foolish old men who still dreamt of love and went eagerly to China to claim young brides, to return cleaned out of their pitiful savings, the laughing stock of all. Young, pretty women were plentiful in China because Singapore money converted richly into the Chinese *renminbi*. Ah Heng Cheh's pitiful savings had been cleaned out, many years ago, not by gullibility of love but by compassion: she had felt sorry for a couple in trouble and had paid them good money for a useless bit of land.

Kwan said slowly, looking hard at his sister, 'How come you care so much for Ah Heng Cheh?' And from Yin Ling's fondness for the old servant it was just a step to the uncomfortable subject of her relationship with their mother. Kwan slipped easily into the role of a mediator. 'Now that you're going to get married, you might stop hating Mother.'

'I don't hate Mother.'

'She thinks you do. She says you love Ah Heng Cheh and hate her.'

'That's not true!'

Mothers tease their children with tales of how they were found in dustbins, laughing to see the small faces grow red and the tears shoot out in distress. Her mother's tale was caustic, not playful, and seared Yin Ling's soul: 'As soon as you were born, I put you in a dustbin. Ah Heng Cheh found you and brought you back.' She remembered bursting into tears and clinging to her mother. 'Go to Ah Heng Cheh,' Alice Fong had said. 'She's your mother, since you will only listen to her, not me.' She remembered screaming, 'No! No!' as her mother tried to push her away. The next day she asked her brother what Ah Heng Cheh's surname was. Her brother said knowledgeably, 'Her name is Madam Yap Siew Heng. I've seen it in her passport.' Armed with that knowledge, Yin Ling went on a rampage of retaliation. She scratched out the family surname from her name on all the covers of her school writing books and, in bold block letters, replaced it with Ah Heng Cheh's. 'My name is Yap Yin Ling. My mother's name is Yap Siew Heng.' Her class teacher, not knowing what to make of the bizarre incident, decided to let her off with a scolding. Under the teacher's watchful eye, she had to erase her new identity and restore the old one.

On the threshold of a momentous event like a marriage, daughters made up with their mothers. The filial piety decreed by tradition was so easy: provide for parents, put food in their stomachs, a roof over their heads, accord respect at all times, remember them ever afterwards and teach progeny to revere them in memory. The filial piety enjoined by conscience was much more difficult: love, sincerely and truly, a parent whom you have never understood and who has never understood you. Conscience said: It's up to you to make the first move. This much you owe. But Yin Ling had never managed to leap across the terrible gulf of their separate temperaments, their separate existences, under one roof, in a tiny, cramped flat where they lived together, ate together, sometimes watched TV together, did occasional errands for each other and maintained the appearance of perfect accord while all the time each seethed inside with the question: 'Why can't she understand me?' Or even worse, 'When can I be rid of her?'

Kwan, the clown of the family, the babbler shooting off his mouth at the most inappropriate moments, said suddenly while they were all eating a late-night supper he had bought from the Monckton Food Park, 'It's all Ah Heng Cheh's fault.' Kwan's wife, a good-natured woman who always looked timidly to everyone else to decide what she should say or not say, glanced at her mother-in-law, then quietly continued eating.

Alice Fong looked away.

Yin Ling envied her best friend Gina and her mother. For almost a year, they hardly spoke then suddenly became very close a month before Gina's engagement. The earlier animosities were submerged under an abundance of happy chatter and goodwill over the preparations for the engagement party, including the selection of a diamond for the ring, the area of her mother's undisputed expertise.

'Do you think the problem lies in the English language?' Gina had mused. Her mother spoke only Cantonese.

'My mother speaks English perfectly,' Yin Ling had replied. Indeed, her mother spoke dialect only to Ah Heng Cheh.

Alice Fong's reaction when Yin Ling told her of her engagement to Vincent had been a silence followed by the quiet announcement that if there was to be an engagement party in the coming month she would be unable to attend as she would be going on a trip to South Korea organised by her church. The tears had sprung to Yin Ling's eyes. She wanted to scream, 'It doesn't matter. Ah Heng Cheh will be there, even if it means dragging herself from her deathbed.' Both mother and daughter had then got up, without looking at each other, to return to their separate rooms.

Till one's dying day. The enduring pain of a thoughtless act by one's own flesh and blood is measured in those fearful terms. When Yin Ling was twelve, she did something her mother said she would remember till her dying day. She had submitted a composition, upon the urging of her English language teacher, for a competition organised for schoolchildren by the district community centre, in conjunction with 'Family Values Month'. The regular government campaigns, moving resolutely from 'Courtesy' to 'Clean Public Toilets' to 'Saving Water', had culminated in 'Family Values'. The title of Yin Ling's composition was 'The Person Who Means Most to Me'. It was clear to the judges, going through hundreds of entries, that the three-hundred-word composition by Woon Yin Ling, written in flawless English with a creative flair, came from an unusually sensitive, gifted child. Yin Ling was unanimously judged the winner. The prize was one hundred dollars. Bursting with pride, she read the composition aloud on a flower-bedecked stage, in front of hundreds of teachers and parents, including her mother whom she had persuaded to come. She had intended to hand over the prize money to her as a surprise after the ceremony.

It was only half-way through the reading that she became aware of her horrible mistake. The person who meant most to her was her old servant, not any member of her family. The audience, listening intently and nodding in smiling approval, began to cast sidelong glances at her mother, sitting quietly in the front row, looking straight ahead. Yin Ling's clear, girlish voice rang out with the narration of one joyful or humorous episode after another concerning the old servant. She described Ah Heng Cheh in elegant and luminous prose of a quality seldom achieved by a twelve-year-old.

When she came to Singapore at the age of nineteen to serve my grandmother's family, she had already reached her full height, which was actually very little. For at twelve, I am much taller than Ah Heng Cheh. She is very neat, and wears only black trousers and long-sleeved white or grey cotton blouses. For important occasions, such as going to pray in the Buan Ki Temple, she has a specially starched white blouse and black silk trousers. Her ear-lobes are never without two tiny jade studs, looking like green tear-drops, her left wrist is never without a jade bangle. She calls it her 'lucky bangle'. It began as a very pale green, but gets brighter every year, meaning that the god of prosperity is looking upon her with favour. Sometimes she lets me touch her jade bangle. I like to lay my cheek against it, to feel its comforting smoothness and coolness.

She went on to read about how Ah Heng Cheh had made a patchwork blanket for her, from hundreds of tiny pieces of material saved over the years, with a magical tale attached to each triangle, square and hexagon; how Ah Heng Cheh had caused a small fishbone lodged in her throat to disappear mysteriously by writing with her forefinger the Chinese character for 'cat' on her throat; how she had pinched Yin Ling and Kwan at their grandfather's funeral, to make them cry and appear respectful.

Yin Ling read on and on from the winning composition, and still there was no mention of her mother. At the end, an uneasy hush descended on the audience, before someone broke it by starting to clap. The applause was warm and sustained, leaving the unease behind. Red with embarrassment and almost ready to cry, Yin Ling bowed and ran off the stage. Early the next morning, as she got ready to go to school, she saw, placed beside her schoolbag, the envelope containing the prize money. Her mother had returned it, unopened.

*

Ah Heng Cheh had another dream. This time she was making her way through cold, dark water, not across dry, dusty land. It was a stream, or a lake – she could not tell in the darkness. On her back was her god. He was urging her to go faster. Astride her, he dug his toes impatiently into her sides to goad her on.

'Do be reasonable,' she said irritably. 'Are you aware that you're getting heavier and heavier?' And indeed he was. At one point she had to pause for breath.

A man giving a woman a ride on his back across a stream, through a rice-field, through a forest, a parent piggy-backing a child, a grown-up child his aged parent, a god a mortal – she had seen all these in her home, back in the ancestral country. But never an old woman, almost on the brink of her grave, carrying her god as a burden on her back.

Four

Vincent said, 'Ling, you'll never guess.' He often invited her to guess yet one more triumph in a life bright with promise. Was it the exemplary progress in his Ph.D. studies, his supervisor having told him that his thesis was highly publishable? The overtures of friendly interest made by the Minister for National Development who was clearly singling him out for future political leadership? The acquisition, on pure impulse, of a new Volvo? Yin Ling's guesses, seldom correct, enhanced his pleasure.

But this time Vincent's invitation to guess had nothing to do with himself. 'Remember the bearded, unkempt foreigner we saw that evening at the Monckton Food Park months ago? The guy who got involved in that incident with a Filipino maid? Guess what?'

She remembered him. She had not stopped thinking of him. The blue eyes in blazing defence of a woman who had run instinctively to him, a stranger, for help; the protective arms; the voice raised on her behalf while others slunk away, fearing to be involved. Eyes, arms, voice – they were not just fragments of recollection but had come together gradually into a whole, enduring image.

Vincent said, 'He is one of the best brains in economics from the US. The University of California at Berkeley. Professor Benjamin Gallagher. First in his field. He could be one of the examiners for my thesis.'

It turned out that Ben Gallagher had just started his teaching stint at the University of Singapore, one of an increasing number of Americans recruited for the tertiary educational institutions. The shrewd, pragmatic MTC, on record for making some blunt remarks in the past about American 'unruliness', had openly praised the quality of American higher education, instantly opening a two-way flow of eager Singapore students to any American university that would accept them and eager American academics to Singapore for change and stimulation.

Yin Ling had not yet seen Ben Gallagher in the campus. It was a huge one, with the arts block, where she worked, separated from the Economics Department by a sprawl of buildings, including the huge students' canteen. But she would look out for him. Between lectures and tutorials for her master's programme and while she waited to meet Vincent, she would look out for him.

'Mad. The man's absolutely crazy,' Vincent continued. 'Do you remember me telling you about another eccentric American, a Dr Kevin Wolff, in Engineering? The man who went around in bright pink trousers?' There had not been many such on the campus, and they stood out from the more sedate British. The university code of dress for staff and students generally succeeded in erasing whatever profligacies of colour and style might pop up, so that in the end the students walking along the well-kept roads and covered walkways, going in and out of lectures and tutorials, sitting down in the campus canteen, looked very respectable.

Nowadays, eccentricities of dress in foreign guests were tolerated, but not of behaviour that spilled over into brazen, meddlesome criticism of the host society. One Dr Larry Donahue from London University had made the mistake of writing an unflattering article on the state of the arts in

Singapore; three days after it appeared, he received a note from the dean of the faculty saying his contract would not be renewed. Offensive behaviour and non-renewability of contract had become invariably tied up as cause and effect.

Vincent harped on Ben Gallagher's eccentricity. 'Remember how untidy he looked that evening? Well, somebody told me he was ten times worse when he first arrived. Long hair, bushy beard, shirt not tucked in, sandals. Divorced. Real messy one, I hear. Drinks like a fish. No wonder he looks old for his age. Only in his thirties, but debauchery adds another ten years at least. Has an eye for the local girls. Remember the call-girl at his table in the food park? The dean's going to have to rein him in a bit.' The dean had already spoken gently to Professor Benjamin Gallagher, who subsequently went for a haircut, kept his shirts tucked in, at least for his lectures, and wore shoes and socks.

'Mad as a hatter,' said Vincent. 'Do you know, in the middle of a lecture recently, he suddenly sat on the table and recited a poem in an obscure European language, which he then translated and tried to get the students to comment on?' The bewildered students had not known how to react. They could only giggle. But they did not dare giggle when the Professor, in the middle of another lecture, descended ferociously on the front row, knocking the notebooks from their hands one by one. Somebody gasped. Another gave a startled shout, which was quickly swallowed. They all stared, shifted about, looked at each other, but did not dare look at the Professor.

'Stop writing down every word I say and listen instead!' he roared. He picked up a notebook and began to read from it. The student had taken down the lecture verbatim, including an opening remark and a silly joke. Professor Gallagher threw back his head and laughed uproariously. Then he stopped and glared at all the silent, staring faces ranged before him.

'Think, for God's sake,' he said. 'Think. Speak up. Ask questions. Challenge me.' To his friends later, he groaned, 'I've never come across a more quiescent class of students.' The students continued to shift uneasily in their seats. But they all acknowledged he was a first-rate lecturer. They also liked his unconventionality. They began to approach him, outside the lecture rooms, to talk and ask questions.

Vincent said again, with a worried frown, 'He may be one of the examiners for my thesis.' For him eccentricity was too unpredictable. He would have to find out what Professor Gallagher liked and disliked about his students' work.

Deciding to begin in the most appropriate way, Vincent included Professor Benjamin Gallagher on the guest list to the next dinner at his home. He regularly invited friends and university staff for dinner or drinks, revelling in the special privileges of his former position as president of the Students' Union and of his present position as a doctoral candidate. He even invited, with impunity, the dean himself. He was aware, with a warm inward glow, that undergraduates, shuffling around with their books and files of notes and their inadequate monthly allowances, looked upon him with awe, especially when his sleek red sports car screeched to a halt in its allotted parking space, while his fellow postgraduate students, far behind in wealth and social lustre, and resentful at never being invited to his dinners, had long since subsided into a hostile, envious silence.

His mother made him send out proper invitation cards. 'Mr Vincent Chee Wen Siong requests the pleasure of the company of . . .' She forbade catered food, which she considered inferior, and hired a chef from the well-known Grand Winchester Hotel to do the cooking, personally supervising the provision of food, wine and flowers. 'Watch,' she said. Like her son, Mrs Chee used the single word imperative to

48

draw attention to a scene of interest, to warn, advise, coax, instruct. She told Yin Ling, who would soon be her daughter-in-law, to watch her as she went through all the meticulous preparations for a dinner party, in anticipation of her own role as hostess after marriage. Flee, flee, an inner voice said to Yin Ling, from the tyranny of silver and crystal and ivory chopsticks. She made every excuse to stay away from the older woman, and kept close to Vincent's side each time she was at the big house at 2-B Rochester Park. The intimidating voice followed her through every room, urging, warning, instructing, admonishing.

But it could be such a gentle, friendly voice. 'Come here,' Mrs Chee had said once, when Yin Ling was visiting and Vincent had left the room to look for something. She put a finger to her lips to signal an approaching conspiracy as, with elaborate secrecy, she led Yin Ling out of the room. They stopped in front of a tiny opening under a staircase, which they would only be able to enter by stooping low. A piece of red tapestry hung over it. 'My son doesn't know,' she said, and showed Yin Ling a tiny utility room, probably meant for storing brooms and dustpans. It had been converted into a splendid home, with flowers and ornaments, for her gods, now deposed by her son's Christian god and the Christian god's mother, whose images had pride of place in the big house. Proudly she showed Yin Ling the Kitchen God, the Monkey God, the Goddess of Mercy and other minor deities, whom she had faithfully revered and cherished throughout their years of diminished influence. Under one roof, the gods of two family generations co-existed uneasily.

A delicious sense of sharing linked the two women standing before a secret room of the refugee gods. Mrs Chee said, her eyes moistening a little, 'You know, I became a Christian to please my son, but when I die . . .' On her deathbed, this woman, loyal to her gods to the end, wanted solace from *them*, and not the alien, alienating gods of a foreign religion.

Yin Ling moved instinctively towards the older woman, wanting to grasp her hands and to say – she did not know what she wanted to say. All she knew was that it would be about themselves, not the gods. 'There must be so much we could like about each other,' she would say. It was only a fleeting moment that would have allowed the touch – she was ready to snatch eagerly at it – and it was gone in an instant. The wetness vanished from Mrs Chee's eyes, as did the softness from her face, for she had responded, for just a moment, to the secret cry of the heart. Yin Ling stepped back, rejected.

'Let's go,' said Mrs Chee stiffly, and it was all over. She turned her face, severe once more, to meet the tyranny of the silver and the crystal, and the promised loyalty to the new god. Vincent's god. 'Yin Ling,' she said, with undue hauteur, probably to compensate for the unguardedness of a moment ago, 'you will remember, of course, that my son likes his rice steamed, not boiled.'

'Can't we be on our own after we're married?'

The request was preposterous and she never made it again. He was an only son, his mother could not live alone, he was ever aware of his responsibility, the house at 2-B Rochester Park had been and would always be the family home, etc. Vincent gave his reasons slowly, patiently. Then he said, a little curtly, 'I hope you understand, Ling, that I make the major decisions.'

The major decisions would include dress and hair: she was never to wear short skirts again and he preferred her to keep her hair long and coiled in a bun.

She had almost decided to call off the engagement. She was

actually trembling under the weight of so drastic a decision, having paced the floor many times, going through the reasons again and again in her head. She called Gina for advice. Her friend said, 'You're mad,' and spoke crudely of the market value of men, and Vincent Chee Wen Siong's enormous marketability was without question. Of the fifty selected by *Lifestyle* as Singapore's most eligible bachelors, he easily came in among the top ten. Ever down-to-earth and hard-headed, Gina said, 'Who do you think you are, Woon Yin Ling?' She spoke as concerned, caring friend, not harsh critic. 'Come on, be realistic. There is no better catch than Vincent.' She became more vocal, as Yin Ling fell into a deep, troubled silence. 'Let me be brutally blunt. You're going from HDB to prime District 10.' Gina's metaphors for love and marriage ever remained earthbound, tied to the hard economics of acquisition and competition. At least she was frank. Others bemoaned society's materialism, but quietly fattened their bank accounts, and purchased this or that property in Canada or Australia. She continued, 'The man's rich, handsome, has status, is a rising star in politics. *And he's crazy about you.* You're the luckiest girl in Singapore.'

'I'm confused. I don't know what to say or how to feel any more,' Yin Ling said.

'You're confused all right,' said Gina scornfully. She added quickly, 'I don't mean to disparage you in any way – you're beautiful and intelligent and warm and sensitive – but . . .' The 'but' encompassed the enormous gap, so visible to everyone on the campus, that would not have been there if Vincent Chee Wen Siong's choice had been Singapore's top model or the Harvard-educated daughter of a tycoon or the niece of the Minister for National Development. Incompatibility raised eyebrows, set tongues wagging and their incongruity was only a shade less than that of another courting couple on the campus, the young, handsome dean of the law faculty and the assistant bursar, a widow nine years his senior.

Vincent's mother had made no secret of her preference for a girl from Hong Kong, daughter of a shipping magnate, whom Vincent had dated briefly. 'What to do,' she had sighed. 'It's fate.' Perhaps she had consulted her secret gods in the secret room under the staircase and they had told her that her son was not fated to marry the Hong Kong girl.

'Why have you chosen me, of all girls?'

The question had to be asked, sooner or later, impelled by a whole host of impulses – curiosity, vanity, a posture of humility to please a vain man. For answer, Vincent swept her into his arms for a long, ardent kiss. 'I love you very much, that's why,' he said simply – oh, why couldn't there be more such simple, spontaneous moments? – and added, spoiling everything, 'When you become the wife of Vincent Chee Wen Siong . . .' In one of her good dreams, Vincent said, 'I love you.' Just that, without any qualifier.

Could it have been Ah Heng Cheh who drove Yin Ling to the final decision? Ah Heng Cheh, in one of her most lucid moments, had become suddenly aware of the magnitude of Vincent's generosity in employing a maid to take care of her. She asked about the cost, in terms of the maid's salary and upkeep. It was a sum too large for her mind to absorb; she turned it over and over in her head, frowning in concentration. At last she turned to Yin Ling and said, 'Never in my life have I come across such kindness. This man has the heart of a god. I am too old to return the kindness. You must do it on my behalf.'

On becoming the wife of Vincent Chee Wen Siong, the first thing Yin Ling would have to learn would be to be a good hostess at his many dinner parties. When the next occasion arrived, Vincent said, 'Ling, I hope you don't mind, no ladies allowed.' He preferred all-male parties, when he brought out the best wine and passed around the best cigars. The chief guest this time would be the unconventional Professor Benjamin Gallagher; around him, Vincent decided to group those of his guests best suited to provoke the Professor into lively discussion after dinner. Vincent would watch with benign amusement when the Singaporeans provoked the foreigner into explosions of even greater eccentricity. The topic would most likely be politics.

Outspoken Professor Clive Vasoo of the Sociology Department, known for his elegant style, would surely enliven the discussion with his fine sarcasm. His elegance had been carefully cultivated, making him stand out among a multitude of Singapore academics whose arguments got lost in bad grammar and worse pronunciation. Ideally Professor Vasoo should be set against Chong Boo, a lecturer at Yussof Polytechnic, unabashed defender of the most strongly criticised of government policies, whose speech grew more incoherent as his loyalty became more aggressive.

Let Clive Vasoo and Chong Boo get at each other's throats after dinner, and let the free-talking American join in the fray. Throw in, too, the playful, irreverent Y. T. Lam, the best-known architect in Singapore, the awesomely knowledgeable and astute Professor Su Tian from the History Department, the garrulous and highly successful lawyer Michael Cheong, who was less interested in politics than in sex. Michael Cheong only needed an admiring circle of female listeners for his rowdy tales and risqué jokes to complete his enjoyment of any social event.

'No ladies this time,' said Vincent, to the protesting Michael Cheong, who rather liked his reputation as a ladies' man and sought to reinforce it at every party by conspicuously directing his long, narrow, languid eyes to *décolletage* or leg.

But it turned out that there would be ladies after all. Chong Boo had asked to be allowed to bring his wife, since it would be their last evening together before she returned to Australia to look after their two children there; they were at a boarding-school in Perth. Then Vincent decided, at the last minute, to invite Christopher, Gina's husband, who immediately assumed that his wife was included in the invitation.

'You'll have to be there to take care of the ladies, Ling,' Vincent said. He went on to say, in a mood of continuing high spirits that made him say things he shouldn't, 'You know, you could read your poems to them – bring out your little black book . . .' He noticed a swift turn of her neck, a frown darkening her brow. But in his present expansive mood, he cheerfully chose to disregard all signs of annoyance from his fiancée. They were inconsequential.

The secret book would ever be the cause of friction between them. After their marriage, he thought he might be able to persuade her to put her gift for writing to better use. In his mind he was already shaping the intention to get her to fine-comb his thesis for any grammatical mistakes, any awkwardness of style. With her creative flair, she might even be able to improve the style and make it a really first-rate publication.

Years later, Ben would recount the story of the dinner party in vivid detail. He even remembered the day and date, Friday, 17 July 1984, just a few months after his arrival in Singapore. It was an extraordinary dinner party, he said, because of Yin Ling.

Her version of the events of that day was slightly different. Ben said he remembered being introduced to Vincent's fiancée, a quiet, pretty girl, and later noticing her in one part of the room with the other ladies, looking so thoroughly bored that he felt sorry for her. She said she was not bored for an instant that evening: she had successfully shut out the ladies' chatter about fashion and food and unreliable Filipino maids, yet appeared to be listening politely to them while in fact she was listening to the men discuss politics. To her delight, they moved energetically through local politics to international affairs, philosophy, religion. She was enthralled. Shy and reticent, she read books which, like her poetry, she hid from Vincent. At his kindest he might just say, 'I didn't know you liked this kind of serious stuff,' but at his worst, if he had had a bad day at the university or had quarrelled with his mother, he might frown and say, 'Just what are you trying to prove?'

She listened to the men's conversations and revelled in the noisy energy of their arguments. She despised some for their fatuity, a few she admired for their robust intelligence and incisive wit. One of these days, she might write a poem about reincarnation in her little black book: in the next life, she would prefer to be born a man.

She listened to Clive Vasoo and Chong Boo and after a while lost interest. She had heard it all before. Chong Boo listed the amazing achievements of MTC and his team, who had transformed a tiny island with no resources – which a none-too-friendly politician from a neighbouring country had compared to a vulnerable little fish in a region of big fish – into one of the most successful economies in the world. Then Clive Vasoo, drawing languidly on his pipe, smiling sardonically at the man opposite him said, in the most casual tone, 'How strange, if you think our society is so wonderful, that you have sent your two children to school in Australia.'

Eventually, they turned away from each other to refill glasses, talk to others, look at the many beautiful Chinese paintings on the wall; the quarrel was over. Vincent came in with a new bottle of wine, Michael Cheong with a story about sex, to restore conviviality. Everyone became interested in

Michael Cheong's story. The ladies stopped talking among themselves and turned to face the story-teller. Michael called affably to them, 'Hey, ladies, why don't you join us?'

It must have been the effect of the drink. He began by telling of a Singaporean gentleman who went to Bangkok for illicit sex. Then, in the middle of the telling, apparently without being aware of it, the 'he' of his narrative merged into the 'I' of confessed truth. 'I was offered this young girl,' said Michael Cheong, 'who was no bigger than a child. She stood up to this height only.' He indicated with his hand, enjoying the rapt attention of his audience. 'The girl came with a virginity certificate.' Michael watched for the impact, and smiled. There were guffaws and giggles. Everybody had a question to ask or a comment to make. One of the ladies giggled. 'Just a piece of paper. Two doctors' signatures,' said Michael. 'Didn't you know about those hotels in Bangkok that cater to this special preference? Ageing men from Japan, in particular. Ageing Americans too,' he said, turning to Ben Gallagher. 'You Americans know what to get out of the East. You know, all that stuff about a virgin's power to revitalise. The *ying* and *yang* thing. Young *ying* rejuvenating old *yang*.'

Someone gave a hoot and said, 'Wow, recyclable virginity.'

The look of intense disgust on the American's face tickled Michael and he held forth in a new flow of narrative exuberance. 'A special method,' he said, lowering his voice for effect. 'You know how they do it? Chicken blood. I swear to you it's true! Chicken blood, cleverly hidden, then allowed to trickle down the inside of the thigh at the right moment. Ha, Ha!'

Michael raised his voice to apologise to the listening ladies: 'Sorry, ladies! Just close your ears to our dirty stories.'

And still the tale had more surprises. 'In the middle of the night,' said Michael, swaying with the pleasure of drink and attention, 'I woke up to find the girl gone. Gone. Vamoosed. She was supposed to be with me all night. Fully paid for. My first thought was that she had run away with my watch and wallet but they were there, on the bedside table. Then – now you're never going to believe this . . .' Michael rose to the full height of his narrative powers, surveying the circle of enthralled faces. He was prolonging the suspense unneces-sarily. 'You can't guess what I saw next—'

'Go on, Michael,' said Clive Vasoo impatiently.

'The ladies are all eagerly waiting,' said Christopher.

'Well,' said Michael, his face aglow, 'I heard small sounds coming from the bathroom. The bathroom door was slightly ajar. I got up to investigate and guess what I saw.'

'For goodness' sake,' said Clive Vasoo.

'The girl was squatting on the bathroom floor,' said Michael. 'It was only then that I saw how young she was. Twelve or thirteen, no more. She was playing Five Stones. You know – the game played by poor village children who don't have toys? I watched the little girl. She was playing and singing softly to herself. I let her continue playing and returned to bed. Now, don't you think that was some story?'

'What about the sex? You never told us about the sex,' said Christopher, and this time it was he who yelled across to the ladies, 'Ladies, get ready to cover your ears!'

It was at this point that the extraordinary happened. According to Ben, who said he remembered everything vividly, Yin Ling marched up to Michael, stood before him and said, 'You bastard.' She then lectured him in a clear unfaltering voice on the disgusting exploitation of children. She even put out an arm, as if to shove or hit him. Yin Ling's recollection was slightly different. She remembered swinging an arm across that obnoxious smiling face, that desecrator of innocent little bodies. She thought she said, 'You bastard,' twice. The second time Vincent, breaking out of the paralysis of shock, stood up to pull her away. Ben remembered her turning at this point to shout something at Michael; she remembered facing the entire gathering of males and saying, 'You disgust me, all of you.' But both Ben and she agreed in their recollection of everyone's shocked reaction. The total silence and stillness in the room was broken only when Vincent took Yin Ling's arm, then signalled to Gina to take her out. Next he went over to Michael to apologise on her behalf.

'It's okay,' said Michael weakly, and slumped heavily into a chair. He looked stricken, his face ashen. He took out a handkerchief from his pocket and wiped his brow. 'I'm sorry,' he said, in a small voice. They all thought he was going to cry.

As Yin Ling was led away, she felt Ben Gallagher staring at her. It was clearly the stare of recollection, of that moment in the food park when both had turned to stare at each other. She saw his mouth open slightly, as if to say, 'Wait a second, we've met before, tell me where.' She knew, as Gina gently led her up the stairs, that his gaze never left her.

Later, as Vincent parked outside her home, there was a long silence. Then he said, 'We'll forget the whole incident. We won't refer to it.'

She had managed to maintain her cold, defiant silence all the way home in the car, but now as Vincent spoke and made a tentative movement to touch her arm, she burst into tears. She had expected him to explode for spoiling his party, but instead he had reached across to reassure her. It would have been even more reassuring if he had stopped then, and taken her into his arms. Taken her and held her close. She would have sobbed out the frightening strangeness of the evening's events and felt so much better, warm and forgiven, in his arms. But Vincent measured out forgiveness, as he did love, in small, careful doses. 'We'll not talk about it again,' he repeated, looking straight ahead. Then he opened the car door for her to get out.

But that long, intense stare from Ben Gallagher as Gina had led her away had spoken reassurance in large, generous doses. It had said many things – above all, about the excitement and joy of discovery. It had said, 'Please, let us meet. I want to see you again.'

Five

In the university campus, rumours about MTC – the latest concerned some impending crackdown against a theatre group that had gone too far in the political lampooning – went underground, meaning that they could only be whispered behind cupped hands in the walkways, lecture theatres, tutorial rooms, libraries, canteens and lounges. Some of the whisperers had taken to looking over their shoulders.

Two non-Singaporean members of the theatre group, Malaysians, were likely to have their student passes revoked. One was going to lose his bursary as well. He was certain, once his defiant mask had dropped, to howl all the way home to Malaysia. Hit them where it hurts. See whether they will have the temerity to strut around and mock the government once it has smashed their rice-bowl.

The reputedly outspoken student bi-monthly, *Dialogue*, a loose compendium of political and social commentaries, critiques, book reviews, poems and short stories, had been cleansed of anything even remotely scurrilous. The university deans could breathe more freely. There were rumours, too, about officials in MTC's inner circle, including one about a man who was so terrified of not achieving the correct temperature for MTC's beer that, according to his wife, he had started getting ulcers.

Another rumour concerned MTC's wife, a beautiful, gentle woman but for whose influence the man might have been even more overbearing. It seemed that the only time MTC's voice faltered and his face softened was when he spoke of his wife's frail health.

Sliding down the scale of augustness to target lesser luminaries in political and academic life, the rumours focused on the deans of the university – one would soon be relieved of his post, another had gone on a secret trip to China for some undisclosed illness – as if the immaculateness of the campus, said to be among the best in the world, needed an earthy reminder of humanity, even if these rumours, too, went underground.

The rumours about the expatriate lecturers, mainly the Americans and the British, could be openly discussed. After only a semester at the university, Professor Ben Gallagher had gathered around himself more tantalising tales than all the other foreign lecturers put together. The trouble, said some-one, was that the American would not blend in, and insisted on sticking out. Unlike the proverbial nail that got knocked down as soon as it popped up, the Professor's oddities, at least for now, were a honey-pot for the harmless, if irritating, flies of gossip. But if he didn't mind others did. The dean of the faculty, a neat, courteous, impeccably dressed man, was irritated by the presence of flies in his pristine setting.

Even the tea-woman had stories to tell about Ben Gallagher. She liked him immensely for his generosity in tips and for greeting her in her Teochew dialect every morning, but whispered something about him being seen with a young woman in his office in the campus late one night. It was the security guard who had noticed them and told her. She promptly told the cleaning woman, who told some students with whom she was friendly, and then it was all over the campus. Professor Ben Gallagher, brilliant economics lecturer from Berkeley, typical reckless, unconventional American, was fooling around with the local girls. 'One of those good-time girls. Door locked. Came out only after a long time,' the security guard had said, with a knowing wink. There was also Holly Tsung, a lecturer from Hong Kong University on sabbatical at Singapore University. She was pretty and vivacious and was often seen in Professor Gallagher's office or having a cup of coffee with him in the canteen. It was rumoured that Holly Tsung was determined to hook the Professor before her sabbatical ended.

The escapades, both of students and lecturers, remained at the level of harmless gossip unless, of course, somebody lodged a formal complaint. Nobody had ever lodged any complaint against a foreigner. 'They all come here and have a good time. Good salary, good living, good time. They pick up the girls in the bars and at the food centres,' said the knowledgeable security guard, who, over the years, had seen foreigners driving these good-time girls around in their cars and taking them up to their rooms.

But the most tantalising rumours about Professor Ben Gallagher concerned not his love life but his political interference. He had taken to making blunt comments about local government. The dean had admonished him: 'There's no ruling against this, but we generally discourage it,' he said. He had been well prepared for this meeting with the formidably eloquent, exasperating American lecturer, by getting his secretary to lay out the cutting from the Forum page of the *National Times* in readiness. He pointed to the newspaper cutting in front of him on his desk. 'It may be better, Professor Gallagher, to refrain from writing to the press on such matters in the future.' After reading a report in the *National Times* about a man being caned for vandalism, the Professor had shot off a letter to the newspaper to protest against the brutality. 'In this day and age,' he had written grandiloquently,

62

'we should not tolerate relics from a dark and barbaric past.' He was already planning another letter to the newspaper, this time to protest at the unfair treatment of Filipino maids. Back at home, the Professor, from youth, had taken up cudgels on behalf of Vietnam draft-dodgers, exploited Mexican workers, Chinese women illegally employed in sweatshops. Once he had been hit with a baseball bat for his pains, but he had soon bounced back, ready to get into the fray again. Others left radicalism with youth, and settled into good jobs and the good life; although Ben had been married briefly, he continued to expend his prodigious energy on a hundred causes, while making a name for himself as a brilliant student and, later, a brilliant academic. His affairs were numerous and messy but although he spoke ardently of his causes he never spoke of the affairs.

The dean continued, 'You should have obtained clearance from your department head before sending the letter. Technically, therefore, you were in breach of our rules. As I've said, it would be wiser to refrain from sending such letters in the future.'

He was too polite to say what a fellow dean had snarled, red-faced, to a foreign staff member guilty of a similar infraction: 'You foreigners should mind your own business. Don't presume to tell us what we should or should not do.' Decades after colonial rule had ended, the old acceptance of western superiority was unfortunately still around and was regularly attacked by academics and students at conferences and seminars. Kick all of them out. Don't allow any more in. That might have been the rousing cry of some hot-tempered members of MTC's circle, but 'No,' MTC had said, 'we need their expertise. But they should know their limits.' So he stretched out one hand in welcome and clenched the other to show the famously ruthless knuckles at the ready.

Professor Gallagher, facing the dean across his desk, made the supreme mistake of saying, 'But in our society, in any free society—'

The dean was now obliged to drop his gentle tone and gracious smile. He said, curtly, 'Professor Gallagher, in *our* society, you will do as we require.' He stopped short of warning, 'Don't interfere, or your contract will be terminated.' Instead he rose and saw the foreigner to the door. He had succeeded with the long hair, unkempt beard and the untucked shirts; once he reined in the meddlesomeness as well, this foreigner, who was a superb lecturer and did not mind how many additional hours were added to his teaching load, might be a real asset to the faculty. Lecturers could be awkward: the dean thought contemptuously of others who had kicked up a fuss over a meagre hour or two added to their weekly schedule. This new lecturer seemed not even to notice, making the work of the administrative head, Mrs Khalid, so much easier. Mrs Khalid said that, all things considered, she liked Professor Ben Gallagher. It was even said that she had become possessive of him, and that she pulled a face, rolling her eyes to the ceiling, each time she saw Holly Tsung going up to the Professor with her high-pitched laugh and detestable Hong Kong accent.

Once he was out of the dean's hearing, the Professor, who was beginning to enjoy his stay in Singapore, shook his head and gave a little laugh of derision. As soon as he was back in his office, he sat down and typed a second letter of protest to the *National Times*, and sent it off. After a few days, he knew the editors had decided not to publish it.

His colleague, Dr Harold Jamieson, who came from Chicago and had been in Singapore for many years, said, 'Listen, Ben, I wouldn't if I were you. It's not worth it.' Expatriate lecturers came to the country wide-eyed with noble anger and purpose, but soon settled into the ease and comfort the society afforded. They were even able, eventually, to reflect with satisfaction on their peculiarly advantageous position: how nice to be able to enjoy a pleasant life created by an unpleasant government and leave the job of criticising the unpleasantness to the locals.

Dr Harold Jamieson had settled comfortably into local life, and enjoyed the local food, which he said his wife was crazy about. Joanne had reached that delightful stage of integration when she could eat expertly, with only the fingers, the famous fish-head curry laid out on a banana leaf. 'See?' she had demonstrated, giggling, then asked for a picture to be taken to send to the folks back home. For good measure, she wore Indian clothes for the occasion, usually a loose cotton blouse and trousers, and sported a bright red *pottu* on her forehead.

Harold himself valued the cleanliness of the streets and the drinking water – he had nearly died of diarrhoea in India during a vacation there. 'You can eat off the streets, drink tap water,' he had written home. His wife ranked – after the fish-head curry – the safety and security of the streets for women and young girls, even late at night. 'Our Pam goes out with her friends and comes home after midnight, but I never worry.' In any other city in the world, Joanne said, her eyes opened wide into two perfect circles of breathless gratitude, their daughter would have been raped or drugged or had her throat slit. Satiated with all the benefits of her new home, she could list yet one more: the luxury of having a serving-maid twenty-four hours of the day. 'Our Raphaela is a gem. When the time comes for her to return to the Philippines, I'll get Harold to try to extend the work permit somehow.'

The Jamiesons paid the ultimate, extravagant tribute: 'We love Singapore and the East so much, we'll be strangers back home.'

Each time he met Ben, Harold said jocularly, 'I wouldn't if I were you,' assuming that his friend and colleague had just come out of a scrape and was about to get into another.

But to the relief of his friends, Ben began to put aside politics and concentrate on something else. 'This is a marvellous poem,' he said, waving a neatly typed sheet of paper. 'Why did you editors reject it?' He was the only academic in the campus who strolled in to the activities of other departments, attending talks and seminars organised by the History Department, the Chinese Language Department, the Tamil Culture Society; he even took part in a play staged by the Drama Society. He was particularly interested in the students' magazine *Dialogue*, having heard of its bold, fearless articles challenging government policies but was puzzled to discover that none matched its reputation. A member of the selection and editorial committee had just shown him a poem anonymously submitted.

Ben looked at the sheet of paper in his hand.

'The Uncertainty Principle. I've never met a student in Singapore who's even heard of Heisenberg. The writer of this poem even weaves it into a Chinese myth.' He read the poem a third time.

Strange, lost god
A neither-here-nor-there god
Under the snub nose and child's cheeks
Is there a Sky-God's visage
Too terrible to behold?
Strange, lost god
Come off it, I say.
Stop being victim of
The Uncertainty Principle
Take on the certainty of

A particle or a wave
End Ah Heng Cheh's pain
And mine
And show us the way home.

He turned the sheet of paper this way and that, looking for a signature.

The editorial committee member said, 'The writer, whoever he or she is, has been sending in poems over the last few months. Too obscure. Also, we can't publish anonymous submissions. No return address.' He opened a drawer and drew out more typewritten sheets.

The Professor read each carefully. He gave a long, slow, appreciative whistle. 'Marvellous stuff,' he said, 'for the writer's readiness to reveal so much. Here's another one about Ah Heng Cheh. I wonder who this tortured soul is?' His interest was roused.

That afternoon Ben Gallagher put up a notice on the board outside the room used by the *Dialogue* editorial committee. It said: 'To Ah Heng Cheh. Could you please contact me? Ben Gallagher.' It gave his office telephone number.

The note stayed there for a week, eliciting no response. Undaunted, the Professor put up another: 'To Ah Heng Cheh. Could you PLEASE contact me. I'm extremely interested in the poem. PLEASE call me at once. Ben Gallagher.' He left both his office and home numbers.

After four days, in frustration, he put up a third note. He hated the distraction that the suspense was causing in his life. The anonymous poet remained silent. Ben had another idea. He stopped putting up notes. Instead, he pinned up a sealed envelope bearing the words 'To the Lost Snub-nosed God' written boldly on it. Inside a note said, 'You are all screwed up. You need help.'

Yin Ling's initial reaction was of anger and shock. How dared he? And then, in slow degrees, the anger gave way to pure elation. That someone could be so stirred by her poems that they would resort to confrontation to entice the writer out of anonymity was satisfying. That the someone was a man who loved her poems when her fiancé made fun of them was thrilling beyond belief. She geared herself for a suitable response to his provocative message.

The next day, Ben found the sealed envelope gone. In its place was another, bearing his name. Excitedly he pulled it down from the noticeboard and tore it open. There was a folded sheet inside, with only three words: 'How dare you?' He knew then, with certainty, that the writer was a woman. He waited eagerly for a call, another note, convinced that the anger had not been fully discharged with those three words. He saw, in his mind's eye, a pale, intense girl, no different from any of the pale, slender Singaporean girls moving about in the campus with their files and books. He had often watched them, these pretty girls who looked like teenagers although they were in their twenties, with their smooth, lovely skins and sleek, shining hair, walking by themselves or with their boyfriends, and wondered about the lives they led. Perhaps she was one of his students.

What did she look like? In one of her poems, she had described herself as 'all ugly and twisted', like an old gnarled tree on the campus whose branches had mysteriously bent downwards and curved inwards to curl around the trunk, like enormous, scaly reptiles, presenting no smooth surface for young lovers in the campus to lean on. 'Nobody loves me!' the poor ugly tree had moaned, as in a fairy-tale. 'All ugly and twisted!' And she had gone up to it and said, 'That makes two of us.'

The intensity of her inner pain gave the anonymous poet an exceptional beauty.

He waited for a week, then a month. The writer seemed to have vanished.

Then something came up to break the hold of the intriguing poem (kept on his bedside table) which hit a chord deeper than mere curiosity and worked him up to an even greater pitch of fervour. He was in a bar with some colleagues and their friends, drinking beer. The conversation, as usual, moved desultorily over a wide range of topics, and at one point conjured in Ben Gallagher's mind an image of a young, beautiful woman, white-faced with anger but tearful and trembling as she stood before a man and called him a bastard. The image was fleeting because another, even more compelling, suddenly took its place.

'I can't believe it. They can't do it to a human being,' exclaimed Ben Gallagher angrily. The person who had painted the image so vividly for everyone, a lawyer named Derek Lee, nodded. It was true. He had personally seen the man after the caning. Eight strokes. The man's back was raw. He had tentatively touched it with a finger and the man had screamed.

He was an illiterate worker from Bangladesh, one of hundreds brought illegally into the country by unscrupulous locals who took their money under false promises of getting jobs for them, then disappeared, leaving them to bear the brunt of the law. The poor man had sold his farm to raise the money to come to Singapore; now broken, in body and spirit, he had to go home. Derek Lee said, 'It's those lying bastards who should get the cane, not the poor fools who trust them. The man was confused. He kept waving some documents he had been given. Total forgeries, nonsensical, worthless. He was crying all the time.' Derek Lee had slipped some money into his hand.

Ben listened with a deep frown, then looked around the table and said, 'Look, this is serious. We can't let the abuse go on. Let's do something.' It was at this point that everyone sensed trouble and quietly changed the subject, turning to more innocuous topics. Soon everyone was talking animatedly about the World Cup.

Derek Lee came out of it briefly to tap Ben on the arm and whisper, 'I wouldn't if I were you,' adding, 'It's a real problem, these people slipping into Singapore in search of work. A real headache for the government. Remove the law, because everyone criticises it for being draconian, and you get an influx of immigrants overnight. Or rampant vandalism.' He was using the exact words of the Minister for National Development from a recent TV appearance. Ben had met a hundred Derek Lees in Singapore who publicly defended stern official policy and in private softened it with generous disbursements of money to charity.

Vincent said to Yin Ling, 'The crazy American Professor. You know the latest?' He had not, as he promised, mentioned her strange behaviour on the evening of the dinner party; indeed, he had expunged the evening from their shared memory, as if it had never taken place. That one failed dinner party should not tarnish the lustre of a dozen successful ones. With the exception of Michael Cheong, whose name would be avoided – although that did not mean the end of his friendship with Michael, who was basically a decent fellow – all the dinner guests, especially the crazy Professor, could still be talked about.

Vincent liked to talk as he uncoiled Yin Ling's hair or ran his fingers along the smooth skin of cheeks, neck, breasts, legs.

She waited to hear the latest about Ben Gallagher. She had closed her fingers on the offensive note from the sealed envelope, crushed it into a tight ball and thrown it away. She realised, with a start, that she had not stopped thinking about him.

Vincent said, kissing her neck, 'That man's courting trouble.' He still had not found out whether the Professor was going to be one of the examiners for his thesis so he would tread carefully and talk about the man's misdemeanour only to his fiancée. 'It seems he actually visited the Bangladeshi worker. Took a picture of the cane marks on the back and legs. Said he could send it to some international human rights group. Wrote a nasty letter, which might be seen as libellous.'

The dean had been trying frantically to intercept the letter. Fortunately the *National Times* had refused to publish it. Ben Gallagher was summoned to his office and issued with a final warning: one more act of interference in local affairs, and his contract would be terminated. The dean would personally put into his hands a one-way ticket for the next flight home. And at this stage, the dean had felt all the regret of an act of negligence when he had recommended the recruitment of the American to his faculty: he had not requested a proper investigation of the man's background, which would have shown up his radicalism.

Vincent said, with a slight frown, for he had decided he was no longer in the mood for love, 'The trouble is, he may still end up as one of my examiners.'

The next day, Ben Gallagher found a sealed envelope with his name on it, pinned to the noticeboard in his department. Inside was a note, written in a neat hand, that said, 'I will be with Ah Heng Cheh at the Sai Haw Villa tomorrow afternoon at three. She thinks she has found a home for her god. But she will change her mind once more. Or he will.'

71

Six

Kwan, who had arrived on a visit just as Yin Ling and Ah Heng Cheh were on their way out, said, 'Where're you going?' He was annoyed that Yin Ling could not stay, for he had taken the afternoon off especially to discuss a serious matter: the money owing to him, as a result of the exorbitant cost of keeping Ah Heng Cheh alive. An old servant, with no money to leave, was gobbling up other people's by taking an unconscionably long time to die. Kwan could generally be counted on to play the part of the affable peace-keeper in the family, but he turned nasty as soon as he sat down and did his accounts. Ah Heng Cheh had had an expensive operation some months ago, and Yin Ling had borrowed the money from Kwan, on the understanding that it would soon be returned. Kwan expected interest on the loan. The dollar signs danced about inside his head and in his eyes, like musical notes, and came pouring out of his mouth in an unremitting stream.

'I have no money,' Yin Ling said.

'I thought—' expostulated Kwan, but the name was not uttered.

Kwan disliked Vincent; he disliked Vincent even more as the donor of large sums of money. But the man's love for his sister was incredible, given the difference in their status, and called for admiration, no matter how grudging. 'Give credit where credit is due,' Kwan said to his wife, who obligingly echoed him. So he gave credit especially to the flamboyant rich heir with the sports car and the Ph.D. studies for employing a full-time maid for the old servant and, as he had recently found out from his mother, for funding a new water-heater in her flat.

'I can't go to Vincent for any more money,' said Yin Ling miserably. 'He's given so much already.' One night she had sat down with pencil and paper to work out the total cost of his love for her. As the list of things bought by him or billed to him became longer and longer, together with actual cash handouts, which he always put tactfully on the dressing-table in her room when she was not looking, she felt a sense of mounting panic. Finally she laid down her pencil and pushed the piece of paper away. In one of her dreams, Vincent actually held it up to her and said, 'More. Much more,' and he told her what she had forgotten to include in her sums, adding, 'Don't you see? It would cost you too much to leave me now.'

Facing Kwan, Yin Ling suddenly had an idea: 'Would you be willing to take Ah Heng Cheh's property instead?' It was too much to speak of that tiny bit of useless land, tucked away in some obscure part of the island, covered with *lallang* grass and still bearing the remnants of a disused well, as 'property', and Kwan, not exactly in the best of moods, let out a derisive laugh. The sum borrowed was substantial; he needed cash immediately; he would not want to be landed with something he could not sell quickly. Who would want it? For the hundredth time, he railed against that unscrupulous couple, probably long dead, who, more than fifty years ago, had cheated a poor servant of a sum of money that would have grown tenfold, a hundredfold, if properly invested.

Alice Fong came out of her taciturnity to show some concern for her unloved daughter. 'Sell off that property for whatever sum. It will help to take care of the medical expenses. It's not fair to you or Vincent to have to bear everything.' Although she gave the appearance of being interested in nothing, Alice Fong watched everything.

All the way in the taxi to Sai Haw Villa Ah Heng Cheh was as excited as a child. When she was happy, she talked endlessly. Only two evenings before, she had come suddenly to Yin Ling's room and sat down on her bed. Her eyes bright and sparkling, she began to describe the place that might be the elusive home for her god. Yin Ling listened in amazement to a description rich in detail. Ah Heng Cheh spoke eagerly of a place full of gods and goddesses, as well as mortals, some towering into the sky like giants, some tiny like children, hidden away in caves or foliage. Not all the gods were good: there was one with a very fierce black face and rolling eyes, who carried a long spear from which hung a row of skewered bodies. There was a very beautiful goddess who had a robe of pink and blue, standing amidst pink and white lotuses, so that you could not see her feet, but her hands were exquisite with long, tapering fingers, like the stems of flowers. There was a woman, a mere peasant, who was so filial to her mother-in-law that she lifted her blouse and gave her whatever nourishing milk she had, while her own hungry baby lay wailing on the ground.

Ah Heng Cheh talked on and on, her face bright with joyous recollection. She waved her arms about excitedly; she went up to Yin Ling and shook her by the shoulder, impatient for understanding. It was some time before Yin Ling realised that she was talking about Sai Haw Villa, a theme park for tourists, to which she had taken the old woman many years ago. Some fragment of what she had seen that day must have floated back to her and linked up with her homeless god. It was the height of presumption that her god, small and obscure, could aspire to a place among such a glorious pantheon. The mighty god Tua Peh Kong, with the enormous sunburst of golden spears on his back framing his entire body in a magnificent halo, would laugh him to scorn. 'I want to be sure first,' said Ah Heng Cheh earnestly, 'so I will not take him yet. I want to be sure for his sake.'

Ben stared.

'Oh, my God,' he said, as he moved towards them from his waiting place near the entrance. 'Oh, my God . . .' he said again, and burst into laughter. It was the rich, pure laugh of surprise and pleasure. 'Yin Ling,' he said. He remembered her name. It had been a cursory introduction, but he remembered her name.

She smiled. 'This is Ah Heng Cheh,' she said. Ben sprang forward to shake Ah Heng Cheh's hand. The Old One looked quizzically at him, then at Yin Ling, who bent down to say something to her. She frowned in concentration, then stretched out her hand and took his.

'Ah Heng Cheh, I'm so pleased to meet you,' said Ben, smiling, and she nodded and smiled back. Then she disregarded him. Squinting in the hot afternoon sun, she said she wanted to be in the shade.

Still breathless, Ben said, 'I had no idea.' The strange, keen desire he had felt that evening to see her again returned and blended with joyous astonishment to produce something like shock. Continuing to stare at Yin Ling, he could only repeat, 'I had no idea.' She smiled. Ben knew that he must seem very rude with all the staring, but he could not help it. The different voices in the strangely haunting poems – sad, bitter, confused, rapturous – all came together to attach themselves to a most unlikely face: pure, childlike, like clear water, yet with a hint of dangerously stirring life underneath. The picture of the face

75

flushed with anger on the evening of the dinner party, with one hand raised as if to strike, came back, too, to superimpose itself on the calmly smiling face now turned to meet his. There had been few times in his life when he was too overwhelmed for words, and this was one of them. He stood facing a young, slender, pale-looking girl, and he could not speak.

He put a hand to his head. She said something to him and broke the spell. He moved forward with a small abrupt movement, then stopped. He would have liked to grab her hands, perhaps take her into his arms. His initial shock was changing to physical need. But this was Singapore. She was someone's fiancée. He followed her as she led Ah Heng Cheh to a seat in the shade of a massive structure that cleverly simulated a mountain face in which, for the benefit of tourists and locals alike, the illustrious legends of a long ago time and far-away home were carved.

Ah Heng Cheh fanned herself vigorously with a handkerchief, complaining about the heat.

Yin Ling, her eyes looking straight into Ben Gallagher's, said, 'It was well before that dinner party. It was at the Monckton Food Park.'

It took a while for his mind, throbbing with the afternoon's surprises, to absorb this. A slight movement towards him, an inviting smile would have been sufficient; the reminder, loaded with intimacy, made him reel. Suddenly he felt reckless with joy. He moved towards the girl, and was then pulled back by the alarm bells ringing in his head. He decided to ignore them. The bells warned shrilly, 'This is Singapore,' but he dismissed them with a jaunty, 'Singapore, hell,' leant forward again, took the girl in his arms and kissed her, at the precise moment when Ah Heng Cheh's gaze was turned to meet the Monkey God's, a short distance away.

Seven

The love-making would take place in his room or, if he didn't want his bed messed up, in either of the guest-rooms or, as had happened twice, in the back of his car. But never again in her room. Vincent had no objection to making love in an HDB flat where a room was small enough for the sounds of sex to be heard outside; he just disliked the thought, during moments so intimate, of being under the same roof as the cold mother and the scheming, greedy brother. The demented old servant was harmless, but even her presence could be disconcerting, as suddenly one night, without first knocking, she had walked into Yin Ling's room, causing them to reach for their clothes and scramble up from the bed. The Old One, her wispy white hair loosened from her bun and floating around her face, had insisted on sitting in a chair in a corner of the room. There they were, looking foolish, their clothes hurriedly pulled around them, waiting for her to do or say something, while she continued to sit quietly, saying nothing, and turned a romantic evening into farce. He had laughed about it later, but that was it: no more love-making in the flat.

A deep sense of noble purpose always gave impetus to their love-making which, over the months since their engagement, had taken on a definite pattern, with a distinct sequence of steps. Vincent worked his passion systematically downwards, beginning with her hair, which he loved to uncoil and with which he could do a dozen playful things, then her cheeks, lips, neck, shoulders, breasts, belly. Lying calmly, she had the strange feeling of being an expanse of staked territory, unfolding to the advance of his hands. He liked her to lie back calmly and receptively, having nothing but contempt for women who took the initiative and did unseemly things. 'Call me old-fashioned, if you like,' he had said, smiling, 'but I want *my* woman to steer clear of all feminists.'

He stopped at her lower belly, where her panties had been pushed down and rucked up to a precisely drawn line at which his religion, which advocated sexual intactness until after the sacrament of holy matrimony, said, 'Stop right there.' Vincent, priding himself on self-control, stopped. Theirs would be one of the few marriages in modern-day, western-ised Singapore when bride and groom would go virgin to the marriage bed. It was a secret that needed no disclosure, and he was proud of it. The rampant Michael Cheong would have laughed immoderately at the quaintness. 'It belonged to our parents' time,' he would have guffawed in his characteristic crude style. 'Just what sort of fossilised code of sexual morality do you carry around with you?'

But Vincent had laid down the guiding principles of his life; they were working very well and he was not about to jeopardise his well-being by any violation. Actually, they were his father's principles; his father should get the credit. When Dato Chee Kim Leong (the title of Dato had been conferred by the Sultan of Johor in the annual birthday honours) had converted to Christianity, his fortunes changed. God show-ered him with one blessing after another, including business success, the honour of being singled out by the Sultan of Johor as a personal friend, and relief from a chronic pain in the shoulder – which had disappeared mysteriously after prayers in church. But as soon as he did something the

Church forbade, God withdrew the blessings. 'It was uncanny,' he had confided to Vincent, then fifteen, making him promise not to tell his mother. Just one sinful act and the very next day, for no apparent reason, a business venture had got into trouble. Vincent's father cursed the bad companions who had persuaded him to go with them to Bersih Street, the vilest street in Singapore, then notorious for its brothels. But he had quickly come to his senses. He had sworn never to sin again. God forgave him, and the business partner, again for no apparent reason, suddenly relented and made good the losses. 'Uncanny, I tell you,' Vincent's father said to his young impressed son. 'It wasn't a coincidence. It's happened many times.'

From this episode in his father's life, Vincent had come to the conclusion that sexual weakness was the surest way to incur divine displeasure, and had himself remained strong ever since, pushing his fiancée's panties down only to permitted pubis line. When the love-making was over, it gave him a special feeling of victory to be able to reflect that, once again, he had stood strong against temptation, and could help his fiancée put on her clothes without the slightest tinge of sheepishness or guilt.

The delicate question of whether it was all right for young engaged couples to make love was referred to his parish priest, Father da Costa. Rumours had circulated for some time about the mistress, a widow, whom he kept in a house in Johor Baru, which Vincent steadfastly repulsed as vicious and totally unfounded. He liked Father da Costa and invited him occasionally for a beer. On the matter of pre-marital sex, Father da Costa had said that God understood and forgave human weakness but it would be better to show self-discipline and restraint. Best of all, one should avoid even the temptation of sin. In the secrecy of the confessional, kneeling before Father da Costa or Father Alban Kee, Vincent could humbly but truthfully say, 'I did not avoid the occasion of sin. But I did not sin. There was no . . .' and either priest would understand. A man could be guilty of lust in his head alone, but nowadays, priests tended to be more understanding of young people. Concupiscence might course fearfully and powerfully through Vincent Chee's veins, like a raging flood, but he never broke into the forbidden, sanctified area, frenzied desire combining with caution to produce only a great deal of harmless thrashing around. When it became a habit, it also became a pleasure. Afterwards, he rolled off her in great, sighing contentment, and lay still for a long while, eyes closed, languorously aware of her movements as she dressed and made herself presentable to go out of the room to get him a warm beer, which he enjoyed after love-making.

Sometimes he smiled to hear her and his formidable mother exchange polite words on her way downstairs to the kitchen. His mother's advice on the whole matter, unlike Father da Costa's, was pragmatic: 'Don't get her pregnant,' meaning that pregnancy gave a girl bargaining clout. Mrs Chee liked and did not like Yin Ling: the girl was sincere, respectful and not in the least calculating or manipulative. But – even after one closed an eye to the demeaning background, to the repulsive mother and brother – she was strange and unpredictable and likely to give Mrs Chee's son a lot of trouble.

Yin Ling was in the mood for giving trouble and felt ready to deliver a sharp little pinch to an obnoxiously growing complacency. When Vincent rolled over, congratulated himself for self-restraint and disparaged others for lack of it, she knew the moment had come to strike. She got up, went to her handbag and pulled out a little pamphlet on sexual morality issued by the Catholic Church which she showed him, saying, 'It says that that is a sin, too.' The pamphlet kept its gently dignified tone throughout and referred only to the casting of seed.

'Come here,' said Vincent, with a return of desire, for when animated, her face was truly lovely; besides, he liked it very much when she came out of her usual quiet, introspective mood to challenge or tease him, and he liked it even more when the towel fell off, and a switch of hair fell down a shoulder and over a breast. It would only be later, in his review of events, that her sharp little comments and playful jibes, now conducive to desire, would be seen in the true context of their malice.

He was wild about her. Now, kissing her in his car parked in a large dimly lit area among a dozen other lovers' cars – unnecessarily so, since the privacy of his bedroom was only a two-minute drive away – he said, 'Why have I chosen you? My colleagues and friends have asked me, my relatives, my mother and you. Why? Because you are the most beautiful, the sexiest woman in the world.' She hated the banality and beat down the rising irritation. 'It's true,' he said generously. 'Yours is the kind of *natural* beauty I value.' He held her face in his hands and itemised her eyes, skin, smile, hair, slenderness. 'Look at Gina,' he said contemptuously. 'All that paint and gaudiness.' Carried away by his rhetoric, he went on to name other artificial women, always returning to the unadorned, pure beauty of his fiancée. 'Call me old-fashioned, if you like,' he said, 'but I'll permit makeup only for the wedding day, simply because it is expected and Mother would hit the roof otherwise. Otherwise just a little for evening functions.' In a moment of rebellion, she thought – as he proceeded to undo her bra – she might have her long hair cut off, load her eyes with mascara, rouge her cheeks and raise her hemline by several inches for the pure pleasure of watching his shocked reaction.

Artificiality of behaviour was even more contemptible to Vincent. He spoke of girls he had dated who had all failed the test because they turned out to be scheming or insincere, money-minded, manipulative or spoilt. The Hong Kong girl favoured by his mother had been the most spoilt of all. So the reasons for his choosing her were to be inferred from his rejection of the others: the Hong Kong girl was arrogant and demanding, so Yin Ling must have pleased him because she was simple, humble and co-operative. One Lina Neoh, an air stewardess, was clearly more interested in his sports car, his big house, his status, so Yin Ling must have been chosen because she loved him for himself, divested of the wealth.

'There you are, Chosen One,' he said, smiling at her.

'It's not too late to change your mind,' she said.

But he was not listening to her. It might have been the rousing effects of the movie they had just seen, which, even after cuts by the Censorship Board, reeked of sex, or it might have been the additional excitement of being among clandestine lovers, of being at the mercy of the Peeping Toms, including the perverts, shining torches into the startled faces in the darkness of the back seat. An efficient police force generally kept the lovers' haunts safe, but sick voyeurs were always prowling around. His mother would have been horrified. 'Your own private air-conditioned bedroom, and you parked your car in a public place full of bad, dangerous people? Vincent, you're mad.'

In the car, worked up to an impossible pitch by the recollection of a particularly compelling scene in the movie, he was all over her. As his mouth and hands worked on her body, he liked to ask her 'What are you thinking about?'

But she was thinking of something she had seen from the car as they drove along busy York Road. Professor Ben Gallagher and Holly Tsung were coming out of Yorkville Cold

Storage, carrying shopping bags. They were dressed casually and laughing together. She had wanted to turn back for a longer look as the car sped past, but had refrained from doing so.

She said, 'Nothing,' the irritation overtaken by the guilt, for she was conscious of a massive lie.

She had not stopped thinking of Ben since that meeting in Sai Haw Villa: she could recollect, in every detail, as of a movie scene in slow motion, the approach of the beard, the gentle pressure of his lips, the startled yielding of hers, the second startled movement as she turned round quickly because she thought Ah Heng Cheh was looking, and her sigh of relief when she saw that the Old One's face was turned towards a statue that had attracted her attention.

But the picture of him and Holly Tsung, laughing together, kept intruding and soured the joy. *If only*. Jealousy expressed itself in the same language as longing. If only there were no others. Vincent said, 'You are very quiet this evening.' She hated his probing, particularly tonight. Why are you quiet? Has anything happened? Is something the matter? Don't you enjoy my love-making? A man's sense of insecurity during his love-making was worse than anything else, for it made him querulous. She had learnt to deal with it.

'Thank you,' she said. The expression of thanks did the trick.

'Oh, don't think about it,' he said. 'Your brother shouldn't bother you any more.' He had written out a cheque for Kwan, as full settlement for the loan, drawing his attention to the amount of interest included in the sum payable to a precise decimal point.

Vincent's rescue of Yin Ling would be in exactly three months. He had left the decision of an auspicious wedding date to his mother to please her. She would consult the gods to whom he knew she was still loyal and pretend that she had done nothing of that sort.

And on Vincent's insistence, Ah Heng Cheh would come to live with them at 2-B Rochester Park. 'Thank you,' Yin Ling said again, miserably, overcome by the enormity of an unpayable debt.

Eight

Yin Ling said, 'I won't be long,' and left, ostensibly for the washroom sited at the other end of the Sai Haw Villa sprawl of exhibits. For she had grasped that Ben and Ah Heng Cheh wanted to know each other better, each presently resorting to much sizing up of the other and perhaps thinking, What would this person be to me but for her?

She stood in the middle, in dear connection to both. She left, feeling happy, and the gap that had been her place when they had all stood looking at a tableau of statues demonstrating filial piety, narrowed as the tall American, perspiring in the unaccustomed heat, moved closer to the little old Chinese woman, less than half his height, with the neat bun and perfectly starched clothes, and tried to make conversation with her.

Ben had learnt some words and a few sentences in her dialect, mainly greetings packed with goodwill and generous wishes for good health, prosperity and long years. She responded with much smiling and vigorous nodding, afterwards remarking to Yin Ling that she couldn't understand what the *ang moh* was saying; it was the *ang moh*'s thick tongue and thick beard that got in the way. She mimicked the thick tongue and plucked at the air around her chin to demonstrate the thick beard, making Yin Ling laugh.

Ah Heng Cheh remembered seeing an *ang moh* when she was a little girl in China. He, too, had had a beard and bright blue eyes, and wore a long black robe and a small image of his Christian god hanging from his neck. The village children, including herself, had followed the strange-looking foreigner as he walked about in their village, wanting to have a closer look at his eyes, like glass, and bushy beard, like a furry animal. They followed as a group, for safety, giggling and whispering among themselves, stopping when he stopped and turned to look at them, continuing to follow once his back was turned. She was the bravest of them all, though the tiniest. 'I went up to the stranger,' Ah Heng Cheh chuckled, when telling the story to Yin Ling and Kwan as children, 'and began to pull at the little tufts of hair on his hands. Such a lot of it! Like the fur on an animal's back.' It must have been this recollection that made Ah Heng Cheh now point, laughing, to the hairs on Ben's wrist, as his hand stretched out to her in friendship. They laughed and nodded at each other, their heads bobbing merrily up and down, like two amiable clowns in a children's pantomime. Then Ah Heng Cheh, the fascinated child once more, moved forward, selected one of the hairs and lifted it delicately between forefinger and thumb. She kept it held up and looked into Ben's face, laughing all the while. Ben grinned, intending to indulge the old woman as long as she wanted and thinking that, in his short stay so far in a superbly run, dreadfully predictable society, the unpredictable sometimes happened in the most delightful way. In a short while, the old woman was going to get tired of the childish diversion and return to her strange preoccupation of staking out a place for her god in this sprawling, garish amusement park. Meanwhile, he would humour her.

Meanwhile, too, they were attracting the stares of the other visitors to the park: a family group had stopped to look, giggle and comment. The combination of an *ang moh* and an old Chinese woman, who didn't speak each other's language – in the local idiom, a hen and a duck in comical squawking-quacking incomprehension – would be odd enough; the intimate horseplay made it odder, provoking the questions of the insatiably curious: Who could they be? What could have brought them together? What were they doing here?

Yin Ling's return provoked an 'Ah!' of instant understanding. The curiosity was over and the family group moved on. Local girl and foreigner: Singapore was full of them. The old woman was probably the girl's grandmother who, in her time, would have been forbidden by her parents to marry anyone outside her dialect group; now she had no choice but to move with the times and countenance her granddaughter's association with a hairy, blue-eyed foreigner. Someone in the family group, more curious than the others, turned round to have a last look and saw more confirming evidence of the old woman's concession to the young: she was actually having a picture taken with the foreigner by the Villa's roving photographer, standing between him and her granddaughter.

Ah Heng Cheh, fanning herself with her handkerchief, said she was tired: could she rest in the shade for a while? But she was not ready to go home yet.

Ben said, 'You know what I think? She's doing it for us.' Perhaps the god in the old woman's possession was a god of love; perhaps Ah Heng Cheh had witnessed their kiss, though she pretended not to, and had gone into a generous conspiracy with her god. Shall we pretend, for her sake, that there is a strong chance that Sai Haw Villa is your home, and take our time to decide? And the god, because love was his portfolio, not money, longevity or power, had agreed.

This was the second visit. Perhaps there might be more? Presumptuous, he thought. Yin Ling, sharp, bright and determined under that gentle exterior, was probably making use of him to provide some diversion to an intolerably tedious life with that bore of a fiancé. The thought tortured him.

But, at this moment, he didn't care. He allowed wish to spin into pleasing thought, then into firm conviction. Struck by the joyful things happening to him, he meant to enjoy every one to the full. The girl, risking so much by this tryst with him, using the old servant's presence to give everything an innocent colouring, must be interested in him, and interest was a sure prelude to love. He was wild to find out. He said again, 'She's doing it for us,' investing the 'us' with a new intimacy.

Yin Ling pointed at the life-size statues before them, painted in bright colours. 'How do you like our Singaporean tales of filial piety?' and immediately his buoyancy subsided into caution. She was nothing if not unpredictable. He had to tread carefully. He had been smacked down hard by the dean, by fellow Americans residing in Singapore, by the local people themselves for presumptuously bringing to bear his western perspective upon Asian cultural values. When in Rome . . . But unlike the Romans, Singaporeans did not demand that degree of accommodation from visitors. All they required was what MTC had already publicly voiced: 'Foreigner, don't foist your ideas of what is good and bad on us.' Someone had written a letter to the *National Times*, decrying senseless violence in American society and extolling Asian virtue, and Ben had instantly shot off a spirited reply, which was also a counter-attack: no society has a monopoly on the virtues of hard work, family closeness, filial piety. And he had dared to refer to examples of Asian barbarity, both past and present. When his letter appeared in the newspaper, the dean studied it carefully, then decided that this time he would not raise the matter with the American, sighing heavily over the continuing recalci-trance.

Yin Ling was challenging Ben. For reasons of her own, she was shifting into intellectual, debating mode. Perhaps with that pompous fiancé she had never had the chance to exercise her lively, questing mind. Heisenberg, Nietzsche, Kuhn: never having heard of them, the fiancé would have tried to put a saving face on his ignorance by simply turning everything round: 'Just what are you trying to prove?'

Suddenly Ben realised he didn't care for polemic any more. West versus East: never the twain shall meet. Newly prosperous societies like little Singapore rising in proud challenge of their former colonial masters. He remembered hearing Chong Boo talk gloatingly, at the dinner party, about a young Singaporean couple who employed a British nanny to take care of their two small children. The *National Times* ran pictures of them: a blonde, blue-eyed girl in white uniform, called Brenda Applethorpe, and two black-haired little boys called Ken-yi and Lu-yi. Chong Boo had hooted with glee at this truly historic turning of the tables: his own mother and an aunt had once worked as *amahs* for the white man.

Ben liked to engage in robust debate with bellicose Singaporeans like Chong Boo for the pure pleasure of it but there were too few of them around. Oh, for some really good friendly, or not-so-friendly, verbal jousting in a too-compliant society! But now the need sank under the greater urgency to please this girl, to say the right thing just to see her smile and the glow of pleasure in her eyes. It was unthinkable that she thought and felt like Chong Boo, but if she did he would help her hoist that ruthless MTC up on to the pedestal just to see her smile.

He could spend hours looking at her, watching her changing moods – moving shadows under clear, unmoving water. He thought, with a terrible pang, How can I bear it? She was going to be married in three months. Ah Heng Cheh and her god, if they were on his side, had three months.

He was aware of the stories circulating about him and various women, which were multiplying, but for her sake nobody would know about his passionate interest in this girl, engaged to someone else.

Yin Ling said, looking at the filial piety tableau, 'As a schoolgirl, I wrote about this and made fun of it. Later I felt sorry for being so mean.' The story in the tableau of the young woman who breastfed her old mother-in-law and allowed her own baby to starve to death had come in for the greatest ridicule. Yin Ling, eleven years old, fumed on behalf of the poor baby. Then, when she took up her pen again to write about the filial young man who every night took off his shirt and invited all the mosquitoes to bite him so that, satiated with his blood, they would leave his old mother alone, she laughed. Stupid young man. There were surely a hundred other ways of saving his mother from the mosquitoes; he was subjecting his body to needless torture.

But when she came to the story of the young man who wanted to reach a fish hidden under thick ice for his old father's dinner by stripping naked and lying on the ice to try to melt it with his body heat, Yin Ling relented and was ashamed of herself for being so mean. A god took pity on the young man, came down from heaven, melted the ice and thus allowed him to take home the fish to feed his father.

Yin Ling's eyes had filled with tears. She saw how wrong she had been. The ludicrousness of the tale was nothing. The kindness was everything. The eleven-year-old sat down and wrote another composition, this time of retraction and contrition. She handed it shyly to her teacher, a voluntary piece of homework – unheard-of. Her English language teachers at the Convent of St Elizabeth had received superb pieces of her work throughout her years at the school and had not known what to make of them, or of her. On the happy occasion of National Day, she had written a sombre poem that seemed too bleak for a ten-year-old; on death, she had written a ten-line paean of celebration and joy, upsetting the teacher who was superstitious and did not like reading about coffins and dead people coming back.

Woon Yin Ling's strange outpourings of heart and imagination came in a stream, uninvited, always written in her neat, firm hand, sometimes attached to the regular weekly compositions with less fearful subjects under conventional classroom titles like 'A Picnic on the Beach' or 'Helping Mother at Home'. Her classmates struggled with the intricacies of English grammar; she streaked ahead with flawless work that had some of her teachers running to their dictionaries. One day, her favourite teacher, Sister St Anne, in a lesson on general knowledge, invited questions and she stood up shyly to ask why a good god permitted evil in the world. Her teachers still whispered among themselves about her outburst of rebellious rage when she had savagely struck out the family name on her exercise books, and replaced it with one they later found to be an old servant's. Woon Yin Ling, star student, problem student. The teachers forgave her odd behaviour, impressed by her brilliance. Even then she was showing signs of a troubled nature, so that years later, after she had married Vincent Chee Wen Siong, rising political star, and the strange rumours had begun to circulate, her teachers were able to say, 'We knew all along.'

Yin Ling continued to surprise Ben. Seemingly shy, she broke out of her diffidence in the most unexpected ways. Who could forget that scene at the dinner party when she broke through her society's strictures to accost, accuse and berate men? Yet he had also seen her, timid as a mouse, beside her all-important fiancé. Engaged to be married in three months to a man she did not love, she was secretly, daringly meeting another whom she did. She did, she must – he could not bear it otherwise.

Again Ben became aware of desire spiralling wildly into hope. As the moment came for them to leave the villa he felt an overwhelming desire to stretch the hour of the visit into two, three, the whole day. He said, 'Could I take you and Ah Heng Cheh for a coffee somewhere?' It was a wild hope indeed: she must have made the two visits to Sai Haw Villa in time snatched between the hours reserved for that possessive, overbearing fiancé, possibly on permission grudgingly given. He wondered at her adroit manoeuvring.

Yin Ling said no, they had to go home now. But it was provocative, for her eyes said yes and sparkled with the daring of a dangerous, carefully hatched conspiracy: another time, soon. And then she was gone.

That brief, wondrous kiss of their first meeting, in front of a grotesque monkey statue – he had watched for a chance to repeat it in some dark cavern in the Courts of Hell perhaps, or in the shadow of a clustering of colossal gods or demons. He had been disappointed. It was as if the girl, shocked but tantalised by the brief contact, was saying, 'This is a strange new world I'm in with you. Don't hurry me.' Her eyes, face, every movement of her limbs said, 'I like being with you like this. Let's not do anything to spoil it.'

Where was she leading him? Reckless with hope, he didn't care. Again, caution said, 'This is Singapore. You are an *ang moh*. She is engaged to be married.' It might have added, 'To Vincent Chee Wen Siong, protégé of the Minister for National Development and, therefore, with enormous clout, enough to thrash an *ang moh* and make you wish you had never come to Singapore.' But a more compelling image, her sweet, exposed beauty, took precedence. Only this time, he was part of the picture, ardent and ecstatic. She was tender and loving, and Ah Heng Cheh was not present.

Nine

Alice Fong received a visit from Mrs Chee, for which she put the blame on her daughter. When Yin Ling arrived home from the university, the door was open even before she put her key to it, and her mother was standing beside it. She looked at Yin Ling and said coldy, 'I will not have anything like that happen again.'

Alice Fong had caught flu and had taken sick leave for some days. Yin Ling must have mentioned it to Vincent, who must have mentioned it to his mother. Mrs Chee, listening and saying nothing, secretly decided that this was the most opportune time to act. In her chauffeured Mercedes, bearing an expensive gift of ginseng, the best possible thing for a convalescent, she descended on the woman who – horror of horrors – would be related to her in three months' time. She had prepared well for this irksome but necessary visit, as she would later tell her friends, carefully rehearsing her request all the way to the woman's HDB flat: convince your daughter that she cannot bring the old servant with her to 2-B Rochester Park. We are a close, respectable family. At my time in life, I cannot bear too much change. My doctors tell me I have a weak heart. It was the right mix of seriousness, dignity and candour, and she memorised it with admirable concentration to ensure that every word, every inflection was in place.

The smell of stale urine in the lift – or could it be stale vomit? – hit her as soon as she stepped in, and she immediately pulled a handkerchief out of her handbag to cover her nose. Walking up two flights of stairs, which were covered with litter despite the government's frequent anti-littering campaigns, she was almost knocked down by a small child running away from another in a noisy game. Mrs Chee struggled on bravely, the handkerchief still pressed to her nose, bent on her mission.

The careful rehearsal had included gracious enquiries to Alice Fong about her health and the humble gift for her speedy recovery, and Mrs Chee delivered them smoothly and smilingly. Alice Fong, wearing an old grey cardigan and looking pale, had shown surprise then mobilised all her faculties to repel any attack by this alien visitor. She said, 'Thank you. Sit down. Would you like some coffee?' and was done with the obligatory courtesies.

'No, thank you. I won't be long,' said Mrs Chee, and instantly made the first of several blunders by giving in to her curiosity. Vincent had told her about the appalling conditions of the small, cramped HDB flat, and now her eyes darted here and there, trying to identify those generous gifts from her son that were making life more comfortable for everyone under that roof – the air-conditioner, a tall standing fan, even the new-looking furniture.

Alice Fong quietly watched the obnoxious woman, perfectly coiffured, glittering with her jade and diamonds, reeking of Chanel, doing a surveillance of her plain home, and knew she had to take the lead and make the first strike. She said, without any inflection in her voice, 'You have come to see me about something. What is it?'

Caught off-guard, Mrs Chee moved her eyes back to fix them on the face opposite hers and was instantly struck by how cold a person could be. It was most fortunate that the woman's daughter was not like her. Mrs Chee opened her mouth to speak and realised, with a little start of dismay, that she had forgotten the rehearsed speech. She said, in a rush of words, sounding harsher than she had intended, 'The old servant can't come to stay with us at 2-B Rochester Park.'

She had begun on the wrong foot, and knew it. Alice Fong, her face devoid of all expression, voiced cool surprise: 'You have come all this way to tell me this? I have nothing whatsoever to do with my daughter's life.'

'As her mother, surely . . .' stammered Mrs Chee and fell deeper into the trap of her own making, for Alice Fong threw back her words in all the ruthlessness of their logic: 'As his mother, you surely have enough influence to have made all this unnecessary in the first place.'

Mrs Chee, nonplussed, opened and closed her mouth several times, but nothing came out. She wanted to speak of her love for her son, and his love for her – there was no closer mother–son relationship anywhere in Singapore! – but she did not know where to begin. With her friends she talked interminably about her precious Vincent. 'My son asked me to adopt his Christian religion and I did,' she said. 'I would not have done it for anybody else.' When he was fifteen, Vincent had been hospitalised for some leg injury. She had slept on a mattress on the floor beside his bed, waking to his every need, making the nurses redundant. She wanted to talk about her son to everybody, including Alice Fong. But the woman, cold as a tombstone, stopped joy at its source. Mrs Chee thought, I hate her more than ever. She stood up and Alice Fong stood up with her.

In the short distance to the door, each swore inwardly that any meeting in the future would be confined to the two obligatory occasions of the wedding and the family dinner after the couple came back from their honeymoon. They would be joyless occasions, with everyone surreptitiously

96

looking at their watches. The birth of a grandchild would necessitate another tedious round of *ang pow* giving and celebratory meals, but neither wanted to think so far ahead at this stage.

Almost at the door, Mrs Chee said, 'Oh!' as she suddenly saw Ah Heng Cheh standing a short distance away, staring at her. Ah Heng Cheh, her remaining years depending on this powerful woman, could not have appeared at a worse time. She looked dishevelled, having got up from a long, fitful afternoon sleep, and she smelt. 'Stale saliva,' Mrs Chee was later to say, with a shudder. Worse, she was holding in her arms the statue of her god, discoloured, pitiful, misshapen – an outcast god unfit to be under the same roof, much less in the sacred room under the staircase, with Mrs Chee's respectable gods. 'Oh!' said Mrs Chee, and fled.

It had been a thoroughly bad visit. She had failed. On her way to the waiting Mercedes, she made little noises of agitation, then wept. The handkerchief was out again, to deal with the smells of this horrible place – the tears, too, inflicted by its horrible residents. The horrors were not over: walking down a flight of stairs, Mrs Chee stepped on a soiled banana leaf bearing the remnants of a curried meal. 'Oh, God, oh, God,' she moaned, trying to shake it off the heel of her shoe.

Perhaps the gods would be kind and save her son from a disastrous marriage to this strange girl, with her strange mother and servant. Mrs Chee was prepared to go several notches below the ideal set by the daughter of the Hong Kong shipping magnate. She would not mind, for instance, any decent, well-behaved girl from the HDB, provided she was devoted to Vincent, had a good education and was not burdened with a demented old servant who was taking too long to die. Perhaps, thought Mrs Chee, with something approaching desperation, she should enter into some kind of bargaining with the Christian god himself. Her good friend Mrs Maria Fernandez had recommended going through the Blessed Virgin Mary, with a novena of masses in her honour: even gods listened to their mothers. But, sighed Mrs Chee, she was more at ease with the gods of her childhood, whom she had watched her mother, and her grandmother, persuade, cajole, beg, flatter, importune and even trick into granting their requests.

On the way to the car, Mrs Chee passed two children, one carrying a large basket containing small, neat, conical packages in newspaper. Mrs Chee knew what these were. The children looked tired and the basket was still almost full, which meant that, going from door to door selling their *nasi lemak* or vegetarian noodles, they had found few buyers. Their mother was probably a widow or an abandoned wife and made the *nasi lemak* in between caring for the baby and doing piecework for a garment factory. Mrs Chee, from the opulence of 2-B Rochester Park, was familiar with the struggles of the other side, mainly through stories told by her cleaning woman and Arasu, the chauffeur.

She stopped the children and bought up the entire basket, which she would give to Arasu for him to take home to his family. Through her tears, she smiled kindly upon the startled faces of the children. They shifted about, then looked at each other. The older of the children, a serious-faced girl of ten or eleven, shyly took the large note that Mrs Chee had pulled out of her purse. She whispered something to her small brother, who was clearly in charge of the takings. He pulled out some money from his pocket, and they went into urgent consultation, not knowing how much change they should give back to the lady.

Mrs Chee laughed and said, 'For goodness' sake, children, I don't want the change!', closed the girl's fingers tightly over the note, and waved them away. They said, 'Thank you,' together, very politely, then hurried off.

On her way through the heartlands of Singapore's poor, Mrs Chee dispensed largesse liberally. 'My mother always taught me to be kind to the poor,' she said. An old man in a torn singlet and dirty khaki shorts ambled up, and Mrs Chee opened her purse once more.

It was in her nature to be generous; it was also in her nature to be shrewd. One day, playing *mahjong* with her friends, she had hit on a plan for parlaying her acts of generosity into a force of high-stakes bargaining with the gods. She selected her *mahjong* friends with care, settling upon three equally respectable, equally well-endowed friends – Mrs Gracie Han, the wife of a retired banker, Mrs Lee Ai Geok who owned a chain of antiques shops, and Madam Florence Lim, wife of the late president of the National Turf Club, who had homes in Los Angeles and London. Mrs Chee, holding up a large silk pouch to show her friends, all seated in readiness for a game, had announced her plan, 'All losses are mine. All winnings go in here. For charity,' and started a trend among the caring rich who said it suited them perfectly, since they played *mahjong* to kill time, not to win friends' money. Over the years, the Little Sisters of the Poor, the Seng Tee Loke Old People's Home and the Singapore Buddhist Orphanage had benefited from Mrs Chee's magnanimity.

Each act of compassion and kindness increased her accreditation with the gods. Relieve suffering. Value life. Once her charitable project had got off the ground, Mrs Chee began to consider how she might honour the second part of the god's injunctions. She sternly instructed her two Filipino maids never to wantonly kill the snakes and rats that sometimes came into her garden. She scolded Arasu for killing a wounded pigeon that had fallen on top of the Mercedes and made a mess on it. She bought cages of doves for release during temple festivals, watching, eyes wet with joy, as they fluttered, then soared into the dazzling freedom of the vast blue sky.

She was steadily building up merit in preparation for the tremendous favour she was going to ask her gods. 'You want this from us. What will you give us in return?' they were sure to ask, and she could say proudly, 'Not *will*, but *have*. It's already done!' and show them the merit amassed, like handsome savings in a bank, ready to be drawn upon.

Arasu said, 'Ma'am?' solicitously, for the tears of agitation at the recollection of the failed visit had returned and she was blowing her nose. Nowadays, because she had taken on the problems of the young, her moods swung wildly and gave her headaches.

'I'm all right, Arasu,' she said.

She did not forget to give him the basket of food for his family, and enquired after one of his sons, who had had a minor accident. Then she sat up straight, dried her eyes, repaired her makeup and told him briskly to drive her straight to the Kek Lok Thong Temple, and not let Vincent know either of the visit to Yin Ling's mother or the visit to the temple.

Alice Fong did not see the need to hide anything from her daughter. Both the stark truth of the present and the grim prospect for the future had to be told. So Alice Fong, as soon as she had discharged her displeasure about the visit, recounted it in its every unpleasant detail, then went on to say, 'Vincent says yes now. A man in love will promise anything. But give him a year, two years. If Ah Heng Cheh has not died by then you'll be in trouble. His mother will give you

100

hell. And I can't have her, as you know. I am not well. I went to see the doctor yesterday. It's not flu.'

It was like her mother to deliver rebuke, advice, warning and devastating news all in the same monotone. Yin Ling almost dropped her bag of books and files to the floor as she rushed forward and asked, 'What did the doctor say? Is it bad? Why didn't you tell me?' She stopped. Even then, her mother did not allow herself to be touched.

Alice Fong sat stiffly on the sofa, her cardigan pulled tightly around her. 'It's all right,' she said quietly, not looking at her daughter.

'Does Kwan know?'

'There's no reason for him to know.'

'He's your son.' This would have been no more than a banality to her mother, and would therefore have been better left unsaid. She could see her mother, pulling her grey cardigan more tightly around herself, wincing at the effusions of concern and sympathy. Kwan could swing from the melodrama of noisy grief to grave inquisition all within half an hour. Had she prepared a will? Would her church, which received 10 per cent of her salary every month, be named as beneficiary?

'I shouldn't have told you.'

'But, Mother—'

'Please don't let Vincent know.' She disdained to mention his mother, but that was understood.

'I won't. But, Mother—'

'We won't talk any more about the matter.'

Now Yin Ling remembered the recent persistent coughing from her mother's room and the efforts she had made to suppress it. She remembered too an array of medicine bottles on a small tray on the kitchen table. How remiss she had been!

Yin Ling sat down beside her mother on the sofa. They were silent for a while. 'Mother . . .' Her hand had laid itself on her mother's, which was clenched in a fist on her lap. To her joy, her mother made no attempt to move away. To her greater joy, the fingers slowly unclenched and moved to respond to hers. She would have liked then to throw herself into her mother's arms, the terrified twelve-year-old all over again, who, after she had seen the prize money returned, had wanted to run screaming into her mother's room and deny the truth of the prize-winning composition: 'It's you, Mother, I swear it's you and not Ah Heng Cheh.' She had stopped in front of her mother's closed door, then turned, walked away, dried her tears and got ready to go to school. She would restrain herself now, too, and be content with the tiny opening of that closed door. Strong emotion would only frighten off her mother. So they sat quietly together side by side, their hands clasped, but only for a short while, for Alice Fong got up abruptly, said it was time to take her medicine and left to go back to her room.

But she had a request to make first. 'Let me know if Mrs Chee has a cold or is indisposed in any way.'

That happened exactly a week later. Vincent told Yin Ling about a fall his mother had had in the bathroom in which she had sprained her ankle. It swelled badly and she had to be confined to the house for three days. On the second day she received a gift from Alice Fong through Yin Ling. The ginseng was of a different brand, but equally expensive.

Ten

Vincent said, 'Take it down.' The president of the Students' Union, Daniel Koh, hesitated, looking foolish and unhappy. He tried to say something, standing uncertainly under the huge white banner strung between two lamp-posts announcing in large red and black letters: 'Lecture by opposition member Tiger Dragon Khoo! Hear the Tiger roar! See the Dragon breathe fire!'

As past president, Vincent Chee had no right to throw his weight about, telling present presidents what to do or what not to do. But his reputed connections with the Minister for National Development, who in turn was reputed to be MTC's blue-eyed boy, as well as his high standing with the university authorities, inspired respect and fear. Daniel Koh, a cowed, diminished figure who bore little resemblance to the confident, eloquent populist of a year ago, riding high on the shoulders of supporters to garner the highest number of voters ever recorded in the history of student elections, shifted about and avoided looking at Vincent. Then he muttered something to some fellow unionists who were hanging around in the background, and they began to remove the objectionable banner. Poor Daniel had thought it more than a good idea to invite an opposition member to give a talk to the students; he had thought it brave as well, and had received several congratulatory claps on the back for a decision that was sure to provoke much excitement in the campus, since university students had always been described by opposition parties as weak, cowardly, spineless, for their fear of speaking up. Tiger Dragon Khoo would be a refreshing change from the government's party men, who droned on and on either about government achievements or threats to the achievements. They never deviated from these two topics and came with impressive coloured charts and columns of statistics, which they flashed on overhead projectors. The student audience always clapped politely, but for V. S. Ponnusamy – the leader of the opposition – or Tiger Dragon Khoo, they stood up and cheered lustily. V. S. Ponnusamy delicately twirled a white gardenia and alternated his shrill denunciations of MTC with sly, almost gentle references to high government malfeasance cleverly hidden all these years, and Tiger Dragon Khoo, in the midst of his screaming invectives, would tear open his shirt to reveal a ferocious tattoo of a tiger and a dragon entwined. He made the crowd go wild – laughing, hooting and stamping their feet. The political rallies of the government attracted a trickle of people, those of the opposition a flood, causing roads to be clogged with honking cars. The local newspapers never carried reports of these rallies, but the crowds kept swelling.

But, at the end of the day, Singaporeans, although wanting to deflate the government ego, thought of the safe streets, the clean water, their subsidised flats, the money growing in their bank accounts, and they voted accordingly.

'Did you have any idea at all of what you were doing?' Vincent scolded, and perhaps it was to impress his fiancée, standing by his side, that he continued to berate Daniel Koh, who was looking more foolish by the minute and now deeply regretting his bravado. He was sure to get into trouble. He was on a study grant from the university and he feared it might be withdrawn. Could Vincent Chee put in a word for him? After the mess was over, he would approach Vincent Chee for help.

Vincent watched Daniel Koh and his fellow unionists meekly pulling down the banner and rolling it up. It was already late evening, but they would have to start taking the necessary action following the decision to cancel the talk. The flyers on the university noticeboards would have to be taken down, and new flyers apologising for the cancellation put up in their place. A phone call would have to be made to Tiger Dragon Khoo. 'I'll do it personally,' said Daniel Koh miserably.

Tiger Dragon Khoo was sure to scream, 'See what I mean? Typical Singaporeans. Cowards. MTC has all of you grovelling in the dirt at his feet.'

Daniel Koh, with the rolled banner under his arm, stood in abject wretchedness before Vincent Chee, for a last dose of stern advice. 'Concentrate on your studies and avoid this sort of trouble in future,' said Vincent, relishing his role of respected mentor.

'Yes, Mr Chee,' said Daniel, then looked up to see Vincent Chee's fiancée looking at him with a smile, gentle, warm, reassuring, that said, 'You're all right. Everything's all right.' It was gone in a second, but it saved the evening for Daniel Koh, who said later to a friend, 'I liked her from that moment.'

In the falling darkness, as he walked back to his parked car with Yin Ling at his side, Vincent said, 'Singaporeans may rail against MTC but in their hearts they appreciate what he has done.' He could have given a convincing example but he did not want to hurt her feelings: her mother and her mother's relatives had been living in squalid Chinatown tenements or in *kampongs* with no proper sanitation, until the government had built HDB flats, thus enabling them to move out of the squalor and, for the first time in their lives, they had had the benefit of electricity, running water and flush toilets.

Yin Ling said, 'I think MTC's not the callous, ruthless person that people make him out to be.'

Vincent turned to look at her, surprised. 'Oh?' His fiancée never ceased to astonish him. He demanded an explanation for a perception that pleased him although it ran counter to the majority view: MTC, all head and no heart, MTC in whose veins ran the severe black ink of dictatorial authority and cold efficiency, and not a drop of human kindness.

Now it was her turn to hide something from him, for it might offend him that it was she and not he who had been honoured with a face-to-face encounter with the great founder of modern Singapore – MTC himself. It would more than offend Vincent if he knew that Ben Gallagher had been involved too.

It had happened in this way.

Yin Ling, Ah Heng Cheh and Ben had been waiting for a taxi outside Sai Haw Villa. While there was always a continuous stream of taxis plying outside the popular tourist place, that day none had appeared. They had waited for twenty minutes, and Ah Heng Cheh was getting fretful, when Ben decided to walk to a busier road some distance away, where there were sure to be some taxis, and end their torturous wait in the afternoon heat. Fanning Ah Heng Cheh, Yin Ling was startled to see a Mercedes draw up in front of them. The driver got out and said, pointing to Ah Heng Cheh, 'Is she ill? Does she need transport anywhere?' Too astounded to reply instantly because she had recognised the stern personage sitting at the back of the car, Yin Ling said something about their getting a taxi soon, and the driver nodded and returned to the Mercedes, which then sped away.

Sitting in the car in the dim light of one of the many street-lamps dotting the vast campus, Vincent said, 'I heard that Professor Ben Gallagher was at one of the university plays, cheering them on.' A trap? Or just the usual sharing of campus news and gossip? Yin Ling felt that she gave herself away easily. The mere mention of a name, a place, a time could instantly elicit in her the give-away flushed cheek, evasive eye, faltering tongue. The mere thought of him – oh, grown so dear over only three hurried meetings at the villa: she was keeping count – was enough to quicken her breath; the mere recollection of a dream in which he had appeared only as a blurred face or a soundless voice was enough to make her dart for something, open her bag, adjust her collar, do anything to hide the spreading flush. In the campus, her friends talked about Professor Ben Gallagher more than any of the other lecturers, and breathlessly ran out of adjectives to describe him: crazy, eccentric, mad, interesting, brave, refreshing, brazen, daring, reckless, insane, simply gorgeous, sexy. She was learning to keep a straight face while the chatter went on around her. The truth might be troublesome, was threatening to break out all over her face, and then, of course, she would again have to pretend to drop something or rummage about in her bag.

Might the truth be preposterously daring one of these days, make her look at her friends straight in the eyes and announce, 'Never mind your speculations about him and Holly Tsung. Ben Gallagher and I are seeing each other secretly,' then watch the expressions on their faces. But the truth, like rumours, mostly went underground in people's lives in this respectable society and sloshed about uncomfortably. Only edited and sanitised truth, as befitted their society's clean image, stayed at the surface. Everybody coped better with that version of the truth.

Suddenly Yin Ling remembered Michael Cheong's tales of

his private life in the brothels of Bangkok, which had bubbled up for everybody to see as soon as drunken good humour took over. Gina's father didn't drink and therefore didn't let down his guard, but his daughter unabashedly let others peer into the dark gutter of his wild years of womanising and gambling at the races, which at one time had plunged his family into acute poverty. 'My mother made rice dumplings to sell in the market,' said Gina. 'I love my mother. I hate my father.'

The secret life of Yin Ling's own father had gone to the grave with him. Or perhaps her mother knew, but would not tell her.

And Ah Heng Cheh? Did an old servant with a blameless life have a secret or two too shameful to be told? She remembered once that, in his uncouth way, Kwan had told her he had heard from their mother, who had heard from their grandmother, that Ah Heng Cheh had lost her virginity as a young girl to a rapacious relative. That had been just before she set sail for Singapore. Perhaps that was why she had been sent away.

Vincent Chee? He had told her about his dates with an air stewardess and the Hong Kong girl. 'No secrets from each other,' he had said, at the start of their relationship. 'You have nothing to fear.' What he had meant was that deception and betrayal, if they occurred, could only come from his side, with all its disproportionate advantage and therefore temptation. Now things had taken an unexpected turn and he was the one feeling insecure. Vincent could be sly: was he setting her a trap? In the dimly lit darkness, he said, 'Ben Gallagher's playing with fire,' and she thought he cast a quick sidelong glance at her.

108

Eleven

Ben knew that between four-thirty and five in the afternoon Yin Ling would be at the university library, in the philosophy section, sitting on a bench or leaning against the wall, reading a book and waiting for her fiancé to pick her up. He had seen her there twice since that memorable meeting in Sai Haw Villa; the first time when he thought she assiduously avoided looking at him, the second when he decided to walk over to her but stopped at the sight of Vincent Chee approaching. A slender girl with a pale-coloured cardigan draped over her shoulders, sitting on a low stool, bent over her book, the afternoon sunlight streaming in through the window slats and shining on her coil of hair and part of her face – the picture stayed in his memory for years and grew dear.

Nowadays all sorts of thoughts about her occurred to him, sometimes in the most unexpected way, as in the middle of a lecture, causing his heart to quicken, a sudden trailing off of his voice and a reddening of the tips of his ears, which would not go unnoticed by those incorrigibly curious female students who were for ever watching him and suppressing giggles. He never saw girls who watched so avidly or giggled so much, and was vaguely aware that he had been voted by them the most eligible lecturer in the campus.

'Do you think it is Holly Tsung?' they whispered. They had seen him with her several times on the campus. They had also seen him with other members of the university's female teaching staff. 'Big Romeo, that American. It must be Holly. She's the prettiest.'

He became self-consciously aware of a tear in the seam of a sleeve, a spread of ink on a shirt pocket where he had put a leaking pen, a tiny flake of food lodged in his beard through the reaction of the most avid of his watchers, a pretty girl named Faridah. She grew bold and began going to his office more often than was warranted by tutorials and work assignments. After each visit, she would leave behind a personal item such as a pencil-case or sunglasses and telephone him later to ask about it, then hurry over to collect it. One small item, a ring with some mysterious Egyptian sign that she liked to play with during tutorials, had served for four visits. The relentless amnesia would have continued if she had not decided one day that it was time to take action. Over the months, the Professor's numerous acts of courtesy, friendliness and goodwill towards her had built up into the solid evidence she needed to prove that he was interested in her. She now believed that the time had come to act on the evidence. 'Do you have a girlfriend?' she asked boldly.

'No,' he said.

She brightened visibly. 'Do you have somebody you think about all the time?'

'Yes,' he said and added, 'but I'm afraid she already has someone else.' He swore he could hear her resolve in her mind, as she stared at him in shocked silence, 'I'll find out who she is.' Faridah had done some quick eliminations: the woman could not be Ms Manjeet Kaur of the Geography Department, Dr Louise Reynolds from the English Remedial Unit, Miss Holly Tsung, the lecturer on sabbatical from Hong Kong University. Could it be Mrs Khalid from Administration, who made no secret of her admiration for the handsome American professor? But Mrs Khalid was happily married.

Girls like Faridah, giggly and silly, could turn vicious and attack rivals with their lethal fingernails: he imagined Faridah descending with fury upon Yin Ling and screaming, 'You leave him alone. You have a boyfriend already. How many more do you want?'

He needed a precise slot of time in the relentless march to her wedding in three months, and a precise measure of space in the vastness of the campus that she would vacate in three months for the greater vastness of her new life in which he could never hope to see her again. These were coalescing into a precious opportunity for him to strike.

He struck, coming upon her as she was sitting on her favourite low stool reading – he managed to see the book's title before she snapped it shut and looked up at him; it was *Socratic Dialogues* – and at once noticed how beautiful she was. A girl on the threshold of marriage looked her most radiant; this girl, pouring her pain into secret poems, took her radiance from elsewhere. He had seen romantic novels poking out of the bags of some of his female students as they sat for lectures and tutorials; this one, with her sad, gentle face and tumultuous soul, sought calm in the work of ancient philosophers while waiting for her fiancé to take her home in his red sports car. Yin Ling would never cease to intrigue him.

The tiny opportunity shrank. For even before he began speaking to her, he saw her eyes dart instinctively to her watch – how close was it to the time when her fiancé would come striding up? – then glance around the room: how many people were looking on, to tell her fiancé later that they had seen her talking to Professor Ben Gallagher? This girl, bright, intense, passionate, moved among strangulating shadows.

He felt an overwhelming urge to confront her with the

untruths with which she had surrounded herself: 'Why do you continue to be with this man?', then stage a lightning rescue: 'Come with me.' Then he thought, I, too, have my untruths that need confronting. And this is Singapore. You have a good job. This girl is about to get married.

Groping for a conversation topic, Ben said to Yin Ling, 'Did you read this story in the *National Times* about Madam Leow trying to track down her son's killer?' He pulled out a copy of the newspaper, open at the page of the report, which showed a picture of a solemn-faced, middle-aged woman.

While cycling to do an errand for her, Madam Leow's fourteen-year-old son had been knocked down by a hit-and-run motorist and left to die. Frustrated by the inability of the police to find the killer, the woman had taken on the task herself. Every day she stood silently on the spot where the boy had died beside four placards mounted on wooden stands, in the four official languages of Singapore, appealing for witnesses to the accident. Her message in English said, 'Please help. Please help end a mother's pain.'

The incident was one of many, reported daily in the newspapers, about accidents and burglaries, the preying on naïve, trusting old women by confidence tricksters with magic stones, and the outraging of female modesty in buses by men unzipping their trousers or rubbing themselves against terrified girls. It was a piling up of shameful debris that should have been the target of the government's anti-littering campaigns rather than the piles of rubbish left by picnickers on beaches or by careless hawkers on the streets of this proud, clean, successful city.

Sensitive, gentle Singaporeans, like Yin Ling, skipped the trumpeting reports of government successes and dwelt on these raw, chastening reminders of a people as weak and bad as any. But Yin Ling never wrote impassioned letters to the

Forum pages of the *National Times*. Instead she went to her secret notebook and wrote her poems, sharing the agony of a widow who had lost her only son to cancer but continued to set the table for two every day; of a young, desperate mother who had left her newborn baby outside a police station but was caught because she had hung around for a last look at the baby. Yin Ling sent them anonymously to *Dialogue*, where Ben read them and waited, futilely, to see them in print.

In a lower voice, Ben said, 'I shall be there at eight o'clock tomorrow evening,' meaning that he would go to the place of the accident, near the junction of Tennant Road and Rajagopal Street, where Madam Leow stood in lonely vigil every day until midnight. No curious onlooker, he planned to say something kind and encouraging to the grieving mother, and he wanted Yin Ling to be with him then. The normality of a regular date was out of the question; a meeting disguised with nobility of purpose might work. Thus frustrated love was making him desperate and devious and he knew, in the weeks ahead, that he would plot and scheme shamelessly, employ every trick of manipulation and subterfuge to meet her.

In his dream, he disregarded the shrill warning bells, plucked her away from Vincent Chee, walked with her along the lovely beaches of Changi, along the brightly lit streets of charming Little India, got gloriously lost with her in the lush greenery of the Botanic Gardens with their hundred-year-old trees. In his working hours he plotted, with an increasing sense of urgency, to snatch whatever little time she had away from her fiancé. It was a hurried, whispered invitation, and he was out of the library in a few minutes, not wanting to risk meeting Vincent. She had looked surprised and said nothing, but her eyes had betrayed interest and excitement. He would ever be fascinated by her eyes: large, deep, haunting, and burning with their secret fire. In one of his dreams, she was wearing sunglasses and he pulled them off saying, 'Don't. Don't hide.'

Looking into her eyes, he had felt a surge of confidence. She would be there. She would not disappoint him. She would extricate herself from whatever activity her fiancé had planned for them, leave the old servant sleeping peacefully at home and slip out quietly. Love had turned fugitive, and they would adjust their behaviour accordingly. They were playing a high-stakes game, and were fired by it.

Ben stamped his feet and waved his arms about to beat off the mosquitoes. There was a local joke that they only went after *ang moh* blood. The pests would eventually be vanquished by the teams of fumigators from the Ministry of Health fanning out to all parts of the island to kill them, but right now they were buzzing around him in a swarm. He was a short distance from Madam Leow, still standing stoically beside her pleading messages. There was a stool nearby, also an umbrella and a basket with a flask, a cup and a folded towel, but in the hour that he had been there he never saw her sit down or take a sip from the flask. She stood, eerily silent and still, looking out into the night, crying to an indifferent universe: What do you care? Her strength came apparently from a love that had first melted helplessly in the crucible of her grief, then cooled to form a cold, hard, shining weapon of revenge. Ben thought, Pity the culprit if the police catch him for this woman will slay him first. He had gone to her to say something kind, but she had repelled him by her stern demeanour, continuing to look straight ahead and ignoring the curiosity of motorists as they slowed down to watch. Ben felt ashamed of himself. He had come to show sympathy for one woman but could think only of another. He glanced at his watch. So she was not coming after all. He would like to believe she had tried and given up: her fiancé's possessive surveillance, like a finely meshed net, allowed no escape.

Suddenly aware of the inquisitive looks thrown in his direction by motorists and pedestrians, Ben gave a snort of annoyance. Perhaps they thought he was a journalist from a foreign newspaper, out to get a sensational story, a tourist with a strange tale to tell the folks back home, a crazy, idle *ang moh* who had nothing better to do than watch out for the bizarre in the endlessly fascinating East.

He was none of these: he was just a big fool who had allowed hope to overtake reality.

His hope held, as he made his way back slowly to his car in a nearby car park, looking back once, twice, then with every few steps he took. That beautiful, familiar face – what wouldn't he give to see it now? He started. It was a girl, of about the same age, with the same slender build. He looked at her walking past Madame Leow in silent vigil, looked at her intently, as if that would make her stop suddenly, turn round, wave at him and wait for him to hurry over and say, 'I knew it was you. I knew you would come.' Another woman passed by; no, it was not her. He reached his car and was about to open the door when he heard her voice and spun round. She had run to catch up with him and was out of breath. The pale-coloured cardigan was around her shoulders. 'I'm so glad you're still here. I'm sorry,' she said breathlessly. She pointed to a taxi a short distance away, waiting by the road. 'Two minutes,' she gasped. 'I've just two minutes.' So it was snatched time all over again – two minutes here, five there, half an hour in the library, one hour in Sai Haw Villa.

Suddenly Ben felt angry. He was living on the leftovers of her time and energy. He wanted to say, 'Damn everything. I don't have to take this any more,' but he saw the pale, stricken look on her face. He wanted to say, with some remnant of the anger, 'Damn the taxi, send it away, I'll take you to wherever you want to go.' Then he realised she was trying to tell him something, but couldn't. They stood awkwardly together by his car, the pretext of noble purpose in coming to this place now exposed, for neither wanted to spend the precious two minutes on any other – and they could feel the impatience of the taxi-driver by the road.

He took her hands in his and saw how cold and frightened she was. He wanted to pack into the two minutes a reckless promise for future meetings, 'I'll be wherever you want me to be, at whatever time,' an extraction of a promise even more reckless, 'Tell me that, no matter what happens, you'll always want to see me,' and a kiss, for he could dream of nothing these days but holding her close in his arms, breathlessly, silently.

She pre-empted all three by breaking away abruptly and saying, in a hurried whisper, 'My mother's in the taxi. We're on our way home from the doctor's.'

He felt a surge of pity, then of gratitude and love: all came together in an overpowering impulse to grab this girl and hold her in a long embrace, long enough to allow a gentle easing of his overcharged heart. For he needed – oh, so much! – to ease it against her warmth. What excuse had she given her mother for getting out of the taxi to meet him in secret? Could the woman be peering at them now through the darkness, trying to detect danger and issue warning? This girl whom he had thought of confronting with her untruths was negotiating them, as in a deadly minefield, one at a time, for his sake.

She said, 'I'll be taking Ah Heng Cheh to Sai Haw Villa on Thursday afternoon,' then ran back to the taxi.

He understood now. Their meetings would have to be confined to a public place, during a slot of daytime, covered by the respectable purpose of enabling an old servant to help her god find his way home. Outside this safe structure – a warm nest out of the storm – Yin Ling was lost.

He told himself it would not be for long. In a short while she would have to leave it, trample it into the ground, break out. At that moment Ben hated Sai Haw Villa for the garishness of its displays and the stridency of its messages about filial piety and obeisance to powerful gods.

He would not have minded accompanying her to any of the places, dismal beyond belief, that she had mentioned in her poems: a derelict shop-house, one in a row soon to be torn down where an old man had been robbed of his meagre life-savings then murdered; a strange temple or a shrine somewhere in a remote part of the island, consecrated to the memory of babies not allowed to be born; that spot on the campus grounds where stood the deformed, shunned tree that spoke her language of love and sympathy. He thought of a particular poem she had shown him, which had made the excitement of his discovery of her flare into something like yearning, though the poem, written a year ago, was clearly not meant for him:

I want to tell you something
Mine is a lonely message
In a bottle, storm tossed,
Cast by the sea at your feet.
I know
You will go on your way.
You will not break the bottle,
Much less break the code.

Had it been meant for that boorish Vincent, who only understood the language of raw power and domination? Or

117

for a secret lover who came and went, never understanding the cry from her heart, bottled up and thrown upon the waves? He felt suddenly jealous.

He claimed the poem for himself; she had shown it to him, therefore she must have meant it for him. Years later, she would reveal to him (he wished she hadn't) that the lines had been penned for neither mortal man nor immortal god but for an unknown being, hidden in shadows, to whom she was always appealing for answers to tearful questions. *Seek and you shall find. Knock and it shall be opened to you.* She did not seek justice, redress, good health or fortune. She sought answers to questions. Why did good people suffer? Why did bad people prosper? Why did good people die? What happened to people when they died? By adulthood the questions had shaped into darkly sinister ones. Is there a god? Isn't there only nothingness and a void at the end? Is there meaning at all?

The being had eluded her questions. But it had not always been elusive, hiding in the shadows. During a brief period of her school life in the St Elizabeth convent, he had taken on the bright reassuring presence of a loving father and shepherd, the gentle-faced, bearded god with his hair parted in the middle and falling gracefully to his shoulders, so familiar from the myriad statues in the convent, the holy pictures and medals that the nuns distributed. She had told him that even as a schoolgirl she was already asking the gentle Saviour to help her understand the many confusing things she saw around her. Her classmates prayed for good grades in the examinations; her prayer was, 'God, if you are all-knowing and all-caring, please help me understand,' but she had gone away dispirited. She was only fourteen, but a crisis of meaning had already entered her life. Sister St Anne, her English language teacher, had been nonplussed by her questions.

'You think too much,' she had said, tapping the girl's forehead with a forefinger. 'You ask too many questions. Here' – the friendly nun had picked up her hand and pressed it against her heart – 'here. This is more important. Loving God is more important than asking questions about Him.'

'I was an arrogant girl, wanting to know everything,' she had said, smiling at the recollection, and he had smiled back, loving her. 'I would open the Bible at random to find the answer to a question, and then read, to my dismay, something totally irrelevant. 'Why do even babies have to suffer?' For answer, I had the tale of Jonah's three days in the belly of a whale, or the miracle of the loaves and fishes. I would go away feeling let down.' She had been impossible, in those days, arguing with the good-natured nuns and a kindly priest called Father Anthony. The god, inviting the hungry, sick and troubled to go to him, ignored her and went on his way, leaving her stamping her feet in vexation. She stopped looking for answers. In time, the god too would become irrelevant and fade away; his footprints on the sand were gone but the unhappy bottle was there still.

Ben thought, watching her taxi speed away, So it will have to be Sai Haw Villa, dammit. But he felt happy. The earlier mood of disappointment and annoyance had vanished. He began to whistle and wax sentimental, seeing a tiny, storm-tossed bottle that he would not wait for the sea to cast at his feet but would go plunging into the waves to seize as his own.

Twelve

The Ten Courts of Hell, ten tableaux of incredible tortures meted out to men and women who had had the effrontery to offend the gods, were the centrepiece of Sai Haw Villa. It was the only display not outside in the open air and bright sunshine but set in the semi-darkness of dimly lit caverns, the better to highlight the burning coals and dancing flames of hell, the blood from decapitated, disembowelled or impaled bodies splattered on pure white snow, the gleam of knives, spears, axes, hoes, pitchforks and tridents at the ready or in action. The aim of the display was to instil a proper sense of awe at the power of gods presiding over mortals. The creator had even made the horror auditory, installing tapes of bloodcurdling screams, wails and sobs.

This was Ah Heng Cheh's latest choice for a home for her god although she had decided on a shrine at the entrance, rather than the Ten Courts themselves, bright not darkened, which was dedicated to a variety of male deities, all with ferocious staring faces and vengeful weapons, fitting guardians of hell. Here, Ah Heng Cheh said, she would pause and pray, and make offerings on behalf of her god, who seemed to be showing signs of affinity with the deities so unlike him in appearance and demeanour. A gentle, snub-nosed, child-faced god with his deformity of arm among these? thought Yin Ling. They would eat him up in a moment, since they claimed no divine compassion, only power.

Still Ah Heng Cheh insisted, clearly impressed by the scale and extravagance of the offerings in the shrine. Here the visitors converged, in the capacity of devotees, not sightseers, putting aside camera for devotional joss-stick. The joss-sticks were bigger and longer, the gold and silver paper flowers larger and brighter, the heaps of coins on the ground higher. Someone had draped a heavy garland of jasmine, dahlias and marigolds, threaded with tinsel, round the neck of the most ferocious god of all, whose eyes were two enormous white discs with burning black centres and whose fangs dripped blood. Garlands were for alien gods, not these, who preferred billowing joss-stick smoke and sumptuous food – the wor-shipper might have come after doing a similar obeisance at a Hindu shrine then perhaps proceeded to a Christian church with a third garland, playing safe in this multi-religious society.

Ah Heng Cheh preferred to stick to her one god, on whose behalf she had brought, in a paper bag, a bunch of joss-sticks, some plastic flowers and two red candles. A lesser god, he needed help, and she would never be found wanting. 'Is this where you want to be at last?' she asked him, and watched for signs of his answer.

'What *are* these signs?' Vincent had asked Yin Ling, suddenly curious about his fiancée's weird old servant. 'It is one thing, Ling, to be loyal to an old woman living in the past, and another to subscribe to her superstitions.'

'What *are* these signs?' Ben, too, asked.

'I don't know,' Yin Ling said. 'Ah Heng Cheh doesn't tell me certain things. But I think they have to do with what her prayer-sticks say or what her dreams tell her.'

Ah Heng Cheh began her rituals at the shrine, which would take at least half an hour.

Ben said, 'I'm beginning to love her. She's doing it for us,' and as soon as they were out of the sunlight and in the welcome darkness of the First Court of Hell, he turned Yin Ling's face towards his and kissed her.

'I have an idea,' he said. 'Listen to it and don't say no.' It was preposterous and tantalising. 'We don't stop coming to this place till we have seen all the Ten Courts of Hell. And we are allowed to do only one Court at a time.'

Ten visits in two months or so before the wedding – neither could refer openly to the rapidly approaching event, which hung ominously in the air. Ten visits of at least sixty minutes each. And if she allowed him to drive her and Ah Heng Cheh back in his car instead of taking a taxi, that would be another ten times, say, fifteen minutes of extra time. Ben joyfully did mental sums. A total of an extra one hundred and forty minutes or two and a half hours. Love had its calculus of hours and minutes, dollars and cents, which clacked away busily, like the noisy counters in the Chinese abacus.

Now it was Yin Ling's turn at the negotiating table. Every Thursday afternoon, she took Ah Heng Cheh to visit a sickly friend, in the Seng Tee Loke Old People's Home, someone Ah Heng Cheh claimed had come from China in the same ship as herself, though that was doubtful. It had been an easy switch from the Seng Tee Loke Old People's Home to Sai Haw Villa that needed no accounting to Vincent, since no time was being taken away from their regular weekly schedule of activities together. Vincent had kindly offered to take them and fetch them home, then shown great relief when Yin Ling turned him down. So far so good. But Vincent's indefatigable mother was planning an elaborate schedule of wedding preparations, including several visits to the dressmaker for the wedding gown and the long *cheongsam*, into which Yin Ling would change midway through the wedding dinner, as well as visits to the bank vaults to view her jewels, which would be

loaned to Yin Ling for the wedding. The schedule, meticulously planned and executed, was sure to eat into Yin Ling's
precious Thursday afternoons. Ten visits? They would be
lucky to have eight, seven, four.

'Wait a minute,' said Ben. 'Are you saying that this is all the
time you have for me?' He was already making the claims of
the lover.

She wanted to say, 'Wait a minute. What is this that I hear
about you and Holly Tsung?' The fleeting glimpse of them
outside Yorkville Cold Storage on York Road returned, with
more remembered details, screaming evidence of a liaison:
the casual clothes they were wearing, he in T-shirt and shorts,
she in some skimpy blouse and shorts, both wearing sandals,
carrying the grocery shopping bags of cosy domesticity.

Yin Ling thought desperately, No. No. Their first time
together in the tantalising semi-darkness of the Courts of Hell,
where a man and a woman could stand close together, could
turn to face each other for a kiss, without attracting the
attention of other visitors, must not be spoilt by any intrusions.
She was shocked at how easily she gave in to jealousy – a new
feeling. She would beat it down and relegate it to an outside
world quite separate from her private, precious one. Her
world had split into two, a fearful outer and a joyous inner.
The outer world seemed, thankfully, far away – Vincent,
Vincent's political ambitions, Vincent's increasingly sharp,
loaded questions, Vincent's querulous mother and her frenetic
preparations for the wedding, the wedding itself at which the
Minister for National Development and a couple of Members
of Parliament would be present, her mother's cancer, still in
the early stages but worrisome, the new life in the splendid
home at 2-B Rochester Park in which Ah Heng Cheh might or
might not be allowed, Ben's women, Ben's messy affairs,
Ben's clashes with the university authorities that might cost

him his job and force him to leave Singapore for ever. It was a frightening world, which receded when confronted with the urgency of the present moment, shimmering with possibilities. Confined to a small space in semi-darkness, before a scene of suffering souls, and a small slot of time that would end when her watch alarm sounded telling her to fetch Ah Heng Cheh and go home, this tremulously thrilling present must be relished in its every second.

She thought, with a wildly beating heart, It may just be possible. I may yet find the courage. But every time the daring possibility of leaving Vincent occurred to her, the hateful outside world would break in, with its chilling rebuke, 'Are you mad?' and try to drive away the madness.

There were tales of women in flight from the altar at the last minute or in their bridal cars driving round and round until the wedding guests could wait no longer and the families screamed for an explanation. They were rare tales indeed and rarer still in Singapore where men and women, with their university education and their respectability, went about their lives in an orderly manner, returning quickly to the orderliness if they were so foolish as to succumb to passion's madness. In her mind, she tried the first words: 'Vincent, I think we should talk,' but she could not even manage this first step, much less the wild flight in her wedding dress.

Ben said, 'What are you thinking about?'

'Nothing,' she said.

When they came out into the bright sunshine once more, Ben emptied a pocketful of coins into a plastic box placed on a table near the exit, with a crudely written plea for donations that would surely be rewarded by gods' blessings. He was so happy that he felt his generosity must cut a swath through the poor and needy of the world. He dragged Yin Ling to a little booth where a stout man with bad teeth told fortunes. For a few dollars each, his clients' palms were photocopied, the photocopies fed into a computer, and their fortunes rolled out in English on pink paper. Ben's eyes skipped the extravagant promises of wealth and prosperity, the confident analyses of character and temperament in terms of lofty Oriental virtues, to concentrate on predictions regarding his love life.

'"You will achieve much happiness, contentment and fulfilment",' he read jauntily, holding up his piece of pink paper. It was his excuse to touch her again. 'Who's talking about "will", future tense?' he said, pressing her to his side. And it was then that, despite an overwhelming joy, she asked, 'Would you tell me about Holly Tsung?'

He touched her lower lip with a forefinger. 'We'll not talk about Holly,' he said, 'or Vincent.'

Thirteen

Ben wanted some ground rules. 'Let's agree on a few things,' he said. 'Number one, as soon as we step into Sai Haw Villa, we drop everything.' He meant any mention of other relationships: of Vincent or Holly. The rule would stretch to forbid mention of any place or person connected with either: so Rochester Park and the Minister for National Development were out, as were Hong Kong and Yorkville Cold Storage. Love guarded its interests jealously and crushed out everything else; it searched past, present, future for every sign of threat and crushed it systematically. Ben never thought he could be so insanely jealous. He thought, My God, this girl is driving me crazy.

Their time together was so precious they could not afford to fritter it away on argument or quarrelling. 'Don't you see how ridiculous it all is?' he said. 'We have our time here by the whim of an old woman and her god and we spend it talking about others.' Yin Ling liked the 'we' of their growing closeness, the 'others' of its exclusiveness, making their world a precious cosmology of two; she began to get hungry for more proof of his growing attachment and greedily analysed his speech, searched his every look for it.

'What's number two?' she said, feeling light-hearted and happy.

'Actually, there's no number two,' he said, and since the only other visitors in the semi-darkness of the Courts of Hell

126

were a pair of elderly tourists who had no interest in observing a young Singaporean girl and an *ang moh*, he spun her round again to face him and was delighted at how readily she responded.

One of the elderly tourists, a rosy-cheeked, grey-haired lady in neat skirt and blouse, smiled benignly upon the young couple so comfortably nestled against each other.

Yin Ling, peeping over Ben's shoulder, saw the tourists looking at them and smiled back. She was radiantly, recklessly happy. This was only the Second – or was it the Third? – Court of Hell: they would never be able to complete all ten and reach Heaven at the end, represented by a pleasant pavilion with a curving roof. There the gatekeeper, represented by an old woman dressed in a blue robe, would administer the Potion of Forgetting and Forgiving to the sufferer, thus releasing him from his pain and preparing him at last for Heaven.

No Potion of Forgetting or Forgiveness for her. In a dream, Vincent and his mother were already assailing her: 'What do you think you are doing? Everybody's talking about you and the *ang moh*!' Her own mother's voice joined theirs: 'You are playing with fire.' Vincent's voice rose above everyone else's: '*You* rebuked Michael Cheong for being immoral and made him lose face.' But recklessness had its own special joy. 'I have never been so happy in my life. Leave me alone,' was all the defence she needed, and thereafter she shut her ears to the warning voices.

A group of three visitors stopped beside them to gaze at the dismal scene they were standing beside, and to peer, in particular, at the crushed body of a woman in a mortar, her limp legs hanging over the edge, her mouth opened wide in a scream that coincided with a shriek of pain that came from the audio tapes.

Ben and Yin Ling had jumped apart as soon as the visitors appeared. The startled guilt of lovers was in itself a pleasure, and so they stood, trembling with their secret joy and suppressing an urge to laugh, while waiting for the interlopers to move on to the next Court of Hell, which they did, still shaking their heads over the crushed body.

'Rule number two, proper behaviour in the presence of gods,' said Yin Ling, instantly inviting another round of misbehaviour, as Ben said, giddy with happiness and disregarding an approaching group of noisy, chattering tourists, 'Come here,' and this time kissed her deeply, daringly.

Fourteen

It was not ground rules this time. It was a proposed schedule, written out on a piece of paper.

'So little time together,' said Ben, 'and there's so much I want to know about you.'

The proposed plan was cast in the bold language of the confident lover: 'By 4th Court of Hell, YL must show/read the secret poems. Skip 5th Court for YL to attend V. S. Ponnusamy's rally in Bukit Merbok. Would love to attend political rally with her! By 6th Court YL must reveal her thoughts and feelings about her fellow Singaporeans. Skip 7th Court to smuggle YL into apartment for homecooked candlelit dinner. Can make great pasta! Before 10th and last Court?'

The large question mark for the last Court stood out on the paper, wobbling with uncertainty, then trembling with daring hope: suppose at the end of the long, dark, winding cavern, she suddenly made up her mind, turned to him and said, 'It's done. I've done it!' He said, giving her the piece of paper, 'So, what do you think?'

What did she think? Her thoughts were less relevant than her feelings, for she experienced then a tremendous surge of joy. This man loved and desired her so much that he was resorting to a slew of stratagems to keep her by his side, masking them with a show of playfulness. But even as her heart was singing, she took a pen from her bag, scratching out the rally and the candlelit dinner. 'I'm sorry,' she said. 'We agreed. We can't be anywhere without Ah Heng Cheh and her god.'

He hated Ah Heng Cheh and her god then. He wanted Yin Ling to break free, to go with him into the vast open spaces of lovers' exploration and discovery, but she stayed determinedly in her little confining space. He was reminded of a small timid animal that had been confined so long it had forgotten how to be free.

She gave him back the outrageous proposal, and he let it fall, a limp failure, to the ground. His moods swung wildly and dangerously; he needed to check himself by looking at her, touching her. She pressed her face to his shoulder. 'Rule number two. Stick to Sai Haw Villa.'

He let his arm fall to his side. She took something out of her bag. 'By a perfect coincidence,' she said, 'I have brought this' – it was her precious book of secret poems – 'and we happen to be at the Fourth Court of Hell. So your first wish is granted.'

Ben said sulkily, 'Not one of your poems was written for me. I don't want to see them.' Love, hungry for attention or confirmation, used the childish ploy of petulance and succeeded.

She said, 'This one's for you. I wrote it last night.'

'Is it sad? All your poems are so sad,' he said.

'Read it.'

It was entitled 'The Rhetoric of Our Love'.

Our shared sense of cosmic yearning
Has turned this into a suprasensual union
Lifted above Earth's space-time.
But if in the cosmos' vast dust-pan
Man's history is but a speck,
And a man's history but a speck
Of a speck of that speck,
Then what chance has this,
Our one hour

130

Against Time's merciless obliteration?

Only the lovers' bold impulse
To pull it out in time
And fix it upon
An eternal star.

In the brief ensuing silence, he felt tears prick his eyes and blinked them away quickly, overcome by her touching naïveté. Less than two months before her marriage, this girl celebrated her love for another in a poem of outrageous claims, hopeless longing and massive untruths. The vaunted suprasensuality was an outright lie. They had become as earthy as they could get, retiring into the darkest of shadows allowed by the Fourth Court of Hell, to press together in contact and desire: his hand was already inside her blouse and upon a breast and she was pressing herself closer. The lover's bold impulse to save the threatened love from cruel obliteration? Another massive untruth and a false promise too, for neither had the guts. She would never be able to fly out of that elaborate gilded cage, even if the door were left open. And he was not sure if he wanted her to. A woman cast out of her society for her folly, later to wake up hollow-eyed with regret and misery, would be more than he could handle. What could he offer her in return for so much love and sacrifice? Nothing.

He kissed the head that lay on his shoulder and said, 'I love you so much I wish I didn't.'

With Vincent, Yin Ling had rejoiced in the pure surrender of the three simple words, only to have the purity sullied by the hundred qualifying conditions attached to them: I love you, but first you must love my mother and 2-B Rochester Park. I love you, but first you must give up those worthless secret poems. I love you but, but, but . . .

131

This man said, 'I love you so much it hurts,' qualifying the pledge only with his pain.

It drove her closer to a resolution of the situation that had its own special pain – oh, how could she have imagined her soul would be in such turmoil? – so that she was at a loss for words, and clung to him, trembling with joy and trepidation as she watched the storm-clouds come closer.

Fifteen

Ben said, 'See, we're almost at the end,' and from where they stood, they could see part of the Heavenly Pavilion where the gatekeeper awaited with the Potion of Forgetting and Forgiving. It was bright with natural sunshine, unlike the Ten Courts. Indeed, it shimmered with the promise of eternal joy. Ben turned her round sharply to face him. 'Come with me. I need you. Don't you see? Don't leave me.'

She noticed that he expressed his love, longing, anger and frustration always in three words, never more.

Her spirit soared to the love of this man, from a foreign land, who had come into her life unexpectedly and too late. It was a call of pure love that enticed her spirit and made it sing and soar, a cosmic yearning, no longer tied to the smallness and meanness of earthbound things. As a girl at school, during an art lesson when they had to express their dearest dream in a painting, she had drawn a picture of herself and the gentle Saviour with the beard and middle-parted hair, in loving closeness, among a froth of clouds and a sunburst of haloes. The art teacher, Sister St Dolores, going through a pile of eager paintings of pretty houses with modern furniture, gardens and swimming pools, was astonished to see it. It was entitled 'Love'.

Yin Ling caught glimmerings of this perfect love in Madam Leow who stood, in solitary grief, day after day on the spot where her son had died, and in Ah Heng Cheh, who said she would not die until she had fulfilled the wish of her little god. No buts and ifs hung upon *their* loving.

'Come with me,' Ben said to her a month and a half before her wedding, and her spirit swelled. The radiant-faced god of love, high up in the vast blue sky, was stretching out his arms to her, but he had to reckon with his rivals, dark and serious-faced because their realms of influence were not love but hard cash, property and status, duty to mothers and servants and sheer survival on a cold, hard planet – and a colder, harder bit of that planet called Singapore. These rival gods grabbed her by the arm and pulled her away, saying, 'Are you mad? Are you throwing away everything?'

Ben said, 'I've been thinking. I can't give you the same life of wealth and prestige, but we could live reasonably well on my salary. You could go on with your studies, at Berkeley, if you wish to.' He was speaking in the language of the rival gods now. They talked, with some embarrassment, about the messy financial situation following the divorce from his wife of two years, which involved a jointly owned house and which remained messier than ever, with lawyers and acrimony.

It was horribly unrealistic of them therefore, standing together in the last Court of Hell, to think that the call of that radiant-faced god in the security of his pure white clouds, could be heeded. Everywhere around them, the other gods, earthbound, were shrieking their warnings.

'I'm scared,' she said, hating herself for it, and he, not relinquishing the frantic urgency of his searching mouth and hands, said, 'I know.'

Sixteen

A h Heng Cheh's dreams went far back in time, crossing seas, traversing vast stretches of land. She saw herself as a pig-tailed little girl in her ancestral village in China, hiding in a temple, being fed rice by a stern-faced woman who, she knew, was not her mother. The woman, with a show of bad temper, kneaded the boiled rice into little round balls and pushed them into her mouth, saying angrily, 'Eat, eat,' almost choking her. The dreams whizzed wildly to and fro in time; now she was a child, now a young woman in a ship bound for Singapore, sick all the way, vomiting and being vomited on, for there was a group of three women with her who were all sick. Truth of memory had no place in dreams for although she recollected clearly that in real life they had all made it safely, like her, to Singapore, she saw them, in her dreams, fly in an arc through the air, like three bedraggled birds, and fall to their deaths in the churning waves.

One man in the ship made it more than safely. Years later, Ah Heng Cheh was able to say, each time the name of the remarkable millionaire-philanthropist Tan Puat Hoe came up, that they had been in the same ship. He was a skinny, bright-eyed boy with nothing but the shirt on his back, standing on the deck every day to stare out at the far horizon, already smelling fame and fortune. Tan Puat Hoe and his sons and the grandsons now owned the largest hotels in Singapore, and their names were mentioned frequently by politicians in speeches because of their immense donations to charity. But in her dreams he, too, was cast into the sea, like the unfortunate, vomiting women.

In Singapore, she had served Yin Ling's family through four generations, which the dreams scrambled in a crazy time mix, so that the old were young again and the young took on the grey hair and seamed faces of the old. She herself was child, young woman, old woman, one melting into another, like trembling shadows in water. But her god was always the same. Carried with her other belongings in a tin trunk secured tightly with rope when she came to Singapore, he never changed in her dreams, although, nowadays, the dreams of him were not happy ones.

'Please don't harm him. He's never done anybody harm,' she pleaded. An ugly-looking child with a snotty nose, wearing a ragged shirt and shorts, had seized the statue from her and was now raising it high in the air. The child's face said, 'I want to see how it breaks.'

'Let me,' said Ah Heng Cheh, in a soothing voice pulling a handkerchief out of her blouse pocket. Nimble as a darting goldfish, she had run after the naughty, laughing Alice Fong, and later her children, Kwan and Yin Ling. 'Let me,' said Ah Heng Cheh gently, taking her clean handkerchief to the child's nose. The child pushed her away. 'No! No!' she screamed then, as another child ran up and snatched the statue away. Then another appeared, and another. Soon the place – a patch of wasteground, with a huge rubbish dump – was full of menacing children, passing the god among them in boisterous play. He was tossed about in the air, a plaything. Ah Heng Cheh ran frantically from one child to another, to save him.

'Oh, no, no!' She looked around. The children had vanished, and so had her god. Then she heard a pitiful wail and looked up to see him lying inside a bird-cage, one of a multitude hanging from the roof of some old building. She had never seen so many bird-cages in her life, like a vast overhead bamboo forest. 'I'll save you,' she said. She had seen a long wooden pole somewhere; she went to get it, then prodded the cage in which her god was imprisoned. He looked so tiny and lost.

'You know it's all your fault, don't you?' he said petulantly. 'Our troubles started with you forcing me to befriend those gods in Sai Haw Villa.'

'Forgive me,' she said humbly. 'I'll save you.'

An old man came running up, red-faced with anger. 'Stop that!' he said, wresting the pole from her. 'What do you think you're doing? Now go away.'

'But that's my god!' said Ah Heng Cheh tearfully. 'Why are you all doing this to him? He's never harmed anyone.'

She saw, to her alarm, that a bird was in the cage, fluffing up its feathers and circling her god menacingly. The bird became two birds, four, a dozen: soon a whole horde was encircling her god. They were small, normally peaceful singing birds, but they had turned vicious, and were attacking him with their beaks. She saw them peck away furiously at his eyes, then his stomach. Peck, peck, went the sharp, hard beaks, making holes in his stomach, pulling out his entrails and draping them across him. Blinded, disembowelled, the god uttered not a sound.

'Have mercy!' wailed Ah Heng Cheh. The old man stood by indifferently, smoking. 'Have mercy!' sobbed Ah Heng Cheh. She saw somebody in the distance and recognised him instantly. 'Kwan!' she shouted. 'Please come and save my god!'

'Is he already dead?' asked Kwan. 'A dead god is not worth any money.'

Fortunately, the god was not dead. After Kwan knocked off

the murderous birds with the wooden pole, the god sat up in the cage, alive and whole once more. Ah Heng Cheh wept with relief and joy. She saw Kwan studying him with great interest.

'He's special,' said Kwan. 'Can't you see? There's a name for special gods because they have gold under their tongues and behind their eyes.' He examined the god closely. 'Ah Heng Cheh, you are a very lucky woman. You can sell him for a lot of money!'

Ah Heng Cheh snatched back her god. 'What do you mean?' she said angrily. 'This god's not for sale. This god wants to go home!'

'Wait a minute,' said Kwan, and he no longer looked like the Kwan she had taken care of and loved. 'He's mine. I saved him. Give him back!'

Ah Heng Cheh fled.

'Stop!' said Kwan, and gave chase. She ran and ran. She could hear the running footsteps behind her. Then the footsteps and the shouting became fainter and faded away. A darkness and silence had descended. 'Let's take a rest,' said Ah Heng Cheh, and sat down on what seemed to be grass, a little damp but otherwise comfortable. She held her god tightly in her arms, then rocked him gently, making little soothing sounds.

Ah Heng Cheh looked around her. In the distance, she could see the light of street-lamps and tall buildings outlined against the night sky. She could hear the faint sounds of moving motor vehicles, which suddenly gathered into a single impatient honk followed by something like a man's angry shout. Where was she? A large drop of water fell on her nose, another on her god's forehead and then the rain pelted down mercilessly.

'Oh, oh,' cried Ah Heng Cheh in alarm, scrambling up. She decided to walk in the direction of the lights and the tall buildings, clutching her god. She thought, in panic, Where am I? What's happening? for she found herself in the midst of moving, honking cars. One screeched to a halt in front of her. It was difficult to see anything in the rain, despite the light from the car headlamps, but she could feel faces staring at her. Then somebody grabbed her arm and led her away, guiding her through the cars.

It was a stranger, carrying an umbrella. 'Old Auntie, come with me,' he said, holding the umbrella over her with one hand and clutching her arm tightly with the other. He led her out of the rain and into a brightly lit shop, where several men and women sat drinking coffee and eating hot buns. 'Sit down here,' he said, offering her a chair beside a table. 'I'll get you a towel.' She sat down, dripping wet. Everybody was staring at her. In her dreams, she flew across fields, ran down roads, negotiated rivers with the strength and ease of the young. Now she was immobilised by the clinging wetness of her clothes, the cold, hard ground under her feet, the relentless-ness of unkind stares. The stranger returned with a large towel, accompanied by a woman, presumably his wife, carrying a cup of hot water. 'Old Auntie, you'll be all right,' said the stranger kindly, and she burst into tears. She wept loudly.

'I want to die,' she sobbed. 'Will somebody take my god to his home and let me die in peace?'

The kind stranger said soothingly, 'Old Auntie, don't cry. We'll take you home. Come, drink this hot water.'

His wife said, 'Would you like something to eat?' She had thoughtfully towelled the god dry too. She hurried off, then came back with a warm blanket, which she put gently round Ah Heng Cheh's shoulders.

Feeling drowsy, Ah Heng Cheh began to drift into a fitful sleep. She heard voices and moving feet and opened her eyes to see Yin Ling kneeling beside her, looking anxiously into her face. 'Ah Heng Cheh, you frightened me. What on earth happened?' cried Yin Ling.

Ah Heng Cheh heard another familiar voice and turned to see Yin Ling's *ang moh* friend, the bearded one. Had he entered her dreams too?

Ben said, 'We'd better take her home at once.'

Yin Ling said to the kind stranger and his wife, who were the proprietors of Sin Sin Coffee Shop, open twenty-four hours a day to serve night-shift workers but not lost old women, 'We can never thank you enough.' Ben was already helping Ah Heng Cheh to her feet and picking up her god to put back safely in her arms.

The couple, mistaking Yin Ling and Ben for a couple, told them about a grandmother, aged ninety, who also went wandering off on her own. The woman said to Yin Ling, 'You and your husband had better make sure it doesn't happen again. My grandmother was almost knocked down by a motorcycle!'

The man applauded the cloth label bearing address and telephone number on Ah Heng Cheh's sleeve. It had been sewn on by the resourceful Romualda. 'Very good idea,' he said amiably. 'We didn't think of doing it for my wife's grandmother.'

During the ride home, Ben was ashamed because his first thought was: This is the first time she's with me in my car and she has to be at the back, with her old servant. Ah Heng Cheh was talking to herself agitatedly. Ben thought, I don't care. This could be our last time together. He turned round suddenly, leaving only one hand on the wheel and tried to touch her – her face, hand, knee, any part of her. A second

140

before he turned back he glimpsed Ah Heng Cheh lean towards him. He could not see her face clearly but felt the heat of the anger that animated it. He heard it, too, in the words she was now hurling at him, and caught sight of an accusing finger shaking at him. Perhaps she was already regretting her part in their complicity, and was now joining the warning voices: 'Beware this foreigner. You can only come to grief with him.'

Yin Ling said, 'Ssh, ssh,' trying to calm her, but the old woman's voice got shriller and her forefinger more accusing.

Ben said, 'Tonight's adventure has been too much for her. We'll be home in a short while.'

'How is she?' Vincent had called Yin Ling on a whim – he seldom telephoned after ten at night – and found out from Alice Fong about Ah Heng Cheh's strange escapade. He had driven over immediately.

The old woman was sleeping peacefully. She was none the worse for the adventure, and there was no need to get a doctor. Alice Fong had found a hot-water bottle, prepared a flask of hot water, then returned to her room and gone back to bed.

Vincent said, frowning a little, not wanting to look at Yin Ling, 'Let me get this straight. You had a call from a stranger close to midnight. He had found Ah Heng Cheh wandering in the rain. You decided to call Professor Ben Gallagher for help. Why didn't you call me?' The other question, 'How did you get his phone number?', was already on the tip of his tongue, but for the time being he would concentrate on the outline of a development that was beginning to send out foul vapours. He did not like it one bit. His instincts said, 'Go slowly and carefully. Only in this way will you get to the bottom of it.' He repeated, 'Why didn't you call me?'

Her heart was pounding so wildly she thought speech would be impossible, or incoherent at best, but she surprised herself by saying calmly and distinctly, 'I didn't want to disturb you.'

His instincts said, 'Keep calm. Anger won't help.' But this was too much. 'Disturb me!' he exploded. 'Since when have I regarded anything I do for Ah Heng Cheh as a disturbance?'

The truth was troublesome, and Yin Ling had kept it to herself. Now she would allow it to come forth in the ruthless unambiguity of words.

She said, 'I have been seeing Ben Gallagher.'

It took him a while to digest the enormity of the confession. He looked at her steadily. He had learnt to ascertain the truth of her every utterance, whether of contrition, guilt, embarrassment, defiance, doubt, need, yearning, by looking at her face as she spoke, and he had never been wrong. Now he was not sure. He said, 'What do you mean "seeing" him?' Women like Yin Ling, transparent and guileless, sometimes exaggerated their wrongdoings when caught. Once, when doubting his word and harbouring angry thoughts of him, she had made a tearful confession out of all proportion to the deed, and he had accepted her apology, secretly pleased. She was as open and trusting as a child. His mother, with her unerring judgement, had once told him, 'This I must say of your girlfriend. She is a very good person.' And she gave half a dozen examples of devious young women whose cunning little zigzags to find out this or that, to ask for this favour or that, contrasted so sharply with the straight, clear lines of Yin Ling's dealings with her.

This thought filled Vincent with something like hope, suppressing his anger, as he stood before his fiancée, demanding truth. Love needed hope; fear, too, needed it. Once he had been totally secure in his relationship with her;

now he felt the ground shake a little under his feet – a new sensation. The hope began to shape itself around a strong possibility, which he would put to her for confirmation: she was seeing Ben Gallagher over her poetry, of course, meeting him in the *Dialogue* office. He knew she had been anonymously submitting her poems to that stupid magazine, which few bothered to buy and which, he was told, would soon fold. And he knew, too, that the American went to the *Dialogue* office sometimes, to chat with the editors, and had attended many literary events organised by the English Literature Department. Damn the poetry! Damn *Dialogue*. And damn the American. But if that was the reason for their meetings, even if they had been regular, it meant that the situation was still manageable. He would put an end to it.

Then she told him about the meetings in Sai Haw Villa.

Vincent remained silent for a long while, looking at the ground. Then, his face taut, he said, 'Let me get this clear. Ah Heng Cheh suddenly gets it into her head that her god's home is somewhere in the sprawling grounds of Sai Haw Villa, to which you took her on a visit many years ago. She asks you to take her there again. She has asked you a total of three, four times, and each time you have asked him to go along?' It was no longer possible for Vincent to refer to his rival by name. 'May I ask why it didn't occur to you to ask me?'

As her fiancé, he had first claim to her dependence and trust. It was understood that she could always ask, and he would always give. Her answer again would have to be defensive: 'I didn't want to disturb you,' and would violate that bond of understanding and provoke the same explosion of displeasure. So she remained silent and continued to stare at the ground.

'May I ask,' said Vincent, his voice dangerously calm, 'how many more times Ah Heng Cheh needs to go to Sai Haw Villa to decide on the final resting place for her god, and whether you intend to ask him along each time?'

He had cast all of them, including the god, in the roles of cheap conspirators, and she resented it. But her resentment stayed locked in her throat, for her predominant feeling now was of desperate hope. If only! The tumult inside her head and heart had drained her face of colour and chilled her hands, which she kept pressed tightly together. If only he would say, 'It's all over with us. The wedding's off.'

I love you so much, I wish I didn't. When he made it, Ben's declaration had fired her with new resolve. Now, as always in the presence of her fiancé, fear returned. How weak she was! If only. The drastic action would have to come from him.

Gratitude had made her weak and now it came charging back to enfeeble her resolve even further. If it had been merely the casting off of a trap, the flying away from a cage, she would have been equal to it. 'You bastard,' she could have said, as fiercely as she had denounced Michael Cheong, and walked away. But it was a silken trap, of a hundred fine, lovingly woven threads, a gilded cage in which she had been more than pampered and indulged. And Vincent had also extended his generosity to those most dearly connected to her. When she had told him of her mother's cancer, his first reaction had been to comfort her and say, 'Don't worry about the cost of the treatment.' Then he had asked, with gentle tact, 'Does she intend to keep her job? Tell her, if she decides to quit, not to worry. I could help . . .' The cost of Gina's uncle's cancer treatment had been a staggering fifty thousand dollars. The extent of Vincent's giving had overwhelmed her. 'Stop!' Yin Ling had cried, but he had only said, 'I do it for you,' and continued.

One day, while walking home from the market with Ah Heng Cheh, she had turned back, walked to a booth selling the national lottery tickets and bought a few. The first prize, a huge sum, would have been more than enough to buy her freedom from the terrible cage. Vincent, of course, would have remonstrated, 'What debt? You know you owe me nothing,' and she would still have pressed the prize money into his hands and said, 'Thank you for everything. Goodbye.'

But it had all become too complicated to be solved by a simple financial transaction. The thought of the flagrant ingratitude of flying away and never coming back, of wounding a generous man who loved her, made her feel sick and fold in her wings.

Her brother would have said, 'Don't even think of it! You don't have a cent. You know the truth of the mortgage on Mother's flat, don't you?'

Her mother would have asked, with no hint of feeling, 'What are you going to do about Ah Heng Cheh?'

Gina would have shaken her by the shoulders and demanded, 'Are you out of your mind?'

Ben would have stormed in and yelled, 'Can't you see? It's all a ploy. He's using his money to trap you,' and stormed out, still yelling, 'Don't let his money bludgeon you into submission!'

The cacophony of voices would only add to her pain. Yin Ling waited, watching Vincent from the corner of her eye. He had started pacing the floor. He said at last, stopping in front of her, 'I want you to answer this question truthfully. Is there anything between the two of you?'

She had known the question would come with the end of the floor pacing. She saw him clenching and unclenching a fist in his pain at asking it.

Yin Ling felt an invading chill, though she remained calm. 'No,' she said.

Vincent looked at her and felt a surge of relief. He believed

145

her. It was Ah Heng Cheh, of course. It was always Ah Heng Cheh. She went to extremes for her old servant, for reasons connected to her troubled childhood and bad relationship with her mother, about which, out of delicacy, he had never asked her. Fearing to impose on him further, she had accepted the offer of the American. She was all right. It was Ben Gallagher who was creating all the trouble.

The relief grew by the minute, allowing Vincent to gather his thoughts, as well as his feelings, ready for the next stage of dealing with a crisis that had arisen so unexpectedly: 'Well, then, I want you to stop all these meetings. They're a waste of time, surely.' He was the lecturing, hectoring, stronger partner once more. He might have been saying, 'I want you to stop wearing all those short skirts of Gina's,' or 'I want you to stop spoiling that maid Romualda. She's getting lazy.'

He found comfort in his accustomed role and began to elaborate at length. 'Ah Heng Cheh's been giving you this trouble for a long time now. She's very old and can't be around for long. We'll have to put up with her, of course. I understand and respect your gratitude to her. In fact, it speaks very well of you. But from now on, if you need to go anywhere or do anything in relation to Ah Heng Cheh, you call me. Is that clear?'

From now on. I want you to. Is that clear. He never swerved from the language of authority and power, which, however, he now hastened to soften, by going up to her and taking her in his arms. Taut and quivering with anger, fear, resentment or guilt, she responded instantly to his touch and let go in a flood of tears.

He held her close, saying softly, 'It's all right.' A good sign, he thought, and continued to hold her, stroking her hair, which had fallen over her face. An almost amusing thought flitted into his mind: Mother wouldn't forgive me for this. In

146

forgiving his fiancée, he would earn his mother's unforgiveness. He knew about her secret prayers to her gods on his account. 'A god-given opportunity for you to break off with her, and you let it go by? Oh, son, how could you? She's a good person. But, oh, son, how could you?'

Yin Ling's sobs subsided and Vincent decided to bring in the second part of the planned admonition, in an appropriate blend of gentleness and firmness: 'I think you should know this. He has a very bad reputation. I need not elaborate.' His relief was complete and made possible a full return of authority: 'I want you to stop seeing him because I don't want to see your reputation tarnished.'

It was a lot of nonsense, he thought irritably, and he, Vincent Chee Wen Siong, only a month and a half before a wedding that everybody in the campus was talking about and which *Lifestyle* had requested to feature, should not have to be bothered by it. But, he reasoned, in a month and a half, all this bother would be over and forgotten. Yin Ling could be irritating with her naïveté, and Ben Gallagher was malicious, and meant to cause as much chaos as possible in Singapore before he left. Which might be much sooner than he thought. Already the dossier on him was building up. A copy of the letter he had sent to the international human rights group on behalf of the caned Bangladeshi was in the hands of the Minister for National Security. The rumours about his women might come in useful to build a case against him when the time came. Best of all, it had been confirmed that he would not be one of Vincent's examiners.

Vincent Chee Wen Siong's fiancée leaving him for the crazy American professor? Vincent Chee Wen Siong, one of Singapore's fifty most eligible, most successful young men, personal friend of the Minister for National Development, dumped for an *ang moh* with a messy secret life, no money, years older? The humiliation of being a laughing stock on the campus, the loss of face among his friends and his mother's friends could not be lived down in a lifetime. Vincent decided that nobody must know of this unfortunate series of events. He would ensure that the secret was kept at all costs. He would not tell his mother. He would bring forward the wedding date if he could. But that would upset his mother's plans. The important thing to do now was to wait out the rest of the stay of the American, watch his fall as the authorities closed in on him, ensure that Yin Ling got into no more scrapes, get married, then re-educate his new wife. It would be a long, tedious, step-by-careful-step process, but he would do it. She needed to be prepared for her role as his spouse in his political life.

He was beginning to see that loving a difficult woman was both noble and a burden – but he would take her in hand. She would be perfectly all right once the cause of all the trouble passed out of their lives – and into oblivion.

How strange that so much upheaval could be traced to so insignificant a person – an illiterate, senile old servant who had been around too long.

Seventeen

Yin Ling was viewing the bridal bedroom, especially prepared for them by Vincent's mother. The lady, indefatigable in her pursuit of excellence in home décor, had made a blunt assessment of her future daughter-in-law's capability in that area: 'You have neither the talent nor the inclination to do it.' She had taken it upon herself to go shopping in the best furnishing houses in Singapore and decide on the precise colour scheme of the bridal bed on which the first grandson would be conceived to carry on the family name.

It was not the aesthetic motive alone that had prompted her to do this: by herself in the bedroom, Mrs Chee surreptitiously sewed into the lining of the bridal bedspread a small, temple-blessed amulet to guarantee the births of many male grand-children.

Realising she ought to pay more attention to Vincent's mother, Yin Ling tried to drive out all the thoughts that were buzzing in her head like persistent bees, but one would not go away. Curiously, it had to do with Gina. She saw her friend staring at the expensive curtains, the bedspread, the ornamental cushions, the rugs, the vases, and whispering, 'Lucky you. Which other girl in Singapore has a mother-in-law doing all this for her?' Gina's remonstration, always made with that narrowing of her shrewd eyes, was by now a running refrain. The best deal! Any girl would die for it! Don't be a fool.

She threw a sidelong glance at her mother-in-law's face, to check on her mood. The sheer pleasure of doing up the room in her favourite colours, with the expert advice of the best interior decorator in Singapore, had combined with her distaste for her troublesome, undeserving soon-to-be-daughter-in-law to confuse Mrs Chee and produce a mood in her that swung wildly between eager talkativeness and distant hauteur.

'Here's your room,' she said coldly, then launched into an enthusiastic description of how she had succeeded in getting the salespeople in a particular furnishing shop to call up their various branches all over the island to find the exact colour sample she wanted.

Yin Ling thought, She's not so bad, really, remembering the brief time of warm sharing when Mrs Chee had, upon impulse, taken her to the secret shrine under the staircase and shown her the beloved gods hidden there. A motley pantheon, they had had the power to melt the hardness and draw up to the surface the truth of her heart's yearnings. Underneath that sleek, perfumed, hard elegance was a frightened, confused woman. *You know, I became a Christian to please my son, but when I die* . . . Yin Ling thought, We could learn to love each other. But the look on Mrs Chee's face, as she drew attention to this or that item in the splendid bridal room, was already set in determined severity. Yin Ling wanted badly to see the stern lines soften and reconfigure into the touchingly honest look of that day in front of the staircase gods. Gratitude should do the trick. She expressed warm appreciation of all the hard work that had gone into the wedding preparations, and meant every word. Hyperbole should do the trick even better, considering the woman's vanity. Yin Ling used up her entire stock of superlatives to break the rigidity of that face – kindest, most generous, greatest surprise, perfect taste – wincing a little at the extravagance of her language. She saw, to her dismay, a darkening of Mrs Chee's brow, a grim tightening of the lines around her mouth.

'Come with me,' said Mrs Chee.

She led Yin Ling to an ornamental table where a large, handsome, leatherbound book lay.

'I know you're not a Christian,' said Mrs Chee stiffly, 'but my son and I are.' She took Yin Ling's hand and placed it on the Bible. 'Swear,' said Mrs Chee, her lower lip trembling with the vexatiousness of the business, which she had dragged out of an unwilling Vincent, 'that you will not do anything to shame my son and our family name.'

Eighteen

On the phone, Ben was aggressive. Yin Ling listened silently. *Weak. Weak.* His accusing brush made a wide sweep and tarred everybody – herself, her husband-to-be, the dean, who was clearly plotting something against him, all Singaporeans too weak to follow the truth of their hearts. Playing games they did not care about by rules they did not believe in. Himself? The weakest of all – for going along with them, for being compromised by a soulless culture. I give you the tallest buildings, cleanest roads, sleekest condominiums, fattest bank accounts, said MTC, and you give up your soul, your dreams and your fight. What does it profit a man if he keeps his soul but loses out in a competitive world? Is it not better to have food instead of fire in the belly? A whole generation of Singaporeans said, 'Yes,' and was carried along on an easy, seductive tide. The Clive Vasoos, Chong Boos, Michael Cheongs, Derek Lees and Vincent Chees, even the Yin Lings agreed, probably, too, the V. S. Ponnusamys and Tiger Dragon Khoos, who raged against MTC now but might be seduced into the enemy's camp by promises of plum jobs and cushy ambassadorships. Foreigners, like the Jamiesons, came in with their noble talk and postured on the high moral ground of their ideals of freedom but were quickly sucked in too, lapping up the goodies cast before them. Only Ah Heng Cheh clung to her dream and refused to be borne along. Ah Heng Cheh was the only one Ben respected.

Yin Ling said, 'Ben, are you all right?' for he was raging wildly. She spoke softly on the phone, afraid that her mother, in the next room, would hear. Perhaps Vincent would hear too, through some secret and ingenious device of phone-tapping, with the connivance of Romualda. A month before her wedding, with every detail of the arrangements meticulously set in place by her efficient mother-in-law, Yin Ling was aware of her detachment from it all. She had submitted, indifferently, to the fittings for the bridal gown and the wedding-dinner *cheongsam*, to visits to the Grand Winchester Hotel, where she watched quietly as her mother-in-law harangued the banqueting manager, to visits to the bank vault and selection from the awesome collection of jewels, an unappreciative presence at life's rich feast.

In later years, she would remember the frenzied preparations for her wedding as just so many indistinct images blurring into each other, like the reflections in a stirred pool, mere background for the private yearnings in her heart that swam up in sharp, painful focus.

And then, a month before her wedding, in the privacy of her room, she had called Ben. There had been the agony of indecision when she had picked up the phone, put it down, then picked it up again at least a dozen times. 'You have already made up your mind. What else is there to say?' he might have expostulated. She would have an answer to that, carefully rehearsed. He might also have sneered, 'A bell-jar. You're in a bell-jar. You can't run away. Or won't.' She would have an answer to that too. Instead he was ranting and raging about everybody and everything in Singapore. She regretted the call.

'Ben, have you been drinking?'

'The hell I have. What do you expect me to do?'

But the sound of her voice, like the sight of her face, softened him. He subsided into pleading. 'Don't,' he said abjectly. 'Don't. I can't bear the thought of losing you.'

Why couldn't she say it? He had declared his love. There was only one more thing she wanted to hear from him. *There's nothing between Holly Tsung and myself.* Women were greedy. They demanded both affirmation and denial, love and renunciation.

Gina had told her, in an offhand manner, that she had seen Ben Gallagher and Holly Tsung having lunch together in a bistro. She added that someone had seen them together at V. S. Ponnusamy's rally.

'When was that?' Yin Ling had asked, maintaining her calm.

She needed to put his betrayal in context, to decide how much to excuse, how much to forgive, what further action to take. A woman told the truth if she claimed to have renounced money and prestige for love; she lied if she denied the power of jealousy. No woman inhabited second place in a man's heart gladly; to share first place with Holly Tsung in Ben Gallagher's affection was equally unacceptable – even now.

'Choose,' Ben had once said to her, in his undisguised jealousy of Vincent.

'Choose,' she wanted to say to him now.

'You tell me.'

'You tell me first.'

It had become a game, like that played by children drawing lines in the sand, eyeing each other warily. In the end, love was no more than a game with familiar rules, no different from the down-to-earth business transactions it despised, carrying its own calculus with the mean little algorithms of profit and loss. They were now facing each other across the drawn line in the sand, clicking away at their abacuses. In

154

their equations of love, they were holding Vincent and Holly in suspension, still indeterminate factors but soon to be assigned their respective places in the mathematics. Perhaps Vincent and Holly were doing the same with them, working hard on their own abacuses. Love was everybody's business and everybody's game.

But only Ah Heng Cheh really understood the game and bestowed upon her little god perfect love, willing to die, poor and forsaken, for him. The rest pretended and made all sorts of excuses and adjustments as they stumbled along.

Ben said, 'What's the use of talking any more? We're going round in circles. As usual.'

She said, 'I'm sorry,' and instantly saw her mistake.

The two words were deadly, closing all negotiations, for they put a finality upon a situation, sealing it, whereas the truth was that she wanted even the merest crack to allow the tiniest hope to slip through. She wanted to retract them, to say something to repair the damage, but Ben cut in savagely, 'I'm going out to the Heron to get thoroughly drunk. And let that coward do as he likes.'

Somebody had told him that the dean had been quietly looking for a replacement and had already interviewed several promising candidates.

Later he rang back. Yin Ling said, 'For goodness' sake, where are you?' for she could hear a lot of background noise, including loud raucous laughter.

'The Heron,' said Ben. He was very drunk. He said, 'I can't stop thinking of you. It's driving me crazy.'

Desire spiralled crazily into jealousy: standing at a public phone in a noisy pub, he told her angrily that he wanted to kill Vincent. 'Why did you call me?' he demanded. 'Why don't you leave me alone? Come with me,' he begged.

One part of her said, 'Oh, Ben, Ben,' while another said mournfully, 'How can I leave my bell-jar?'

'I need you,' he said miserably, and she knew that the restraint they had both enjoined upon themselves in the intimate darkness of the Courts of Hell, when they had come together to touch and be warm against each other, was melting away rapidly. In later years, the sensation of his hand upon a breast under her blouse would be an enduring memory for both; now he used it to claim her aggressively: 'How can you just walk away? Didn't it mean anything to you?' It was their secret, and here he was spilling it out with his beer in a public place.

She remembered the thrill of his warm hand firm upon her left breast, the greater *frisson* when it glided slowly to her back to undo her bra in one swift move. She remembered his sharp intake of breath as he lifted her blouse to look upon her beauty and press his lips to it. Her one thought then had been, If Vincent saw us now . . . which trailed off in a spasm of thrill and terror, and then they were innocuous sightseers once more, the only betraying signs being the flush on her cheeks and the reddened tips of his ears.

Nineteen

Alice Fong said, 'I'd like to talk to you.'

Yin Ling realised, with a start, that her mother rarely addressed her by her name, as if that would raise expectations of a term of endearment. Despite the cancer, Alice Fong had not stopped working, insisting she felt well. Sometimes she allowed Yin Ling to take her for her appointments with the doctor; mostly she went alone, solitary and proud till the end. She was beholden to nobody; that would ever be her consolation.

Alice Fong said, 'I do not like to interfere in your affairs, but you are playing with fire.' She had seen them that evening as she sat waiting in the taxi and peered into the darkness; there were all the signs of a dangerous, clandestine meeting. Then she had had the confirming evidence of a secret telephone call made to him. In her grey cardigan, noiselessly pacing the floor, Alice Fong caught a few words here and there that were enough to make her decide to act. Though disinclined to interfere in anyone's affairs, she had yet felt it was a maternal duty she had to perform. She said, 'I hope you know what you are doing. Your wedding is in three weeks.' A grim reminder of that coming event was in the new blue-grey silk *cheongsam* she had made for the wedding dinner, hanging in a plastic bag in her closet. 'I don't want to see you suffer in any way. If you need prayers for help, my friends will be happy to oblige.'

She met regularly with the prayer groups from her church,

who sought divine help for those in distress. Her daughter, an adamant unbeliever, was an outsider in the worst sense of the word, but would not be excluded. Warning, advice, offer of help. As usual Alice Fong put them all together in an uninflected delivery.

Yin Ling felt the tears spring into her eyes. She wanted so much to repeat that rare moment when she had laid her hand on her mother's and it had slowly uncurled in response. 'Mother, how are you feeling? What did the doctor say?'

But Alice Fong only said, 'Remember what I've just said.'

'Mother,' said Yin Ling, with desperate malice, 'why don't you throw away that ugly grey cardigan and get another?'

Her mother looked at her coldly, and got up to return to her room.

Ah Heng Cheh laid out the new grey silk blouse and the new black silk trousers on her bed. She understood they were to be worn at a wedding but had difficulty remembering whose.

'Mine,' said Yin Ling. 'I'm marrying Vincent Chee in three weeks.'

Ah Heng Cheh's face lit up with recollection and gratitude. The precise sum of Vincent's generosity to her was lodged permanently in some part of her memory. 'I'm a useless old woman. You must repay him on my behalf,' she repeated humbly. Then she made another request, equally humbly, but it had nothing to do with the important matter of her future after Yin Ling's marriage.

She began talking at length about some place far away, unvisited, with an old disused well that had seen death and sorrow. A newborn child, unwanted because female, had been cast into it by her distraught mother, many, many years ago. It was some time before Yin Ling understood. Ah Heng Cheh was talking, of course, about her property. The *lallang*

158

there had grown, thick, coarse and relentless, over the disused well, hiding it from sight.

Perhaps her god, after the disappointment with the Sai Haw Villa, was asking to be taken *there*, in his continuing, heartbreaking search for a home.

Twenty

During their love-making, Yin Ling noticed something different. Vincent's silence and the tautness of his face, which gave it a frightening pallor in the dark, were the warning signals. He was lying beside her breathing heavily, having fallen off her after the predictable half-hour of working around the chastely rucked panties. Two weeks to their wedding, he was maintaining his vow of premarital chastity to his god. Then, with what sounded like a savage grunt, he was upon her again and this time he pushed down the panties all the way, pulled them roughly off her legs, flung them aside, and was on her and in her, pushing with the frenzy of an unleashed animal. She gave a gasp, less from the searing pain than from the shock of it all: two weeks to their wedding, her husband-to-be was relinquishing, in a split-second decision, a faithfully kept vow. It was not a mere succumbing to flesh: it was the working out of some fearful, pent-up rage.

In the darkness, shocked by the assault – for assault it was – she shuddered under the weight of his attacking body and the exploding pain in hers. There was no place for tenderness in such a ferocious, systematic working out of lust's need, which peaked with a roaring accusation that terrified and confused her: 'The bastard!'

So jealousy was asserting itself, with his fierce staking of territory: 'This woman's body is mine.'

160

She had tried to understand his pain but wondered in shock if she could find it in her heart to forgive him for hers, now filling her entire body. The man's pride had been damaged, and sex – the real thing, not the ersatz kind in which he had indulged as a compromise with his god – was his way of salving it.

Vincent rolled off her once more, lay still with an arm across his eyes, and said again, 'The bastard.' His anger made him sit up abruptly and spew abuse. He was almost shouting: 'Gave everybody the impression he was so chaste and pure, gave moral instructions and counsel and all the time he was fucking his mistress in a love-nest in Johor Baru.'

Father da Costa, trusted chaplain of the Cathedral of Divine Saviour, Vincent's confidant, mentor and spiritual guide, was rotten to the core. A hypocrite. The same Father da Costa who had advised him about the sanctity of pre-marital chastity.

Now she understood. By a curious turn of logic, he had decided that the best revenge was to join the priest, to subscribe to his philosophy of public uprightness and private fornication. As soon as he had made the decision, he lost not a second in taking revenge and he took it on her body.

Alone by herself in her room, Yin Ling wrote a letter. *Please forgive me. I can't go through with it,* was all it said. She went to bed with a violent headache and had a dream in which her mother-in-law, dressed like the old gatekeeper in the Heavenly Pavilion, forced her to drink a bitter brew. 'To make you change,' she said severely, 'into a good person who will no longer shame my son.' She pointed to the woman whose smashed body lay in a mortar under a pestle and said, 'See what happened to her? It was for much less, you know.'

She saw someone moving about in the shadows, then stepping out. It was Ben. He pulled her by the hand and they ran away, with the angry mother-in-law giving chase. They saw Vincent join her. 'We'll catch them!' shouted Vincent. 'They won't escape us!'

Then, 'Caught you!' he cried triumphantly, pulling Ben, naked, off her. She, too, was naked, lying on the ground indecently splayed, the pain still inside her but quickly distilling into a knot of pure pleasure.

Her mother-in-law came up, wringing her hands and lamenting, 'When will all this end?'

She turned and saw her own mother, who took off her grey cardigan and covered her nakedness with it. 'I am a sick woman,' she said. 'Let me die without shame.'

And now joining in the general uproar was Ah Heng Cheh who came running up to ask, 'Where is the *ang moh*? He promised to help my god find his way home.'

'He's in the last Court of Hell,' said Vincent with savage triumph, 'the worst of all. And then he goes back to the first one, to start all over again. There's no better punishment for him.'

Twenty-one

Yin Ling pleaded illness. Indeed, the tumult in her soul was causing her head to throb, her throat to constrict, her stomach to churn.

'Are you sure you're okay?' said Vincent. He was truly concerned. He wanted to drive over with medicine and loving words. But there was something in his voice that said, 'That was good. I'd like it again.'

If only! If only he could see the note, which she held, trembling, now, he would explode in her face: 'All right, the wedding's off. You'll have to live with disgrace and regret all your life.'

Her heart was pounding so violently that she could hardly pick up the phone to call. She would only have the courage to do this once. She would make it a very simple call. 'Ben,' she would say, 'the wedding's off. I want you to take me away.'

She picked up the phone and called. There was no answer. She hovered over the phone, calling at regular intervals. It was the university break, and she knew he had not made plans to go anywhere. She was glad she was alone, for the wildness in her eye would surely provoke comment and concern. She paced the floor, sat on her bed, got up, read the note again and again. Her handwriting, not neat as usual but almost illegible in the terror of the message, swam crazily before her eyes: *Please forgive me. I can't go through with it.* Holding it, she tried to block out from her mind the shocked faces of

Vincent and his mother, her mother, Kwan, Gina and a hundred, perhaps a thousand others in Singapore, since the wedding, to be held in less than a fortnight, had been well publicised.

I want you to take me away. She realised, with a start, that she had forgotten about Ah Heng Cheh. *I want you to take me away as soon as I put Ah Heng Cheh in a home.* She picked up the phone again. It must have been the hundredth attempt. This time somebody answered. 'Ben—' she began, and heard a woman's voice. She put down the phone instantly, and stood very still. Her thoughts scrambled together in the chaos of sudden bewilderment, but mercifully settled into something resembling hope. Could it have been a wrong number? Or perhaps the female voice was his housekeeper's?

She picked up the phone once again and dialled, preparing to ask, in as casual a voice as she could, to speak to Professor Ben Gallagher.

The same woman answered.

'May I speak to Ben Gallagher?'

'Who shall I say it is?' said the woman, and she immediately recognised the Hong Kong accent.

Yin Ling put down the phone. Her thoughts and feelings were once again in a tumultuous spiral, threatening to distil into a stream of pure gall that she would have to swallow.

She dialled once more.

'Who is it?' It was Ben, and he sounded very drunk.

She heard Holly's voice, 'Some woman's been trying to get you, Ben,' and Ben's response, 'Hell, who is it?'

She put down the phone and sat on the bed. She sat for a long time, allowing her tears to flow freely.

Twenty-two

A week before the wedding, Vincent said, 'You know, of course, that Ah Heng Cheh is welcome.'

Yin Ling said nothing, and he went on, 'You mustn't mind what my mother says. She has a sharp tongue but a kind heart. She has given her word that she will not oppose my decision any more.'

He stroked her hair and kissed her face. 'We'll forget everything that has happened.' He was apologetic about the honeymoon having to be delayed to enable him to complete the last chapter of his Ph.D. dissertation and send it off. It would be a grand tour of Europe.

'By the way,' said Vincent casually, without looking at her, 'Professor Ben Gallagher left suddenly for Hong Kong. Never told anybody. Just packed and left.'

Twenty-three

S he ignored the frantic ringing of the telephone – it was probably her mother-in-law calling to check on some detail regarding the wedding, in three days' time, or Vincent simply calling to say goodnight – to concentrate on what she was doing. She read the last poem in the precious private book, before consigning it, together with the others, to the flames, actually only a small fire contained in an old ceramic pot with a lid so that the smoke or the smell would not wake her mother.

She had entitled it 'A Gladness Restored', and had written it after the last meeting at Sai Haw Villa, before all the painful events that could only now invest it with a bitter flavour.

My outer shell was smooth
And so fragile
It would have crumbled
Into the emptiness within
At a touch.
But your touch was healing.
There is stirring life
Restored
In the empty shell.

If at some time in the future they met again, would she be able to recite, from memory, the poem she had put in her handbag to show him? He hadn't seen it because she had grabbed the wrong bag before rushing out with Ah Heng Cheh to catch a taxi.

Yin Ling watched the sheets blacken, then curl and crumble into ashes in the little darting tongues of fire in the ceramic pot. She poured a glass of water into the pot and listened to the last faint, sad hiss of a vanished dream.

Twenty-four

On her wedding day in the Cathedral of the Divine Saviour, standing beside Vincent to pronounce her marriage vows, Yin Ling tried to dismiss from her mind the postcard from Hong Kong she had received the day before. The words danced before her eyes. 'Congratulations on your wedding.' The banality, in a large scrawl, took up almost all the space on the postcard, so that the subsequent words had to be squeezed together, becoming almost undecipherable: *'I was the storm-tossed bottle cast at your feet.'*

She saw that Vincent avoided looking at Father da Costa throughout the ceremony. For a fleeting moment, as he turned to look at her, his eyes caught sight of the stain on her bridal dress, below the left breast, where the dead baby's blood had not been completely wiped off. But he dismissed it. Nothing would spoil the day for him.

He was beaming with joy when he lifted his bride's veil and kissed her tenderly. She was so glad about the veil, for it had allowed the tears to be hidden; by the time Vincent lifted it, they had dried.

Oh, Ben, Ben.

Part Two

One

In the later months of her pregnancy, Yin Ling's belly swelled amazingly, a huge, perfectly round melon, hard and smooth, pulling up the front of her dress to well above her knees so that finally she resorted to long, all-covering kaftans.

Once she looked into the mirror to study her new appearance. Standing naked in a crumpled mass of dropped bra, panties and kaftan, she stared at herself in the mirror, slowly turning this way and that. The sight of her stomach, blown up into a grotesque hemisphere of a drum, the skin stretched in an incredible tightness, exercising a special tyrannising power over the rest of her body – breasts, pubis, thighs – distorting it fearfully, caused her to turn her eyes away.

She had never liked to look at pregnant women, huge, misshapen, waddling along on slippers or sandals, a far cry from the slim, radiant girls of bridal photographs, and now she wondered, with an uneasy shudder, if the aversion would translate into maternal indifference. Women waxed lyrical over the first stirrings, the first vigorous kick – Gina chattered endlessly about her experience – but Yin Ling merely wondered, and waited, thought hard and long, about matters unrelated to the growing child in her womb.

Gina had conceived her second baby almost as soon as she had delivered the first, provoking much good-natured ribaldry among her friends. 'Stop groaning,' they said. 'Who told you to be so naughty?'

'I didn't expect it at all. Then one morning, wham – boom!' It was not clear whether the graphic imagery of violent explosion referred to conception or sex.

At a dinner party in the Shangri-la restaurant given by Vincent, to which Gina came wearing a billowing maternity dress, the talk had quickly turned to sex. All the young husbands, apparently fired, had gone home to make love and explode joyously in their wives. She wondered whether the child now stirring in her womb was the result of that random act. Or of an act – she would die of guilt and shame if anybody knew! – in the dark secrecy of one night's dream, when a woman could receive the touch of one man and think of another, indeed, more than think, so that later, when the stirring life began in her womb, she wondered about its fount. Treachery of spirit, treachery of flesh – perhaps there was no difference. The possibility had shocked her so deeply that she shivered and sought to hide it by tightening her embrace of her husband, so trustingly asleep beside her.

From the start, Vincent had participated fully in the intimacy of the pregnancy, outdoing every concerned husband and expectant father in his eager reading of doctors' reports, his instant springing into action at the merest sign of a cough from his wife, the merest hint of loss of appetite. Pregnant women were notoriously demanding in their craving for this or that food, usually unavailable, sending their husbands on a wild search. The men remained undaunted, if only so that they could regale friends and relatives later with amusing tales of pregnancy's whimsy. One evening, Gina had had a sudden urge for the special boiled squid and *kang kong* obtainable only from a stall at a hawkers' centre at the other end of the

172

island. Her husband duly sped off in his car only to discover that the whole centre had relocated.

Vincent was always asking, 'Would you like to eat anything special?' meaning that he would have gladly flown in the finest shark's-fin or bird's-nest or abalone from Taiwan, China or Japan if his pregnant wife so wished. His mother remonstrated, 'Enough! Enough!' but in a good-natured way: she had gone to much trouble herself to boil special herbs for her daughter-in-law.

Vincent's friends teased, 'You didn't invent fatherhood, you know.'

Yin Ling's old gratitude had taken on a new dimension: 'He loves our child so much.'

In the last stages of her pregnancy, Vincent had a special way of sharing in it, which she thought rather amusing. He would kneel before her as she sat on a chair or on the bed and lay his head against the roundness, his hands cupped around its contours. The sounds coming from the child inside – once he swore he heard the curled foetus doing a joyous somersault in warm amniotic fluid – conferred on him a special pleasure.

In those days his love overflowed. He looked so well and happy that everybody noticed and commented. As soon as he was home from his work in the office of the Minister for National Development, who had been promoted to Deputy Prime Minister, he would yell, 'Ling, where are you?' and bound upstairs, two steps at a time, tearing off his tie and undoing the buttons on his cuffs to go to her and press his face against the growing child in her.

'Why are you always sitting by the window?' he said once gently. 'You ought to be exercising more, you know.' He chose this moment to make an apology, also very gently.

'Sorry you had to give it up, but it couldn't have been otherwise.'

I didn't give up my master's studies, she thought, with some resentment, which was dulled into listless quiescence by the overwhelming experience of the pregnancy.

There had been the interruption in the writing of her dissertation by the wedding although, as Vincent promised, it could be picked up later. But, ever since, something had happened to delay it, including the honeymoon, the major renovations to 2-B Rochester Park, Vincent's new job and now the pregnancy. In the end she thought, Hell, do I care any more? and settled quietly into her new life.

'You can pick it up after our baby's born,' said Vincent cheerfully. 'I made inquiries at the university. There's a three-year grace period, I think. But I could make an appeal, if necessary.'

She wanted to say, wearily, Why don't you stop pretending?

Vincent said, his face still pressed close to his heir, 'We'll register him in the National Singapore Kindergarten as soon as he arrives.' He did not want to risk his son's place in Singapore's most prestigious and popular nursery. His mother had told him in authoritative tones that it would be a boy. As soon as Yin Ling had announced the pregnancy, Mrs Chee had gone to her gods to ask, but pretended that it was unerring intuition.

Yin Ling thought much about sex, strangely, in the last month of her pregnancy; not with the tremulous expectancy of the last weeks before her marriage, but with a certain cool, analytical detachment, based on her observation of how closely it was tied to a man's mood swings caused by his job. She could tell what Vincent's day in the office of the Deputy Prime Minister was like by the frequency and nature of his love-making. Extreme high spirits at one end and brooding anger at the other expressed themselves in a display of ferocious energy that made her wonder if the growing child might be harmed. Sex cleared Vincent's mind marvellously, for as soon as he rolled off her he was able to say, 'I'll give that impertinent woman' – the Deputy Prime Minister's personal secretary whom he detested – 'a piece of my mind tomorrow morning,' or 'I know how I'll conclude my report, which I understand is going right up, maybe even to MTC himself.'

In those days, Vincent's sexual energy was prodigious, riding on a tide of the pure joy not only of his securing the coveted job with the Deputy Prime Minister against unbelievable competition, but of the promise of Singapore's most reputable publishing house to publish his Ph.D. dissertation, which they had called a landmark study. He would do his wife the supreme honour of involving her in the editorial work – 'Nobody in Singapore has the same feel for the English language,' he had already told the publisher – and duly acknowledge her contribution in his preface.

His face pressed to her belly, his arms encircling it, Vincent confided his dreams to Yin Ling. The Deputy Prime Minister had been given the special task of waging a counter-campaign against Singapore's enemies, mainly foreign journalists who had been writing scurrilous reports and articles. One American journalist had been in Singapore for two and a half days and had written extensively about the climate of fear in the society, claiming interviews with a whole spectrum of the population, including civil servants, professionals, businessmen and artists, who had spoken only on condition of anonymity. All lies, half-truths, clever distortions, said Vincent. A smear campaign against Singapore. And the opposition parties were joining forces with Singapore's enemies.

An article had appeared in the *Hong Kong Tribune*, by Professor Ben Gallagher, criticising Singapore's woeful human-rights record. But no mention of that man or anything even remotely connected with him would ever pass Vincent's lips. If Vincent could have done so, he would have legislated Sai Haw Villa out of existence and living memory. Since he could not, he sought to obliterate other memories – for instance, that of the dinner party at his home, more than a year ago, in which the American had featured so conspicuously, by the simple decision to take his friends to restaurants instead. He had heard about the American lecturing in Hong Kong University and possibly being shacked up with Holly Tsung; he disdained to hear more.

And Ah Heng Cheh, a daily reminder of the complicity, whom he had not entirely forgiven for her part in it, even if it had been unwitting, was, most fortunately, no longer living at 2-B Rochester Park.

Two

Ah Heng Cheh's fate had been decided by two incidents, small in themselves but which created a storm of displeasure, resulting in her having to leave 2-B Rochester Park. It had never welcomed her or her god in the first place.

It was Mrs Lee Ai Geok, the most regular of Mrs Chee's *mahjong*-playing friends, who had first noticed her standing at the door. Mrs Lee was shuffling the *mahjong* tiles on the table and listening to the chatter of the other three players when she looked up and caught sight of her. There she stood, a wildly staring, stricken look on her face, her clothes in woeful disarray, her long hair floating about her face in stiff strands. Long, loosened hair invariably marked the female lunatic or ghost; in the case of very old women, its spectral whiteness brought an even more terrifying aura of death and desolation.

Suddenly appearing at the door, at an hour well past midnight, Ah Heng Cheh became the perfect incarnation of the special fears of those who stay up long after others in the house have gone to sleep and who slowly become conscious of the night's silence, wondering what will emerge from it to shape into some fearful presence at the door or window. Only the day before, at their afternoon game (it was only in daytime that such stories could be told), Mrs Lee had told the true story of a Madam Kan who had collapsed and died at the *mahjong* table and whose ghost was subsequently seen by her friends, once at the table itself, in her favourite place facing the window. The detail of Madam Kan's dead fingers refusing to let go of the winning *mahjong* tile, which would have secured her a perfect 'Thirteen Wonders' game and won her hundreds of dollars, had made it an amusing rather than a frightening ghost story. Mrs Lee and her friends had laughed merrily. But that had been in broad daylight.

Looking at Ah Heng Cheh now, eerily still and silent at the door, Mrs Lee gave a little gasp and turned pale. Mrs Gracie Han and Madam Florence Lim looked up at the same time, glanced in the direction of Mrs Lee's gaze and turned pale too. All three said later that their hair stood on end and that their skin tingled with goose-bumps. For the strange old servant of Mrs Chee's daughter-in-law seemed no longer to belong to this world: she had become a walking apparition, moving in shadows.

Mrs Chee was the last to notice. She swung round and saw Ah Heng Cheh take a few steps towards them. She said sharply, 'Ah Heng Cheh, what are you doing up here?' Up there was the *mahjong* room, her bedroom and other rooms strictly forbidden to one whose presence in the house was irksome enough to be relegated to an annexe near the garage, constructed for the sole purpose of ensuring that Mrs Chee would never have to look even once upon the detestable old servant. How had the Old One found her way up there?

Ah Heng Cheh said something incoherent, pointed to something indiscernible, then sat down on a nearby chair. The sitting position was, if anything, even worse than the standing one by the door, giving the Old One, as she sat very still and stared at them all, a preternatural authority.

Mrs Chee said again, her sharpness undiminished by the rising panic in her voice, 'What are you doing here? Go back to your room.'

Ah Heng Cheh got up and chose as her victim Madam Florence Lim, who had a notoriously weak heart. Madam Lim's heart began to beat very fast and she had to reach for the Tiger Balm in her handbag, but all Ah Heng Cheh did was to walk up and stand behind her chair and peer over her shoulder. Madam Lim moved both her hands about to wave the apparition away, uttering agitated little sounds. Mrs Chee said, her voice rising in a hysterics of shock and fury, 'Ah Heng Cheh, I order you to leave this second,' as to a wayward child. But it was too late: her *mahjong* friends had been frightened away from 2-B Rochester Park.

'The old are to be forgiven,' they said, citing personal experiences of demented parents or relatives, but still, they did not want to risk another such encounter with Ah Heng Cheh. Mrs Lee Ai Geok had a great-aunt who threw tantrums, like a three-year-old.

But the *mahjong* incident was nothing compared to the incident involving the staircase gods, three days later, after which Mrs Chee, sobbing as if her heart would break, threatened to leave the house if Ah Heng Cheh did not.

In deference to her son, Mrs Chee had decided to forget Ah Heng Cheh's transgression of that *mahjong* night, or at least postpone any decision till after the birth of the baby. 'Let it be understood,' she said grimly, wiping her tears and receiving the cup of hot ginseng tea that Vincent had told the maid to brew for her, 'that I'm doing it for my son only.' She might have added, 'Also for my grandson,' thereby establishing the precise limits of her loving: 'Flesh and blood in here. All others, including my daughter-in-law, out there.' A situation where she thus excluded a succession of daughters-in-law over the years but kept all the grandchildren close to her loving heart was entirely conceivable. In her will she had already made an important stipulation: all her jewels would go

179

to her son only, and her son's sons, and their sons' sons, in an unending line, in demonstration of the sacred link between blood and property.

Mrs Chee, trying to recover from the bad experience of the *mahjong* evening, sought help from her gods, praying to them for strength and patience. She never knew what to say to the Christian god of her adoption, and thus sat stiffly beside her son in church, rising and kneeling when he did. But with the familiar gods of her childhood, she was articulate, voluble, audacious. 'Please let my grandson be delivered safely. Let my son prosper in his job and achieve his dream. Let me enjoy many years of good health and peace of mind. Let Ah Heng Cheh have a speedy and peaceful end.' Birth, life, good fortune, death – all featured significantly in Mrs Chee's ardent pleas to her gods. She attached a sly inducement: 'Grant my wishes and I'll build you a proper shrine.' It would be impossible to have anything more than this secret staircase worship in a house presided over by her son's Christian god, but she was already thinking of a special shrine that she might persuade the guardians of the Kek Lok Thong Temple to allow her to erect for them, in return for a large donation. She would go about it quietly, but it would be the most beautiful shrine, a fitting home for deserving gods.

Mrs Chee, finishing her prayers, reverently stuck a joss-stick in a small porcelain urn in front of her row of gods, represented variously by statuettes, effigies, carved images on jade and marble. It was while she was delicately removing a solitary rose petal that had dropped between two tiny gold urns that she first saw evidence of Ah Heng Cheh's trespass amounting to sacrilege. One of her gods, a black-faced deity, passed down by her grandmother to her mother to herself, had been rudely pushed to the back of the altar, his place taken by Ah Heng Cheh's god of the snub nose, child's face and deformed body. The god grinned at Mrs Chee and she screamed. As the full extent of the blasphemy dawned on her, she let out one scream after another, her fists clenched, the veins in her throat throbbing fearfully. The two Filipino maids, who were in different parts of the house, rushed to her, crying, 'Mam, Mam.' The chauffeur, Arasu, who was cleaning the Mercedes in the garage, rushed in too.

Mrs Chee took to her room and refused to see anyone. Her message to her son, relayed by the Filipino maids, was, 'Either she goes or I do.'

The secret of her staircase gods was now known to her son, but that was no longer relevant to the larger issue at hand. Mrs Chee kept saying to herself, alternately wringing her hands and pressing her handkerchief to her mouth: 'What have I done to deserve all this suffering?' The fact that the perpetrator of the suffering was an old servant, the lowest of the low, who had come under her roof as interloper, continued to astonish her and force her to conclude, in a burst of self-pity mixed with self-blame, that in a previous life she must have committed the most heinous of deeds to deserve such a fate in this. She would later tell her friends, her eyes brimming with tears, 'Don't love any of your children too much. It only brings suffering.'

Vincent said to Yin Ling, 'What do you think we should do?', adding, 'All this shouldn't be happening now, with our baby due soon.' He laid his hand gently on her stomach, and the child inside responded with a kick, delighting him. He prided himself, secretly, on a magnanimity far greater than his mother could ever have shown: for his wife's strange old servant had desecrated *his* God too. The statues of the Holy Family, standing on a table beside the Bible, had been knocked down to make way for Ah Heng Cheh's god; there he stood, incongruous beside the Holy Book, the fallen St Joseph, lying

181

face-down on the table, and the Virgin Mary, with the Child Jesus in her arms, in a similarly ignominious position. It was the Filipino maid, with the cleaning rag, who first noticed the violation. She swung round to face him as he was hurrying past, on his way downstairs to the Mercedes waiting to take him to his office, and gasped, 'Sir, look!' He saw the devastation, instantly raised a forefinger to his lips to signal secrecy and told her to restore things as best she could. 'Take it back to her room,' he whispered, referring to the usurping god, 'and don't tell anyone.' Thinking that Ah Heng Cheh would live one more year at the most, he decided he could tolerate her senility and wondered how the Old One could have sneaked out of her room in the annexe with her god to wreak such damage. In an even happier mood, he would have concentrated on the comicality of it all, for regaling to his friends later. He would tell Yin Ling at a suitable time. For now, he was quietly making inquiries about old people's homes. Meanwhile, all his energies should be conserved for the demands of his new responsible job – the Deputy Prime Minister said MTC would probably ask to see him one of these days. In a house of women, with their never-ending problems, he could afford to be magnanimous and stay coolly, authoritatively in control.

Yin Ling said, 'I'm sorry for all the trouble.' She had wanted to apologise on behalf of Ah Heng Cheh, but her mother-in-law had resolutely refused to see her. 'Ah Heng Cheh,' she had said wearily to the old servant, who was reacting to all the commotion around with a tight-lipped, grim-faced petulance, like a child angry because unfairly · scolded, 'why are you causing all this trouble?'

Her brother Kwan would have said triumphantly, 'I told you so. Things would be different if she had her own money.' He was still harping on the folly of throwing away all her savings on that useless bit of land. Her mother would have said, with none of the spiteful triumph but with all of the grave displeasure of a parent never heeded, 'What's the use of your telling me all this now?'

It must have been the general dispiritedness brought by the pregnancy and a continuing disappointment – there had been no communication from Hong Kong after that card on her wedding day – that made Yin Ling go on to say, with something like reproach in her voice, 'Ah Heng Cheh, Vincent was doing us a great favour when he agreed to let you stay here.'

She regretted her words immediately for the old woman turned round slowly to look at her and said coldly, 'So you, too, are against me?' and thereafter fell into a determined, grim silence.

'Ah Heng Cheh . . .' It was like in the old days when Yin Ling was a little girl, scolded, smacked, pinched for a naughty act, and crying to be reinstated as the favourite.

Ah Heng Cheh said, with cool hauteur, 'I know when I'm not wanted.'

It was raining heavily and Yin Ling, waking up with a start from a dream in which she saw Ah Heng Cheh out on a road amidst a snarl of honking cars in pouring rain, was seized with a sudden fear. She slipped out of bed quietly so as not to wake Vincent, hurriedly put on a robe and went downstairs.

The house, being immense, required some skilful negotiations in darkness for her to reach the annexe. To her alarm, she saw that Ah Heng Cheh was not in her room, though the light was on.

'Oh my God!' she gasped.

An arrangement for one of the maids to sleep in her room would have saved much anxiety but Ah Heng Cheh had

183

insisted on being alone. Yin Ling had a vision of the Old One lying smashed on a dark road somewhere with her god, in pelting rain, and was about to return to wake Vincent when she heard a scuffling sound and turned to see the familiar face and hear the familiar voice a short distance away. 'Oh my God,' she gasped again, this time in relief.

Ah Heng Cheh was in the darkness of a sheltered part of the annexe, sitting on a tin trunk, secured with rope, and clasping her god, wrapped in a towel. She was in her best clothes, the grey silk blouse and black silk trousers given her to wear at the wedding dinner. Sitting in the dark shadows, Ah Heng Cheh said, in a clear, even voice, 'I'm going to the Seng Tee Loke Old People's Home. I won't trouble any of you any more.'

And she continued to sit silently on her tin trunk, waiting for dawn to break.

Three

It was as if her soul had left her body – as if *two* souls had left their bodies, since the child inside her had reached full-term and was about to be born at any time now. She was a detached presence, watching herself walk through the large maternity ward of the First Singapore Hospital, between the long rows of beds, gliding along effortlessly, despite the weight of her belly, as in a slow-motion sequence of a movie where a taut, hurrying body becomes a graceful floating presence.

The women sitting or lying on their beds turned to look in curiosity at her, a stranger in their midst despite her similar condition, for they sensed she came from the ward at the other end of the hospital wing, with its private, luxuriously fitted rooms. Looking at them, she thought of the time, only a little more than a year ago, when as a bride, resplendent in gown and jewels, she had walked into their midst in the HDB heartlands and walked out again, the baby blood on her bridal gown. She smiled at them.

They would have looked away in annoyance or embarrassment if her smile had carried the arrogance of wealth and power: See my baby in a first-class ward, yours in a government-subsidised one. See my baby to be registered in a first-class kindergarten, yours in a government-run one. But the friendliness and goodwill were apparent. One of the women, a hawker's assistant who was having her fourth baby, called out a cheerful greeting. Yin Ling walked over to her bed and sat on it, then all the women in the ward were talking and laughing, a cheerful sorority ready to lend support to one another in the coming trauma. For trauma it would be for each of them, even when women no longer died in childbirth, as long as they were still unsure of their babies' wholeness: a harelip? a supernumerary thumb? a cruel twist or kink in the bloodline somewhere that would show up later when the poor baby turned blue, turned yellow, vomited whatever it was fed?

The hawker's assistant, who was already forty years old, spoke of her fear about having a baby at this late age, but said it would be her last try for the longed-for male child. The woman on the bed next to hers, whose belly was an enormous mountain crushing the rest of her body, said she wanted the birth of her twins to be over as quickly as possible so that she could go back to her work as a car-park attendant; her husband was unemployed and she needed the job to support her family. The reason for her husband's unemployment came out quickly in a ready unburdening of the heart to a sympathetic audience: he had just come out of drug rehabilitation and was showing all the signs of having to go back. Then all her life's sorrows tumbled out, and they had mostly to do with money, the high cost of living. The woman spoke emotionally of how much her school-going children were costing her in terms of books, bus fares and shoes. 'I lost all my jewellery recently,' she sobbed. But it had not been to the pawnshop but to a pair of confidence tricksters she had met at the market, who convinced her they had magic powers and could multiply cash or jewellery many times over. She had taken off a gold chain, a pair of ear-rings, a bracelet and two rings, which they put under a piece of cloth together with a cut lime and a magic stone. 'I felt dizzy and when I opened

186

my eyes they were gone. So was my jewellery.' When reporting theft to the police every tricked woman invariably recounted giddy spells that made them do things against their will. In time, if too many complaints against confidence tricksters came in, the government might start a campaign to warn and educate the public.

The woman, heavy with her twins, began to weep, and the others crowded round, offering sympathy, tea, homecooked food from a tiffin-carrier. Then they all turned to look at Yin Ling as if to say, 'You, from the other side, you will never understand,' and seemed relieved when a nurse came hurrying up, said, 'Mrs Vincent Chee, you should be in your room. Your doctor is due in a few minutes,' and waited to escort her back.

Her husband and her mother-in-law would have been horrified that she had ventured out to an unfamiliar part of the hospital. As her delicate condition warranted concessions, her mother-in-law would not have said, in a huff, 'Quite mad, I tell you! Suppose the labour pains had begun then?' but would have thrown a shawl over her shoulders and hurried her back.

Yin Ling, sitting in a chair in her room, waiting for the doctor, put a hand on her belly to touch her coming child. Its progress closely monitored by the doctors at every stage of its development, its nursery already prepared with an expensive cot, wallpaper, pictures, rugs, toys, her child would arrive in the world to a welcome never known by the hawker's assistant's baby, or the car-park attendant's twins. Certainly not by that poor little abandoned newborn in the rubbish dump. Did the god who had said that he cared for the sparrows in the air and the lilies in the field decide on the fates of Baby Xiang Min (Vincent had decided on the name after much discussion with his mother) and Baby No Name of the rubbish dump? Her thoughts shaped into a poem which, as soon as she had written it on a paper napkin from the hospital dinner tray, was consigned to the same fiery fate as its predecessors:

'Let the dicing begin,' he said,
And the other agreed.
To put an end to the suspense.
Outcome couldn't be worse.
'Whatever happens, we'll still be friends.'
So said both, and so doubted both.
A neutral hand threw the dice,
All watched, drew breath, crowded
To look upon the fateful upturned faces of dice.
'I'm the winner!' he shouted,
And the other was silent.
Both prepared for the journey
To Earth.
The winner to the Princess of Wales,
The loser to the beggar woman of Calcutta,
The hour of birth was soon.

Yin Ling bent over her belly and put both hands on it gently, to caress the child curled inside her. It would soon burst upon the world in a crying, frenzied thrashing of limbs. Could one apologise to an unborn child? For she was guilty of thinking more about a dead child than the living one inside her. Other mothers spoke loving, welcoming words to their unborn, while she was lost in her troubled thoughts of a god who perhaps played dice with the world after all.

Vincent had insisted on being present at the birth. His mother had not been too pleased with the idea. Having expressed a readiness to go along with modern trends in Singapore, she had meant only trends related to food, fashion and entertainment, and not that atrocious one of the husband witnessing his wife give birth. She liked to tell of how her mother had made sure that no male in the household would ever catch sight of the midwife carrying out of the confinement room a chamberpot containing the soiled towels of afterbirth; the midwife did the emptying only at night, in stealth. Mrs Chee grimaced at the thought of her son's exposure to all the gory rawness of a woman's legs violently parted; all her life she had ensured that a woman's private smells and stains never brought bad luck to the men in the house by sternly instructing the maids to wash their clothes in separate tubs.

'I don't understand you young people,' she had said, with a shudder, when Gina told her that her husband had not only been present at the birth of their baby but had taken pictures of its various stages.

'Would you like to see them?' said Gina.

'Heavens, no!' cried Mrs Chee.

She was the first to set eyes upon the touching scene, which, as she later told her friends, moved her to tears: her son, holding his firstborn, wrapped in a towel, sitting beside her daughter-in-law lying upon a mound of pillows, exhausted by the birth.

The baby's birth, in one marvellous stroke, wiped out whatever ill-will had accrued since the wedding. Mrs Chee was ready to slip into her role as most concerned mother-in-law, providing endless ginseng, bird's-nest and other nutritious brews, and as most loving grandmother ready to scold nurses and maids if they so much as held the baby too tightly.

Yin Ling waited. She waited for her husband and her mother-in-law to be gone so that she could have the baby all to herself. She wanted to hold it close for a long time and to gaze at it.

The nurses said, in laughing remonstrance, 'Mrs Vincent Chee, we must take the baby away for its wash. And you must have a rest,' but still she would not let go, staring at her newborn, wrapped in a towel, asleep in her arms.

The waves of pain that had buffeted her body the night before, when the birth pangs began, causing her to gasp and groan, were nothing compared to the waves of some powerful feeling, as yet indescribable, now washing over her, one after another, tearing loose her moorings and throwing her upon the buoyancy of the vast ocean as, almost giddy with joy and trepidation, she held the child in her arms and looked into the small face, still furrowed, and the small fists, still clenched from the fearful throes of birth.

A new world had broken upon her; she reacted to it by a flow of quiet tears, which swelled into convulsive sobbing, as she pressed her face upon her newborn child still sleeping peacefully in her arms.

Four

It was impossible! How could one love another so much? It was an overpowering, obsessive love that allowed no rest. It permeated her whole being and commandeered all the resources of her body, mind and soul for his service alone.

The Filipino maid Raphaela practically had to wrest the baby from her, laughing in the delight of an observation she was to share with the other Filipino maids in the neighbourhood: 'Mam, you love Baby Xiang Min so much, but time for his bath now, Mam!'

The baby absorbed all her energy; she had to be reminded that others, too, had legitimate claims on her time. 'Mam, Sir says he'll be back in fifteen minutes to pick you up for Minister's dinner.'

'Mam, your brother says to return his call, Mam.'

And still she would not let go of her baby. She wanted to continue to hold him close to her, to smell the top of his head with its fine wisps of baby hair, to smell the breath of his baby mouth. She wanted to press her lips to his brow, to uncurl his tiny fingers, one by one, then feel them curl tightly once more around her forefinger, to gaze at the closed eyes and watch for the tiny movements under the eyelids, signifying the onset of a dream. But what were baby dreams like?

If there was an infant deity whose every whimper in the cradle was a command, whose every inch of growth was observed and recorded by watchful, adoring eyes, it was her newborn.

In the pale light of the moon coming through the curtains and falling on his face as he slept in his cot, she sang to him. She sang a song that Ah Heng Cheh had taught her, so long ago, of a small bird in a forest, lost and found, and of good obedient children rewarded with delicious rice dumplings with meat stuffing. Perhaps it was to make up for maternal shortcomings during the long months of pregnancy when, unlike other mothers, she had neither sung nor spoken to him, and even winced a little when he struck out in his amniotic bubble to reach her: I am your very own. Flesh of your flesh. Her indifference had frightened her. Here was a child who ought to have been luckier in the celestial game of dice and been sent to a more loving mother on the face of this wide earth.

The change of heart had come late, but not too late. Up to the point of his expulsion from her body, when she had felt an immense relief, she had remained detached. Exhausted, she had fallen into a long, deep sleep. Other mothers would have willingly delayed rest to hold their newborn, still wet with the slime of birth, for that first wondrous moment of touch and connection; instead she had turned away from him to crawl into the warm nest of sleep's oblivion. Marriage, childbirth: she had discharged her duties to a demanding world and only wanted to be left on her own. For her, the much-feared melancholy that came after birth had descended far too soon. Her last thought before the warm, enclosing darkness was: Oh, how tired I am! If I never wake up, I shall not mind. And the last image in her mind, strangely, was a peaceful, happy one, a composite of favourite images of girlhood drawn from romantic poetry: she saw herself, a pale-faced corpse in white, with white flowers strewn on her body, lying in a boat pushed out into the quiet sea.

When she opened her eyes at last, she saw Vincent beside her with the baby in his arms, wrapped in a towel. He had no words in his profound joy, only a smile as he laid the warm bundle in her arms. For the rest of her life, she would remember – oh, with such tender remorse! – the thought that came with that simple act of love and pride: If I have not loved you, I will do so now – as if loving were an act of will. It was at this moment, too, that the change of heart towards her child took place. It was probably a flight of maternal fancy, but she was convinced that, from that precise moment, the tiny heart began to beat in conjunction with hers.

She laid her wet cheek upon her son's, and wished that Vincent's camera had not intruded upon so private a time. Click, click, went the camera, relentlessly ever afterwards, in an extravaganza of chronicling that filled a dozen bulky baby albums foisted upon hapless guests by the excitable grand-mother, Mrs Chee.

'My darling,' said Vincent, 'the nurse is here to take Xiang Min back,' but she would not let go of her newborn. *Flesh of my flesh*. The mysteries of existence had coalesced in this tiny, helpless baby in her arms. An invisible blob of tissue only months before, it had directed itself to grow limbs, fingers, toes, eyes, mouth. Like millions all over the world at that very moment, it had come into existence from the void, and if there were a benign god who did not play dice, he might have said, raising a hand in blessing, 'Goodness, peace and joy to you all the days of your life, little one.' She would protect him, her little one, all the days of her life.

She remembered a picture in the *National Times* some years ago, showing a picture of a beautiful American child, golden-haired, cherub-cheeked, aged eighteen months, perched on his mother's knee, and beside it, another picture, taken twenty years later, of a grim-faced young man, both a victim and perpetrator of crimes that shocked the tiny, peaceful community in which he lived. She remembered thinking then, with much sadness, Who would have thought? and saying a prayer for Todd Lincoln McCaughey. Such inappropriate thoughts! How she wished they would not intrude upon her joy.

Over the months, Yin Ling jealously guarded her time with her son. She liked it best when she was alone with him, watching him sleep, listening to the synchronicity of their breathing as he lay against the gentle rise and fall of her breast. She had seen mothers breastfeeding their infants and had not liked the sight. Once, many years ago, on a train, she had seen a toddler running to his mother, pushing up her blouse and pushing his face into her breasts, small, dried, depleted bags of skin. She remembered her horror. She had stared at the toddler, who stared back defiantly, sucking one breast and playing with the other, while his mother, thin and tired, her own hunger unassuaged, looked out dully upon rubber trees whizzing past the window. But the remembrance of that dead baby at her breast on her wedding day was different. The dice had not favoured that baby. If it was true that pain in this life paid for pain inflicted on others in an earlier one, had the dice been loaded to punish Baby No Name?

How her mind strayed with such thoughts! Who would have imagined, looking upon her now, in the most elegantly fitted nursery in Singapore, sitting in a two-thousand-dollar rocking-chair bought from Robinson's Department Store, that such morbid thoughts were inhabiting her mind?

Only Ben would have understood them. For he had told her, many times, 'You have the queerest thoughts, but I love them.' And he had picked up her hand and kissed the tip of each finger, as if each was an endearing queer thought. She wondered, pressing her lips tenderly to her baby's head, What would he think to see me now? In the midst of her new happiness, the old pain of his loss lingered, but no longer with the power to draw tears, to make the dreams at night a sadness to wake up to in the morning.

There had been the card for her wedding, the long silence and then the card shortly after the baby's birth, as if he had decided that his contact with her, from wherever he was in the world (he had apparently left Hong Kong) would be limited to the major events in her life. Congratulations on your wedding. Congratulations on the birth of your son. Congratulations on the birth of your second son. The felicitations down the years would become worthless, because whatever interest they had begun with would long have been dulled by habit.

If he had left a forwarding address, she might have replied: 'Aren't congratulations due to you too? Tell me. Please tell me where you are now, what you are doing, who you are married to (if).' Like men and women standing on the cooled cinders of old passions, they might still be friends, linked by the occasional card or letter, rich in news about themselves. In the old days, each had always approached the other with such anticipation, to attune thought and speech perfectly, in the brief, precious time together. There would be a little less of the pain of remembrance as the months went by, and even less over the years, until finally, one morning, she would wake up and say truthfully, 'It's gone.' New love healed the wounds of the old. But, it would be a child, not another man, who would heal her. It might have been for her future child that she had written one particular poem consigned so hurriedly to the flames:

But your touch was healing.
There is stirring life
Restored
In the empty shell.

She marvelled at the life-giving stream that passed from her body to that of the child at her breast. Her mother-in-law had asked to see the milk to ascertain the salutary effects of the ginseng, shark's-fin and bird's-nest so painstakingly brewed for her since her baby's coming home from hospital, and had been much satisfied with its abundance. 'I'm happy, that's why,' Yin Ling wanted to say. 'It's the abundance of my new happiness.' Her newborn fed eagerly, his baby mouth tugging greedily and sending joyous little ripples through her, a sensation that she had felt only once before, in a secret place, in a secret time. Invisible cords supposedly connected those who loved each other impossibly, so that even when separated by vast stretches of land or water each felt the tiniest tug of the joy or sorrow, pleasure or pain of the other. Were such cords stronger between mother and child than between man and woman?

Suddenly she thought of the woman who waited in silent vigil on the spot where her son had been killed to catch his killer. The cords in her case traversed not only the boundaries of land and water but life and death. From where he was, the dead son pleaded, and she went into a frenzy of revenge. Had someone, unable to endure the sight of her pain, come forward at last with information that revealed the killer?

Yin Ling hated it when others intruded upon moments of delicious intimacy with her baby. The maid and her mother-in-law had taken the hint and now signalled their entry in her room by polite knocking. Vincent, claiming all the privileges of husband and father, descended boisterously upon them, watching, with undisguised fascination, the nipples, dark, turgid and rich with sustenance, and the eager clamping by the small, hungry mouth. In a good mood he was given to saying the most mawkish things, and he now declared, with a lascivious guffaw, that he would reclaim his rightful territory as soon as possible. Buoyancy of spirits always passed into sexual desire. He waited for the baby to finish feeding at her body, then it was his turn. In those days she watched, with a degree of amused detachment, the greedy claims made on her woman's body: she would resist no longer, she would give all.

Now she understood something that had puzzled her in her schooldays in the Convent of St Elizabeth: every statue of the Blessed Virgin Mary holding the infant Jesus showed flatness where full, rounded, life-giving breasts with their swollen nipples should be. Breasts had too much provocative ambiguity.

Newborns had to be protected from bad luck and in return gave good luck. She had a sneaking suspicion that her mother-in-law had had a secret consultation with her staircase gods and sewn a little amulet into the mattress in her baby's cot to ward off malignant spirits in the air and on the earth. 'Tell me, share with me your secret. I will not tell Vincent,' she would have liked to say and her mother-in-law might have said in reply, 'It's nothing, nothing. You in your world, me in mine.'

She had a sneaking suspicion, too, that the cleaning woman from the house next door had bought a lottery ticket based on her son's birthdate or weight or the numerological significance of his name, and had won some money. Yin Ling had overheard her excited sharing of the good news with Arasu, the chauffeur.

But more than good luck, her baby brought peace. Babies, by the mere fact of their birth, could claim that redemptive power. Some babies. Not poor Todd Lincoln McCaughey. But her newborn son did. For the First Month celebration, her mother, who had sworn she would never step inside 2-B Rochester Park, did so, and her mother-in-law, who had looked away or curled her lip at each mention of Alice Fong, not only smiled but invited her, with all sincerity, to come again. Mrs Chee, being the grandmother on the paternal side, had right of first place in the giving of *ang pows* to the baby on this most important event of infancy. She did so, intoning good wishes for the brightest of futures, the greatest of good fortune, then slipped the rich gift of money, in a red paper packet with gold designs, into a pocket on the baby's vest. Then it was Alice Fong's turn. With a smile that nobody remembered ever seeing before, she, too, pushed her *ang pow* into the vest pocket, with kind words for her grandson. Kwan was next, whispering to Yin Ling, 'Good for you', probably thinking that she had successfully planned and executed this clever strategy of reconciliation. He complimented her especially on the excellent luncheon to which they all sat down after the *ang pow* ceremony. It was indeed a strange sight – her mother-in-law, her mother, her brother, her husband, all sitting down and talking to one another with real goodwill, and all getting up in a body to have a last look at the child sleeping in his cot before the visit ended.

But Ah Heng Cheh, since her departure to the Seng Tee Loke Old People's Home, had remained angry and resentful, refusing all invitations to 2-B Rochester Park to see the baby, and sitting in tight-lipped sullenness through every visit paid her.

Five

Kwan said, 'I can't believe she can do this to you, after all you've done for her.'

Mrs Chee said, 'I'd rather not talk about her,' meaning that Ah Heng Cheh's leaving 2-B Rochester Park for the Seng Tee Loke Old People's Home *of her own free will* was the best thing that could have happened, putting an end to all the trouble. '*Omi-tho-hoot!*' she would say, clasping her hands fervently, or 'Hallelujah!', depending on which of her two gods she felt the need to express gratitude to. Upon the Old One's death, she would make a brief appearance at the funeral and donate a handsome sum of money to the Seng Tee Loke Old People's Home. Meanwhile, Ah Heng Cheh no longer existed.

Alice Fong said, 'There are limits,' meaning that Yin Ling had gone well beyond duty to the old family servant and should not now be subjecting herself to so much anxiety and indignity. She disdained to speak further, not wanting to touch on the old painful subject of a daughter's affection so disproportionately claimed by another.

Kwan said, with rising irritation, though he admitted it was none of his business, 'Let me get it right. You have gone eight times, maybe more, to the home to see Ah Heng Cheh, and each time she has refused to see you.'

It was a strange scene: Yin Ling, carrying her little infant son dressed in his best for the visit, storming the resolutely shut gates of Ah Heng Cheh's displeasure. She had had to call three times before Ah Heng Cheh would come to the phone.

'Please let me see you and talk to you.'

'No.'

'I need to talk to you.'

'There is nothing to talk about.'

'Don't you want to see my son?'

'No.'

'Ah Heng Cheh, you *must* let me see you and talk to you. It's very important to me.'

'No. Go away.'

Those of Ah Heng Cheh's fellow inmates at the home who were not too old or infirm to continue to be interested in the world around them watched these scenes with intense interest. Frail old men and women, *sans* hair and teeth but not that spark of life that ever looked round to be rekindled, they watched and were gratified that sometimes it was the young who came pleading. A few felt it incumbent upon themselves to play peace-maker.

'Show some pity for her and the child.'

'Whatever happened belongs to the past. Forgive and forget.'

'We old must forgive the young.'

It had never happened before at an old people's home. One Ah Koo Cheh, aged eighty-three, had not had visitors for the last ten years and every night railed against ungrateful children. Another, an old man whom everybody called Uncle Three Moles, had six sons and daughters, all professionals and doing well in the world, who visited only occasionally. 'Revere the old,' admonished the leaders in a campaign directed at the heedless young, 'Preserve the traditional value of filial piety,' but privately they understood the enormous difficulties faced by busy young people. Uncle Three Moles said two sons and a daughter had emigrated with their families to Canada, precisely to avoid these difficulties. The further the better. Australia was too close to Singapore. Ah Heng Cheh, not even a parent, a mere servant, the lowest of the low, stood tall and proud against the visitor from the world of the rich and important and arrogantly waved her back to her chauffeur-driven car.

Such a thing was unheard of.

Kwan continued, his face red with exasperation, 'Let me get it right. You, the wife of Vincent Chee Wen Siong, of 2-B Rochester Park, go all the way to the Seng Tee Loke Old People's Home and beg to be admitted into the company of an old and destitute servant who, in the first place, would not have been there without your husband's money. She turns you away each time, and you go crawling back. How can you tolerate it? The old bitch.'

As long as Ah Heng Cheh remained in the family, Kwan's language, even at the height of exasperation, had been restrained. Now that she was in an old people's home, he could view the situation with undisguised brutality, use any number of savage epithets he liked. The savagery was in proportion to his exasperation with his sister. He almost wanted to swing round and say, 'Would you do a fraction of this for your own mother?'

He himself had never been to an old people's home, but always knew when he passed one because of the smell of strong disinfectant and stale old bodies. Hearing about a Christian organisation's plan to build a hospice for the destitute on a plot of land close to his condominium, he had his own plans to round up support from all the residents for a strong petition to prevent such contamination of bright affluence.

'The old bitch,' he said again. 'The absolute, unending power of a penniless servant who refuses to die.'

'You shut your mouth,' said Yin Ling angrily.

Kwan said, 'I wash my hands off everything,' and left.

Then Ah Heng Cheh discovered a new source of power to do with food. On Yin Ling's tenth visit to the home, she said, 'If you want to sit down and talk to me, you must bring me . . .' and named her favourite dish of pork fried with ginger, which she had enjoyed at 2-B Rochester Park.

Yin Ling was delighted. If only Ah Heng Cheh had told her of the problem earlier. In old people's homes, the food, at best, was indifferent. She duly brought the requested dish, carefully placed in a special container to keep it warm. It had been cooked to perfection by the Filipino maid, Laura, whom her mother-in-law had sent to do an expensive course on fine Chinese cooking.

'Ah Heng Cheh, here's the pork and ginger. Doesn't it smell nice?' The aroma had brought some of the inmates crowding around to look and smell, old men and women who, having lost everything else, were determined to enjoy good food till the end. Yin Ling, holding the container lid, watched for Ah Heng Cheh's reaction. The old servant, who was sitting imperiously in a chair, looked at the food and said, 'The portion is too small. Are you being deliberately mean?' In her memory there must have lurked a scene of a mistress who haughtily pushed away the food set before her – 'The soup is too salty' or 'The fish is too oily' – and rebuked her for being slow, stupid or lazy.

For subsequent visits, Ah Heng Cheh demanded black mushrooms in oyster sauce, button mushrooms with *tofu* and leek, steamed pomfret, braised pig's knuckles in vinegar, chicken's feet in black sauce, king prawns seasoned in tamarind and deep fried fine *ee-fu* noodles, sweet and sour fish, abalone soup, roasted duck, bitter gourd stuffed with minced pork. She indicated the requisite quantity by raising cupped hands in the air to enclose an immense amount of space, and the quality by saying that the food had to be fit for gods.

Ah Heng Cheh was fattening her god for his journey home.

'Surely he does not need so much food?' said Yin Ling, with a smile. She had seen the god being offered tiny rice cakes and sweetmeats, token food only, doll-size, in delicate plates and bowls. She spoke hesitantly, humbly, afraid to offend the Old One so soon after being allowed into her presence.

'My god does not need to be told how much food he needs,' said Ah Heng Cheh curtly.

Ah Heng Cheh's wits seemed to have sharpened in the home. Yin Ling did not remember her having been so manipulative. She was using her god and the gift of food as a clever ploy to gain friends in the home. Yin Ling knew that, as soon as she left, the divinely appointed food went straight into the stomachs of mortals. Of course, Ah Heng Cheh's god was given time to partake of the feast, but after that, the food could be claimed by mortals. Ah Heng Cheh gave the signal that her god had finished eating, then allowed her friends, by now taut with anticipation, to descend joyfully upon the meal. 'Eat, everybody. Don't worry, there's enough for all,' said Ah Heng Cheh magisterially.

'What about you? Here we are, greedy demons, eating up your share,' said Ah Kum Cheh, who had taken pains to befriend Ah Heng Cheh and was now her best friend at the home.

'Don't worry about me,' said Ah Heng Cheh, smiling and waving a hand magnanimously.

Yin Ling's visiting day at the home was banquet day when the usual modest lunch of steamed white rice, one meat dish and one vegetable dish could be abandoned. Those inmates outside Ah Heng Cheh's privileged circle became envious and angry, complaining loudly to the supervisor, a Madam Thong – who made sure that she too benefited from the largesse of that wealthy visitor.

'She's the greediest,' Ah Kum Cheh whispered. 'She selects the best for herself.'

'Why are you so petty?' said Ah Heng Cheh reproachfully. 'Let everyone eat and be happy.' She had not been so happy for a long time. 'Let *them* come to us,' she said to her little god, who, on account of the food offerings, had his own altar in the home. 'About time. We have been wandering about for too long.' Still homeless, but satiated with good food, the god said he was satisfied. His answers to her questions nowadays, which came through the prayer sticks she shook out of their urn, told of contentment.

Everybody watched out for Yin Ling's visit. Even before the lids of the containers were lifted, they knew if it was braised mushroom, roast pork or fried chicken and they quarrelled over the food, like children.

'How lucky you are, Ah Heng Cheh.'

'How generous you are.'

'You have such a good heart.'

Ah Heng Cheh, with a laugh, dismissed the accolades.

'Ah Heng Cheh, are you sure your god is not tired of all this food?' said Yin Ling, keeping up the pretence, although her mother-in-law had been asking questions and making comments.

'I hope you don't mind, Yin Ling . . .' Now, her mother-in-law approached her with formal politeness, a temporary state, she hoped, between the past hostility and the future amity her son was making more likely every day.

'Why are you taking all this food to Ah Heng Cheh? Surely

204

it's too much for her. She's only got one tooth on her lower gum.' Mrs Chee was probably thinking of that evening at the Monckton Food Centre when her son had painstakingly cut up the roasted pork on Ah Heng Cheh's plate into very small, manageable pieces. Mrs Chee complained to her *mahjong* friends who, since Ah Heng Cheh's departure, had returned for the regular weekly sessions, that although she did not mind the expense, the cooking was taking up the Filipino maid's valuable working time. 'No complaints,' she would say, if asked for an assessment of her daughter-in-law. 'She's very respectful and considerate and attentive, but . . .' Her daughter-in-law was strange. '*Tow hong,*' she might have said to her friends, twirling her finger against her forehead to indicate a crazed mind. She had not as yet told her son of Yin Ling's strange act involving the dead baby on the way to the wedding, preferring to consign this and all bizarre incidents to memory's inaccessible chambers. 'She has given me the most beautiful and brightest-looking grandson in the world,' said Mrs Chee, smiling. 'I'll love her for that if for nothing else.'

The ultimate test of her mother-in-law's love, Yin Ling thought, would be for her to take herself and her little son to that secret home of her gods under the staircase, for that was where her heart truly was. But it was a sanctum that would be closed for ever to others.

In the midst of playing with his son, who would be one year old soon and whom everybody proclaimed to be the cutest and cleverest baby in Singapore, Vincent said, 'Darling, there's something I need to ask you.'

Even in the midst of the new happiness and peace, she shuddered at such a request, instantly connecting it with that time in her life when she almost left him for another – oh, why had he stopped writing? – and fearing its threat to the peace.

'Are you still in touch with him? Does he write? Do you still think of him? *Do you still love him?*'

But Vincent only asked, 'Why were you so anxious to take Xiang Min to see Ah Heng Cheh?' All those futile visits, all that nonsensical bribery with food.

'I wanted her to give him her blessing.'

'Did she?'

'Yes.'

'What did she do?' Vincent would have taken offence if his precious son, baptised with holy water in the Cathedral of the Divine Saviour and given the name Bernard Augustine, had been subjected to some crude ritual involving joss-sticks or, worse, made to imbibe some temple-blessed water. His mother's secret amulets for himself were tolerable, but Vincent would allow none for his precious son.

'She put her hand on the top of his head and gave him an *ang pow*.'

That was all right. He had long ago given up trying to wean his wife from her bizarre attachment to the old servant, which fortunately would not last for much longer, given that Ah Heng Cheh was approaching ninety and in frail health. His wife's oddities of behaviour were nothing to her immense usefulness: her fine linguistic editing of his thesis had yielded a first-rate work that no editor at the Singapore Cambridge Publishing House could have achieved. Beside the wives of any of his friends and colleagues, Yin Ling stood out with her fine mind, her radiant beauty, her quiet demeanour. At a recent function where the Deputy Prime Minister was guest of honour, he had proudly shown her off and watched with immense satisfaction his being taken up by her intellectuality and poise. Later the Deputy Prime Minister had told him, 'I was highly impressed by your wife.'

He loved her so much! Motherhood had brought out the best in her.

'So Ah Heng Cheh blessed our little son?' He was prepared to be totally indulgent.

Nowadays Yin Ling's untruths to him were more of omission than commission. It had not been only the putting of a hand on the little boy's head and the giving of an *ang pow*. Ah Heng Cheh had brought out her strange little god to touch and bless the boy too. She had also tied a piece of red string round the god's wrist and then the child's. Thus would they be ever linked. 'Love, prosperity, happiness!' Ah Heng Cheh had intoned. Child and god stared at each other, then broke into smiles. Xiang Min gurgled, and attempted to chew the red string on the god's wrist. Yin Ling laughed delightedly.

This she omitted to tell Vincent. She was so pleased she had succeeded in getting Ah Heng Cheh's blessing for him. It was important to her.

'I'm a useless old woman, soon to die,' Ah Heng Cheh had said. 'Why have you come to a useless old woman?' but had given her blessing anyway.

At the same time that her husband affectionately pulled her down on the bed with one arm while embracing his son with the other, he said, 'I hope you know your limits.'

Limits! Limits! In the old days she would have burst into rebellious rage, even if only in the privacy of her own heart. These days, Vincent put up severe warning signs against any threat to his illustrious respectability in society with one hand, and with the other dispensed generous rewards for good wifely behaviour. Yin Ling knew she must be the most richly endowed wife in Singapore, provoking the envy of Gina and other wives who clustered round to look at each new gift of diamonds or rubies or emeralds at the numerous parties to which Vincent liked to take her. Now, in her new happiness, which had nothing to do with the jewels or the new luxury seaside apartments that Vincent was planning to buy in her name, she thought, I'll submit, and simply kissed the top of her son's head and put her forefinger in his hand for his small fingers to curl around.

Oh, she loved him so much!

She wrote a poem about her son, not about heavenly benisons from old servants and their gods but about little boys' everyday activities. She saw him a few years hence, her happiness and peace by no means diminished as she watched him growing, and marvelled at how an old love, aching with the pain of its passion, could slowly become a new one, quiet and confident, centred upon a little child.

> *I could hug you, press you close,*
> *Only I don't want to disturb*
> *Your peaceful slumber.*
> *Dirt-encrusted stick fallen from limp hand*
> *That just now was gun, horse, magic wand,*
> *Sweaty handkerchief fallen from face,*
> *That just now was robber chief mask,*
> *Lump of garden dirt still on your forehead*
> *Defiant of gravity's law.*
> *Chocolate-moustached,*
> *You murmur in your sleep*
> *Perhaps still dreaming of that game*
> *In the tree-house in the garden.*
> *A soft kiss will not disturb your slumber.*

She had seen mothers revelling in the simple joys of motherhood; she would claim all of them, down to the thrill of putting Elastoplast on a bruised knee, emptying a small boy's pocket of its treasure trove of stones and twigs, dead beetles and melted Smarties, telling stories to calm a child unable to sleep. She who had stormed heaven with her pained questions would now find her peace in the everyday joys of earth. She would no longer look up, puzzled and questing, into the vast, fearful void, but downwards, to the familiar smells and sights of home.

Xiang Min, growing up through the years, lovable through infancy, robust boyhood and serious manhood: what did the future hold for her son? What did the future hold for her?

There was a story she once read that she had never forgotten. A woman married young and prosperously, but without loving her husband very much. Still, it was not too bad a marriage. Everybody was good to her. When she was thirty, somebody came secretly into her life. It was only a very brief affair, and the man went away as suddenly as he had come. She never saw him again. But, oh, such passion, such happiness! Afterwards, nothing mattered any more. Her life was over. She went through the remaining years, thirty in all, lifeless, spiritless, the walking dead. She walked upon the earth as one still alive, breathing, talking, eating, sleeping, sometimes even laughing, but inwardly she was a cold, dead thing, without life, meaning or hope. Such was her love for the man. Before she died, she gave instructions for these words to be carved on her tombstone: 'She died at thirty, and was buried at sixty.'

The story had haunted Yin Ling for years. It was the saddest story she had ever read about love. She made the resolution, holding her son tightly in her arms, 'No such fate for me,' and embraced the life she had chosen.

Alice Fong called to make a request: 'If you can spare the time, could you please come over.'

Her mother's cancer was in remission; indeed, Alice Fong gave the impression that she was cured, dismissing any expressions of concern from her son or daughter, who came with money and special nourishing food; Alice Fong irritated them by turning all gifts over to her church. 'I don't need them,' she said and, turning to her little grandson, would say, with uncharacteristic feeling, 'He makes his grandmother happy. That is my therapy.'

Yin Ling came hurrying over. A death warrant? For cancers could unexpectedly reassert themselves in even more deadly forms. Trouble from Kwan? He had been harassing his mother about some messy legal matters related to her flat, which he believed she was secretly intending to will to her church.

As soon as Yin Ling arrived, Alice Fong made her sit down, then went to a drawer and took out a sheaf of postcards and letters, tied together with a rubber-band. Without a word, she handed the stack to her daughter.

Yin Ling gasped. She recognised the handwriting, saw the postmarks from a number of different countries – Hong Kong, China, France, Italy, Poland, the UK, the US, Malaysia too. Had it crossed his mind, when he was in Malaysia, to come to Singapore, just a bridge away? The messages, just now only fragments dancing before her eyes, would have to wait for lingering attention in private. Right now, she wanted to confront her mother and shout, 'Why didn't you let me know? Why have you been keeping these from me?'

She had a quick look at the dates on the postcards. They spanned a long period. He *had* been writing after all. He had never stopped thinking of her.

'Mother, how could you do this to me?' She was shouting now. 'You had no right—'

'I had every right – and duty – to protect my daughter,' said Alice Fong coldly. 'Why are you still playing with fire? Why are you allowing this man to threaten your marriage and your happiness?'

'There is no threat,' screamed Yin Ling. 'I'm not playing with fire. There's nothing between us any more.'

'Then I should have thrown all the cards and letters into the fire,' said Alice Fong. 'This man is dangerous. He's obsessed with you. He will destroy you.'

So her mother had been reading her postcards. Possibly even her letters. She remembered her mother's stealthy footsteps outside her door during those tempestuous days before her wedding when she was talking to Ben on the phone and shouting at him above the din in the Heron. Her mother would justify everything with duty.

'I have a duty to my grandson,' said Alice Fong, and she took the little boy from her daughter to hold in her arms. 'I can't stand by and watch his future being destroyed by irresponsible adults.'

Yin Ling stood still, pale with shock, clutching the letters. Mistaking the shock for anger, Alice Fong went on, 'You can say anything you like, but I will not allow anything to harm the life of my grandson.' The strength of her assertion brought on a fit of violent coughing. She handed back the baby, sat down on the sofa and rubbed her chest. Immediately Yin Ling went to her mother's side to assist her. She continued coughing, her face a dull red.

'When was your last visit to the doctor? What did he say?'

Usually Alice Fong would wave away these inquiries, but this time she said, slowly and hesitantly, 'He thinks it's spreading. I may need an operation.'

Yin Ling thought, I'm sick of all this. Her mother was using the cancer to gain attention while her natural taciturnity repelled it. The visits to the doctors, mentioned only in passing to her children, the reports and diagnoses conveyed only partially, the bottles of medicine and packets of pills put on the tops of cupboards with all the appearance of being bravely kept out of sight, but clearly visible – all this was aimed at provoking inquiries and solicitous comments.

Most came from Kwan. 'What's this? I haven't seen this X-ray before. What's happening, Mother?' Once he had stood on a stool and brought down a whole tray of bottles from a cupboard top. 'What's this? Are you taking all this, Mother? How come you never told us?'

Suddenly Yin Ling felt an overwhelming pity for her mother. Locked into her joyless world, she could not keep out the loneliness and now sought desperately to assuage it. Her church prayer group that met every Thursday and went on a trip to South Korea every year, her cancer, her grandson – they were all means for assuaging the frightening loneliness. And the letters. She could have destroyed all of them and never let anyone know. Instead, she saved them up, then summoned her daughter for a dramatic confrontation. It was as if she was looking for any excuse to emerge from her self-imposed solitude.

Alice Fong got up from her chair, had a last fit of coughing and said, 'I will not have you shout at me again. I hope this is clear.'

'I'm sorry, Mother.' She was the confused, resentful twelve-year-old all over again. She thought, Something is wrong with me. My husband, my mother, my brother, my mother-in-law – I am at odds with all.

'Wait,' said Alice Fong, as her daughter was about to step out of the door. 'You can't expect me to be party to your guilt. If you want to continue receiving letters from that man, you must use another address.'

'As you like, Mother.'

All the way back home in the Mercedes, driven by Arasu, Yin Ling held her son close, while the stack of letters nestled safe in her handbag against her side. His scrawl, which had floated in disconnected fragments before her eyes half an hour ago, had flared into a searing presence in her head, making the veins at her temples throb. She tightened her embrace of her son, who had fallen asleep in her arms, and heard again her mother's words: 'That man is obsessed with you. He will destroy you and your family.'

You have no idea, Ben had written on the postcard, disregarding the discretion that postcards demanded, *how much I love and miss you*. She had read all the postcards and letters in the privacy of her son's room, as he lay asleep in his cot; it would have been a simple matter to shove them all under a pillow if anyone had entered the room then. She had arranged them in the order of the dates in which they had been written, noting the time interval between each, the shortest being probably a few hours, for three postcards had been sent in the course of a day, and the longest a fortnight when he seemed to have been held up somewhere in an obscure part of India, possibly in an ashram. She noted, too, the changes in mood and tone, which swung violently from deep despair to wild elation, from bitter accusation to tender remembrance. By now, only a few hours after receiving them, she knew them all by heart and could actually reorder them, in any way, by topic, tone, depth of feeling, strength of hope.

Six

It's pathetic, really pathetic! All the news I get from you is from a friend in Hong Kong who gets it from a friend in Singapore who gets it from *Lifestyle* magazine or other friends in Singapore.

So he must have found out about her wedding and the birth of her son in that way. She could see him scouring copies of *Lifestyle* and the *National Times*, for sometimes Vincent made it into the newspapers too. Not once had Ben mentioned Vincent nor Xiang Min since that congratulatory card shortly after the birth.

Vincent said, 'I love you.' Stinting in his professions of affection before their marriage, he now loaded her with them. He had not thought a dedication appropriate in an academic treatise, but he had dedicated the book to her anyway, 'To my wife, for all the love and support,' and placated his mother by telling her that while wives were honoured in dry, academic stuff, mothers deserved nothing less than a blockbuster novel, which he would write one day, on her account. Mrs Chee, not exactly mollified, had said, 'You young people do what you like.'

Vincent said, uncoiling his wife's hair and gathering it up in sensuous play, 'I love you very much.'

'I love you too,' she said, with a little shuddering *frisson*, for it was the first time she had said it. No, she told herself, she was not telling him an untruth. She did love him – in her own way. It was frightening how love needed to be qualifed to be true. But that was how things had become – the hidden true life and the open false one trying to co-exist peacefully. She sometimes thought that the four chambers of the heart were meant to serve the different needs: two to beat to necessity's tempo, two to love's.

I can't forget you. How many times have I said it? I don't know and I don't care. I can't sleep, I can't work, I've lost interest in everything. Yesterday I had a letter from the human rights people pursuing the case of that poor caned Bangladeshi. I threw it away. I can't bear the thought that while I'm in torment, you are happy and contented.

She had searched all the postcards and letters, but Holly Tsung had not come up. Not even the remotest hint.

I'm mad. It's a greater madness to know and persist in it. Why do I keep writing to you – I must have sent a hundred cards and letters by now – and deliberately leave out a return address? Why do I keep pouring out my heart with no return address for you to tell me how yours is faring? You know why? I know how it's faring and I don't want to know. Consider this scenario which I want to avoid like hell: I tear open the envelope with tremulous hope, in the language of you Charlotte Brontë aficionados (did you know you used the expression three times in your poems?), read your letter with a wild hope (my expression), then cast it away as just so much vile shit (my language of angry despair). So, if you don't mind, I'll continue the lunacy of this one-way communication.

Lightly running his fingers along the curve of a breast, Vincent said, 'You know, we should be thinking of a companion for Xiang Min. He's going to be two soon. He'll need a cutesy little brother or sister. Is my little cutesy wifey ready?' He, who took lessons from expert trainers in public speaking, had taken to the lover's coy language of diminutives. These days, in her peace, she had stopped being unreasonably irritated by other people's speech habits. In difficult, earlier times, she might have snapped, 'Stop that,' or winced.

I am ready! I am ready to receive your response, no matter how devastating. Tremulous hope or not, I'm going to tear open the envelope bravely. Sorry, you will say. Sorry, but it's too late. I live a happy, prosperous and peaceful life now. You cannot be part of it. I have decided I must take the risk of hearing even that. I need to hear what your heart says. So here goes. Please write to this address. Please write something, anything.

In the darkness, Vincent whispered, 'You know something? It's so much better now.' He meant the love-making. It had been fraught with anxiety just before and just after their marriage, with Vincent blaming Father da Costa for ruining his sex life: that hypocritical, renegade priest was still keeping his public celibate life in easy harmony with his private unruly one. The bishop knew but pretended not to. His mistress, it was said, was getting bolder and demanding to be seen with him at certain social gatherings. There would be one other Vincent would blame, but never openly because of the shame. His name would never again be mentioned in Vincent's house.

I dreamt of you. Yet again. Three dreams in a row, two sad, one happy. I'll only tell you the happy one. You can easily guess it. The Tenth Court of Hell, the nth Inn of Heavenly Happiness for me. Every detail is etched in my memory; it was the most detailed dream in my life, down to the strand of hair on the shoulder of your pale blue blouse, which I would have kept for remembrance if you had let me. Remember? But what's the use of asking you anything when you never want to write back? WRITE BACK!

Yin Ling said to Vincent, 'I'm pregnant.' He was overjoyed. He embraced her, then told his mother.

Mrs Chee said, 'It's good for the little one to have a brother or sister to play with.' The gods in her private shrine under the staircase had told her she would be blessed with many grandchildren.

Yin Ling told her mother who, since the day she handed over the packet of postcards and letters, had slipped back into cold severity, coming out of it only at the sight of her little grandson. Alice Fong said, 'That is good news. That will be good for Xiang Min.'

Yin Ling told Gina who immediately exclaimed, 'Good! Let it be a boy. Two sons. Then a daughter. Perfect family. Everybody happy.'

Tell you what! Forget all that I've written, all those outpourings of pain and hope. Forget what I wanted to know about *your* pain and hope. Forget all those things related to that most insidious of organs, the heart. It ever misleads you. From now on, we'll write as mere acquaintances interested to get news about each other. Simple, innocuous news. What you have been doing. What a typical day is. What you ate for lunch, wore, watched on TV, etc., etc. You can make it like

217

routine diary jottings. 'Went to Takashimaya in the morning to buy a pair of red sandals. Lunch at Bistro. A shampoo at Mervin's. Watched the ten o'clock news.' As dry and impersonal as you like. That will be enough for me AS LONG AS YOU WRITE.

Yin Ling was quiet. She said to her husband, 'This must be such a disappointment to you. I'm sorry.'

He embraced her, saying, 'Never mind. The important thing is that you're okay.'

The miscarriage had been sudden. It had occurred when Yin Ling had stopped at a children's playground in an HDB estate, to allow Xiang Min to play with some small children there. They had been on their way to see Ah Heng Cheh in the Mercedes, driven by Arasu, when the little boy, seeing the children at play, jumped up and down excitedly, wanting to be taken to join them. In the playground, watching her son with two small children digging in a sandpit, she had suddenly felt a warm trickle down her left leg, had looked down to see the blood and bent quickly to wipe it off, glad that nobody had noticed. The doctor had said, 'This sort of thing happens. Don't worry. You are healthy. You will get pregnant again.'

Her mother-in-law said the same consoling thing. 'Both of you are young and healthy. There will be plenty of time,' and kindly brewed restorative ginseng and bird's-nest for her. Privately, Mrs Chee said to Vincent, 'It's that old people's home. The atmosphere is not good. Why don't you tell her not to go so often?'

Alice Fong said, 'Do be more careful. You mustn't carry Xiang Min. He's grown too big and heavy for you to carry in your condition.'

Yin Ling could never have shared the thought that had

come to her then with mother or husband or mother-in-law: 'I'm glad it's turned out this way. I couldn't bear another pregnancy.'

What's the matter with you? What's happened to the warm, generous, honest person I knew? Can't you even write one line? Have you grown so callous? Write one line, I challenge you, even if it is this: 'I've stopped thinking of you.' Write it! I challenge you!

It was an unusual request, but Vincent acceded to it immediately and wholeheartedly. The magazine *Lifestyle*, which, years back, had listed Vincent Chee Wen Siong as one of Singapore's Fifty Most Eligible Bachelors and had later run a feature on the wedding, wanted to do a follow-up piece on the children born to those eligible bachelors now enjoying fatherhood. Baby Xiang Min, at two years, topped the list. Yin Ling was hesitant, but was argued down by her husband and mother-in-law. Mrs Chee, who claimed that at least four features of the baby's face and at least three traits of behaviour were direct inheritance from the Chee side, said, 'That baby who won the first prize in the Esso baby show. Our Xiang Min is a hundred times cuter.'

All right, all right, I give up! I know your silence is your way of saying, 'I don't think of you any more. Please don't threaten my safe and happy and prosperous life in any way.' All right, but may I make a request, a plea? I miss them so much! I mean your poems. I know them all by heart, those you chose to share with me. I'd hoped you'd show me all. Please, please send a poem. I can't imagine you giving up your secret writing. One might as well tell you to give up

219

breathing! PLEASE SEND A POEM! I'll be at the above address to end of November, then it's Los Angeles. You might have thrown away the LA address, so here it is once more. Don't throw it away this time. Parched, crumbling earth slaking its thirst at a spring. That's what your poem will do for me. I remember the imagery – it was from the poem you recited to me at the Eighth Court of Hell. You said you hadn't written it yet, and probably never would. Tell you what. If you write back, I'll send you the poem. I remember every word. Good trade. A poem for a letter. A one-line letter. So PLEASE WRITE!

Xiang Min said, 'I love my mummy.'

'How much?' Both grandmothers invariably asked about the extent, smiling to see the little boy's demonstration of it, which sometimes resulted in his toppling over or falling down with a bump. He stretched his arms upwards, then outwards, standing on tiptoe. Then he ran to touch this table or that corner of the wall, as if needing points of reference for the measurement of the vastness of his love. Lastly, he ran to his mother and flung himself into her arms. Often she had to hide her face in his, to cover the tears.

I promise you I will not bother you again if you do this for me. Tell me about Ah Heng Cheh. I think of her often too. Is she dead? Is she still alive? And well? Is she still looking for a home for her god? Or has he already gone home?

She sat down and wrote back, on a single sheet of notepaper, which she hurriedly slipped into an envelope, and posted to the address in Los Angeles:

Ah Heng Cheh is still alive. She is well. Her god is still with her. They are both residing in the Seng Tee Loke Old People's Home.

She gave Gina's address for the reply.

Seven

'Darling,' said Vincent, 'could you do me a favour?' As usual the favour for her husband had to do with his ambition and her talent: she had edited his Ph.D. thesis for publication, checked his numerous speeches for delivery at various official functions, even written the less serious ones for him with touches of wit, quotations from Shakespeare and other poets. She helped regularly with the linguistic and creative aspects of a government newsletter started by the office of the Deputy Prime Minister – the DPM.

Each time she sat down to work on any of these favours for her husband, she could imagine Ben saying, with fine sarcasm, 'So that's how you're using your rich gifts – to write propaganda.'

'Darling,' said Vincent, 'I know your generous nature will not refuse to help poor Justin.'

He brought 'poor Justin' to see her shortly after, and she understood why he constantly used the epithet of commiseration for this sixteen-year-old boy: no nephew of the august DPM, the second most important person in Singapore, should have been so puny, troubled and maligned. The youth had plucked eyebrows, two fine arches over large, limpid, long-lashed eyes, which stared at her with a strange blend of melancholy and defiance. The style of his hair, neither too short nor too long, and of his shirt, which was made of some delicate material but might arguably be presented as an item of male clothing, was a desperate compromise with a stern, unaccepting world. The compromise was necessary only during the day, when he went to school or was under the supervision of his mother or the chauffeur, who had been given strict instructions not to let the boy out of his sight.

As soon as night came and he was sure that his mother was asleep (his father was seldom at home), the compromise was joyfully abandoned, and he slipped out of the house with hair dyed or curled exactly as he liked, in a daring outfit, usually of red leather, and high-heeled boots, to be happy with his friends at the Nightingale or the Omar Khayyam along the waterfront. Here he talked, laughed, teased and was truly happy. Some Singaporeans, writing in the Forum pages of the *National Times*, had urged the authorities to close down these notorious gathering-places: they gave Singapore a bad name. 'These places are corrupters of our young,' one incensed reader had written. 'It is an irony that Singapore, which has invested so heavily in moral education in the schools, is letting it go to nought in Sodom and Gomorrah.' The police sometimes conducted raids on them and took away people for suspected prostitution or drugs; it was during one such raid that Justin had been caught and his parents discovered, to their horror, what he had been secretly doing. Fortunately, when the police found out that he was the nephew of the DPM, they got in touch with his parents for a discreet but polite warning. Margaret – his mother and the sister of the DPM – who ran her own law firm, was terrified that any future foray on Justin's part might bring shame to the family; his father, the top executive of Shell Oil, struck him once or twice across the face, then buried his own face in his hands. 'Be calm, for goodness' sake,' the DPM had advised, at a family conference. The boy was due to sit the all-important O-level examinations at the end of the year. Their primary concern should be to make sure that he passed well and then they could send him abroad to continue his studies, under close supervision, of course. 'Stop crying, Margaret,' the DPM said tersely to his sister. To his brother-in-law he said, even more tersely, 'You might consider, Boon, giving a little more attention to your son.' Boon spent half his time travelling for his job and the remaining half on the golf course. The DPM made sure that he himself spent as much time as possible with his two daughters. A discreet and circumspect man, he had nevertheless one morning spoken privately of the problem to Vincent. It was clear that he trusted the bright, hard-working, reliable young man at all levels. Vincent was deeply moved. He said immediately, 'Why don't you let my wife help him prepare for the exams? She's extremely good in English literature and the fine points of the English language, and she's very patient.'

The DPM was moved in his turn. 'You are very generous. Let me speak to his mother.'

The boy was quietly defiant, sitting very still and looking unblinkingly into Yin Ling's eyes. It was a well-developed strategy of defence – to stare expressionlessly through any long tirade. His mother would shake him violently by the shoulder and scream, 'Stop staring like an idiot! Didn't you hear what I've just said?' but her hysteria only strengthened his resolve to stare down a hateful world.

'I hate you,' he said at last to Yin Ling, still with the blank face. 'It's no use your talking to me, because I hate you and everyone.' He came each time in the chauffeured family car with a great show of reluctance, and sat through each lesson impassively, staring ahead or slowly turning those long, unblinking eyes upon her as she talked to him.

'What are you doing?' she said, in the middle of a lesson on

Hamlet. She made him show her what was in his hand – a small rounded stone that he was rubbing against his leg. The deliberate distractions got more and more self-destructive: on one occasion, he kept jabbing the back of his left hand with a long needle; on another, he drew weird, esoteric symbols along his arm with a purple marker pen. 'Stop it,' she said severely. 'You're doing all this to irritate me.' Gradually she began to realise that Justin had the finest mind she had encountered in any young person, which he hid behind the imbecile stare.

She tried every trick to win him, and suddenly realised she was enjoying the challenge of breaking through to this difficult boy, but he remained impervious. He stopped mutilating himself, but continued the exasperating stare.

She even showed him her poems. 'I've shown them to only one person,' she said. 'Actually, I burnt them all. These are what I remember of them. But some are recent.' He said nothing, but when she went out of the room briefly, she returned to see him leafing through the sheets.

She said to him one afternoon, 'You're wasting your time and mine. I'm going to tell Uncle Vincent I don't want to be your private tutor any more.' She used the courteous 'uncle' whenever she mentioned her husband to the boy. He said nothing. 'In fact, I don't even have the energy or the inclination for today's lesson,' she went on. 'I'd rather use the hour and a half to go to see Ah Heng Cheh instead. So, if you don't mind, Justin, I'm going to call your chauffeur now and tell him to take you home.'

The boy said, without any change of expression, 'The theme of *Tess of the D'Urbervilles* is the total indifference of the universe to human affairs. There are several incidents in the novel to show that Hardy wanted the reader to be aware of this . . .' In a previous lesson on English literature, she had asked him to do some homework on one of the texts for the O-level exams, and he had, as usual, remained silent. 'The accident that killed the family horse, for instance,' Justin continued, 'and Tess and her brother mourning its death under a night sky full of stars indifferently looking down . . .'

Yin Ling now had a clear image of the boy. He was like several children she heard of who were bright beyond the ability of the teachers to teach and stimulate them, thoroughly bored day after day and who finally gave trouble. Justin's homosexuality must have given even greater cause for alarm and concern.

Unable to contain her excitement, Yin Ling said, 'That's very good, Justin. But I still want to go to see Ah Heng Cheh and send you home.' Justin looked for a bag he always carried with him, took out something and handed it to her. 'Last week's homework,' he said. 'I'm sorry I didn't give it to you earlier.'

It was a composition she had asked him to write as exam revision.

'Well!' said Yin Ling. 'This is a surprise. Well!'

'May I go with you to see Ah Heng Cheh?'

'You keep surprising me, Justin. But why not? I'm sure she won't mind. It depends on her mood, though.'

'Will she show me her god?'

He, like Ben, had been most taken by her poems on Ah Heng Cheh and her little homeless god.

'I had a friend,' Justin said, and it was amazing how the blankness gave way all of a sudden to a swirl of emotion, which condensed into tears filling his eyes and flowing down his cheeks, 'who died last year. I could have been the one you were writing about.'

So he liked, too, the poem she had written when she read in the *National Times* of the huge commemorative patchwork

226

quilt, covering half a football field and bearing the names of those who had died of Aids with messages of love from grieving family, friends and lovers. It had come all the way to Singapore from the United States, before continuing its journey of remembrance round the world. She had gone to see the quilt and taken part in the candlelit procession around it, impressed by the pain that must have gone into those little pieces of needlework to form a riot of colour more suited for celebration than mourning. 'If you don't mind, darling,' her husband had said, 'you go on your own. I'm not sure I care for this sort of thing.'

Her mother-in-law had asked, 'Where's Yin Ling gone?' and when told, had clucked her tongue and said, 'Motherhood should have cured her of her strange habits.'

'I've learnt to let her do as she likes,' said Vincent. 'When she's happy, she's at her best.'

She had called her poem 'Masterpiece', scribbling it on rough notepaper during a solitary hour in the room adjoining the bedroom where her husband lay sound asleep.

He said he had something very important to do
So he went into hiding,
Punished fingers, eyes,
With holding, threading a needle,
Needle's eye mocked his squinting eyes
Needle's point his finger
Stabbed to rawness
On the cloth held taut in the wooden frame.
Taut his heart too with the ache
Of the beloved's name at last
Swimming into view through a haze
Of tears.
He used only purple and red

These being the beloved's favourite colours
And stitched in a small grey pebble
This being their last secret.
At last it was ready
No masterpiece, more
A child's reluctant needlework at school.
He saw it that day in the exhibition hall
Fitted into the giant quilt of remembrance
One hundred messages
In needlepoint, cross-stitch, satin-stitch, herringbone
On cloth, wool, leather, silk, denim
The message the same
For the hundred deaths the same
Though nobody said 'Aids' once.
Loss, grief, remorse
All bordered in loving gold
Guilt's gilt quilt
He broke down
Not in sorrow
But in new sorrow of the old shame
Of always the inadequate offering
Against the magnitude
Of their loving.

As soon as she had finished the poem, she had thought that Ben would have taken her to task for the self-indulgence. ' "Guilt's gilt quilt"?' he would have echoed, stroking his beard. But of course she would never send him the poem.

Justin said, 'It's a real coincidence. I used blue and yellow, though. Those were Alex's favourite colours. And I stitched in a message, forty-two words on a square inch of a paper, which I folded to form the tiniest square in the world.' Yin Ling could see the boy, alone in his room in that big bungalow in Ashtonbury Park, working with a needle and thread late into the night, perhaps in the light of a small torch so that his mother would not know.

'I would have done something for Jackie, too, except they allowed only one offering per person.' Had the boy, at sixteen, already had lovers? Alex, Jackie. Wistfully androgynous names. She remembered reading about a Professor Balasingam, a top surgeon in a Singapore hospital who performed sex-change operations and claimed as his greatest success a man who did not have to change his name with his new life because he was called Kim. She had not known many gays but had always been fascinated by their lives on the fringe. Vincent had told her that the government did not approve of them but was not quite sure how to deal with them, Singapore's top architect being gay, as was a leading sociologist at the university. As long as they were discreet and made no public issue of it, said Vincent, the government was prepared to turn a blind eye. One of these days MTC was going to ask for a confidential report on the gay population in Singapore.

Yin Ling looked at Justin, nephew of the DPM, and wondered what the secret life of this sixteen-year-old student was like. She could imagine MTC summoning the DPM into his office and saying, 'What is this I hear about . . .'

She was beginning to like him very much. One day, after a lesson, he said, 'Let me show you something,' and he rolled up his shirt to show a tattoo on his chest, which comprised a simple intertwining of the letters A and J.

She said, 'If you do your homework and get good grades at school, we can spend more time talking – I like talking to you. And more time for visits to Ah Heng Cheh.'

'It's a deal,' he said. At the old people's home, he was neither interested nor uninterested. He stood around patiently and politely, waiting for her. He had seen Ah Heng Cheh's god and was clearly unimpressed, the reality not quite matching the image he had formed from her poems.

'Xiang Min, this is Justin. Say hello to Justin,' said Yin Ling, when her little boy ran in during a lesson, pursued by the Filipino maid. The child rushed into her arms squealing, and vigorously pushed the maid away.

Justin was comfortable with small children. He drew pictures for Xiang Min and allowed the little boy to climb up on his knee and explore the contents of his bag. Mrs Chee, who had peeped in once and seen, to her dismay, her grandson perched on Justin's lap, had later voiced her concern to her son.

'Don't be silly, Mother,' said Vincent.

Mrs Chee said, 'I'm still uneasy. I wish I could tell Yin Ling things directly, but . . .'

Vincent said to his wife, 'The DPM's very pleased with the progress Justin is making. Only four months and he's improved vastly in his grades at school! I'm so proud of you, darling!' He embraced her, very pleased indeed. With each day, he became more convinced of her worth. 'Darling, there's something that would please the DPM even more.' Vincent ordered his requests on an ascending scale of the DPM's pleasure. He wondered whether Yin Ling could do something about Justin's behaviour. He was no longer slipping out at night and going to those dreadful places on the waterfront, but could she persuade him to give up those dreadful plucked eyebrows and long fingernails, those fancy shirts and boots?

She thought, I'm getting very fond of the boy. He said to her one day, 'You told me I was the only other person you had shown your poems to. Who was he, or she?'

'Someone who came into my life years ago.' Would she tell

him her favourite story of that woman with the heartbreaking epitaph, 'She died at thirty and was buried at sixty'? But, unlike that poor woman, she was heartwhole again.

'Did you love him?'

'I suppose I did. I almost wanted to run away with him.'

She had told Gina about Ben in a roundabout way; with this sixteen-year-old boy she found herself talking plainly and simply.

'Then you did love him. Why did you marry Uncle Vincent instead?' Leave one man, marry another, follow the heart's cry – as if life were that simple.

'I don't know.' But she thought she did. The anger and pain of being abandoned, of that last phone call, of his sudden departure for Hong Kong, had only now been assuaged by those pleading cards and letters. Pride had to be reclaimed first, even before love. In her less generous moments, Yin Ling had almost written back to say, 'Now you know what it feels like.' *Now you know.*

Justin said, 'Tell me about this person and I will tell you about Alex.' There was a new camaraderie between teacher and student, between those who had loved and lost. Justin had met Alex while on holiday in Hawaii with his cousins. Alex was an interior decorator, fifteen years older, and they had kept up a secret, intense correspondence, even during those months when he lay in hospital, dying of Aids. 'Alex knew exactly what he wanted for his funeral,' said Justin eagerly, 'down to the hymns and the colour to be worn by the funeral guests.' It was Justin's dearest wish to visit his grave in Los Angeles and lay some peach-coloured carnations there – Alex had told him his favourite flower. He had the money to fly to LA, Justin said, because his grandmother, who loved him very much, was always giving him big *ang pows*.

'Now you tell me about the person you love, Yin Ling.' He

231

only used the polite 'Auntie' in Vincent's presence. 'I think you still love him very much. I can tell by watching you when you talk about him.'

'There's nothing to talk about, Justin. We made our decisions. At least, I did. He doesn't write any more. I told him he mustn't write any more.' But it had been a difficult decision – those cards and letters had been her sustenance – and she had not told him the truth. That would have been a confession: 'I don't want to receive any more letters from you because each reminds me of how much I love you.' Instead she had written an outright lie: 'Please don't write any more, because I've stopped thinking of you at last.'

'If I get good grades, will you tell me about this person you secretly love? Really tell, I mean. From the heart, with the heart.'

It had become a game – good grades in exchange for a whole range of good things, including the sharing of the heart's secrets.

'If he comes to Singapore again, will you see him?'

'I don't know, Justin. You do ask difficult questions! I don't know.'

' "Don't know" always means "Yes". People say "I don't know" when they mean "Yes" but are too embarrassed or confused to say so. Are you confused?'

'I don't know – there I go again. You're tying me up in knots, Justin. So no more questions. Get back to work.'

'When are you going to see Ah Heng Cheh again?'

'Very soon. Now, *work*!'

Ah Heng Cheh was still demanding good food for her god, but now her mind was turning to something else. She said she had had a dream; Ah Heng Cheh's dreams could be troublesome, resulting in this or that demand for her god, and this one turned out to be the most troublesome of all. She had been visited by the ghost of the baby girl who, so many years ago, had been drowned by her distraught mother in the well that was now covered by grass in Ah Heng Cheh's land, her only possession on the face of the earth. The Old One said that, in her dream, she had seen the ghost of the child talking to her god and telling him his home was with her, in that disused well, in a forgotten corner of Singapore. Ah Heng Cheh wanted to visit the spot with her god and offer food and joss-sticks. Her god was sure to tell her if that was truly where he wanted to be at last.

'How can it be?' said Yin Ling. 'It's just an old well. Surely that's no home for a god?'

The flattery did not work. 'You used to believe my dreams,' said Ah Heng Cheh sourly.

'I still do,' said Yin Ling earnestly. She was in a happy mood that had nothing to do with Ah Heng Cheh. Ben had ignored her request and had written back, 'I don't believe you. I know neither of us can stop thinking of the other,' and continued sending his letters through Gina. How happy they made her! There was no happier secret life for a woman than to know she was loved against all reason or hope; she would dwell tenderly on that thought all the days of her life. She owed an enormous debt of gratitude to Gina for agreeing to let her use her address for the receiving of those secret letters. Gina had gone about her new role with admirable discretion. She had written to Ben to provide her address, resisting the temptation to go beyond the one line that Yin Ling had requested: 'Could you in future send all letters to . . .' Gina received then passed over the letters with elaborate secrecy, bursting to tell her husband but solemnly promising not to. She rather relished the role of intermediary between a happily married woman and her secret admirer, thinking it no bad thing if a woman could keep her marriage while enjoying another's devotion.

'One of these days,' said Gina, ruminating, 'I might take a secret lover. Heck, who cares? Life must be lived greedily.'

People said to Yin Ling, 'Why, you're looking more beautiful than ever! Motherhood's done wonders for you.' The truth of her glowing looks was known only to Gina, who thought that marriage was compatible with illicit love, if it was handled discreetly and sensibly.

Ah Heng Cheh never once complimented Yin Ling on her obvious good health. Instead, she launched into one bitter tirade after another. 'Nobody believes me. Everybody takes advantage of me. Even you. I might as well be dead. Every night I pray, "Let me die soon and not be a bother to anyone any more." And I tell my god, "You will have to be on your own. You will have to find your way home yourself."'

'Tell you what, Ah Heng Cheh,' said Yin Ling, struck by an idea, 'if you have one more dream of the baby ghost at the well, I promise I'll take you and your god there.' She had made the condition before she realised how silly it was.

'One doesn't dictate to the spirits of the dead how many times they must appear in dreams,' said Ah Heng Cheh testily. 'If you have no intention of granting my request, say so, instead of talking nonsense like this.'

It was no use talking to her any more. Ah Heng Cheh was in one of her difficult moods and was clearly determined to stay in it. Jealousy was a strategy of those who loved; Ah Heng Cheh used it unabashedly, turning her full attention to one Ah Bah, a son of her best friend Ah Kum Cheh, who often visited his mother at the home. He was an odd-job labourer and, in the course of his visits, had befriended Ah Heng Cheh, offering her a share of the food he brought for his mother in a large tiffin-carrier.

'Ah Heng Cheh has been giving us such expensive food, and you are offering her our poor fare!' said Ah Kum Cheh, in deep humility.

'Nonsense!' said Ah Heng Cheh, and spoke in the friendliest possible way to the man, who later asked his mother about the rich visitor with the expensive food gifts.

Ah Heng Cheh spoke endlessly of the new friend Ah Bah. He did this, he did that for her. He cared for her. Yin Ling said sharply, 'That's not nice, Ah Heng Cheh. You're just trying to make me jealous. That's not at all like you.'

Each was accusing the other of a change of heart.

'You don't believe my dreams. Please don't come any more.'

Her mother, brother, husband, mother-in-law, her friend Gina, the whole of Singapore would have been aghast: 'You go regularly to visit an old servant at a home with all that expensive food, regarding this as a special favour from her, and then when everybody at the home is satiated with it, she tells you you can't come any more. And you begin your second round of begging.'

The unmentioned thought in everyone's mind was: 'Yin Ling has brought this on herself,' and the unasked question, 'Why is the Old One taking so long to die?'

On her next visit, Ah Heng Cheh was cheerful.

'You may not want to grant me my wish,' said the Old One, with a triumphant smile, 'but there is someone who will. In fact, we are getting ready to go now.' She was indeed dressed for going out, and was holding a black umbrella. 'There are still people in this world who care about a helpless old woman,' the Old One continued pointedly.

Yin Ling was standing at the doorway of the visiting room and turned to see him. He was standing by a window at the other end of the room. He lifted a hand in greeting and her only thought, in a rush of feeling that caused her to lose her balance and grab at the door, was, Why, his beard's gone grey.

Eight

Ghosts, whether adult or infant, did no haunting during the daytime. Only in the shades of twilight or night did they come out, riding on a cold wind that made the hair on the skin of the living stand on end, standing in silent vigil by their graves. Even in the darkest of nights, the coldest of winds, the baby girl who was drowned in a well would instil no fear. Now, in bright sunshine, invited to appear by Ah Heng Cheh holding a lit joss-stick, the ghost provoked only pity. Had some villager in that faraway time in Singapore gone to draw water, peered at the small, crumpled body in the dark depths, then run off to tell others? Yin Ling thought of the dead baby boy she had cradled in her arms against her wedding dress.

Ah Heng Cheh's story might not even be true. Many of the spirits she prayed to were probably only characters in the tales told and retold down the generations. A tragic couple in a Chinese opera, for instance, passed into enduring myth and was honoured in a little shrine on a small island off Singapore that still attracted the faithful, especially during the Feast of the Hungry Ghosts. Ah Heng Cheh might have nurtured a nothing into an awesome child ghost that spoke imperiously to adults in their dreams and even made decisions for their gods. The nurturing had a quality both touching and pathetic: Ah Heng Cheh claimed that the dead baby had been a dear daughter in an earlier life, and remembered her name, which meant 'Little

Flower'. As if in compensation, her tragic death on entry into the world had invested her with immense power.

For the special occasion of the visit to this powerful child ghost, Ah Heng Cheh's god was dressed in his best, in a gold silk robe that Yin Ling had never seen before. Or perhaps it was the same robe he had worn for the ceremony of the blessing of her baby son, when Ah Heng Chch had tied his wrist to Xiang Min's with lucky red string. The god looked at her amiably, remembering their many journeys of search together. 'You in your world, I and Ah Heng Cheh in ours,' he said, 'but do let's all be kind and jolly together!' And perhaps his friendly gaze included the American, too: 'You in your even more remote world, but now that we're all here together, let's be kind to each other.' Ah Heng Cheh went fussily about the ceremony of invocation, which involved placing beside the well joss-sticks, a candle, a plastic bowl of bright candy, some paper money and her god, dressed in his best, in grinning collusion with a child ghost on his journey home.

Ben relit the candle, which had gone out in a gust of wind, and fumbled for something that Ah Heng Cheh indicated she wanted, which was a handful of coins, the money of the living, to be offered with the paper money for the dead. They were American coins but would do.

Yin Ling held an umbrella over Ah Heng Cheh, knowing the Old One was averse to the afternoon sun. It gave Ben his cue to speak: 'Isn't it the same umbrella she used at the Sai Haw Villa? I recognise the blue flowers at the edge.'

Each had been waiting for the other to say something. Almost within touching distance, they circled each other warily, fearful of a wrong word said and retracted too late, of unkind words colliding. Physical presence was always daunting: it tied up their tongues where imagination or tender recollection had loosed them and allowed free play with words. Or perhaps the sheer joy of seeing each other again made speech irrelevant. Ben, who had poured his feelings in angry, rushing streams into his letters, continued to make observations about Ah Heng Cheh's umbrella and the edging of blue flowers.

Eventually Yin Ling observed, 'Your beard's gone grey.'

He said, 'You've lost weight.'

Umbrellas, beards, weight, derelict wells, child ghosts, the afternoon heat – they tiptoed around the danger. Why have you come to Singapore? Why shouldn't I come to Singapore? Didn't you understand I couldn't write letters, only receive them? Am I expected to believe you couldn't have written *one* decent letter in all this time? Have you any idea how much I suffered? Have you any idea how much *I* suffered?

Neither was ready yet to ask the hundred questions screaming inside them; they would have mired themselves deeper in the self-centredness and vanity of lovers who saw only their own wounds. One wrong word, one false step, and the whole fragile structure of negotiation would tumble down once more. Words never did lovers much good, invariably dragging them back to the past, which ever demanded explanation for this or that; they had much better concentrate on the here and now of the physical presence.

Ben was mesmerised by the physical presence, and the small-talk dropped to the ground at his feet as he stared at Yin Ling.

'Ben, you're making me nervous.'

'You're beautiful.'

Exhausted by the long plane flight from home, in a forgotten part of Singapore, far away from the throbbing life of the city-state, presiding over an old woman's ceremony of conjuration for a dead baby, Ben Gallagher suspended all thought and feeling to concentrate on one thing: comparing the face now before him with the face he had remembered and hungered for in his restless travelling from city to city. He wanted to take that face in his hands and kiss it, as he once had, but knew he could not for the circumstances had changed. Damn the circumstances! They had names – marriage, husband, child, duty. He had not changed, and neither had she: he could tell instantly by her eyes, which ever betrayed her. Ah Heng Cheh had not changed either, or her god. So damn the circumstances.

He had to make a decision, and make it quickly. There was no time to lose in a situation that might never come again. Ben realised, with an inward groan, that his relationship with this woman, whom he loved with an aching despair, had been no more than a series of urgent attempts to gain time.

It was a simple decision.

'Ground rules all over again,' he said, trying for jocularity. 'To show appreciation to Ah Heng Cheh and her god, without whom we could never have met, we should enjoy every moment of our time together.' *Without whom we*. He might have been making a formal speech of acknowledgement at some university function. The sonorous tone, at odds with his personality, was perhaps necessary to establish the seriousness of purpose.

'So we will have no questions, no arguments, but only talk about happy things, and laugh. For instance, Ah Heng Cheh's umbrella. My beard. Your beauty.' His eyes were now bright with the excitement of the moment – she had once told him that, in a good mood, he looked sinister, for his eyes became narrower, the lines around them deeper, the eyelashes darker, giving him the aspect of a brooding Heathcliffe or a Byzantine monk.

He saw her looking at him and instinctively moved closer, longing to take her hand at least and bring it to his lips, but he recovered quickly and said: 'A poem about a child goddess at a well must be forming in your mind. Do you remember that woman whose son was killed in a hit-and-run and who stood on the spot day after day?' He said that he had read in a Hong Kong newspaper that the culprit had finally been caught.

Yin Ling had not known. She realised, with a start, that she had grown hungry for the sight of his face, the sound of his voice. She had it now. The hunger, too, was for a touch but that, like the rest, in the face of unremitting reality had to be given up. But from deep inside her, a small, persistent voice of hope and need that she thought had died refused to be silenced. It did not want to give up. It did not say, 'Leave it all to Fate,' wearily acknowledging defeat. Instead, it said, 'Who knows?' and kept hope alive.

Love did not conquer all: it buckled up in the face of an unforgiving society, and fell back on compromises. But at least, that way, it kept itself alive.

'Why are you seeing him again? What do you want? Don't you realise it will lead nowhere?' Gina's worldly wisdom, which approved the receiving of secret letters, would have warned against the writer appearing in person: as survey after survey had shown, no married woman's guilty liaison lasted twelve months. No passion, no matter how ardent, could be sustained beyond six. For a woman bore in her body, which was made for nurturing others, love and guilt in equal parts. She might try to beat down the guilt, but it would rise again each time, invading her every waking hour and filling every moment spent with her lover, with a fretful fear, until he said, 'What's the matter with you?' and she crept away from his bed to her husband's, and cried to hold her children in her arms. Gina would have cautioned, 'If you run away with this *ang moh*, your remorse regarding your husband and son will kill you within a year.' And Yin Ling knew it was true. Singapore

241

was dominated by the acknowledged gods of common sense, duty, money, security, power, who could not be put to flight by love.

In the end it would always be the good marriage saved, the contrite wife received back, the joint property, so carefully built up over the years, kept intact, the family name untainted by shame, the well-being of the children protected. Let passion have its brief hour, but in the long days ahead, it had no place. In the end, said everyone philosophically, it comes down to that heat in the groin, fleeting and passing, which the family is not. All else passes away, except family.

Yin Ling suddenly thought of the Epitaph Woman – *died at thirty, buried at sixty*. There must have been a moment when, pining for her lover, she had thought of running away to him. What had caused her to turn her back on her dream and live her remaining years in sorrow? There must have been a child. Thirty years later, when the child, now a grown man or woman, gazed upon that sad epitaph, he or she must have wondered at it. The god of passion must have sneered at the dying, unfulfilled woman, 'Serves you right. Thirty years of the heart's slow bleeding. The price of duty.' The pragmatic god must have come to her defence: 'Consider the alternative. One false decision born of one moment of dubious pleasure, leading to lives ruined everywhere. This woman did the right thing!' The god would have harped upon the worst outcome of a wrong decision: guilt and remorse. The social sanctity of marriage doomed a married woman's secret love from the start. Passion, guilt, regret. It was not fair that the god of love exacted so much more from a woman than from a man.

If Yin Ling and Ben had had the stomach to sit down back then and work out together the practical side of love, like the businessman doing his sums of profit and loss on his computer, would they have cast it in the crude language of economics, with each claiming, 'I stand to lose more than you,' totting up loss of property, financial support, salary, work opportunities? Lovers liked to believe they were above the economic imperative, while all the time they were subjected to it and eventually succumbed to it.

She believed she was above it. She would give up without a second thought all the affluence and privilege of 2-B Rochester Park, the promise of more as her husband rose, a shining star in the political firmament.

But she could not give up her son. The fear of losing him would be her only strength against the onslaught of the maverick god of love. For Vincent would fight with every ounce of his energy, every dollar in his bank account to deny her access, much less any claim, to her son. The mere thought so filled her with dread that she had once, while watching her husband tumble on the carpet with the little boy, dashed over to seize him and hold him close.

'What's the matter?' Vincent had asked but, fortunately, had not waited for a reply as she let the boy run back to him.

By the well, Ben watched Yin Ling looking into the far distance, her face grave. He said quickly, urgently, since Ah Heng Cheh's ceremony at the well would be ending soon, 'Do you think you could have a coffee with me? We'd drop Ah Heng Cheh at the home first.' He spoke, without much hope, of a little corner shop near the home selling excellent coffee and curry puffs, and received the expected reply resignedly: 'I think I'd better not. I'm expected home . . .'

I'm expected home before six. I've been invited to this or that function at eight. I'm supposed to . . . she always used the passive voice, to avoid any mention of her husband. 'Vincent expects me to be ready at six' would have violated the rules agreed between them. This beautiful, intense, difficult, unhappy woman had her own private grammar of misery. Ben thought, as he had thought many times, Everything's working against me. I hate everything. It's a hopeless situation. He had become a hearty hater in the cause of love, hating his own rules and wishing he could destroy them all at once, like a bundle of dry sticks broken across his knee. He had chosen the wrong god, or, rather, the god had chosen him. This god was not a cute little winged boy with a bow and arrows, shooting at random. He was a mature, powerful, stubborn, over-confident god, who exacted tribute from his followers, then turned their lives upside down. Better, thought Ben savagely, to give allegiance to a passionate wrong god than a cold right one. Passion. He could not do without it. The fervour he had brought to noble causes since boyhood was nothing in comparison to his passion for this woman.

The long flight home was not till the late evening of the following day but it would be useless asking, 'Can I give you a call?', much less, 'Can I see you one more time?' But it was difficult to be angry with the woman he loved so much.

I know what I'll do, thought Ben grimly. He would spend the hours of waiting at the Heron. He already saw himself at his favourite bar, slouched over his beer.

As they prepared to leave, he longed to touch her hand, cheek, lip, but resisted.

Nine

For a moment, Yin Ling thought of asking Gina to dinner at the Rainbow. The restaurant was directly opposite the Heron and would afford a good view, since Ben liked to sit at one of the outside tables in the fresh air, rather than in the smoky interior. A good view of a man slumped gloomily over his beer. She only knew she wanted – oh, so much! – to look at him again.

But even if Gina agreed, there would be the tedious accounting to Vincent – 'Why all the way to the Rainbow? It's an odd place for two women to have dinner. Besides, the food's lousy,' and, possibly, the even more tedious task of allaying any suspicion. She hated the routine that had imperceptibly become an accepted part of their marriage, she asking permission to do this or that, he giving it after asking where, when, who, why. She hated the why most of all, for its ugly, inquisitorial quality. 'Why?' Vincent would ask, as casually as possible, not looking at her, continuing to play with their son. If she happened to be in a playful or defiant mood, she might retort, 'Why not?' with the same assiduous avoidance of his eyes and the same determined concentration on their son. She liked her husband little then, herself less. Every day she spent with him, sharing in the lustre and promise of 2-B Rochester Park and his ambitions, she felt herself slip a little further into the bleak world of blighted dreams. Vincent's generous cheques to her mother and for the upkeep of Ah Heng Cheh in the Seng Tee Loke Old People's Home, so promptly signed and sent, hastened her descent into the darkness of her confusion and despair.

She was about to give up the idea of seeing him one more time when Gina called and provided the ideal opportunity. Gina had numerous relatives and friends abroad who were always coming on visits. An elderly aunt from Toronto was due to arrive on the night of his departure, and if she asked to go along with Gina to meet the old lady, she might just catch a glimpse of him at the airport. It was insane, all the manoeuvring for a glance from behind a convenient pillar or a crowded airport shop, but once the idea had occurred to her, she knew she had to carry it through.

Gina looked at her suspiciously and said, 'Wait a second. You want to come with me at an inconvenient time to meet Auntie Siew Koon whom you don't care two hoots about?' Then she said brightly, 'I won't ask. I should know, shouldn't I?'

'I'm going to the airport with Gina to meet her aunt from Toronto.' The normality and, above all, respectability of the activity would not provoke the hateful why. She could count on Vincent not making the generous offer to drive her and Gina to the airport for he liked his TV and working late into the night on this or that paper or report, or preparing for this or that meeting. She was safe. Technically, she would be telling him the truth.

She had had no idea how difficult it would be to locate one person in the midst of hundreds in busy Changi airport, for the sole purpose of peeping at him from a safe hiding-place. She stayed long after Gina and her aunt had left and looked out anxiously for the bearded face while trying to appear not to. One or two bearded men looked back at her, which made her turn away abruptly. She stood awkwardly at a souvenir shop, nonchalantly studying a mother-of-pearl jewel box, while her heart thumped wildly. The shop-girl said, 'Can I help you?' and she replied, quickly and nervously, 'Oh, just looking around. Thank you.'

She was about to give up when she spotted him. He was rushing through a gate to the boarding area, carrying a small duffel bag, looking tired. She registered each detail of his appearance and movements for later, to spin into tales to comfort herself and feed hope – the duffel bag for the few things he must have gathered hurriedly for his journey to Singapore and his brief stay, the crumpled clothes, the tired, suffering eyes.

There is something very like shock when a loved one, waving goodbye, is lost to sight at last: the last flash of the face pressed at the car window, the waving hand at the railway or plane window might trigger in the onlooker an overwhelming sadness and a terrible emptiness. Her last sight of him was of his beard, streaked with grey, caught in some harsh light. Ben did not wave, for he did not see her, standing some distance away, behind a stack of boxes outside a shop behind redundant sunglasses. She felt a sharp spasm of something akin to panic as she stared, and the thought occurred to her that this might be his last visit to Singapore.

Ten

Yin Ling managed to suppress an astonished 'What have you done to your hair?' as Justin emerged from the BMW. The knowing smirk on the face of the chauffeur, Danny, whom she had disliked from the start, told of one more tumultuous incident in the boy's running battle with his mother. She pretended not to notice the shorn head, smooth, clean and gleaming, and the jug ears sticking out rather comically – the boy had hidden them until now with carefully arranged hair. She said merely, 'Hi, Justin.'

The sight was unsettling – a monk's sacrificially shaven head atop a young body clad in a fancy red silk shirt and white trousers. For a moment she saw him in the privacy of his bathroom, in front of the mirror, with a whirring shaver bought for the purpose, a miniature plough grimly demolishing row after row of the rich hair, until the last hairs fell to the floor in a soft, dark heap.

As with all Justin's escapades, it had been an act of rebellion, meant to throw the mother into a screaming rage. Margaret had looked up from the afternoon newspaper to see her son descending the stairs, shorn and shining, carrying a file of notes, ready for his weekly lesson at 2-B Rochester Park. 'Justin, what have you done . . .' she began weakly, and started screaming. Danny ran in, then stopped to watch, with quiet amusement, storing up another episode in the lives of the rich and famous to tell his friends later. Margaret shrieked,

'I'm going to call Hamburg at once to tell your father. And I'm going to call Uncle DPM!'

Justin said quietly to Danny, 'Let's go, we'll be late.' His mother, in her lime-green Chanel suit, stared open-mouthed at him through a window as he got into the BMW. From the corner of his eye, he saw her disappear in a flash, presumably to start making those phone calls.

The lesson on Wordsworth proceeded smoothly. Justin said, half-way through, 'I'm waiting,' and Yin Ling said, 'All right. What happened?' The boy enjoyed telling her shocking things for she never looked surprised or displeased. His expression throughout the narration of the shorn head incident was of cool defiance.

'I love my mother. Hate is the obverse of love. She must pay,' he said, quoting from one of the cult books he had picked up in a bookshop. He underlined quotable sentences with a purple marker pen, then copied them in his diary or learnt them by heart. He was obsessed with the thought of his mother paying so that every embarrassment or humiliation inflicted upon him would be cancelled out by the shock meted out to her. Once, having found out that his mother had instructed Danny to trail him, he punctured one of the BMW's tyres, then, for good measure, left a lump of dog excreta on the driver's seat. Danny took his mother out to see for herself the desecration of the gleaming new car, while Justin watched from behind his bedroom curtains.

On another occasion, she had gone to his school to complain about something to his class teachers, after he had pleaded with her not to. Of all the things he disliked most, his mother's presence in his school was the most abhorrent. There she stood before the principal, the vice-principal and Justin's class teacher, scolding and lecturing, flashing her diamond rings and bracelets, and repeatedly referring to her brother, the DPM. 'You know,' Justin had said later to Yin Ling, with a smile, 'I didn't have much respect for the principal, who is a coward and a sycophant, but when he said politely, "Mrs Lam, in Hwa Yik High School, we do things this way," and saw my mother to the door, he earned my respect for ever.'

The next day, at breakfast, his mother had looked up from the newspaper to see him quietly overturning everything on the table. She watched in silent horror as he slowly poured coffee on to the white, lacy tablecloth, then the milk on to the spilt coffee, then the honey over both. Next he picked up a knife and slashed at the butter, toast and fruit, decapitated the flowers in the vase, ground them into a mess with his spoon, mixed them into his cereal and ate it. He went about the destruction slowly, deliberately, almost gracefully, as if it were part of a religious ritual.

His mother said tearfully, 'Justin, why are you doing this to me? Can't you see it's all for your good—' and could speak no more in her distress. Those of her friends who had been afflicted with rebellious offspring put the blame on sins in an earlier life and bravely went through their *karma*. Margaret blamed her son's bad companions. Justin said the inspiration for the kind of payment he exacted came spontaneously; all he did was respond to it. He talked eagerly about some esoteric belief that required precisely this response – remaining open to forces coming from the cosmos, absorbing them into one's soul and acting as directed.

Yin Ling stared at the exasperating boy, with the fine features and the sensitive soul, who quietly picked up a knife to slash around, who read more than his teachers, who cuddled a baby boy perched on his knee. Warped and abnormal: his own mother had uttered the words aloud, and had wondered how two wholesome bodies could have produced such an aberration.

Suddenly Yin Ling thought of that tree in the university campus grounds she had written about, warped and twisted with its ugly snake-coils of roots and branches, standing apart from the normal, pleasing trees. That made the *three* of them. A secretly rebellious married woman, an openly rebellious schoolboy, a defiantly deformed tree. She could add several more misfits to the group clustered on the fringes of a society that was uneasy about them, and begged them not to be different and not to be so troublesome: an old servant who refused to die; a god who could not make up his mind; a foreigner who had dared to love somebody else's wife. Every thought in her head, no matter what it was about, went through any number of twists and turns and ended invariably with *him*. With Ben. And every thought about him invariably ended with the question: Why has he stopped writing?

Justin said to Yin Ling, 'I want you to speak to my mother.'

'What about?'

'Sam.'

So that explained the shaven head. Alex. Jackie. Sam. There would be a long line of them to satisfy this sixteen-year-old's desperate craving for love and understanding. The lovers would come from the dark nooks and corners, the closed closets on the fringes of a society that had decided it could not openly acknowledge them. As long as they remained obscure and went about their lives discreetly, the government would leave them alone. One small group had planned, most unrealistically, to emulate the vociferousness of their brothers in San Francisco and had applied to register themselves as a club. The nephew of the DPM was still too young to be enticed in as a member, but what cachet his presence would lend! The Registrar of Societies had turned down the application without a second thought.

'Sam and I,' said Justin, 'understand each other.' Yin Ling wanted to know more about Sam. Justin said, his face lighting up, 'You must meet him. You'll like Sam.' He said his mother hated Sam and was desperate to break up the relationship. She had stormed off to see Sam's father, a lowly waiter at the Hotel Amber and offered the illiterate man a sum of money to keep his son at home.

'I have no control over him,' the man had said sullenly, in dialect. 'He's twenty years old. Take your money back.'

Sam had told Justin, who went out then to buy the electric shaver.

He brought Sam over the next day to introduce him. Yin Ling thought, My God, Vincent and his mother mustn't see him. The young man shocked her not by his appearance – he had shoulder-length hair, an ear-ring, and a black T-shirt with the words 'The Shitty State of Singapore' in bright pink – but by his language. His speech exploded with profanities picked up from popular American movies, and sounded discordant in the mouth of a local youth trained to show respect at all times.

Yin Ling felt a rising tide of annoyance and could not conceal it. She said, 'You can't think or speak clearly while you're relying on all those swear words. Why don't you calm down and organise your thoughts and words?' Bluntness in the face of so much savagery was risky: the young man, whose eyes blazed hatred and scorn, might have pulled a knife. As it turned out, he merely went on spewing invective, then coolly settled himself on the sofa. He caught sight of an anthology of poems, her favourite, on a nearby table, leafed casually through it and said, 'Stupid stuff.'

Yin Ling said sharply, 'Put it down.'

Sam looked long and hard at her. 'Singapore's top one per

cent. From your luxurious house, your fleet of cars, your grand swimming-pool, your expensive chandeliers and carpets, pictures and crystal' – Sam's eyes swept round the room – 'your travels abroad, your second or third homes in London or Vancouver or Perth, you can talk down to us who live in the HDB dumps, work as waiters . . .' Representing the most disgruntled of the HDB dwellers, Sam both courted and despised the sleek cosmopolitans on the other side.

'I would like you to leave now, if you don't mind,' said Yin Ling.

' "If you don't mind," ' mimicked Sam, in a shrill falsetto. 'And, I might add, your polite English, unlike our rough speech.'

'Get out at once,' said Yin Ling.

Sam effected a mock bow and got ready to leave. 'Aha! The little heir to Rochester Park, the top one per cent!' said Sam as Xiang Min toddled in. He stretched out a hand to ruffle the little boy's hair.

'Don't you dare touch my child,' said Yin Ling in rage.

Sam made another elaborate bow and left.

Later Justin apologised for Sam's behaviour. 'He's all right if you understand him. He just likes to shock people because of this raging misery inside.' He told Yin Ling that Sam's parents had more or less disowned him.

She thought, What about me? What about my raging misery inside? She said, 'I don't ever want to see him here again. And I wish you wouldn't associate with him.'

Justin flashed, with sudden anger, 'So you're on my mother's side?' In the end, his mother had become his sole point of reference, his friends' loyalty judged by the side of the great divide on which they chose to stand.

Yin Ling said coldly, 'I'm on nobody's side. And if you want

253

me to go to your mother and say good things about Sam, then you're being presumptuous.'

'I thought you were my friend,' said Justin bitterly. 'I shall not be coming again.'

A month later he came, looking cowed and sheepish. 'I apologise for my behaviour,' he said, and went on, craftily, to lace the apology with flattery, before going on to make his request: 'You were right about Sam. I admire you for your perceptiveness.'

She had an idea of what had happened: Sam's crude insolence had gone too far even for the smitten boy. Actually, as Justin told her later, it was worse than insolence. Sam had humiliated him in a fast-food outlet, in front of a crowd and made him cry. 'I very rarely cry,' said Justin, 'and when I do, it means a rift that cannot be healed, a total severance.' He demonstrated with a hand slicing the air.

'Who's he?' said Yin Ling, noticing the new person he had brought along, who was loitering uneasily near the entrance, by some pots of bougainvillaea.

'I want you,' said Justin earnestly, 'to speak to my mother about Kok Weng.' Kok Weng, unlike Alex, Jackie and Sam, belonged to the respectable world of academia. He was a lecturer in sociology at the university, and would therefore be more acceptable to his mother. Kok Weng even looked respectable, with a neat hair-cut, white shirt, dark trousers and silver-rimmed glasses. 'Kok Weng wants to be my friend,' continued Justin. 'I want you to tell my mother that he is a good and trustworthy person. I want you to tell her not to subject him to any embarrassment or humiliation.' He must have had a terrifying image of his mother storming into the dean's office and threatening to take up the matter with the vice-chancellor.

Yin Ling thought anxiously, I've grown so fond of the boy. What shall I do?

Justin said that Kok Weng was planning a holiday in Bali in the coming university vacation, which overlapped with the school vacation by a full week. Could Yin Ling persuade his mother to let him go? Apparently Kok Weng had changed his mind about being introduced to Justin's tutor, mentor and intercessor: after playing idly with the bougainvillaea for a minute, he drove off without entering the house. Justin must have dragged him along to 2-B Rochester Park in the first place.

'Please,' said Justin.

She thought of Vincent's disapproval. Mrs Chee had shown unease at Justin's homosexuality, but Vincent's disapproval stemmed from a different source. The DPM had specifically stated that Yin Ling's contact with his nephew should be limited to his schoolwork and preparation for the exams. Nothing outside that. The DPM had a horror of family skeletons escaping from their closet to rattle before a delighted opposition, who would have no qualms in making political capital of them. Hence the DPM rebuked his sister each time for her indiscretion: 'For goodness' sake, Margaret, will you stop shouting? Do you want all the neighbours to hear?'

Vincent would say, 'Darling, don't get involved. It might get messy.'

Justin said sulkily, 'I should think that, as a friend and mentor, you might speak to my mother on my behalf.'

'Let's have some ground rules,' said Yin Ling, aware that messy things were manageable only if you turned them into a game with agreed rules. 'If you work hard, do all the homework I set you, score high grades—'

'You're confusing conditions with rules,' said Justin. The

boy was bright and scored high grades easily if he was not distracted. Yin Ling thought of the distraction Kok Weng brought. He called the boy frequently on the phone. He bought gifts. He would wait for Justin in his Toyota, away from Danny's spying eyes, and take him out when he should have been working.

Yin Ling saw the boy, at sixteen, seventeen or eighteen, violated in spirit and body beyond all healing, disowned by his parents, condemned by his uncle, ending up in the notorious Shining Light District, earning a living hawking his body to tourists and finally succumbing to despair.

'Listen, Justin—' she said anxiously.

He said, 'Just tell me whether you are on my side or my mother's.' He swung wildly in his moods and had assumed a cold implacability.

'Listen, Justin, it's not as simple as that.'

'You're on my mother's side, then. Well, goodbye. I'm not coming for lessons any more.'

Each time he swore he would not come back, he changed his mind. But the contrition he showed was a smokescreen for a ploy that was soon uncovered. One morning the DPM told Vincent to convey his special thanks to Yin Ling for the extra lessons Justin had said he needed. As he returned home, Vincent did so, adding, 'I'm proud of you, darling. The DPM was really pleased by your generosity with your time.'

When Justin came for his next lesson. Yin Ling said severely, 'What's this about extra lessons? Out with it, Justin.'

Justin's truth was unpalatable, to say the least. It had all been Kok Weng's idea. He wanted more time with Justin, a few cosy afternoons in his well-furnished apartment on the university campus. So he had hit upon the idea. The 'extra lessons' took place on the chauffeur's afternoons off so that

Danny could not spy on Justin, whose mother, in any case, trusted the wife of her brother's protégé.

'Justin, you used me,' said Yin Ling sharply. Struck by the magnitude of the deception, she stared at him, eyes blazing.

'We didn't do anything,' said the boy earnestly. 'We just talked. Kok Weng showed me his antique clocks and classical records. He's got a stupendous collection. His poetry too. He reads and writes a lot. Kok Weng understands me better than anybody in the world.'

'This has to stop. Or I'll have to tell your parents.'

'Ho, ho! Who's on the moral high horse?' jeered the boy. 'What about that man you were secretly meeting?'

She regretted trusting a sixteen-year-old. He saw her discomfiture and grew reckless. 'You tell my parents, and I'll tell Uncle Vincent,' he said.

'I thought I liked you,' said Yin Ling angrily, 'but you're a mean, nasty, ungrateful boy.'

'Gratitude? What have you done for me?' sneered Justin. 'I would have got all those As and B pluses anyway. Didn't need you.'

'Get out.'

'I will. And don't count on me coming back.'

Flushed with victory, the boy lingered at the door. He looked at her smiling. 'Kok Weng,' he continued, chanting the name like a mantra, 'read me a poem he found somewhere, which exactly describes Singaporeans like you, dying inside because you deny your heart, but pretending that all is well because you do not dare rebel against society.' The sixteen-year-old had swallowed Kok Weng's words and was now merely regurgitating them. He regurgitated the poem, too, flawlessly, and she listened, her heart quickening because the poem had been the only one published by *Dialogue* and the only one Ben had not connected with her.

257

No place here for the heart, for sure,
Until the unruly lushness
Of its impulses
Has been pruned and shaped
Like the topiary beasts
In the Botanic Gardens,
Clipped, bent, wired

To society's dictation
Of logic and efficiency
Insuppressible the heart, for sure,
It will turn fugitive
And go underground.
On the surface then, the smiling
Pre-programmed garden beasts
Below, creatures of malice slouching towards
A schizoid society.

Justin was turning against her, as had the man she loved.

'You poor thing,' said the boy, with supreme malice and walked jauntily to the waiting BMW.

And at this point her anger gave way to an overpowering sadness. She wanted to shout after the boy, 'Once we understood and liked each other.'

Eleven

Another letter arrived from him. It was the longest ever, feverishly scribbled and bore a devastating air of finality. It said:

I should not have come to see you – Ah Heng Cheh and her god forgive me for using them! – for I'm now more desperate than ever to have you. I think of you all the time, awake or asleep, and plot and scheme for the next meeting. The situation is untenable. I've got to have the truth, once and for all – God, how many times have I said that? How many tedious times have we tried to draw closer to it, then backed off, or circled it wearily? I demand it now. But first let me tell you *my* truth. My truth first, then yours, then ours. Mine is this: I have given up everything – job, home, peace of mind – for you and will give up more gladly, if there's anything more to give or suffer. The world will denounce me as wife-stealer and home-breaker, you as faithless wife and heartless mother, both of us as desecrators of the only remaining decent institution left in this sorry, shabby world. I've come out with those words we've been avoiding all along – marriage, husband, son, family, home-breaker. They stick in my throat but I must yank them out and lay them out in the open if we are to begin finding a solution to our problem. Away from you, I can paint our problem in its truest, harshest colours instead of soft-hueing them with those desperate, stupid ground rules which I suspect I'll invoke once again in your presence. Just seeing you unsettles me and reduces me to an idiot. I need the distance, and your absence, to sound coherent at all. And the justification for all this madness? The weapon to fight an entire hostile world? Love. I say it unabashedly. I've got it all ready to do battle. I even have the tickets to fly myself in and ourselves out. That is the measure of my madness. That is *my* truth. I can't suppress my heart. It simply goes underground, then later emerges, soured and cankered. Yours won't canker; it will bleed for thirty years. Is that your truth? Tell me, once and for all. 'I love you' or 'I have stopped loving you.' Everything else is irrelevant. No buts or ifs. Worse, no perhaps or could-have-beens. Either one or the other. Out with it. Out with *your* truth.

The letter was crushed tightly in her hand. She thought, the tears suddenly gushing, Do I know it?

Twelve

Xiang Min's fever wouldn't subside. Yin Ling watched by his cot all night, applying wet pads to his hot little brow, picking him up and rocking him in her arms each time he became fretful, pacing the floor endlessly with him. The child, approaching his third birthday, had never been ill, enjoying a robust infancy that Mrs Chee attributed to the tonic herbs she had made Yin Ling take regularly during the pregnancy and breastfeeding.

The child, his eyes closed, twisting his head from side to side, began to fret and whimper. Yin Ling said, holding him close, 'Oh, my precious.' Multiply by ten, a hundred times, the pains racking his bones or convulsing his muscles and she would take on all of them to give him even the smallest measure of relief.

Vincent called, almost by the hour, from Geneva where he was attending a conference: 'How is he? What does Dr Neo say?' He sounded anxious; he would have no heart for the conference, for which he had been preparing for weeks. 'Would you like me to come home now? Shall I fly back instantly?'

It was strange that she loved him best when he loved best not herself but others – Ah Heng Cheh, her mother under-going treatment for cancer, their little son.

She said, 'You go on with the conference. I'll call Dr Neo now.'

261

But Dr Charles Neo, Singapore's best-known paediatrician, seemed unable to stop a little boy's raging fever.

'For goodness' sake, what's wrong? Why can't you find out? Surely you can find out?' Yin Ling said. In her worry, she became querulous and peevish. She added silently, You call yourself Singapore's top paediatrician.

The doctor explained patiently that he was still trying to establish the cause of the fever and, meanwhile, the little boy should continue with the prescribed medicine. In his turn, the doctor was tempted to be rude: 'He is not the only child in Singapore with a high fever. Just because you are the wife of Vincent Chee Wen Siong . . .' but he maintained a smiling imperturbability throughout.

'I want to fire him,' Yin Ling screamed on the phone, when Vincent next called. 'I want to get another doctor for Xiang Min.'

Vincent said, as gently as he could, 'Darling, let's not act hastily. The conference ends Thursday evening. I'm taking the first flight back. I'll skip the trip to Berne.'

It was a bad time for Kwan to call with his complaints, the worst possible time for her mother's cancer to reassert itself. Overwhelmed with concern for her child's illness, Yin Ling had little patience for her mother's.

'Are you or are you not coming to see Mother?' said Kwan reproachfully. It would be one of those detestable family conferences, where she and her brother sat down with their mother in urgent consultation when none had ever felt any urgency of loving, only the dull call of duty. Even that might be called into question, for their mother had as good as renounced family ties when she made the preposterous announcement that she was going to South Korea to live among friends there. 'South Korea!' Kwan had exploded. 'You are going to live with strangers?'

And Alice Fong had quietly replied, 'I'm living with them now.'

'Mother, what on earth – for God's sake!' Kwan could not go on.

'If I die there,' Alice Fong said, 'it will be God's will.'

'It's all the doing of those prayer group people,' Kwan said to Yin Ling. 'They've promised her a cure in some sanctuary where a faith-healer purportedly cures all cancer-stricken people. But we know what they're after. They're a bunch of crooks.'

'Does she want to go?'

'She's already making arrangements, tickets, transfer of money. You'd better talk her out of it. They'll clean her out of whatever money shc has.'

'She has very little.'

'The flat. Don't forget the flat. And property prices are rising. You know that the flat is going to double in value? Maybe triple in a few years. There's something going on that I don't like. She won't tell me. She may already have signed her property over to the Church.'

'Let her do whatever makes her happy,' said Yin Ling wearily.

'Happy! She's miserable as hell. And it's all because of you.'

'Me!'

'You'd be surprised. You were always thc favourite child, even though she seemed to favour me.'

Kwan bent truths as easily as wires in his hands, for the shaping of this or that purpose, which Yin Ling now waited to hear.

'You must ask her point blank about the will,' he said. 'She won't tell me. You'd better come over directly.'

Yin Ling thought of her mother's pathetic manoeuvres to

gain attention, of the hands that longed to be held but remained rigidly pressed on the lap.

'I can't. Xiang Min is ill,' she said.

'You're always putting everyone above Mother, aren't you?' sneered Kwan.

'I'm talking about my son,' said Yin Ling sharply. Suddenly she felt an overwhelming tiredness. 'Tell Mother I'll go and see her when Xiang Min's well.'

Dr Charles Neo said that perhaps the boy had better be admitted to hospital. Yin Ling, hollow-eyed and haggard, said, ' "Perhaps"? "Perhaps" my son should be admitted? You're not sure of an important matter like this? "Perhaps"?' Now she was downright rude. 'Dr Neo, you should know better. Tell me the worst. Don't hide the truth from me. Tell me at once.'

The doctor wanted to say, 'If all the mothers of sick kids in Singapore behaved like you, we doctors would call it a day.' Later he was to tell his wife, who had been Yin Ling's classmate in school, 'I think her husband's status is going to her head.' The doctor had heard – who in town had not? – of the way she had lambasted poor Michael Cheong some years back at a dinner party and concluded that an advantageous marriage could turn a gentle girl into a shrew.

Yin Ling slept on a couch next to her son's cot in hospital. She had insisted on bringing his mattress, pillows, blankets and toys to reduce the child's distress at unfamiliar surround-ings, and provoked the sly comment among the nurses, 'Mrs Vincent Chee's throwing her weight around.' Xiang Min went in and out of his fever and had the attention of the best doctors in the hospital. The nurses, whispering among themselves, had a name for Xiang Min's fever which they abbreviated to RKA. It was prevalent among children of the rich and influential. It ran its course after a certain amount of money had been spent in specialists' fees. Doctors like Charles Neo made their fortunes on the Rich Kid's Ailment, and found it worthwhile to smile reassuringly through any amount of fretfulness from the mothers and their entourage of relatives and maids. One of the nurses, who had been trained in England and whose mother still practised the folk medicine learnt from *her* mother, said that the traditional concoction of an easily available root and some herbs, costing one dollar and fifty cents, instantly cured all those village children who had dared contract the Rich Kid's Ailment.

Yin Ling, looking at her son sleeping fitfully in his cot in the children's ward of St John's Hospital, thought, If he should die . . . and choked on a rising sob. She struggled to put out of her imagination the dark images of the dead babies with which she had become acquainted – the baby boy abandoned in the rubbish dump, the baby girl drowned in an ancient well. No, no, she thought fiercely, and would, like the ferocious tigress, tear to shreds anyone responsible for the death of her child. Her Xiang Min must grow up to be the little boy with the mud-covered face playing cowboy or robber, with the pocket full of stones and strings and melting Smarties she had written about so tenderly in her poem. And she would go on to write a poem about a tall young man who would share his mother's love of truth, beauty and goodness and celebrate these, less imperfectly, in his own poetry, which he would read to her in her greying years. Mother and son, in the gentle reciprocity of a fulfilling love, when all other dreams had died.

Vincent, rushing straight to the hospital from the airport, found her crying and his mother beside her, pale with anxiety. It would have been futile conveying to them Dr Neo's reassurance that the boy was in no danger and, of course,

unwise to repeat his wry observation that the danger sometimes came from the irrational overreaction of the mothers and
grandmothers.

Vincent said, kissing her gently, 'He'll be all right, darling,'
and then went to embrace his overwrought mother, secretly
gratified that such an abundance of love surrounded his son
and heir, no matter that it was giving trouble to the good
doctor.

Yin Ling said again, 'I want you to fire that man,' and
Vincent went into another round of placation and reassurance.

The next day they were allowed to take Xiang Min home.

Mrs Chee, hanging around furtively outside the door of the
child's room until she was sure Vincent had gone to work,
tiptoed in. Looking to left and right, putting a finger to her lips
in redundant caution since Vincent's Mercedes had already
roared away, she approached Yin Ling, who had Xiang Min in
her arms. The child looked better but was fretful.

'You've always understood me better than my son in this
matter,' said Mrs Chee. She took out of a paper bag a small
bottle of water, uncorked it and shook out some drops, which
she proceeded to apply to her grandson's forehead, cheeks
and tongue. The little boy screamed when his grandmother
pressed his cheeks to force open his mouth and kicked away
the bottle of holy water, probably acquired at great expense
from the Kek Lok Thong Temple.

'Shush, shush, here's a good little grandson,' cooed Mrs
Chee and succeeded in putting her god's healing touch upon
the child's tongue. The boy bit her and she laughed. 'Shush,
shush, you mustn't do that to your grandmother!' She said to
Yin Ling, 'I know you won't tell Vincent,' and her daughter-in-
law responded with a smile, 'As if I ever have,' paving the way
for the next and more important stage of the ceremony:
rescuing a child from the evil spirits. For, in Mrs Chee's mind,

the cause was as simple as that, despite what this doctor or that specialist at St John's Hospital said. It was the Filipino maid's day off, so there would be privacy for the ceremony of healing. Mrs Chee led the way downstairs, then reverently pulled aside the heavy brocade curtains covering the small staircase shrine of her gods. 'They're waiting,' she said, as if she had prepared them, the row of hidden but always revered gods of her childhood, to receive her grandson.

Yin Ling thought, Five years ago! For it was that long since her mother-in-law had trusted her with sight of the secretly kept gods. She felt a little tremor of joy: it was a renewal of the trust, through her son.

Mrs Chee lit a joss-stick, prayed for a few minutes with her eyes closed and her lips moving imperceptibly, then applied some ash from the joss-stick to the tips of the little boy's ears. *Little child, your spirit that was stolen by the Evil Ones has now been restored to you by the Good Ones. Little child, you will fret no more.*

Xiang Min, who all this time had been gazing in fascination at the brightly painted gods and their paraphernalia of candles, joss-sticks and tea and food offerings, made some small resistance to the administration of the restorative ash, but was otherwise compliant.

That night the child slept peacefully.

Vincent said, 'I'm going to call Father Francis to thank him.' He had no more dealings with Father da Costa who, it was rumoured, was being quietly packed off somewhere by the bishop because his mistress in John Baru was threatening a major scandal. Vincent had requested Father Francis, of the Church of St Ignatius Loyola, to say masses for his little son; the novena had hardly begun when the boy was up and about, playing with his toys, chattering endlessly.

No child who had recovered from an illness gave greater joy to his mother. Yin Ling would not let him out of her sight. The child seemed more alert and energetic than ever, his eyes absorbing everything around him, his mind carefully pondering everything said, every story told. His grandmother said that if he had been born in China under the ancient emperors, he would have been immediately singled out for special nurturing in the imperial household.

However, she was unusually quiet and ill at ease at the celebratory dinner that Vincent gave at his favourite restaurant in the Shangri-la Hotel, to which he had invited Father Francis. 'No thank you,' Mrs Chee said, refusing to eat the suckling pig specially ordered for the occasion. 'No, I'm not hungry,' she said, pushing away the roast duck. She refused every delicacy set before her, frowning as if in displeasure. In the end, she accepted some steamed rice and braised mushrooms.

'Mother, what on earth is the matter?' cried Vincent, scratching his head. 'These are your favourites!'

'Mrs Chee, you must not waste this excellent food,' said the affable Father Francis.

Yin Ling said, 'Leave her alone, she's not hungry.'

Suddenly Vincent lost his temper with his mother. Her peevishness was just too much for him: just because the Catholic priest's novena had been preferred to her gods' methods, with holy amulet or whatever, she was sulking childishly at the celebration dinner. He had tolerated his mother's nonsense long enough, but he had to protect his son from it. 'Mother,' he said irritably, 'I don't expect you to behave like this.'

Mrs Chee looked pained and shifted about uneasily.

'If you like, I can take you home now,' said Vincent, still more irritably.

Yin Ling said sharply, 'Leave her alone!' Vincent and Father Francis turned in surprise to look at her.

Her annoyance with her husband was accompanied by. a warm surge of love for her mother-in-law. The supplication to her god in the temple and under the staircase, she knew, had been reinforced by real personal sacrifice – going on a strict vegetarian diet and abstaining from the pork and duck she loved. The fourteen-day period of self-deprivation had been practised before, in supplication or thanksgiving. This time it was probably both, the child having fully recovered. Mrs Chee, fastidious, self-centred, domineering, had an enormous capacity for love. In the end, that was all that mattered.

Seeing her mother-in-law's eyes redden, Yin Ling said to Vincent, 'You apologise to your mother right now.'

The celebratory dinner had become a fiasco: Vincent was embarrassed, and resentful, making up his mind not to be too indulgent to his wife or his mother in the future. Yin Ling was bad-tempered, Mrs Chee confused and vexed for she did not like it that her daughter-in-law had caused her son this public humiliation, even on her account. Father Francis looked foolish as he made small-talk and tried to rescue everyone.

Yin Ling stretched out her hand under the table to reach for her mother-in-law's, which stayed, coldly, resentfully, out of her reach. She persisted, and the hand relented at last, uncurled and allowed itself to be held.

Yin Ling thought of the Epitaph Woman. Perhaps she, too, had a precious little son who had fallen ill and caused alarm, a mother-in-law and a mother, distant and dear by turns, all three keeping her busy and on her toes, so that she could sometimes take her mind off the loneliness of those long bleak years.

Thirteen

While her son was peacefully sleeping and her husband was at some function from which she had excused herself, Yin Ling wrote:

You said to reply in one of two sentences: 'I love you' or 'I've stopped loving you.' One or the other. Nothing else. I'm going to disobey you and write this longer note instead, in my own language, which you will see is far from absolute and certain. It is hedged with those ifs and maybes that you so detest. But I will only deal with the biggest if. *If there had been no child.* I have decided I cannot leave my son, which would be a certainty if I left my husband. If there had been only Vincent, it might have been otherwise. I think I might have said to my husband, 'Goodbye and forgive me.' But the time for that has passed and I have missed my chance, caught up in my usual manner – alas! – in a whole tangle of untruths about myself. Now there is a child, and there can be no untruth about love for a child, for it transcends everything else. If I lose him, I lose everything.

She read the note six times before posting it secretly.

The reply was back sooner than she expected, and it was only a few words scrawled on a sheet of notepaper: 'It's goodbye then. All my love, Ben.'

Part Three

One

It was a young cub reporter from the *National Times* who had first got wind of the story. She came hurrying to Ah Heng Cheh at the Seng Tee Loke Old People's Home, prompting the other inmates to remark to the Old One, 'My, my, you do get all kinds of visitors. What an important person you must be!'

Soon pictures were all over the local newspapers, some showing Ah Heng Cheh grim-faced, some smiling and exposing the single tooth that remained on her lower gum. The afternoon *Courier* even made it a front-page story with the headline '89-year-old Retired Nanny in Old Folks' Home is Instant Millionaire'.

Yin Ling, the closest and dearest to Ah Heng Cheh, was the last to know about the astonishing development. She should have been alerted to it on her last two visits to the Seng Tee Loke Old People's Home when she had seen Kwan there, laden with gifts of food and toiletries for Ah Heng Cheh. Perspiring in the afternoon heat, Kwan was smiling as he laid out before Ah Heng Cheh rolls of toilet paper, a stack of face towels, a tin of Jacob's Cream Crackers, a half-dozen bottles of Essence of Chicken and a paper bag of mandarin oranges. Ah Heng Cheh said, clucking her tongue, 'You shouldn't have spent so much money on a useless old woman!' and Kwan might have said, 'Useless, true, but fabulously lucky.'

Yin Ling said, 'All right, Kwan. What is it?', upon which he instantly abandoned the pretext, which must have been both too expensive and strenuous for him, dropped the ingratiating smile and drew his sister aside for urgent consultation.

'Four and a half million dollars,' he gasped, wide-eyed, as he gripped her arm, 'and likely to double, if we play our cards right.' It was some time before she understood what he was talking about, and when she did, she turned to look in astonishment at Ah Heng Cheh, who had fallen asleep in her chair in a corner, her head fallen on one side, her hands still holding a fan. 'Who would have thought,' he said again and again, 'that this useless bit of property, in a forgotten corner of Singapore, which Ah Heng Cheh had bought fifty years ago for a few thousand dollars would today be worth four and a half million?'

Yin Ling thought of the time when Ben had stood beside her at the derelict well, lighting Ah Heng Cheh's candle for the baby ghost. Even then, the road had already forked. Choose, he had said. Either choice would have been for love. She had chosen, and must now mourn the loss of that other, forsaken road.

Kwan's excited chatter kept obtruding upon her thoughts. 'That's a profit of more than a thousand per cent! Beats Bintang Basin, even Moorthy Estate – remember the row of old houses and the monsoon drain we played in as children? Works out to at least twelve hundred dollars per square foot! More than three times the cost of my condominium unit!' Kwan could not get over the enormity of Ah Heng Cheh's good luck in having invested in something that now sat in the centre of the primest of prime land in Singapore and he had all the information at his fingertips: the huge American industrial giant that was going to develop the area into a mammoth petrochemical complex, in partnership with a leading local company, the billions they were prepared to invest, their plans to make the Singapore complex their largest operation in Asia. The ground-breaking ceremony would take place soon. It was rumoured that MTC, who usually left the honours, even for massive projects, to his deputies, would himself be present this time.

'To think that Ah Heng Cheh's little bit of land sits right in the centre! They will have to offer her millions, of course.' The tone of certainty was not only for the amount of the offer, but for the family's inclusion in the good fortune, they being Ah Heng Cheh's only connections in Singapore.

Carried away by the wondrous prospect, his eyes narrowing with the intense effort of calculation, Kwan said that four and a half million dollars was actually a conservative estimate. This giant foreign company and its local partner, believe it or not, were now at the mercy of an elderly servant in an old people's home, and would have to send their lawyers, with their fat cheque books, to little old Ah Heng Cheh, saying, 'Name your price.' The prospect was so delightful that Kwan laughed. Then he settled his features into the grimmest expression as he said, still clutching his sister's arm, 'We'll have to make sure she's not taken advantage of. The fat cats in their business suits are totally unscrupulous. You'll have to get Vincent's help. Big lawyers. High-level negotiations. We can't let her be cheated of her pot of gold.'

Gilded by the association, Kwan glowed and beamed, repeating, for the twentieth time, that the cheating couple who made Ah Heng Cheh buy their little bit of land fifty years ago would be turning in their graves now, and their children and grandchildren would be tearing out their hair when the news finally broke. It would only be to his wife that Kwan would groan, striking the wall with an anguished fist, 'If only! If only!' and recall the time, not too long ago, when Yin Ling had wanted him to accept Ah Heng Cheh's land in settlement of a debt. The earlier derision had turned to wonder as he stood surveying the land, covered with prickly grass, and the derelict well, almost sunk out of sight.

Yin Ling saw again, in every vivid detail, the fumbling about for matches to light the candle, for coins to offer to the dead child. She looked at the exact spot by the well where the coins, a handful of American quarters, and a stack of ghost paper money, had been offered, and realised that, although everything had blurred in her mind during their brief time together in this remote spot, now, almost a year later, it took on the aspect of an exquisitely detailed picture, like a framed master, where every blade of grass, every flash of light or droplet of dew called for close, breathless attention. The heart may renounce its dream, but there can be no renouncing by the heart's memory, which guards its precious hoard for ever. In the end, it is dear remembrance that keeps one alive, for thirty years or longer.

Kwan said, 'Tell me exactly what the situation is.'

Yin Ling said, 'What do you mean?' and Kwan instantly launched into a patient and detailed explanation of the necessity for a will: had Ah Heng Cheh made one? Frustrated by his mother's recalcitrance on the matter – those thieving people in her prayer group had probably by now got her signature for her flat and were laughing all the way to church – he was going to make sure that there would be no mess-up in Ah Heng Cheh's case. Ah Heng Cheh's little plot of land was worth twenty times more than that HDB flat.

Yin Ling said, 'You've never once visited Ah Heng Cheh in the four years she's been in the home. And now all this fuss.' In their childhood days, they had played and been unruly and happy together; as adults, they had grown apart, brought together by exigencies that threatened even greater distance.

'Don't you see?' cried Kwan. 'If we don't do something now,

276

Ah Bah will. That crook and his mother have been working on her.' His fears, like a trawling net, ranged far and wide and left no threat uncovered. 'Did Ah Heng Cheh ever mention any relatives in China? Cousins, half-brothers or -sisters? Once the story spreads they will come with their claims. Do you remember that the *National Times* had a story about an old man who died without leaving a will but who left a lot of property including two coffee-shops and—'

Yin Ling said, 'As far as I know, Ah Heng Cheh's made no will.'

'That's precisely it!' cried Kwan. 'It's understood that Ah Heng Cheh leaves everything to you, since you are—'

Yin Ling said, 'Nothing's understood.'

'Please,' said Kwan, trying to beat down an immense swell of exasperation, 'can't you see the danger? There may not be much time left, and Ah Bah and his mother are with Ah Heng Cheh most of the time.' Ah Bah, with his meagre earnings as an odd-job man, was bringing gifts of food and joss-sticks regularly. He was buttering up her god too.

Yin Ling said, 'Ah Heng Cheh's adopted him,' and Kwan let out a shriek.

'There! I told you. He knows exactly what to do. Now he can legally claim the land. He'll try to get her to will it to him. Maybe he's already done so.' The thought was so painful that Kwan went into a paroxysm of anxiety. 'Adopted? You mean legally? Or only in some traditional ritual? Because if it's legal, the land is as good as his. How can you stand by idly and not do anything?' He was getting nowhere so he decided to shift his remonstrations into altruism. 'How can we watch an old servant robbed of her money? She is part of the family, she is old and illiterate and has always depended on us – how can you especially—'

Yin Ling said, 'I don't understand what's going on, but I'll make sure you vultures don't harm Ah Heng Cheh.'

A few years ago when Yin Ling had persisted in the humiliation of being rebuffed in her visits to the Seng Tee Loke Old People's Home Kwan had said in disgust, 'I wash my hands off this whole affair.' But he could not wash his hands of a multi-million-dollar affair, and he paced the floor endlessly, smoking one cigarette after another, in his feverish determination to stop a stranger laying his hands on the millions of an old family servant who, surely, the family should protect. His sister, in her usual headstrong way, was adding to the problem.

The private motivation and public proclamations of noble intent came together in a confused mix of awed ruminations on a figure steadily rising in a heating property market, and ardent avowals to protect an old servant who had served the family for more than fifty years.

Kwan went to see Ah Heng Cheh every day, to get a clearer idea of what the old woman was thinking about concerning the matter, and also to keep an eye on the scheming Ah Bah, who had started taking Ah Heng Cheh to a nearby community centre to watch her favourite opera.

'Remember what I told you?' Kwan said, on the phone. He called Yin Ling after each visit to give the latest on Ah Bah's nefarious schemes. 'This crook will stop at nothing. He's now publicly referring to her as his mother. I tell you, the whole thing is disgusting.' On one visit he had seen Ah Bah's mother, Ah Kum Cheh, massaging Ah Heng Cheh's legs, and Ah Bah ladling steaming soup from a tiffin-carrier into a bowl, and spooning it into her mouth. He had seen fit to issue a warning. He had gone up to Ah Bah and said, 'Ah Heng Cheh has no family except us,' but the other had merely given him an insolent smile. It was clear that the crook's scheme was

278

proceeding according to plan. They had better act fast. A massive counter-attack was needed.

'Mother,' said Kwan earnestly. He sat his mother down for a long session of explanation and exhortation. Alice Fong's plan to go to South Korea, which had so alarmed her children, had appeared to suffer a setback. Her trip had been delayed by some months for reasons she would not tell. When she finally went, it was with great secrecy, and when she returned after only two weeks with even greater secrecy, all she would say was that she was acting according to God's will. On the matter of Ah Heng Cheh's land, her son could not convince her that it would also be doing God's will to save an old servant from a bunch of vultures.

'What can *I* do?' she said desultorily. In his desperation, Kwan scoured his memory for anything he could remember of events in the past linking his mother and the old servant, upon which might be latched a claim. 'She assisted at your birth, you yourself told us that,' he said. 'There was a time when she nearly died, and you got Dr Mehta—'

'Don't talk nonsense,' said Alice Fong quietly. Then she said, 'What about Yin Ling? Ah Heng Cheh listens only to her.'

'That's the whole trouble!' said Kwan, red with exasperation. 'She's doing nothing. She doesn't seem to care. All she has to do is to get Ah Heng Cheh to do a will. I don't believe it!' Kwan cried, with exasperation bordering on apoplexy. 'Millions of dollars at stake, which would have anyone scrambling to do the necessary thing, and my family doesn't care!' He made a bad move when he tried to appeal to his mother through her church, and an even worse one in referring to her cancer. 'You know, Mother, even a fraction of that amount would be useful to your church. I understand they're trying to raise funds for a sister church in South Korea.

279

And you would need a lot of money for specialised treatment. Mary's uncle spent thirty thousand—'

Alice Fong said sharply, 'Stop talking nonsense, Kwan. I don't want to hear about Ah Heng Cheh any more. I've done my duty by her. She's Yin Ling's concern now. I thought I made that clear to all of you a long time ago.'

There and then, Kwan wrote off his mother, but not his sister, for the urgent task that was consuming all his energies. His wife Mary said, 'Darling, you're smoking too much. I'm worried about you.'

His response was to light yet another cigarette and bark out a short, sharp reply: 'Who in Singapore has such an idiotic family?'

In his dreams at night, the money, more than the pot of gold at the end of the rainbow, more than the one-million-dollar first prize offered monthly in the national lottery, for which he regularly bought tickets, danced before him, tantalising, within reach.

Ah Heng Cheh's story excited interest everywhere. One newspaper report said that the American company had doubled its original offer of five million. It was headlined, 'Ah Heng Cheh Sitting on a Gold Mine,' and a cartoon showed a wrinkled old woman atop lodes of gleaming ore. Another said the old servant was far shrewder than anyone could ever suspect: she was coolly biding her time, waiting for the offer to spiral, since the American company and its local partner were already deeply committed to the project and would have no choice but to pay her what she asked.

The foreign media quickly picked up the story. 'Woman in Old Folks' Home in Singapore Holds Billion-dollar American Company to Ransom,' said a newspaper in Hong Kong. The British Broadcasting Corporation sent one of its reporters to the Seng Tee Loke Old People's Home to interview Ah Heng Cheh.

'There's an air of surreality about it all,' the young lady reported, 'seeing an old woman, frail and bent, devoted to a little statuette of a god she carries around, living the most spartan of lives in an old people's home, unaware of the frenzy she has generated, unaware of the phenomenal value of her tiny bit of property, which has stopped the giant bull-dozers in their tracks, for they cannot proceed until she gives her consent and signs, on the dotted line, not her signature, as she is illiterate, but with her thumbprint. This little old woman, who came as a servant from China more than sixty years ago and who has never spent more than ten dollars on herself, is in possession of the most valuable piece of real estate in Singapore.'

Vincent said to Yin Ling, 'What exactly is the situation? The DPM, of course, has read all those reports and is suitably impressed. So what's the situation?' He meant, 'Is there a will?' He realised, with a start, that the old servant's property was worth more than 2-B Rochester Park.

His mother was more forthright. She said to Yin Ling, 'Let's behave sensibly. You are the one closest to her. If there's no will, it's because you haven't bothered about it so far. Now that it's worth so much, you should get the lawyers to look into it. Who else is there to help Ah Heng Cheh if you don't?' To her *mahjong* friends, she confided, 'My daughter-in-law is not at all a greedy person. But she doesn't behave sensibly sometimes.'

In her next visit to the house, Yin Ling explained everything to Ah Heng Cheh. What would she like them to do?

'I know everything,' Ah Heng Cheh said stiffly. 'I had no education, but I know many things.' She added, 'I'm not selling my land to anybody.'

Mrs Chee had coached Yin Ling to make an appealing offer: 'You can make the biggest donation to the Seng Tee Loke Old People's Home that it has ever received.'

Ah Heng Cheh was adamant. It was obduracy, a perverse delight in contrariness and watching others' exasperation, like a wilful child. Vincent and his mother came with Yin Ling to explain, persuade, cajole. They were beginning to share Kwan's belief that some large conspiracy was afoot, involving Ah Bah and his mother Ah Kum Cheh. The two were clearly coaching the Old One on what to say to the reporters, to her family. Ah Heng Cheh seemed to be in their power, completely taken in by their demonstration of devotion, and was now referring to Ah Bah as her son. 'My son did this for me, my son did that for me,' she would say proudly to her fellow inmates at the home, giving an arch look at Kwan or Yin Ling if they happened to be present. 'I had no family, but now I have a son.'

'For goodness' sake, Ah Heng Cheh,' said Yin Ling sharply, 'what's the matter with you? Of course you have a family. You've always had a family.'

'Ah Bah never speaks to me in this way,' said Ah Heng Cheh sullenly, then fell silent. In the midst of new prosperity, she had never looked more discontented, pressing her lips tightly together and turning her face away.

Yin Ling reached out to touch her hands, which were resolutely clenched on her lap, and thought: All my life I have reached out to touch hands clenched into cold, hard fists. In one of his notes, Ben had put himself in the same position of futile beseecher saying, 'Unclench!'

Vincent said, 'We really have to do something. But what?' Everyone wanted to know how much Ah Heng Cheh would get and what she would do with all the money. One report said, 'If Ah Heng Cheh spent $50,000 a year, she would have to live to a hundred and eighty to finish spending all that money.'

'Tell her, someone, please tell her,' cried Kwan, ready to tear out his hair in supreme frustration, 'that if she persists in her insanity, the government can seize the property and pay her whatever compensation they think fit. Probably a very tiny fraction of the present offer. There's a law that they can invoke. I've inquired about that. Tell Ah Heng Cheh nobody can stand in the way of a huge project that has MTC's backing.'

When he next visited her at the home, she chased him away. 'I've told you I won't sell!' she yelled. 'Don't come pestering me!'

Two

Stopping at the Singapore National Kindergarten to pick up Xiang Min on her way to the Seng Tee Loke Old People's Home, Yin Ling glowed with pleasure to see her son, big and tall for his age, running towards her. As usual, he leapt into her arms, almost making her fall over. 'Sweetheart, be careful!' she said, laughingly.

'So what happened to Ah Peh's gold teeth?' said the boy, as soon as they were settled in the car, ready to be driven off by Arasu. They had an understanding by which if he was a good boy and ate up all his food, she would tell him a story about each of Ah Heng Cheh's friends at the home. The story would have two endings, hers and his, and they would decide which was the better, or come up jointly with a third. Ah Peh, who was ninety and had been in the home for more than ten years, had no teeth, much less gold ones, but they were allowed to take liberties in their stories, so Yin Ling had conferred upon him a full set of shining gold teeth, which some robbers were about to yank from the old man's mouth, when it was bedtime and the storytelling ended.

Yin Ling thought, hugging her son, How I love him. At four, he was any mother's pride and joy and every kindergarten teacher's anxiety, for he asked interminable questions and read, in one hour, the entire stock of story books meant for a whole term. Xiang Min said, 'I know what happened to Ah

Peh's gold teeth!' He bounced up and down on his seat and yelled at the top of his voice, 'Arasu! Arasu stole them!'

The good-natured chauffeur turned round and said, 'Naughty boy, I never steal teeth,' chuckling in his recollection of the time when he had unwisely shown his false teeth to the boy.

Yin Ling said, 'Sweetheart, you'll remember not to yell in front of Ah Heng Cheh? She doesn't like noise.'

'Uncle Kwan says Ah Heng Cheh is now a very rich woman,' said the boy, whose eyes and ears picked up everything around him. 'Is she richer than you or Papa or Grandma?'

In the home, they waited as Ah Heng Cheh completed her daily ritual of respect and regard for her little god. When no one was looking, Xiang Min lifted up the god's robe to see if he wore anything underneath and whether he had a penis. Yin Ling was hoping that the Old One, who in the midst of her new prosperity appeared grim-faced and unhappy, would soften at the sight of the little boy. 'Ah, the boy!' she would say, with a smile, as soon as she saw him, and then tell the story of how she brought god and boy together, through a piece of red thread.

Xiang Min would whisper to his mother, 'Mummy, she's telling me the same story again. Can I go out and play?' but would politely refrain from saying or doing anything that his mother said would hurt Ah Heng Cheh's feelings. In one of their stories, Ah Heng Cheh was so upset by something someone said that she wept for a long time.

'Mummy, do I have to eat it?' the child whispered desperately to his mother, when Ah Heng Cheh gave him a biscuit from a smelly old tin.

'Say "Thank you" and hold it in your hand,' she whispered back, 'but you don't have to eat it.'

The old servant's delight in seeing the little boy had given Kwan an idea. He immediately called his sister to discuss it with her. 'Ah Heng Cheh refers to Xiang Min as her grandson. She's so fond of him. Why don't you suggest that she will the land—'

Yin Ling said, 'Don't you dare bring my son into this. We'll let Ah Heng Cheh do exactly what she likes. It is her property.'

'But she's old and senile,' wailed Kwan.

'She's far from senile.'

There was no hint of senility in the firm voice in which Ah Heng Cheh announced her decision. She had requested the presence of the entire family. While they sat before her in a silent, expectant group, Vincent staring hard at her, his mother nervously twisting her rings, Alice Fong looking down at the floor with supreme indifference, Kwan so intently alert that he gripped the sides of his chair and leant forward, never taking his eyes off her, Ah Heng Cheh said calmly, 'The property does not belong to me. It belongs to my god. He has found his home at last.'

She would build a simple little hut there, set up an altar for him and devote the rest of her life to caring for him in his final, permanent home.

Three

hy was it, Ah Heng Cheh had wondered, that in her dreams Nature was never kind to her, always sending bad weather to make a difficult journey even more difficult? It was always either too hot or too cold, either so wet that she was drenched, like a cat she once rescued from a swollen monsoon drain, or so dry that the ground sent up clouds of dust to settle on her face and invade her nostrils.

But nowadays, even Nature ceased to bully her and, like the rest, came flattering her and bestowing on her good things. Here she was in another dream. A cool breeze in gently warm sunshine, exactly as she liked it. She felt as important as a goddess, and could have said, 'Breeze, more, please! Around my armpits, because I tend to sweat there,' or 'Sun, enough, stop shining,' and they would have obeyed her. She was a nobody, an orphan from China who had never known a mother or a father, a servant all her life, who had had to submit to the whims of others, and now she could stand up and command wind and storm.

'Indeed, you are a goddess,' said her little god, who was dressed in his gold silk robe, 'and, I might say, more important, for no goddess has so much money!' The little god was in a mood to please.

'Watch,' said Ah Heng Cheh mischievously. 'Go behind the curtains and watch. You too,' she said to Little Flower, who

287

did not appear as a drowned infant in a well, but as a healthy, laughing child.

They were in a room, which was full of beautiful furniture yet did not seem to be a room, for the well was nearby, broken and covered with tall grass.

Mrs Chee arrived, accompanied by her *mahjong* friends, all bearing large tiffin-carriers of freshly cooked food, filling the air with a wondrous aroma. 'There were four of you,' said Ah Heng Cheh imperiously. 'Why are there only three?'

'Mrs Lee died,' said Mrs Chee sadly. 'She was so excited at getting the winning card that she collapsed and died. Some said she choked on a rice dumpling but we here can testify that she died at the *mahjong* table.'

'Good!' said Ah Heng Cheh spitefully. 'She laughed at me and made fun of me. She said I had the smell of a decaying body and turned up her nose at me.'

'Please forgive her,' said Mrs Chee. 'Please accept this, and this and this, from all of us.' The tiffin-carriers that she and her friends had brought proliferated into a hundred, offering a virtual banquet. Even the emperors of old China had never enjoyed such a sumptuous feast of braised pork, roast duck, steamed chicken, tender bamboo shoots, rare fungus, rarer sea cucumber, pigeon double-boiled in an earthen pot to capture its every essence.

'What's this? Beef? Take it away! How dare you?' cried Ah Heng Cheh, but anyone could see that she was only pretending to throw an ancient taboo at the three supplicants and frighten them into greater meekness. Then she picked up a pair of ivory chopsticks and began prodding fussily at the food in the containers. 'This one is too salty, this one is too bland, this looks and tastes like shit!' She was enjoying herself immensely and, from the corner of her eye, caught the worried look on Mrs Chee's face.

'Oh, no, no! Please don't!' cried Mrs Chee as, at a signal from Ah Heng Cheh, her god and Little Flower ran out from behind the curtain and began a rampage of destruction, overturning the tiffin-carriers and spilling the food on the floor. Food commanded respect; rice thrown upon the floor was a desecration. But the occasion was special and there was no stopping the sweet jauntiness of revenge.

'Ha! Ha!' laughed Ah Heng Cheh. 'That is for saying, "Get rid of her! Either she goes or I go." Your exact words. Don't think I don't know. The walls have ears and they report to me every bad thing you've said about me to your son. You passed me in the kitchen and what did you do? Never mind that you did not greet an old servant, but you hurried past as if I were a leper.'

Mrs Chee said humbly, 'Forgive me,' but the torrent of Ah Heng Cheh's grievance did not stop. Raising her voice to a shriek, she picked up an umbrella from somewhere and began to poke the air in front of her to emphasise every word. 'From the very first day! Every day at your big beautiful house was hell for me. You think I liked staying in that little outhouse you got your son to build for me? An outcast, a leper. You think an old woman has no feelings? I prayed to my god every day to let me die. You think an old servant's heart did not bleed when your maids followed your example and insulted me?'

Mrs Chee snapped out of the supplicant mode for some sharp refutation. 'You were more difficult than any servant,' she said. 'You were well cared for, but never showed any appreciation. Did you know that old Ah Song Cheh was given a small corner of a storeroom to sleep in, on an old bug-infested mattress? And Ah Sum Cheh never had the luxury of eating half the good things you were given. Compared to them, you were treated like an empress!'

'I was given no respect,' said Ah Heng Cheh angrily. 'Give

me plain rice porridge with soy sauce every day but give me respect.'

Mrs Chee was the entreater all over again. 'I'm sorry, please forgive me,' she said.

'I told you!' Ah Heng Cheh whispered softly to her god. 'Money is power.'

Mrs Chee said, 'Please, I'm not asking this favour for myself, but for my son who was good to you and spent a lot of money on you. Remember how many things he bought for your comfort? The doctor's bills he paid?'

Ah Heng Cheh stopped her with a magisterial hand and said, 'I want to make it clear to all of you. Nobody gets a cent of my money. I will not sign anything. Go away,' she said to Kwan, who had just come up, also laden with gifts of food. 'My, my, what do we have here? The most expensive mushrooms. Abalone! Let's see what else. Pig's trotters in ginger. What a feast for an old woman who has no teeth. But it's too late.'

Kwan said, 'Ah Heng Cheh, you took care of us when we were little children. Remember you used to tell us stories? My favourite was the one about the tortoise that fell from the sky and cracked its shell. We were like your children. You pinched us at Kong Kong's funeral because we were laughing and misbehaving. You were more than a mother to us. He' – Kwan swung round and pointed an accusing finger at Ah Bah who had just appeared with a basket from which bunches of joss-sticks were sticking out – 'is an impostor. He's pretending to be your son to lay his hands on your money. Don't be fooled by him – or his mother,' for Ah Kum Cheh walked up then and stood beside Ah Bah. Mother and son stood close together, smirking nastily.

'Here's the proof!' cried Ah Bah triumphantly and he held up a wrist tied with the red string of adoption and belonging.

His mother nodded and said, 'The proof. We are Ah Heng Cheh's family now.'

Kwan swung a fist at Ah Bah and they fell to the ground and rolled about in a fight, like two small boys. Ah Heng Cheh laughed till the tears rolled down her face, while her god and Little Flower watched and cheered.

'Where's Yin Ling?' said Ah Heng Cheh suddenly. 'Why isn't she here?'

'I won! I won!' cried Ah Bah.

'No, you didn't!' cried Kwan, scrambling up. 'I'll fight you again and again, to prevent you from stealing our money. *Our* money.'

'All right, all right,' said Ah Heng Cheh, and her expression softened so much that everyone looked at her hopefully. 'I'll settle the matter once and for all.' She made a signal with an authoritative wave of her hand, and her little god disappeared obediently behind the curtains and came out dragging two huge gunny sacks. They were taller than him and he puffed a little as he pulled them right up to where Ah Heng Cheh was sitting near the well. As everyone watched he took out a knife from a pocket of his robe and ripped them open. Out spilled bundles of money, bound neatly with rubber bands. Everyone stared and gasped.

'See, I told you! Ah Heng Cheh is more powerful than a goddess. She has so much money that it fills ten sacks. There are more behind the curtain. And there are ten pillows on Ah Heng Cheh's bed, all stuffed with money too,' said her god. He turned to look proudly at her. 'Ah Heng Cheh is richer than any one of you now.'

They all gathered to stare at the money on the ground, not daring to touch it until Ah Heng Cheh gave permission. She watched the crowd growing, smiling to see the astonishment on their faces. In the crowd, she saw Vincent, and Alice Fong

291

and the supervisor of the Seng Tee Loke Old People's Home. She saw the nasty sharp-tongued Ah Poon Cheh, the most quarrelsome inmate in the home, who had once made a sarcastic remark to her. They were jostling and pushing each other to have a closer view of the money. Ooh, aah, aah, they went. They had never seen so much money in their lives. The value of each bundle was easily ascertained by its colour: red for tens, blue for fifties, light blue for hundreds. Somebody said, 'Look!' and pointed with a trembling finger at a bundle, lying under the others, which was purple, for thousands. Nobody at the home had seen a thousand-dollar note.

'All right, all of you, listen,' said Ah Heng Cheh. 'I am an old woman. I have no need of money. My god and I will take only what we need for our journey home. We will have some for Little Flower, who says she won't go on the journey with us. The rest is yours.'

They fell upon the money, like children upon scattered sweets, like starving vagrants upon food. Kwan made a rush for the purple bundle and saw, to his disappointment, that it was no longer there. He yelled to his wife and two children to help him scoop up some money. Ah Bah said, 'You think you can outsmart me?' and summoned a whole crowd of relatives from nowhere.

'Ha! Ha!' laughed Ah Heng Cheh, like a naughty child who has played a prank upon adults.

'Ha! Ha!' laughed her god, and was joined by Little Flower, who was clapping her hands and jumping up and down. They watched gleefully as, one by one, the money-gatherers screamed and abandoned their loot. One by one, they flung the bundles back upon the floor.

'*Choy!*' shrieked Mrs Chee, staring at the bundles of ghost paper money in her arms, then throwing them down. They dropped at her feet, and she kicked them away with her high heels. '*Choy! Choy!*' she continued screaming, and frantically tried to shake the touch of death off her clothes.

One of her *mahjong* friends said, 'It's no use. It will stick for ever.'

'Ah Heng Cheh, how can you play such a wicked trick on us?' roared Kwan. 'You are an evil old woman!' He had scooped up exactly ten bundles in his arms and was now stamping in rage upon them.

His wife said worriedly, 'You'd better not show such disrespect to the dead. It's their money.'

'Here's what I think of your gift, Ah Heng Cheh,' said Kwan savagely. He opened his trousers and urinated on it.

'Ha! Ha!' cried Ah Bah. 'I'll do better.' He took off his trousers and defecated.

'All of you go away now,' said Ah Heng Cheh. 'I am satisfied. Indeed, I've never laughed so much in my life.' She turned to her god and said, 'We'll live for a hundred years, to continue laughing.' Suddenly, she looked worried. 'Where's Yin Ling? Why hasn't she come to see me?'

Ah Heng Cheh opened her eyes, blinked and looked around. She was sitting in a chair, and saliva had trickled from the corner of her mouth. She saw Yin Ling and said, 'I wondered why you never came.'

'I've been coming almost every day,' said Yin Ling, smiling. 'Are you well, Ah Heng Cheh?'

'Where is he?' said the Old One, looking around once more, and Yin Ling made the supreme mistake of calling Vincent, who was standing some distance off. He came hurrying forward, but Ah Heng Cheh never looked at him. 'I tied your hands together with red string,' she said earnestly, 'in the presence of my god, remember? His hands were so hairy!' She

293

began to chuckle. 'Like the fur of an animal. I tugged at it and he laughed.'

It would have been bad enough if memory had served truth; confusing it was sure to cause deep displeasure. Already Vincent had turned a little red and was looking the other way.

Four

Xiang Min would not go to sleep but wanted the story of the tortoise told again and again.

'Sweetheart,' said Yin Ling, 'you must go to sleep now, and if you're a good boy . . .' She bargained, as mothers do, with her recalcitrant offspring, but told him the stories he loved, whether or not he ate up his vegetables or allowed the maid to clean inside his ears. He had an insatiable appetite for stories: he did not want his mother's to end and craftily forced her to go on with 'Then what happened next?' each time she paused. All the stories in his books at the Singapore National Kindergarten had been thus stretched – children became parents who became grandparents who died and were resurrected to start all over again – and still the child, his large eyes wide and unblinking, would ask, 'What happened next?'

He preferred the stories about Ah Heng Cheh, such as the one about the single wobbling tooth on her lower jaw, which had endured because two tiny men, the size of pinheads, held it down. In the child's imagination, the dwarfs and elves and giants of *Grimms' Fairy Tales* comported amiably with the Chinese gods and demons and village bumpkins of Ah Heng Cheh's stories. Just when his mother thought he was at last dozing off, he would open his eyes and say reproachfully, 'You forgot the tortoise's tail,' or 'You forgot Ah Heng Cheh's cabbage soup for the tortoise,' determined to preserve a tale's inviolability against adult carelessness.

Ah Heng Cheh's stories had lately become bleak and dark, because they were based on her dreams at night, and were therefore not fit for a child. But there was a wonderful stock of tales from the old days, of wondrous gods and goddesses, of little children who ate magic rice dumplings and never went hungry again, which Yin Ling could tell her little son.

'I know what happened to the tortoise's broken shell!' said the child brightly. 'Miss Ho took some Superglue and mended it.' He and his mother peopled their tales with the good and the bad, the clever and the stupid, the heroic and the cowardly from the worlds of their daily acquaintance. His kindergarten teacher, Miss Ho, was invariably good and helpful, old Ah Peh at the Seng Tee Loke Old People's Home decidedly wicked, Arasu only sometimes stupid. Then 'No, she didn't,' he said. That was his mother's ending and he wanted to provide his own. The broken pieces of the tortoise's shell became a mighty jigsaw puzzle but one piece was missing, and even Ah Heng Cheh's god could not find it. He searched high and low, but there remained this awful hole in the centre of the tortoise's back that was bigger even than Papa's fist. The child was excited, describing the hunt for the missing piece.

Vincent stood at the door holding a letter. It must be urgent to warrant the interruption of the bedtime storytelling. He held it out to her, and her heart leapt in a mixture of alarm and excitement. So his goodbye had not been goodbye after all. *All my love*, he had written, as if wanting to purge himself of a love that had brought only trouble. Had it remained inexhaustible, welling up to show itself once more? Even in the dim light of the child's room, she could see the foreign stamp on the envelope, the familiar scrawl. The first thought that struck her was, He's bypassing Gina, and the second was, Vincent's setting a trap. I must be careful. She hated the intense, lingering look he gave her, and hated even more her struggle to preserve a defiant nonchalance. She slipped: there was an unguarded moment for which her husband must have been watching – her look of disappointment when she suddenly realised that the handwriting on the envelope was not Ben's. She could almost hear Vincent's triumphant sneer, 'You can't lie with your eyes.' He said, 'I'm surprised he took the trouble to write, considering that he left under such disagreeable circumstances,' still looking fixedly at her, resorting to cheap ambiguity to trap her further.

She said quietly, 'I'm not surprised. Justin and I are still friends, despite everything.'

She was doing a dance of wills with her husband – three steps forward, two steps back, one step forward, two back, in a fearful squandering of whatever trust they had built up together. Oh, how tired I am, she thought. Ever since Ah Heng Cheh's blunder in confusing the participants in her ceremony of binding with red thread, he had been watching her for signs of betrayal. Too proud to mention Ben by name, he set his subtle traps, and watched and watched.

He said, dispensing with the subtlety, 'You look disappointed to receive a letter from Justin.'

She said, suddenly angry, 'I'm always happy to receive letters from friends.' And it seemed to her that from that moment, the dance of uneasy tension slid backwards so that they would have to start all over again.

Alone, she read Justin's letter eagerly, the initial disappointment replaced by anxiety for the boy who had been forcibly put in a plane and sent to a college in England to detach him from the vile companions at home. There had been only one postcard from him, so far, in which he had said he would be better off dead. This letter, though, was cheerful. 'I am very happy,' he wrote, and she knew what was coming next. 'Kenneth understands me.'

Kenneth Sim was a Singaporean former actor who had been disgusted by the sterility of the arts under harsh government censorship, had taken up British citizenship, and was now doing well on the London stage. But the real reason for the letter was not to rave about Kenneth:

Did you know that Ah Heng Cheh's story is carried in some London newspapers? Imagine, the strange old servant in the old people's home you took me to visit a few times. Well, a poor woman suddenly has it in her power to cock a snook at a powerful American company, even the government of MTC. How I love it! The report says that the government is actually watching the situation with concern because it's a major business venture with a foreign company, and they don't want to play into the hands of the human rights organisations. I won't ask Uncle DPM; in any case he wants to have nothing more to do with me. And, of course, my mother – you know talking to Mother is like talking to a brick wall! Three cheers for old Ah Heng Cheh! Hip, hip – Kenneth says it has all the ingredients of classic epic irony: a poor old despised servant is raised by the gods to hold a whole nation in thrall. Kenneth says he simply loves the picture of Ah Heng Cheh in her little hut with her god, keeping the huge bull-dozers and other machines of corporate power at bay! Kenneth says [the boy's adulation needed to be fed on frequent invocation of the adored one's name] he could turn the incident into a powerful stage play, only instead of a poor old servant in an old folks' home, it will be a gay man dying of Aids, who suddenly finds himself the centre of intense attention. Suddenly his millions give him a voice; he sits up on his hospital bed and everyone listens. Kenneth is so excited about his idea he's thinking of going back to Singapore to see if something can come of it. I'll go back with him. I don't care if you tell Uncle Vincent or Uncle DPM. Fuck Uncle DPM.

Trying to reclaim some of the dance's lost ground, Vincent said, 'The DPM says it was thanks to your coaching that Justin managed to get so easily into the college. He says the boy is doing well and scoring good grades.' The boy's mother, Margaret, had sent with their chauffeur the gift of a diamond brooch, which Yin Ling had returned.

Shortly afterwards Vincent announced, 'This thing about Ah Heng Cheh could get out of control. The media are just turning it into a circus, and those foreign newspapers that have never liked MTC are watching to see how they can make use of it.'

Vincent liked to divulge important information in carefully controlled doses: the most important he held back for a more opportune hour. MTC had put the DPM in charge of what was beginning to be called 'The Ah Heng Cheh Affair'. It seemed that he had become less active of late, conserving his fighting spirit to battle his wife's disease, which was in an advanced stage. The DPM had turned to Vincent and said, 'I'm putting you in charge. It's becoming messy with all the outside interest and interference. But I know you can handle it. With intelligence, tact, dignity.' The DPM was an elegant man and repeated, 'With dignity.' He had also gone on to hint that this would be a test for Vincent; a major decision regarding his political future depended on his performance.

Filled with exhilaration, Vincent was in a generous mood. He went to his wife to hold her and tell her reassuringly, 'Darling, don't worry. I'll make sure nobody harms Ah Heng Cheh.'

'You mean she will be allowed to stay there with her god as long as she likes?'

'More than that. I'll make sure nobody harasses her. I have been given the authority.' The words rolled easily off his tongue.

Yin Ling had been worried that Ah Heng Cheh would be evicted from the land by government officials, as Kwan had warned, and now felt so relieved and grateful that she could only say, 'Vincent, I don't know why I continue to be so difficult when you've been so good to me.'

And he remembered, stroking her hair, a Sunday sermon that had impressed him, 'My cross'. Everyone in this world has to bear a cross. Rich, in good health, enormously successful, Vincent's cross was a woman he had chosen of his own free will, perhaps against his better judgement, and whom he loved more when the danger of losing her to others was great. She belonged to him, she was his alone; any threat to his possession of her was anathema to him.

He had heard that the American had been back in Singapore, purportedly to provide support to Ah Heng Cheh in the midst of the growing controversy, in the same spirit of bravura as he had been when he had tried to muster support for the caned Bangladeshi. This time, thought Vincent, glad that he had been put in charge of this by the DPM, I'll know what to do.

Five

First it was the hornet men; then it was the mosquito men. The foreign media said it was just a government ploy to get Ah Heng Cheh off the land so that the construction of the giant petrochemicals plant could begin; they had it from highly reliable local sources, who wished to remain anonymous.

There was an old tree by the side of the broken well near Ah Heng Cheh's hut, which the three men, all in blue uniforms and armed with the necessary equipment, insisted had a dangerous hornet's nest among its branches. They told this to Yin Ling, who happened to be with Ah Heng Cheh in the hut, having brought some food, a flask of hot water, some towels and a torch for her: this was one of the nights that the Old One insisted on spending with her god in the hut, instead of being taken back to the Seng Tee Loke Old People's Home. The men pointed to something hidden in the branches of the tree and said they had been instructed to clear it since it could be a menace to children in a small school nearby. They proceeded to spray the place with some vile-smelling chemical.

Ah Heng Cheh choked and spluttered on the acrid fumes, but said firmly, 'I will not leave. They're trying to make me leave but I will not let my god down.' Her god, who was standing on an altar-table surrounded by his favourite oranges, tea and joss-sticks, grinned happily. Ah Heng Cheh said she had proof that this was his final, permanent home, but would not say what the proof was. She also confided that Little Flower had left: her spirit had flown to join her ancestors and was at peace at last.

These days, Yin Ling worried for her old servant because she loved her. I don't know how long we can go on in this way, she thought sadly. Ah Heng Cheh is not eating or sleeping properly. Her dream is consuming her.

Indeed Ah Heng Cheh seemed to be dwindling by the day. She held up her hands, thin and dry as sticks, and said, laughing, 'See, they're like birds' bones!' But her eyes were brighter than ever, burning with the intensity of a dream that was at last about to be fulfilled.

Part of her dream was seeing those of others smashed: there was plenty of malice left in the Old One that needed to be burnt out before she found her peace. The malice had its roots in the unspoken hurt of her childhood in China. It had come with the baggage in the long trip to Singapore, an accumulation of remembered taunts and beatings. In Singapore, her employers had been kind, but there had always been the insults and innuendoes deemed acceptable by even the most tolerant mistress. Ah Heng Cheh absorbed them all silently, and nobody realised that an intelligent, proud and sensitive nature had been struck to the ground and lay there writhing in its pain. Now, in her new position of power, it rose, demanding redress. It grew savage, exaggerating past hurts. Hence, while Ah Heng Cheh had laughed away the eleven-year-old Kwan's provocative behaviour of angrily exposing his penis to her and yelling, 'Yah, yah, you're a beggar!', now she remembered it vividly, quivered in anger and said, 'He must pay. He must do the grovelling.' Kwan and the entire world would grovel before her. Only Yin Ling would be spared.

Ah Heng Cheh had done nothing to stop the hornet men. Now she ran out of the hut with a bamboo pole to shoo the mosquito men away. 'Get off my property!' she shrieked. She would have done the same to the chairman of the American company and his counterpart from the Singapore partner firm if they had come in their Mercedes-Benzes and business suits.

The mosquito men were polite and insisted there was a swampy patch that might be a breeding ground for the insects. They set about flooding the place with more vile-smelling chemicals.

The *International Times* ran a picture of the little woman in a white blouse and black pants, her hair in a neat bun at the back of her head, carrying a long bamboo pole in her skinny hands, making straight for the men who had all adopted a defensive posture. The picture was reproduced in the *National Times*; in the next few days the Forum pages were flooded with letters from concerned Singaporeans. 'Stop harassing an old, defenceless woman,' said one. 'An amiable solution can be reached,' said another, and proceeded to give a detailed suggestion as to how a proper temple could be built to house Ah Heng Cheh's god and how she might be persuaded that she could better honour her god this way. 'Let it be a win-win situation,' the letter concluded. Yet a third asked rhetorically, 'Should a demented old woman's fantasy be allowed to stand in the way of a major, multi-million-dollar national project that is for the good of all Singaporeans?' and proceeded to chastise those who were her legal guardians for not helping her make a proper decision. 'Singaporeans,' the letter concluded, 'we have always been a pragmatic, down-to-earth people. Is an old woman's dream worth 4.6 million dollars, possibly much more?' It elicited an immediate and irate reply. 'That's the trouble with us Singaporeans. We put a price tag on everything.'

303

Ah Heng Cheh said, 'I don't like all these people gathering around and staring at me.' Each time she looked out of her hut, she saw curious onlookers and determined reporters, hoping for a picture or an interview. 'Why are they after me? Have I done anything wrong? This is my property and this is my god.' She peered into the growing dusk, and saw a tall, dark man accompanied by two others. 'Who are they?' she asked Yin Ling. 'I don't like the look of them at all.'

V. S. Ponnusamy had made a scathing speech, widely reported in the foreign media, in which Ah Heng Cheh had represented the oppressed and become a victim of official bullying. He had gone into urgent consultation with his aides and they had decided that the frail old Chinese servant would be an even more potent symbol than the white gardenia: V. S. Ponnusamy sought both an interview and a picture with her.

Standing at the door of the hut, Ah Heng Cheh said, 'If I had a chamberpot of urine or shit, I would throw it at you vultures.'

A young reporter instantly quoted her.

'Yes,' said Ah Heng Cheh savagely. 'No less than shit.' She and her god had themselves been the recipients of the indignity: a lump of excreta had been left in the hut, close to the god's altar. It was probably the work of some prankster, or of Ah Bah who, since Ah Heng Cheh's refusal to talk to him or his mother, had turned vicious. A middle-aged man and a woman, whom Ah Heng Cheh had never seen in her life, had turned up at the doorstep, claiming to be a nephew and a niece, children of Ah Heng Cheh's half-sister in China.

'I have no half-sister,' said Ah Heng Cheh angrily. She looked at them in cold disdain. 'If you are indeed the children or grandchildren of that woman who ill-treated me and shoved rice into my mouth making it bleed, then you get this, not my money,' and she picked up a broom and shoved it at them. She said tearfully to Yin Ling, 'Why are they all doing this to me? I have no one who cares for me but you.' And it was at this point that Yin Ling managed to persuade her to return to the Seng Tee Loke Old People's Home for a bath, a meal and some sleep, before continuing the long, long vigil for her god. Ah Heng Cheh said, still more tearfully, 'I don't know why all this is happening. I am a peaceful person. I just want to die peacefully. Last night,' she said, confiding a secret, 'my god rebuked me. He said, "Your heart has become as hard as stone. It makes you say such unkind, hurtful things."'

Yin Ling said, 'You're tired. Let's go back for a rest.'

She would have preferred a return to 2-B Rochester Park where the Old One would be better cared for, but Ah Heng Cheh had said, 'Never. I would rather sleep on old gunny sacks on the floor and eat plain rice porridge every day than go to live in a place where I am not wanted.'

'Mummy,' said Xiang Min, 'I know how Ah Heng Cheh's story should end.' The story they had created together was far removed from the reality: it made no mention whatsoever of a multi-million-dollar plot of land that was the little god's home, only of a magic stick that Ah Heng Cheh and her god used in their long, long journey, which they could command to be anything, such as an umbrella when it rained or a boat if they came upon a river or a bowl of hot, delicious noodles if they were hungry.

'All right, sweetheart, tell me what it is,' said Yin Ling, stretching out her arms for her son to leap into, which he liked to do.

'I won't tell you!' said the boy mysteriously. 'It will be a surprise.'

'Why don't you draw it for Mummy?' said Yin Ling. She had

recently bought him a box of thirty-six crayons in glorious colours, for he enjoyed drawing as much as telling stories. In his pictures, Ah Heng Cheh had a bun that was twice the size of her head and a tooth that looked about to fall. The boy thought about his mother's suggestion, and shook his head vigorously. Then he burrowed deeper into her arms and bellowed out the answer to Ah Heng Cheh's invariable question each time he was taken to visit her at the home: 'My mummy! I love my mummy best of all!'

Ah Heng Cheh liked to provoke him further. 'But what about old Ah Heng Cheh? Don't you love her a little?'

And the little boy would yell lustily from the shelter of his mother's arms: 'No, I only love my mummy!'

Seeing his mother read the letters in the Forum pages of the *National Times*, the child asked her about them. He could decipher many words and recognised Ah Heng Cheh's name in print, counting the many times it appeared. He read falteringly, ' "The Ah Heng Cheh Saga",' and asked, 'What's a saga, Mummy?' She found herself explaining the meaning of controversy and *cause célèbre* to a little boy of not quite five.

'Let her do as she likes. Her end can't be too far away. Six months? A year?' Decency forbade Singaporeans to talk in this way except privately. But one blunt reader of the *National Times* wrote in to say, 'Why all the fuss? Let an old woman go peacefully to her death. Let nature take its course.'

An official involved in the huge project commented privately, 'Every day that Ah Heng Cheh is alive means the loss of thousands of dollars.'

A sociologist from the Singapore National University did a long scholarly article on the special cultural underpinnings of Ah Heng Cheh's strange decision regarding her god, but mostly people were taken up by the enormity of the sum of money involved. One article in a popular local magazine, carrying the title 'What You Can Do with Ah Heng Cheh's Money,' listed the various things it could buy: a penthouse in one of the upmarket condominium developments in Singapore, a Mercedes, a membership in the Supremo Country Club, a round-the-world trip on the *Queen Elizabeth II*, with plenty of cash to spare.

Yin Ling received a note, scrawled in lurid green ink, that said, 'I would like to meet up with you. Neither Mother nor Uncle DPM knows I'm back. I know you won't tell Uncle Vincent. I want you to meet Kenneth, and talk about his play. Shall we meet in Ah Heng Cheh's hut? Kenneth will be thrilled. Fuck Uncle DPM.'

Vincent thought the time had come to tell Yin Ling. 'Professor Ben Gallagher is in Singapore,' he said, without looking at her. 'We have information that he is planning some big demonstration outside Ah Heng Cheh's hut to embarrass the government. He's clearly out to create big trouble. If I were you, I'd stay out of all this.' He added, 'You remember the Filipino maid who went running to him at the Monckton Food Park after a quarrel with her employer three years back? There's some sordid story about them.' He paused, then went on, in a rapid acceleration of destruction, 'He's come back with that Hong Kong lecturer he was seeing in Singapore. What's her name?' Vincent began rubbing thumb and forefinger together in an effort to jolt memory: 'Holly Tsung, I think. They're clearly in league with the opposition or some human rights' group. I've the proof. As I said, darling, if I were you . . .'

Six

He had come back! He had come back! 'So it's goodbye,' he had written, and she had thought then, No, never goodbye to remembrance. That must remain. But remembrance was not enough for this man who loved so much and so foolishly, and he had come back into a brewing storm.

For Yin Ling no longer trusted her husband. She had noticed the resolute, purposeful lines around Vincent's mouth, the narrowing of the eyes that could not look directly at her, and saw a trap.

He was coming back, once more with the untruth he had depended on for so long: 'I'm doing it for Ah Heng Cheh.' Ah Heng Cheh, forgive him! He had been using her and her god all along, and perhaps they knew it, and perhaps the entire pantheon of gods and demons in the Ten Courts of Hell in the Sai Haw Villa, looking at them as they stood together in the semi-darkness, knew it and had already forgiven him. She still loved Ben Gallagher for the folly of his love, and she waited, breathlessly, for the chance to see him again.

Xiang Min said petulantly, 'Mummy, you're not listening!' and she snapped out of her thoughts with a guilty start. The little boy was still intent on finding an interesting ending to Ah Heng Cheh's story. He was thinking of making the magic stick turn into a giant bird with steps up its side, like an aeroplane, on whose back Ah Heng Cheh and her god could be carried home through the skies. He was determined to resist his mother's request to draw the ending with the new crayons, but would surprise her when she least expected it.

'Mummy,' said Xiang Min crossly, 'you never listen to me any more.'

'Of course I do, sweetheart,' said Yin Ling, holding him very close and pressing her lips to his hair, aware of some impending struggle, in which a child's small tear-stained face would be pressed to hers and his small arms entwined tightly round her neck.

Gina said to her, 'Did you know that he's in Singapore, and he's with Holly Tsung?'

'Has anyone seen her with him?'

'No, but I've heard it from a reliable source.'

Until she saw it with her own eyes, she would continue to believe Ben. 'I love you too much,' he had said, and she would hold that against Gina's insinuations or Vincent's threats.

Standing with Ah Heng Cheh in the hut and peering out of an improvised window, she saw the large crowd gathered outside behind a rope. Vincent had arranged for two police-men to be on sentry duty, to protect Ah Heng Cheh from harassment, as he had promised. 'Trust me,' he had said. 'The DPM has put me in charge.'

On the whole it was a peaceful crowd, with no greater motive than curiosity. Everyone wanted to catch a glimpse of the old servant whose obduracy, it was said in the newspaper reports, had resulted in urgent top-level consultations, in phone calls and faxes flying between Singapore and the United States: how could they persuade the obstinate old woman to sell her land without incurring the anger of the humanitarian societies? Also, everyone wanted to know what MTC would do. Would he, as he had with troublemakers in the past, wait for an opportune moment and come in with knuckledusters? But would even he use the knuckleduster on a helpless old woman, especially when his DPM, who was also the Minister of Education, had just introduced the teaching of core Confucian values, primarily filial piety and respect for the old, in the schools? Not a word had come from MTC, but plenty from the rambunctious opposition, who were already licking their lips in anticipation.

Somebody in the crowd yelled, 'Yin Ling, it's me! Get Ah Heng Cheh to let me in,' and was wise enough not to push against the rope, for the policemen on duty would have pushed him back. Kwan had been denied access each time he had come pleading. The last time Ah Heng Cheh had screamed at him and said, 'I know you only too well. You have no feelings for me,' and shut the door in his face. Only Yin Ling was admitted into the sanctum of her god's home.

Somebody else in the crowd yelled, 'Yin Ling! Yin Ling!' then tried to duck under the restraining rope and was pushed back. 'Yin Ling!' yelled Justin. 'It's me. Kenneth's here too. Let us in. We need to talk to you!' Yin Ling signalled to say, 'It's no use. She allows no one but me,' but Justin continued yelling, 'We want to tell you all about the play!' and he pointed to Kenneth, a short, intense-looking young man with shoulder-length hair dyed blond, an ear-ring and a baseball cap worn backwards, as if to wipe out every Singaporean and Chinese characteristic.

Yin Ling again signalled Ah Heng Cheh's refusal, and saw a look of fury on Kenneth's face as he dragged Justin away.

The crowd increased in size. There was still no menace about it, but a disturbance had started at one end. Two men were pushing each other with a great show of hostility – or, rather, one was doing all the shoving and jostling to provoke the other, who was fending him off.

'Oh, my God,' breathed Yin Ling.

She heard Ben Gallagher shout, 'Leave me alone!' and saw the other man jostle even harder. A second man joined him, then a third. One, as if acting on cue, pushed Ben to the ground and another kicked his shoulder. It might just be animosity asserting itself against a foreigner, especially an *ang moh*, or perhaps, as one foreign newspaper was quick to point out, it was part of some larger plot to create mayhem and an excuse to whisk the old woman out of her hut.

But the motivation behind the attack was not important to Yin Ling beside the stark fact that Ben was hurt. She heard the thud of another ruthless kick and saw blood at the side of his mouth. She thought desperately, I must help him, but remained frozen beside Ah Heng Cheh, who was clinging to her like a frightened child and saying tearfully, 'Why is all this happening?'

The crowd buzzed with excitement, their interest shifting from the old woman at the window of the hut to the American on the ground. Someone in the crowd yelled, then another, and there was a great uproar. Suddenly it seemed that everyone was shouting or running about or cheering on the American's attackers. From the hut, Yin Ling saw a group of men fall upon Ben, who was struggling to get up, saw Justin pushing his way through, waving his arms about and shouting, 'Go for it, you bastards! Fuck you all!' before being knocked down himself.

'Ah Heng Cheh, where are you going?' But the Old One was already out of the door and making her way rapidly towards the centre of the pandemonium.

'Get out of my way! Out! Out!' screeched Ah Heng Cheh, with astonishing energy, as she pushed her way towards the fallen Ben on the ground. She caught the shirt of one of the attackers and began hitting him with her tiny bony fists.

The others got up, backed away and stared at the little old woman. She stood near Ben, who had managed to scramble up, and glared at the circle of faces around her, then let forth a stream of shrill obscenities in her dialect, which would have been amusing except that they came from someone who had, in the freakishness of circumstances, become a national icon. 'Leave him alone, he's my friend!' fumed Ah Heng Cheh, and took Ben's hand to lead him into the hut.

Vincent probably had a different version of what had taken place in the hut, but the truth was that Ben never looked at Yin Ling once. 'I came back this time for Ah Heng Cheh,' he said stiffly, while the old woman fussed over him. He added bitterly, still without looking at Yin Ling, 'Maybe this is the only right thing I've ever done in Singapore,' while she cried silently, 'Look at me, Ben, please look at me!' and her heart said, 'It's too late.'

Ah Heng Cheh, her mind skipping back to an earlier time, became almost skittish, insisting that Ben search his pockets for coins. Smiling, she pointed out her god to him, standing on a ramshackle, if improved altar, then began to look for something.

She found it, a piece of red thread, and signalled to Yin Ling and Ben to come closer, for the tying ceremony, to be witnessed by her god. But Ben declined the red thread of peace, reconciliation and love, and said to Ah Heng Cheh, 'It's too late. I'm only going to be around for as long as *you* need me. Please forgive me.'

Seven

'The time has come,' said Vincent gravely, 'to deal with this matter as a family – I repeat, as a family – before it gets out of hand.'

His mother looked bitter and angry, her face resolutely turned away from her daughter-in-law, once again the cause of all the trouble. Alice Fong, as usual, sat in cold passivity, not looking at anyone; Kwan was perched agitatedly on the edge of his chair, white-knuckled, frowning. All avoided looking at Yin Ling.

'As I have told you,' said Vincent, 'the DPM has put me in charge of the problem' – throughout he referred to Ah Heng Cheh as a problem. 'MTC asked him to handle it, and he has in turn made it my responsibility. At this stage, I need only say that he is using this as a test before making an announcement about my political future.' Vincent's tone was at its most sonorous when he was talking about his political future. 'I have called the family together because everyone has a part to play.' He might have been addressing his colleagues in their business suits in an oak or teak-panelled conference room in Singapore or Berne or Washington. He took his family through the various stages of the DPM's decision to put him in charge of the Ah Heng Cheh Affair, saving the best bit for last: MTC himself approved, and was carefully monitoring the situation, despite his preoccupation with his wife's illness. MTC was watching. Vincent quoted the DPM, ' "Everything

313

depends on you now, and we, and the whole world, are watching." '

'The DPM, of course, is aware of my connection with the principals in the case.' The formality had become horribly, almost comically, exaggerated. He did not mention Ah Heng Cheh or his wife by name, but kept referring to 'the principals'. 'He has asked me to disregard my personal connection and treat the problem as one of great national interest and concern. I had thought it would be easy.'

Now Vincent had no choice but to mention Ben Gallagher by name. He had never discussed the problem of Ben and his wife with any family member, either before or after his marriage, believing it to be no more than a distasteful piece of business mainly attributable to his wife's naïveté and an *ang moh*'s propensity for mischief. With the departure of the American for Hong Kong, he had believed the problem solved. He was in control. At bottom, though, was the realisation, so shocking that he beat it down every time it surfaced, that there might be some truth in his suspicions after all: his wife preferred another man to him. His proud nature rejected the very possibility. The public image of Vincent Chee Wen Siong must not in any way be tarnished. That resolution would guide him all his days. In private, there might have to be some reckoning, and when the distasteful business – he could find no other term for it – was over, he would have to deal with his wife in an appropriate manner. Suddenly Vincent realised, with some sorrow, that contrary to his sanguine hopes, an erosion of trust and love had occurred early on in his marriage. Now he explained carefully that he had evidence that the American, having once befriended Ah Heng Cheh and now out of a job, had returned to Singapore, hoping to take advantage of an old woman's dementia and benefit from her millions.

Kwan sprang up and struck the side of his chair with a fist: 'We must stop him! These *ang mohs*—'

Yin Ling said, 'This is the greatest nonsense I've heard. Ben Gallagher has no interest whatsoever in Ah Heng Cheh's money.'

The rest of the family turned silent, knowing looks upon her: So what we have heard is true. There was something between you and the American.

Mrs Chee must have been thinking, They never tell me things, but these old eyes see, and these old ears hear. I knew there would be trouble from day one, while Alice Fong must have been trying to exonerate herself: I did my duty. I warned you, but you would not listen.

In Vincent's mind, two plans had shaped, which would have their own separate unfoldings, the first to involve the family, with parts authorised for public knowledge, if necessary, the second to involve only himself and Yin Ling, in strictest privacy. She had gone too far this time and after it was all over – how he wished for the whole sordid business, this black miasma in his bright existence, to be over! – and the American out of the way once and for all, he would have to make her pay too. The child had become an important factor in the equation of punishment and redress. He would go about things carefully. Meanwhile, there was the family name, and his political future, to be protected. He continued gravely, 'Yin Ling is not aware of it, but her American friend may be in real trouble soon – I'm not talking about his many affairs in Singapore, including the one with that troublesome Hong Kong lecturer Holly Tsung. The Filipino maid he was supposed to have helped has come forward to accuse him of rape. Possibly of having drugs.'

Yin Ling felt her blood rising to the boil, and she stood up to face her husband, her eyes blazing. 'Vincent, tell us the

315

truth! *You* were responsible for those men who tried to beat up Ben Gallagher yesterday! You were hoping there would be a riot, weren't you, so that you could set the police on Ben as the troublemaker and haul him to prison? Luckily, Ah Heng Cheh went out in time to save him.'

'That proves it!' yelled Kwan. 'He's got the Old One in his power. He means to get her money. We had all better—'

Vincent turned upon his brother-in-law, whom he had always despised, a look of withering scorn. 'You stay out of this,' he said. 'You were asked to come here today only because you're my wife's brother.'

'I apologise for my daughter's behaviour,' said Alice Fong, without looking at anyone. 'Since she's incapable of doing it, Vincent, I apologise to you on her behalf.'

'I knew it was a bad omen,' said Mrs Chee bitterly. 'On the wedding day itself. Such a crazy thing to do. Holding a dead baby. Blood all over the wedding dress.' She had never told anyone in the family, not even her son, about the incident, so that her narration now, half sobbed into a handkerchief pressed to her mouth, had a surreal aspect. Nobody bothered to question her about it but accepted it as part of the strangeness of that day's events.

'There's no need to apologise,' said Vincent loftily. An apology might imply pity, and he would have none of that. 'I know what I'm doing and what I want.' He wanted to add, 'I have not come so far in my career without knowing exactly where I am going,' but desisted. He was beginning to enjoy his position of noble magnanimity. 'Listen carefully,' he continued, moving from the stage of explanation to action. 'There's going to be trouble. The American will stop at nothing to embarrass our government, and profit by the situation. We know that V. S. Ponnusamy has gone to see him. Tiger Dragon Khoo, who had fled to New Zealand, is coming back to join the fray. The *USA Courier* is excited that an American is involved, and is clearly all out to blow up the controversy, make the government look shabby and the American heroic. The DPM has said to me, "All yours, Vincent. It's all yours to deal with. We're watching." '

Vincent's face was flushed with the excitement of the challenge, as he said, surveying the faces ranged before him, 'You are all going to London, to stay in my cousin's flat – he kindly agreed to let us have it for as long as we need it. It's a really comfortable, spacious flat in Kensington.'

Vincent's cousin was a lawyer who was doing well in London. 'I need you to be out of the way while I deal with the problem. You leave in two days' time.'

He looked authoritatively at the stunned faces before him, challenging them to contradict or oppose him. It would take them a while to digest the enormity of the decision made on their behalf, the impact on their day-to-day lives; right now, they could only stare silently at him. He towered above them, a Titan with his new powers.

Alice Fong was the first to break the silence. 'Is it necessary for all of us to go? How can my presence, or absence, make any difference?'

Vincent had a ready answer: 'It is my wish. For your safety and peace of mind. You don't know how far the foreign media will go to harass anyone even remotely connected with the principals in the problem.' He would not say, 'I don't want even the smallest possibility of any of you leaking anything to anyone who may in turn leak it to the press.' He said, by way of reinforcing his authority, 'Even Justin will be got out of the way. I have recommended that he be put on the next flight back to England.' He waited for the impact of so clear a manifestation of his new power to sink in, before continuing, 'The police are watching that new friend of his. A drug addict.'

317

Yin Ling said, 'I'm not going.'

Mrs Chee let out a little gasp, Alice Fong turned round sharply to look at her, and so did Vincent. Flushed with the desire to make yet one more gesture of generous power, Vincent actually put an arm round his wife: 'She's okay. She's been under a lot of stress lately.'

'Don't you dare patronise me!' screamed Yin Ling, shaking off his arm.

Vincent shook his head slowly, in good-natured ruefulness, then signalled for everyone to leave, which they did hurriedly. Alone with her, he cast off all pretence and gathered himself for the climax to the day's accusations. He said, menacingly, 'I've had it up to here with you. Don't think I don't know.'

His orchestration of events to demonstrate his power and determination was not over. Yin Ling realised that someone else had come into the room. Gina, who was not family, had been allowed to listen in, from some hiding-place, upon a private family conference. Gina, unlike her usual confident, brash self, looked uneasy and unhappy. She was holding something, a big brown envelope. Avoiding Yin Ling's eyes, she looked unhappily into Vincent's, as if expecting more instructions.

Yin Ling suddenly remembered that Gina's husband had lately been promoted to a position that gave him an influential position in a national project under Vincent's supervision. Vincent was now Gina's husband's boss.

Gina turned to her, still not looking at her, to say something, and Yin Ling knew exactly what it was going to be: 'I had no choice.'

'Open it, Gina,' said Vincent, with icy authority, and Gina opened the envelope to reveal a stack of handwritten sheets. Yin Ling recognised the handwriting at once. Her heart had always leapt at the sight of the familiar scrawl; now she felt it vault right up into her throat, blocking speech.

'Give it to Yin Ling, Gina,' said Vincent. 'After all, it belongs to her.'

She would deal with the bullying later. Right now all Yin Ling wanted to do was to grab the papers and read what he had said. When had he written those letters? After that sad little note of farewell and renunciation?

But it was just one more note; the stack of paper was something else. The sad little note said, 'I knew by heart all your poems, though you had recited some of them only once to me. I have written them all down to send with one of my own.' All her poems, written out in his hand and sent back to her, with a bitterness to match the joy with which they had first been bestowed. Ben was saying, 'I don't want to be reminded of you in any way.' She let the handwritten pages fall to the floor. She never wanted to see them again.

'I'm sorry,' said Gina tearfully. She would regret for the rest of her life this betrayal of her friend, but right now she could only keep saying, 'I had no choice.'

'All right, Gina, you may go now,' said Vincent coldly.

Alone with his wife, he moved swiftly to accomplish the last stage of the grand strategy. 'Here's a lighter,' he said. 'You will burn these. I don't want to know what they're about, but you will burn each and every bit of paper right now, in front of me.' He needed this powerful symbolism of renunciation to salve his wounded pride. His wife had made him, her husband, lose face. That was the greatest conjugal sin, which his ancestors as well as hers would never have countenanced. Therefore she had to be suitably punished. With her own hands, watched by him, she would have to destroy the damning letter and the poems and then, again watched by him, gather up the bitter ashes.

'I don't want to look at them again,' she said. 'Isn't that enough for you?'

'Burn them,' he said.

'No,' she said.

Vincent put the lighter back in his pocket. But he was not done with her yet. He now sought to have the truth that would either condemn her once and for all, or be the reason, once more, for her to earn his heroic forgiveness: 'Did he make love to you in Ah Heng Cheh's hut?'

'I wish he had,' she shouted defiantly, and he slapped her across the face in a strange mixture of anger and relief – then shame. He had never raised his voice against her, much less his hand.

He said immediately, 'I didn't mean to. You made me.'

And she said, trying to hold back her tears, 'What does it matter now?'

He grabbed her by the shoulders and shook her, as he said, between his teeth, 'Whatever you do, don't disgrace me. I can stand anything but that.'

She said, 'Is that all that our marriage amounts to?' and then they were screaming at each other.

'I'm leaving you,' she shouted.

'You'll leave in exactly the manner I wish,' he shouted back.

Then they stopped, for a small body hurled itself at them. Xiang Min, who must have been listening with mounting terror, had burst in and was now a screaming ball of frenzy, as he rushed at each parent, flailing his arms and yelling, 'No! No! No!' before finally grabbing his mother by her legs and sobbing, 'Mummy, Mummy, don't leave me!'

She said, soothingly, 'Now, now, sweetheart, Mummy's here,' and tried to detach his arms but he clung to her more tightly, still yelling.

That night he had a fever and she slept with him on his bed, waking up throughout the night to put wet pads on his forehead and making sure he was comfortable. He woke up a few times, to ensure that she was still there, each time holding her hand tightly until he fell asleep again.

In the darkness, at the doorway of the child's room, she saw Vincent. He was standing very still. Then he came towards her. 'Is he asleep?' he asked, in a whisper.

'Yes,' she whispered back.

He stood around uncertainly. 'For his sake,' he said, and his voice quavered. His implacable sternness had given way to the softness that he sometimes allowed himself to show. Vincent managed both with equal skill. He now moved up a hand to caress the cheek he had struck and, sensing no resistance, gathered her into his arms. 'We have been through this before,' he said and perhaps he meant it. He went on, holding her very close, 'Please forgive me,' once more tenderly touching the cheek that had felt the force of his anger. His rage had provoked white-faced, dry-eyed rebellion; his gentleness, as always, elicited a flood of tears. She began to sob, and checked herself, not wanting to wake the child, who stirred, murmured something and once again felt for her hand to hold in his sleep.

'Here,' said Vincent, holding out the sheaf of poems that he must have gathered up from the floor. 'Here,' he said again, holding out the lighter.

He led her quietly out of the room where, watched by him, she reduced the papers to a pile of ashes and thought, I did it once before, of my own free will.

321

Eight

'I've just remembered,' said Ah Heng Cheh, 'today is the birthday of my god.'

'You've never told me his name,' said Yin Ling. 'What is it?'

Gods had names that resonated with power. Nine Emperors God, Sky God, Lightning God, even the Kitchen God because he had an important domain and function, which was to report on any misbehaviour he observed in the household and thus bring about due punishment.

Ah Heng Cheh's god, alas, had no home and no name.

'He did a lot of kind things in his time,' said Ah Heng Cheh earnestly. She told the story, as she must have done a hundred times, of how a god saved her when she was a girl in China, from being struck by lightning, of how, snub-nosed, deformed and despised by the other gods, he yet possessed enough power to save a whole village from an evil demon. The god's speciality, however, Ah Heng Cheh said, was not the big act of bravery, but tiny acts of kindness that people easily forgot. He never minded. 'It will make my heart glad to celebrate his birthday,' said Ah Heng Cheh, and hinted slyly at celebratory food, such as steamed chicken, fine noodles and fragrant oranges, which had so far not been offered in the ramshackle little hut that was now the god's home.

'We'll celebrate, then,' said Yin Ling. She would go out and buy the offerings and be back in a short while, and meanwhile

Ah Heng Cheh should keep herself safely locked in the hut and not admit any visitor. Those were Vincent's stern instructions. The reporters and journalists had gone away for the evening but would be back in the morning, with their notebooks and cameras.

'You are very good to me,' said Ah Heng Cheh, clutching her arm. 'Your heart will be filled with happiness, your life with prosperity.'

My heart is breaking, she thought. The Old One's benisons were worse than useless, but Yin Ling would give her the joy of celebrating her god's birthday, since there could not be many more.

Ah Heng Cheh said, looking into a paper bag, 'Why, I have more candles and joss-sticks than I thought.' Her god would be duly honoured. She would not say to a god, 'You're one year older today,' for mortals do not mark a god's passage through time, only their own, but would instead ask him for a peaceful death for herself, which indeed had been too long coming. She said anxiously, 'Come back as soon as you can,' and Yin Ling said, 'I will,' meaning to take no more than an hour to shop and check on Xiang Min, who was sleeping peacefully at home.

Ah Heng Cheh stared. It seemed that in the flickering light of the candles, her god's face became as big as a frying-pan, then shrank to the size of a child's fist, then enlarged again, while his small body remained the same. To her dismay, she saw a huge tear form at the corner of his right eye, glisten and quiver like a jewel, then roll slowly down his cheek. 'You mustn't cry on your birthday,' she said soothingly, as to a child.

Something strange was happening. She could tell by the way her god seemed to be swaying from side to side. She stared at his face: his features were melting and blurring into each other, like the colours of a child's drawing, forgotten and left outside in the rain. She was suddenly aware of huge clouds of smoke surrounding them; the tiny joss-sticks appeared to be spewing out angry billows that were filling the whole hut and sending out an acrid smell that invaded her nostrils and made her choke. It was evil smoke, not the smoke of blessed joss-sticks. Then she heard a roaring sound, and felt a tremendous heat fill her. She looked around and saw bright, leaping flames; they grew taller and advanced upon her and her god, roaring like evil demons that once surrounded her in a dream and made her wake up screaming. She had never seen such tall, menacing flames. 'Help,' cried Ah Heng Cheh weakly, and heard the crash, as of a door being broken down. Two men rushed up and caught hold of her. They began to drag her away. She resisted and broke free of them to run back to rescue her god. 'Don't worry, Old One, we've got him too,' she heard one of the men say, and then all was darkness and silence.

Nine

With his arm in a sling, his forehead raw with the burns sustained in the rescue, Vincent issued a terse press statement from the DPM's office: 'There was a fire at Ah Heng Cheh's hut at eight o'clock yesterday evening, probably caused by the many candles and joss-sticks on an altar. I had gone there to pick up my wife and was fortunately in time to save Ah Heng Cheh from the flames. She is now recovering in hospital.' Vincent gave due credit to Arasu the chauffeur, who also sustained minor injuries. The foreign press was insinuating that it had been arson, and V. S. Ponnusamy was already drawing attention to what he termed suspicious circumstances and calling for an official inquiry into the fire.

'Mother, don't fuss,' said Vincent impatiently, as Mrs Chee bustled around with healing herbs and ointments. This was not the best time to exercise patience, but even as he snapped at his mother, Vincent thought, in the end, it's still the mother, and wondered how many embittered married men came to that conclusion. He would harness the bitterness and convert it into noble energy to work for him.

The doctors were surprised, given her age, that Ah Heng Cheh was still alive. She lay very still in the hospital, her eyes closed, but her eyelids twitched with restlessness and her fingers, mere bones, moved uneasily. Yin Ling and Vincent sat by her bed.

'Ah Heng Cheh, tell us what you want,' Yin Ling whispered in her ear.

'Oh, my God,' breathed Vincent and stood up quickly. Yin Ling looked in the direction of his stare and understood his astonishment. There had been a flurry among the hospital staff, but they had not taken any notice of it. Now MTC stood right before them, surrounded by his bodyguards and aides. He looked older, shorter, less assertive than he did on TV or in the newspapers; it was amazing how reality could cut down to size god or mortal. He had greyed markedly and the lines on his forehead and around his eyes had deepened with sorrow. His wife was in another wing of the hospital but, it was said, had asked to go home to die.

MTC made a quick movement with his hand to signal that there should be no fuss. It was clear that this great man, who never did things without careful, shrewd forethought and planning, had come to see Ah Heng Cheh on impulse. Had it been a sense of mortality, a need to console himself that death was everywhere, a need to compensate for the reluctance to face death in a loved one by confronting it squarely in a stranger? Or simple curiosity, since Ah Heng Cheh's story was all over the media and provoking so much talk and speculation? MTC stood looking at Ah Heng Cheh who stirred, then opened her eyes. She stared at MTC, then blinked in puzzlement. He, who rarely smiled, smiled kindly at her and said in her dialect, 'Ah Heng Cheh, how are you feeling?'

The next minute he was gone, followed by his retinue, and the little incident, lasting exactly two minutes, by the bedside of an old dying servant, the humblest of the humble, would become a legend, passed on and embellished by the doctors and nurses who witnessed it that day.

The foreign newspapers were less kind; one – as soon as it got wind of the visit to Ah Heng Cheh's hospital bed – started a wild theory that MTC had been at the centre of the controversy all the time, and had visited the old woman in an unbelievable piece of government hypocrisy.

'Oh, my God,' Vincent kept repeating. He had tried to get closer to MTC to speak to him, to brief him on what had happened, as he had thought proper, and had been waved down. The aides had moved in protectively to surround the Great One.

Ah Heng Cheh was not expected to last the night. Vincent said, 'The doctors are making her as comfortable as possible.' He looked at his wife, pale and drawn, and felt sorry for her, that she should have to bear another shock, of a death that had already taken place. He said, as gently as he could, 'I've got bad news for you.' She looked up sharply. He stretched out his hand to draw her towards him, but she remained where she was, looking intently at him.

'What is it? Tell me quickly.'

She listened calmly, then bent her head, not in sorrow, for that could wait, but from an overpowering sensation that this was not a kind world. She could see him, a splattered mess at the bottom of the multi-storeyed block of flats, or perhaps he had died whole and intact, despite the height and the impact, as she had once seen, in a newspaper picture of a young suicide whose serene face and gracefully curled-up body were those of someone asleep. The details would come only later – the rejection by his friend Kenneth, the police raid of the sleazy hotel room and the discovery of drugs under the pillows, the hysteria of his mother, the screaming match with his uncle DPM, who had managed to track him down to the hotel, the note they had found pinned to his shirt, scrawled in green ink, raving, incoherent, undecipherable. But Justin was dead at seventeen.

'I'm sorry,' said Vincent and grasped his wife's hand.

She would go through each sorrow dull-eyed and spiritless. Negotiate life one day at a time, she had read somewhere. Indeed, negotiate life, so fearful and treacherous, one part of a day at a time. That was the best one could do. At least she had Xiang Min. At least she had her son.

Ten

In her hospital bed, Ah Heng Cheh, given only hours to live, sat up. It was not the vitality of the miraculously recovered, rather the frenzied energy mysteriously conserved for a last urgent request that would disappear as soon as it was made. Ah Heng Cheh's eyes burned with a preternatural brightness, her voice sharpened into an eerie shrillness, and her bony fingers moved about with an uncanny dexterity that startled the doctors and nurses. It was as if she was galvanised for the last and most important act of life. She said, 'Call Vincent. Call a lawyer. I want to sign over the land to him.'

Vincent said, 'I'm here, Ah Heng Cheh.'

'Then be quick,' she said sharply.

She recognised the faces ranged in front of her, but showed no interest. Mrs Chee had been persuaded to come, Alice Fong had come of her own accord, Kwan had been the first to arrive, hopeful till the end. Vincent said to the assembled family, 'I want you all to understand this. I don't want a cent of Ah Heng Cheh's money. It will go to the setting up of an old people's home that will be named in her honour.'

Committed to the path of exalted purpose and public duty, he disdained to use any of the money to repay himself for what he had spent over the years on her account, even though that was clearly the Old One's wish – she had expressed her sense of obligation to him many times.

'I have kept all the receipts, all the records of the money spent,' said Vincent, hinting that these were available for scrutiny if so desired, and throwing a contemptuous glance in Kwan's direction. He would issue a press statement from the DPM's office about Ah Heng Cheh's will and his intention, and shut the mouths of the detractors once and for all.

Kwan said, 'Surely not all of it – it's just too large a sum.'

But Vincent said savagely, 'I don't want to hear one more word from you. Is that clear?'

'Where's Yin Ling?' asked Ah Heng Cheh. The brightness was fading from her eyes, the shrillness from her voice.

'I'm here,' said Yin Ling, with a sob.

Then there was a commotion at the door, as Kwan shouted, 'Don't let him in! He means to make more trouble!'

'I want to see her!' pleaded Ben, struggling forward.

'You stay out,' began Vincent, white with rage. 'How dare you—'

A clear voice stopped him. 'Let him come.'

Everybody turned to see Ah Heng Cheh sitting up in bed, the brightness in her eyes returned, a darting, fearful flame.

She indicated for Yin Ling to approach her too, saying sharply, 'Hurry up, please!' It was only deference to a dying woman that stopped Vincent rushing forward to station himself between his wife and the American, both standing so close together, bent over Ah Heng Cheh, who was saying something to them in rapid, urgent gasps. To his dying day, Vincent would resent the puzzled, almost pitying looks cast in his direction, as he stood excluded from that last intimate farewell.

Everybody stood a respectful distance from the urgent intimacy of Ah Heng Cheh's last private words, straining to hear but gleaning only gasps and disjointed words. Ben and

Yin Ling, standing close together over the old woman, never once looked at each other.

A thought occurred to Vincent: perhaps Ah Heng Cheh was rescinding her will. He had never really trusted her.

The Old One, having used up her energy, fell back upon the pillows. In death, she looked less serene than she deserved, after all she had gone through in the last few days of her life.

Kwan blubbered, 'She's gone!'

Yin Ling sat down, her face white, her eyes dry. Two deaths. There would be time enough to mourn both. Meanwhile, it was the death of her heart that she was looking upon; it was crying out, as it had that day in Ah Heng Cheh's hut, 'Look at me! Oh, please, look at me!', for he was preparing to go.

'You leave at once,' said Vincent to Ben, 'and don't show yourself in Singapore again.'

'That's not up to you,' said Ben.

'We'll see about that,' said Vincent. 'You know the penalty for rape, don't you, and for having drugs in your possession? If you value your future, you will leave at once.'

'I leave because there's no more reason for me to stay in Singapore,' said Ben angrily, 'and don't talk to me in that way.'

'Get out.'

Much later, Mrs Chee was able to recount to her friends, in hushed whispers, the incident that morning in the hospital, beside Ah Heng Cheh's deathbed, in all the bizarreness of detail. 'Ah Heng Cheh's body not yet cold, and all this clamour,' she would say. 'My son's greatest misfortune was to have married that girl.'

For Yin Ling had calmly stood up, walked over to Ben, said, 'I am leaving too,' and walked out of the hospital with him.

331

Part Four

One

Ben said, 'What a pity – for us, I mean, with all our memories.' They were looking at the pathetic remains of the Sai Haw Villa, pathetic only in the desolation of demolished gods and goddesses, some of whose torsos or heads could be seen carelessly left behind by the demolition workers, despite the stern instructions to dispose of them respectfully. There had even been the ceremony of propitiation in advance of destruction – a spray of joss-sticks and a chanting of prayers before the wrecking balls came in. There would be nothing pathetic about the real-estate value of the demolished park, said to be worth at least half a billion, once the prestigious condominium projects were set up.

But Ben was not really interested in the park, either now or in its past glory: he only wanted to keep looking at Yin Ling and touching her. He said, kissing her, 'You have no idea,' meaning that she could not begin to comprehend the measure of his love for her. He had gone through much, had lost almost everything, but would go through it all again if necessary to have her. In his happiness, he was not aware of how he kept saying the same thing over and over again, in exactly the same words, because he could find no others.

He kept saying 'Do you remember . . .?', an invitation to recollect their secret trysts in the Sai Haw Villa in the past, which were really a prelude to open celebration of the present. And Ben always answered the question himself by saying, 'I remember. I remember very well how, when we looked at those poor men and women being thrown into the cauldrons of boiling oil, or their bodies broken upon grindstones, I could only think of taking you in my arms and kissing you.' Which he would do instantly, ignoring the presence of workers in the distance. One of them turned round and nudged another.

'Ben, there're people around,' said Yin Ling, and her happiness flushed her cheeks and neck and put a brightness in her eyes.

'I would have grabbed you and made love to you under the eyes of those huge gods and goddesses, if you'd let me,' said Ben cheerfully, 'so who cares about a few mortals?'

They had already decided that, for a fortnight, they would not mention 'outsiders', their label for the entire world out there, the world of lawyers and money and custody and accountability, which they would have to reckon with at some time or other.

'A week,' said Yin Ling, and he knew who she was thinking of, for only the night before she had tossed and turned and murmured his name before settling back to sleep in his arms.

'Ten days.'

'Till Sunday.'

It was bargaining that would end, as everything did during those first ecstatic days together, in love.

Ben apologised for the meagreness of the surroundings, a mediocre hotel that offered safety, privacy, a basic measure of comfort and nothing else. He refused to mention the luxurious 2-B Rochester Park, the Shangri-la or the Grand Winchester, which had been her familiar surroundings.

Sitting on the bed and looking around her, she said, 'That dear window,' because they had stood there together, one evening after supper, and watched the flow of people and traffic below, and 'that dear chair,' because they had sat there together, she on his lap, her head fallen on his shoulder while they talked and she had fallen asleep in his arms in that blue plastic chair. She could have attached the term of endearment to each item in that modest little hotel room, including the TV, because Ben would switch it on and lose interest immediately.

'This dear bed,' she said, and he was with her in an instant.

Two

'**D**o you think people recognise us?'

'Probably not. They might recognise Vincent. But not me.' In the old days she had avoided mentioning his name; now she was more relaxed and, although the period of validity for the ground rules to keep out the outside world was by no means over, she mentioned names freely.

'We brought Ah Heng Cheh to eat here a few times and she always insisted on having roasted pork, though she had no teeth.'

At the Monckton Food Park, she pointed out to him the table where he had sat more than seven years ago; then it had been a cheap plastic thing, but now was of handsome grey stone resembling marble. Children and lovers revel in repetition, and Ben loved to hear about when she had first seen him, untidily clothed and bearded, newly arrived in Singapore, eating satay by himself at the table and getting flecks of satay gravy on his beard. 'You saw all that from where you were sitting?'

'Yes.'

In his turn he had described in detail, and most inaccurately, the dress she had worn that evening of the dinner party at 2-B Rochester Park when she had shocked everybody by berating Michael Cheong. But she had not thought to correct him, for lovers' untruths, born of the desire to please, both pleased and touched. In Ben's memory, details of date, place and time became gloriously confused; his love, larger than any of these, subsumed them all.

'Did you have to go to court to be witness for that Filipino girl?' she asked. She told him she remembered him telling the irate employer he would do this. She would go no further in her questions, consigning Vincent's ugly insinuation to the rubbish heap of malicious speculation. But of the other woman he had mentioned, it would be necessary to talk at some time, she being part of the real world that lovers had eventually to face.

Ben said, 'Yes, I remember her, and no, I didn't have to testify. It turned out that she had been stealing the family's money. Jewels too. Sent to jail for a month, I think.'

It was impossible not to pay attention to some of the intrusions of the outside world, which, in the case of the Ah Heng Cheh Affair, took on the form of deliberate, determined silence, and invited more comment than noise. The *National Times*, ever co-operative, must have instantly heeded the request from the DPM's office to report nothing more of the matter, and to let Vincent's press statement about Ah Heng Cheh's will be the last official word on a strange event in the smooth, predictable, reassuring life of Singapore society. The Ah Heng Cheh Affair, despite the excitement it had generated, would soon be swallowed up by a hundred other concerns in this vibrant, forward-looking, ambitious city.

Yin Ling told Ben of the visit of MTC to Ah Heng Cheh on her deathbed. Ben let out a long whistle of astonishment. The most powerful man in the country visiting the poorest of the poor. 'It must have been the lustre of her new wealth,' he said. 'Given the chance, half the world would come to gawk at an old woman with millions to give away.'

Yin Ling said, 'Last night I had a strange dream. It was MTC, broken and crying, by the hospital bed of his wife, and Ah Heng Cheh, alive and well, who came to comfort him.' She told Ben she had a theory: everyone, including the terrifying MTC, had a soft centre, which might lie so deep under a hard carapace that it withered away. But now and again, it was touched into life. Ah Heng Cheh's little god of kindness, in a sudden assertiveness of power, must have said, 'Even he,' and touched MTC there.

Yin Ling thought a lot about Ah Heng Cheh.

There had been no funeral: Ah Heng Cheh's body had been taken from the hospital for cremation on the same day and her ashes were now in an urn in some temple. Kwan, of all people, had taken charge of the arrangements.

Ben and Yin Ling had tried to get permission for Yin Ling to be present at the cremation, but everyone, including Vincent, had banged down the phone in anger or disgust. But Ben was determined to take her to pay her respects to the Old One.

In the middle of the night, he heard her again toss and murmur a name in her sleep. It might have been that of her son, or Ah Heng Cheh, or Ah Heng Cheh's nameless god – who was now in their possession, according to the instructions she had whispered to them with her last breath, when she had summoned them both to her bedside.

'I love you so much,' he whispered to her in the darkness, gathering her into his arms and pressing his face on hers. He thought about all that she had given up and would have to give up for him. The hours of night were the most joyous for him. If he woke he would be immediately seized by a thrill as his hand fell on a smooth shoulder or the warm curve of a breast pressed against him.

Sometimes it was she who sat up in the darkness, startled out of a troubling dream, and was comforted by the sight of him. He would pretend to be asleep, to relish the spontaneity of her love. Women are strange, he concluded, in choosing sleep or death to tell a man of their love when he could least hear them. She said, holding him very tenderly, her lips pressed to his brow, while he listened but kept his eyes resolutely shut, 'Dear, dear Ben. Now I can rewrite the story of the Epitaph Woman.'

Three

'**B**en, what do you think happens after death?'

'You ask me about death right in the middle of making love? You *are* strange.'

'But tell me, what do you think?'

'Don't know. Hardly think about it. Maybe I don't care. But' – bouncing up and pulling her down under the bedclothes again – 'I do care about this.'

'Even as a child, I used to picture an indifferent universe, an endless stretch of grey. Now I think it's a vast blue void. Lovely and bright and free.'

Ben had no interest at the moment in metaphysics, only in her physical presence.

'My strange, ethereal little one,' he said, propping himself up on an elbow to look at her, 'always thinking and lost in thought. Come here.'

Four

They had a visitor to their hotel room, though she would not tell them how she had tracked them there. Gina was almost unrecognisable. She wore no makeup, and her clothes, shoes and handbag appeared to have been flung together. The wordly-wise Gina, who had doled out shrewd advice on men, marriage and money, was so ill at ease that it was some time before she could explain the purpose of her visit.

So this is Gina, Ben thought, when they were introduced – at last he could attach a face to the name on which he had depended for the secret transmission of letters.

Under normal circumstances, Gina would have patted a perfectly coiffured head, then scrutinised Ben closely as the man who had ruined the marriage of her best friend. But now she only said, 'It is good to meet you, Ben,' and turned back to Yin Ling. She said she had only a few minutes to spare and had to give Vincent's message quickly – how had he managed to track them down? – which was: 'No more phone calls to the child. Any communication between Yin Ling and the family must be through his lawyers of Raja, Lim and Peterson.' Gina, of course, would not report the savage condemnation: 'No adulteress touches my child. No whore of an *ang moh* comes anywhere near my son.'

'How is Xiang Min?'

Clearly, the unhappy Gina had been under severe instructions to give no information. She would only say, 'He's back at school, he's well now,' hinting of days when he had been unwell and unable to attend school.

'I need to see him,' said Yin Ling, and began to cry.

'Vincent says you can't,' said Gina miserably.

Ben said, drawing Yin Ling into his arms and kissing the top of her head, 'You'll see your son. I'll make sure of that.'

Gina quavered, 'Vincent's left strict instructions with the principal of the Singapore National Kindergarten that they are not to admit you.'

'We'll see about that,' said Ben.

Suddenly Gina slipped out of her role of messenger and became herself. 'I'm sorry, Yin Ling,' she began, and burst into tears. She said she had never forgiven herself for handing over Ben's last letter and the poems to Vincent; she knew about the burning and was heartbroken with guilt and remorse. She kept saying, wringing her hands, 'I had no choice! I had no choice!' Her voice grew bitter: she said that Vincent was still angry with her for playing her clandestine role and might even now exact payment: he had already hinted at relieving her husband of his new position in a project under his leadership in the DPM's office. 'It's not fair to Christopher. He had nothing to do with it,' said Gina.

It would appear that Vincent was on a rampage of revenge and retribution, and his anger reached a long way, back to the months before the marriage. Arasu had been questioned, even the Filipino maids, to find out if any had been a secret messenger for Ben. But he was doing everything discreetly, to keep his humiliation out of the public eye.

Gina offered her own apologies and a gift. She took out of her handbag a large envelope stuffed with money. She pushed it into Yin Ling's hands, perhaps remembering the many times when she had received generous gifts and loans, and said, 'You left in a hurry, you may need this – it's a token of our friendship from me.' Gina broke down again and sobbed.

Yin Ling said, 'That's so kind of you, Gina, but I really don't need it. As you know, my needs have always been simple. Ben's got some money to see us through until he—'

'Until he runs out and takes on a lecturing stint in the University of Brunei,' Ben broke in. Malaysia, Brunei, Thailand. He would take on a job in any of the nearby countries – no Singapore university or college was likely to accept him now – to allow her to be near her son.

When Gina left, Ben said, 'I have a surprise for you. Or, rather, I will have a surprise for you in half an hour. But I need privacy. I'm going to be in the bathroom.'

When he emerged the tears came again, but now they were tears of joy, as she stood beside the man she loved, and looked at his gift. He had remembered her poems, and written them down for her. Once more they were in her hands, risen from the ashes. Twice she had burnt them; twice he had returned them to her. 'Your poetry is part of you,' said Ben. She would have all the time in the world to write now.

'Let's look at Ah Heng Cheh's god,' he said. 'We haven't paid any attention to the poor fellow since the day he was entrusted to us.'

The god had been only slightly burnt in the fire. In her hospital bed, ready for death, Ah Heng Cheh had kept him close to her side. When she had summoned them to her bedside, she had only wanted to tell them to take good care of him. And to give them the name of the village in China that was her god's real home. She had enunciated it slowly but clearly. 'Please, please, don't fail him,' she had said, and then was gone.

345

Now they mouthed the name of the village in China. They would find it together, once some urgent things had been settled. The little god grinned good-naturedly at them now, his snub nose a little blackened, his gold silk robe half gone. Ben said, 'I doubt he's really a god. But he must be, if Ah Heng Cheh was so clear about the temple in the village he came from.'

Yin Ling said, 'He needs a new robe for his journey home.'

Ben said they might be able to make the trip before they went to Brunei for him to begin work. But the longest, most hazardous journey would be the claiming of Yin Ling's right to see her little boy.

'We'll do it, if it's the last thing we do,' Ben said, then added, 'I really have to thank Ah Heng Cheh's god for giving you to me.'

He lifted his face, closed his eyes, pressed his palms together and said, 'Forgive me, god, for so shamelessly making use of you. Forgive me, Ah Heng Cheh, for making use of you too.' He turned to Yin Ling and said slowly, 'There's somebody else I made use of, and I fear she won't forgive me so easily.' When he had received that heartbreaking note of renunciation from Yin Ling some years ago, 'I choose my son, I choose duty', his first reaction had been to give up and find strength in turning his back on her. His second was to seize upon her reference to Holly Tsung. Her jealousy would be his hope. He would work upon it, to keep alive her love for him, for jealousy both consumed and nurtured. When he was coming to Singapore for the last time, he had let it be known that he was coming with her. He had wanted to make Yin Ling insanely jealous, to drive the indifference out of a heart that had once beaten so wildly for him.

There would have to be forgiveness all round. The god of

346

love left incomparable joy but also an indescribable mess. And one of these days, when everyone was less angry, Yin Ling might even go to each and say, 'Forgive me the pain I caused you,' imagining Kwan to turn away abruptly without saying anything, her mother to look down and press her hands together on her lap, her mother-in-law to look up sharply and say, 'The less said, the better! You are no longer part of the family!' To Vincent, she would say, 'I'm sorry, please forgive the pain and humiliation I have caused you.' If Vincent said, 'You'll be sorrier yet,' and revealed he was planning to deny her access to her child, she would face him squarely and say, once again, 'I'm sorry,' meaning this time that she felt sorry for all those who would stand in her way. She would fight tooth and claw for her son and go down fighting. She had thought that love and duty were irreconcilable, but now she knew that in reality things were much more complicated. Yet she was convinced that one day, not too far off, she would be holding the man she loved with one arm and the little son she had left for him with the other.

'I start tomorrow,' she said with determination.

Five

A lice Fong said, 'This is for you,' pointing to a box of something on the table.

'Mother, we'll have to talk about a few things,' said Yin Ling. She thought she heard a presence in the next room, probably Kwan's; he must have bolted when the doorbell rang and he heard her voice. Since the scandal, she later learnt, he had been going to see their mother every day, doggedly going through the recent events one by one, analysing, arguing, cursing, as if that could somehow change them and throw in his way a fraction of the fabulous wealth to which, as someone brought up by Ah Heng Cheh, he felt he had a claim. Alice Fong sat expressionlessly through each tiresome tirade, and at the end of it, merely said it was time for her medicine or her nap.

'Why don't you see what it is? Mrs Chee sent it through Arasu.'

It was the entire collection of her jewellery, which she had been given by her mother-in-law and various relatives for her wedding, a collection that Mrs Chee might have enhanced, if circumstances had been different and she had proved a good, docile daughter-in-law, into a truly valuable set, fit for showing off at parties and weddings. There were the modest sapphire ear-studs, a wedding gift from Alice Fong, which Mrs Chee had more than once hinted she would be glad to take for redesigning and resetting at her favourite jeweller's, at her expense.

Alice Fong threw a cursory glance at the contents of the box, her eyes resting a little longer on her own gift, and Yin Ling thought that might be as good a starting point as any for the purpose of the visit. 'Do you remember, Mother . . .'

Memories, if they were not sad, could dispel sadness. Attached to the pair of sapphire ear-studs was an incident that had made even Alice Fong smile, and recount to friends or family when she was in the mood to do so. She had later told her daughter about it, and smiled again. She had gone to Weng Poh Jeweller's to select a wedding present, vaguely remembering an occasion when her daughter had admired a pair of sapphire studs on Gina's ear-lobes. She found the pair she wanted and got the salesman to take it out of the glass case for a closer look. Her budget was modest; she was determined to bargain down the listed price to match it. The salesman, sensing her eagerness, was adamant. Alice Fong sat for two hours on an uncomfortable stool in the jeweller's shop and sipped the cup of Chinese tea he offered, but neither side gave in. Alice Fong got up from the stool and made to leave, expecting the man to call her back. But he did not.

That night her desire to get the better of him became greater than the need to secure the studs at a bargain price, so next morning, before the shop opened for business, Alice Fong was waiting outside. She demanded to have the studs at her price, and he knew he was beaten, for no salesman would send away disgruntled the first customer of the day. Not all the joss-sticks he lit at the back of his shop to his god of prosperity could counter the bad luck.

Holding up the sapphire studs, Yin Ling said, 'Mother, do you remember the trick you played on that salesman?' and Alice Fong turned to her daughter, opened her mouth to speak and broke down in tears. She wept for a long time, her hands limp in her daughter's. Holding her mother, Yin Ling thought, Why, I can't remember ever seeing Mother cry. She said, 'Mother, I'm sorry, forgive me,' and felt a hand move up to clutch her arm.

Then Kwan emerged. 'Sorry? You ought to be. Bringing shame to all of us. Causing misery to poor Mother and your husband. Messing up everything, when all you had to do was—'

Her brother wearied Yin Ling to the point of despair. If he had been unabashed about his greed for Ah Heng Cheh's money, that would have been less intolerable than the web of sanctimoniousness he spun around it.

Rousing herself to a last burst of angry contempt, she said, 'You get out of my sight. I have no wish to see or speak to you again.'

Six

The Singapore National Kindergarten lived up to its name as the most security-conscious educational establishment in Singapore: it had a tall, wrought-iron gate at the front of the building and visitors were required to acquire a pass from security personnel before entering the school. The tight security was based on fears more imagined than real. Kidnapping was rarely heard of in Singapore, but because the kindergarten took the children of Singapore's politicians, businessmen and élite, the board of directors had felt they could take no chances.

Ben and Yin Ling stood at the gate, and Yin Ling thought, How different things are now. Yesterday she might have been guest of honour at one of the school's functions, the wife of Vincent Chee Wen Siong, opening an exhibition of art or a new music room; today she was an outcast, forbidden to see her own son. Vincent had given strict instructions to the principal, Madam Ong, that Mrs Vincent Chee Wen Siong should not be allowed to see Bernard Augustine Chee Xiang Min of Class 5A. The caller had added that only Madam Ong and Xiang Min's class teacher were to know of this.

Damage control. Vincent was already referring to his efforts to contain the scandal in terms of some national strategy. The *National Times* was co-operative. In public, he went about his work in the DPM's office as if nothing had happened, responding graciously when the DPM complimented him on his skilful handling of the tricky Ah Heng Cheh Affair, which had completely taken the wind out of V. S. Ponnusamy's sails. 'Sorry about what happened,' the DPM had said, touching Vincent lightly on the shoulder, not wanting to mention anyone by name, least of all the adulterous wife and her American lover.

The two men, accepting both the relief and the pain of having the diseased parts of their respective lives sliced off and cast away, grew closer to each other. The homosexual nephew, who had thrown himself off the fourteenth floor of a tower block, the adulterous wife, who had abandoned husband and son to run away with an *ang moh*, could be consigned to the ash-heap of bitter private memory.

There were rumours that MTC, saddened by his wife's illness, was handing over the reins of power. Buoyed by the prospect of further ascent up the ladder of public life, the DPM and Vincent could only feel a strong affinity with each other.

'Come over for dinner sometime,' said the DPM.

In public, therefore, Vincent was defiant, even jubilant. In private, he gritted his teeth, clenched his hands and swore, 'She will never see the boy again, if that's the last thing I do.' He had set two of his aides to look into the huge dossier on Professor Benjamin Gallagher to see how the reports of his womanising, possible drug possession and his critical articles on human rights in Singapore could be used against him.

'Over my dead body,' he had said, when Mrs Chee, attending to a fretful Xiang Min who cried every night for his mother, had asked if he might be allowed to see her. He had watched over the boy carefully, turning down invitations to important functions to stay at home in the evenings. His message to the boy was simple: Your mother has left us. She can't love us very much. We must try our best to get on without her.

Each time he came to work in the office, he was aware of the silent looks, of a sense of unease among the aides and secretaries. He held his head high, rejecting pity. Clive Vasoo, then Chong Boo had called, saying that they had heard, was Vincent okay, could they help in any way, and Vincent had cut them short: 'Everything's perfectly okay. Hey, Clive, Chong Boo, one of these days, when I'm not so tied up in the office, we'll round up the others and have a drink.'

An idea was brewing in his head, to shut up, once and for all, all those still thinking he needed sympathy by showing that his present situation called for the opposite. The DPM had mentioned the daughter of a cousin who worked in a bank in New York. She was coming to Singapore to visit her family. He had suggested a lunch for Vincent to meet her. At the time, Vincent had not shown much enthusiasm. Now he realised her presence might be invaluable. Clive Vasoo and the rest, coming to his house for drinks and armed with their expressions of sympathy, would be introduced to Miss Fiona Goh, vice-president of Chase Manhattan, New York. They would, of course, speculate among themselves about the relationship. He would let them.

Alone at night in his bed, Vincent sometimes lay awake for a long time and allowed a sob or two to escape him. Someone must pay, he thought, and the first instalment would have to come from her. It would be the pain of not being able to see or speak to her son.

Now Yin Ling said, 'They'll never allow me in.'

'You're not going to leave this place till you have seen your son,' Ben replied. 'I have an idea.' He led her to the side of the building, where the imposing iron gate connected with a pretty wooden fence, painted white and festooned with plants, framed a picture-postcard garden with swings and child-size benches and topiary animals.

'Oh, my God,' gasped Yin Ling, tears starting in her eyes, as she caught sight of Xiang Min in his class, which faced the garden. He was with a group of four other children, making things with coloured paper and glue. The teacher was moving energetically among the children. Ben said, 'Come here. I'm going to help you over that part there. Good thing you're not in high heels.' In a minute, her heart beating so wildly she thought the whole class would hear it, Yin Ling had climbed over the wooden fence and was inside the garden.

She took a few steps forward, then stopped. Hidden behind plants, she stood very still, watching Xiang Min. He was holding a strip of gold paper for another boy to cut. Was he sad? Was he happy? Could she tell from his face whether he missed her?

Suddenly he looked up and saw her. He went pale, staring at her, as at a vision. Then he stood up. Yin Ling's arms were at her sides, and she watched her son move a few steps towards her. By now, one or two in the group had noticed and the teacher suddenly swung round. She let out a gasp. The stern instructions of the principal, like so many alarm bells, rang shrilly in her head, but the sight of the little boy and his mother moving towards each other checked her.

Miss Ho froze as a bearded man appeared from nowhere, and said softly, 'Don't you dare raise the alarm.'

The clatter in the classroom had subsided into a murmur as everyone stood and watched. The little boy's taut, pale face was grim with reproach; his body, with the shoulders raised and hands clenched, had become a wall of resistance, yet the feet inched forward. She longed to gather him into her arms – oh, if only he would leap into them as he used to! – but waited

354

for the smallest signal to spring into action. The next moment she was on her knees, holding him tightly.

The child's hands were rigid by his sides, but he let his mother fall over him, crying with joy. 'Oh, my precious,' she sobbed, and could not go on.

The little boy's chin quivered, but he would not allow tears to roll down his face in view of his teacher and classmates. Yin Ling held his face in her hands and looked into it anxiously. 'Oh, my darling—'

'Mrs Vincent Chee, we have instructions from the principal—'

'You stay out of this!' said Ben, in such a ferocious whisper that Miss Ho fled, presumably to get the principal.

'Xiang Min, look at Mummy. Mummy's here, talk to Mummy—'

'Why did you leave me?'

Xiang Min's eyes brimmed with tears. Yin Ling held him closer and sobbed as if her heart would break.

The child repeated, 'Mummy, why did you leave me?'

And Yin Ling saw, to her horror, a film of hardness creep over his face, settle in his eyes, his brow, his mouth. She picked up his arms to twine them round her neck, but they fell back stiffly to his sides.

'Sweetheart, remember the ending we were trying to find for Ah Heng Cheh's story?'

He shook himself out of her arms, then walked back to join his classmates.

Seven

Ben said, 'Back in Idaho, we'll . . .' Their plans for the immediate future were taking shape. He had been offered a job at Idaho University, which they had decided was better than the University of Brunei since he had a small ranch there, where she might be able to start working on her poetry again, reflect, and breathe a little more easily after the turmoil of the last few months.

Good news came from their lawyers: she would have access to her son. The best news came from Xiang Min himself, in a phone call to his mother. He had only said, 'Mummy,' and choked on his sobs. After the traumatic experience at school, she learnt, he had become a problem at home, screaming, kicking, refusing to eat, until a calming telephone call from his mother convinced his father and grandmother that he needed contact with her. 'Our lawyers will work out something mutually agreeable,' said Vincent, and when he heard that Ben and Yin Ling were planning to leave for the United States, he was elated: time and distance would lessen memory and pain, until the boy woke up one morning cured of all need for his mother.

Mrs Chee was showing open approval of Miss Fiona Goh, but Vincent was having second thoughts. In later years, he would admit that, after Yin Ling, most women seemed less than honest, though they were decidedly less complicated.

One afternoon he was startled to receive a call from her: would he see her?

Just months after the breach, she was asking to be taken back! There could be no greater gratification to a wounded man. For a moment, Vincent allowed himself to wonder why: perhaps the *ang moh* had kicked her out; perhaps she had discovered the extent of the *ang moh*'s womanising and had kicked him out; perhaps they were desperate for money and needed help, or she was desperate for her son and had to come back.

Vincent said, through his secretary, that he would see her, and made an appointment for six o'clock at 2-B Rochester Park.

Impelled by curiosity, he peeped from behind the curtains as she was walking up the driveway, and could not decide whether it was with pity or satisfaction that he looked upon her thin, pale face, shorn of its former beauty. What a lot of weight she had lost. She was unaccompanied – of course, the American would never be admitted into the house.

Yin Ling said, 'Vincent, please forgive me.'

He gave an uncomfortable laugh, and said the first words that came into his head: 'What's the use of that now?'

She looked at him earnestly and said, 'I mean it. I've come back for your forgiveness.'

Vincent thought, Be careful. Think carefully before you say or do anything. She means to come back. But on her terms. He thought, Something's not right. She's been coached by the American. Be careful.

But it was genuinely an act of contrition and a request for forgiveness. Yin Ling stood waiting for Vincent to say something. She would say no more. It would have been inappropriate – or cruel – to say, 'I'm sorry I married you when I didn't love you,' or 'I made gratitude serve for love,' or 'I loved you best when you loved Ah Heng Cheh best,' any of

357

which would have been part of the truth. So she simply repeated, 'Please forgive me. I'm truly sorry.'

He wanted her to go on: words of contrition ought to be followed by an explanation of some sort, which he could seize upon and throw back at her, for something like distilled rage, long lying in wait, was rising in a slow, steady stream, ready to be discharged in the fullness of its power to wound permanently. He looked at her, this woman who, if she had been any one of a thousand others in Singapore, would today be basking in the great fortune of being married to Vincent Chee Wen Siong. She stood a little while longer – he had never offered a seat – looked uneasy and said finally, 'I have to be going now. Thank you for agreeing to see me,' and was walking towards the door.

He watched her go, and could not resist peeping at her once more from behind the curtains. He would have preferred a clear show of defeat and remorse from her, which would have elicited triumph and elation in him. As it was, the matter remained unresolved, puzzling, and he fretted in the continuing lack of certainty. Suddenly he thought, Perhaps she knows about Fiona Goh. It would have given him some satisfaction to know that she knew that Fiona Goh, Debra Hon, Madeline Francis and Chew Sian Ting, a former classmate of hers, were all lined up for his choice.

He saw her open the gate and walk past it, saw, with a shock, the American, who clearly had been waiting for her all this time. He saw them embrace, then walk up the road together.

Ben said, 'I've got news for you.' He inflated trivialities to good news or even the best news to cheer her up. But this time it *was* good news. Justin's mother, Margaret, had previously refused to answer all her calls about where she could visit his ashes – there were four columbaria in

358

Singapore – but had apparently changed her mind. She had taken her son's suicide badly and, it was said, was planning to take up permanent residence with a sister in Vancouver, leaving her husband, who had never been supportive, and a brother who, in the end, showed he was only interested in promoting his own political career. Her message to Yin Ling went beyond the bare information about the columbarium. Justin had left something for her, which she could pick up from the residence at 7, Ashtonbury Park, between noon and four the next day. The maid Philomena would give it to her.

Ben and Yin Ling hurried to collect it. It was a proposal for the play that Justin had told her about, the idea of his friend, Kenneth, based on the Ah Heng Cheh Affair. It was a collection of some loose sheets of paper, scrawled with Justin's signature green ink, and because one sheet bore her name, his mother must have decided that the collection was meant for her and had to be handed over, in compliance with the wishes of the dead. Kenneth had fled back to England immediately after the boy's suicide.

Yin Ling was on her way out when she heard footsteps behind her and turned to see Margaret hurrying towards her. She had clearly come out on impulse, for she stopped and fidgeted in embarrassment, having nothing to say. The lines of bitterness and sorrow were deep upon her face, highlighted by heavy makeup. Her eyes were red and at last she said, 'My son liked and admired you. He had nothing but good things to say of you. I'm sorry you didn't accept it,' meaning the diamond brooch sent back through Arasu.

Yin Ling said, 'Thank you,' and was glad when Margaret turned and walked away, for she had nothing more to say to her.

Ben said, 'Three painful visits in a row. Enough. I'm your manager. I say enough.'

The visit to Ah Heng Cheh, thankfully, was not painful. For

some reason, the family had not wanted to reveal to Yin Ling the resting place of the Old One's ashes, probably to punish her for the harm she had done, but it was not difficult to locate the place. They went together to the Buan Lok Thong Temple where Ah Heng Cheh used to worship, and easily found her urn among a dismal row on a high shelf.

'The dead don't hear, but we'll still say nice things, for the solace of the living,' said Yin Ling.

'I beg your pardon, but the dead do hear,' said Ben, and they engaged in a lively little debate about the capacities of the dead, before being reminded of the purpose of their visit and turning to Ah Heng Cheh, to recount the nice things they had all done together.

'She loved your hairy arms, Ben,' said Yin Ling, her eyes shining.

'She was the sharpest old lady I ever met,' said Ben.

'She once made me feel very guilty,' said Yin Ling. And she told Ben the incident of the prize-winning essay at twelve years old, when she had told the world that she loved her servant more than her mother.

Ben held her close, and spoke to Ah Heng Cheh, in her urn, up in the darkness of the endless rows of the quiet dead: 'All right, Ah Heng Cheh! It's too late now to agree to your red thread binding – remember? – but I promise you I'll make an honest woman of her!' There were two other visitors to the temple, but they pretended to ignore Ben, as he continued to talk to Ah Heng Cheh: 'We'll make your dream come true at last. And that's a promise too.'

They were going together, the following week, to the remote village in China, which they had managed to locate, to return her god to his home. He would have a brand-new silk robe for the important journey.

As it turned out, Ben could not make the journey – he had

been summoned to Idaho for some important matter connected with the new job. Yin Ling flew alone. She sent him a letter as soon as she had accomplished the mission and before she caught the plane for Singapore to meet up with him.

You would never believe it! A tiny village on a hillside, inaccessible by anything except a horse cart! I thought all the bones in my body would be shaken loose. I've also got a sore bum. If it had not been for the kindness of the villagers here, I would not have found the home of Ah Heng Cheh's god. A small temple, as Ah Heng Cheh had described to us, amazingly unchanged over all these years, down to the stone well and the red gate. And, would you believe it, Ben, I saw three other gods ensconced in their little niches there, that looked exactly like Ah Heng Cheh's god! I wonder what it all means. We'll never know. The more we probe a mystery, the more it eludes us, doesn't it? The important thing was that he was home at last, dressed in a handsome new gold robe that the others must have looked upon with envy – one wore only tattered paper. I'll tell you much, much more, when I get home. Maybe you're right after all, about the dead being able to hear. When I said goodbye to her little god, I thought I heard Ah Heng Cheh say something. She wasn't just thanking me; it was something far better. I've been feeling very happy about it since.

Dear, dear Ben. I love you so much. I'm looking forward so much to seeing you again. And do behave, when you meet me at the airport. There's enough scandal already – you don't want to shock more Singaporeans.
All my love,
Yin Ling

Part Five

One

oth Ben and Vincent had hurried to the airport as soon
as they heard the news. They met there, but pretended
not to notice each other.

The released passenger list confirmed and reinforced the
heartbreak of the announcement.

MR AND MRS A. Z. ALBERT

MR AND MRS T. ALBANS

MADAM HONG SIT ANG

MR THOMAS BALASINGAM

MR L. C. BEVA

MR AND MRS A. BOEY

MRS Y. T. CHAN

MISS CAROL CHAN

MISS MOLLY CHAN

MADAM L. T. CHANG

DR KANNAN CHANDRALIKA

MR K. C. DENG

MR TENG IUCK DONG

MR AND MRS PAUL ELIAS

DR K. ELIAS

MISS L. T. ELLIS

MR Y. Y. ENG

MISS C. L. ENG

MRS C. T. ENG

MR AND MRS ANDREW FANG

MR AND MRS Y. L. FANG

MADAM LIANE FALLIANI

MR MALCOLM FAULKNER

MR AND MRS SEE QUEK FOK

MISS J. FONG

MR AND MRS BENNY FUNG

MR AND MRS ALEXANDER GABBY

MADAM T. GAFFAR

MRS YIN LING GALLAGHER . . .

All Ben could think was, *She called herself Gallagher*.

Two

Two weeks after the disaster – the plane had simply exploded in mid-air, and the inquiry would take years – Ben went to 2-B Rochester Park.

'What do you want?' asked Vincent.

His friends said he had aged overnight. His mother said, 'I don't understand why. She was no longer part of the family.'

Vincent looked at Ben, with more weariness than resentment, and asked again, 'What do you want?'

'I don't know,' said Ben. There was a wild look in his eyes, and he pressed his hand against the side of his head. 'I don't know. Anything of hers. There must be lots. Personal effects. Books. Unfinished poems. Anything. She couldn't have taken away everything. I want them all,' he said belligerently. He looked shocking in his sorrow, and perhaps it was this that caused Vincent to relent a little.

'As far as I know, there's nothing left. Everything's been cleared. You can ask my mother, if you like. Or her mother or brother.'

Ben stood around a little longer, looking dazed but still dry-eyed and defiant. He looked around the room, as if it might surrender something of Yin Ling to him.

Vincent said, 'The boy does not know. He must not know. At least, not for a while.' He offered Ben a drink.

Ben said, 'No thanks, I'm going,' but still stood where he was, looking around. They stood facing each other, not wanting to look at each other, linked only by a common sorrow.

Vincent said again, 'Let me get you a drink.'

'I'm going,' said Ben, and started walking towards the door.

As he was closing the gate behind him, he heard a voice and turned round to see the boy, who had something in his hand, a large, rolled-up sheet of white paper. He came running up to Ben, his face flushed with the anticipation of sharing a secret. 'It's for Mummy,' he said. Xiang Min felt that a mild rebuke was in order, which he knew the man would convey to his mother, so he adjusted his features to look severe and said reproachfully, 'Mummy hasn't called.' But the secret was too good to be kept back for long – indeed, he was bursting with it – and it came tumbling out in a torrent of excitement. 'It's for Mummy! It's a surprise for Mummy! She said to draw it, and I said no, but now I've drawn it. I used all the crayons except two, but I wrote Mummy's name and Ah Heng Cheh's name with them.'

He unrolled the paper to reveal a picture, executed in dazzling colours, of a giant bird with outspread wings and a ladder by its side, winging its way through billowy white clouds in a bright blue sky. Xiang Min explained that the ladder was to enable Ah Heng Cheh, her god and Mummy to mount the great bird for it to carry them home, and he pointed proudly to the three figures perched securely, in a row, on the bird's back; Ah Heng Cheh with an enormous bun on her head and an umbrella in her hand, her god in a gold silk robe, and Mummy in a brightly coloured dress, waving and laughing.

Ben said, 'This is a great picture, Xiang Min. Your mother will be thrilled,' and the little boy, who had not smiled for weeks, began to skip beside Ben and laugh.

Then he said, seriously, 'It's to be a surprise. You must put it where Mummy can't find it, so that she finds it all of a sudden and says, "Hey, what's this?" ' He made Ben promise it would be a surprise.

The child was now ready to share confidences. He said something funny had happened in school, to Miss Ho, his teacher, and he had written a story about her, which he would tell his mummy when he next saw her. He also asked questions.

'Do you love my mummy a lot?' he said.

Vincent, peeping from behind the curtains of an upstairs window, heard his son's question and strained to hear the answer. He saw the tops of two heads, one greying, the other black and shiny, close together, as the man knelt and held the boy in a tight embrace. He heard a sob escape the man, while the boy, suddenly looking older than his five years, turned his head a little and pretended to concentrate on a solitary bird high in the sky and catch the last of its tremulous call across the vast blue void.

Epilogue

Ben Gallagher left Singapore in 1992, just a month after Yin Ling's death. He said that everything there reminded him of her. But he was back two years later, in 1994, for exactly the same reason: he wanted to revisit every place they had been together, including the Sai Haw Villa, now a huge condominium development called Paradiso 1 right up to Paradiso 5. He said little of what he had been doing in the two years, except that he had taken the job in Idaho, then left it to put together Yin Ling's poems as a book in her memory. He had published it himself, as American publishers saw little in those strange intense poems by an unknown Singapore woman to attract the American public.

Ben had never talked much about his family in the US; he had an aunt and two sisters, with their families, who had been supportive during the troubled times. He had told them little about his life in Singapore, so for years they talked in hushed, awed whispers among themselves about dear Ben's passion for a young married woman in Singapore who had died in a plane crash.

In an attempt to cope with his sorrow, which the years had done nothing to ease, Ben plunged into a frenetic journey of revisitation and remembrance. He went to the Monckton Food Park several times and also to the modest little hotel on Gim Choo Street where they had stayed during those turbulent weeks; it would be pulled down soon, as part of a massive urban renewal programme.

Ben stayed there for a few days and was pleasantly surprised that the *roti prata* man, at whose side-street stall he and Yin Ling had sometimes had breakfast, remembered them. 'Oh, sir, I'm so sorry,' he said, when Ben told him of the crash.

Vincent had heard of Ben's return and invited him over for a drink. He went, and was appalled that Vincent seemed interested only in the official investigation into the cause of the crash. Vincent said he had read that the families of the American victims had decided to set up their own independent investigation, and asked Ben whether he knew anything about it. He was clearly still high in the political firmament, but it appeared that he was losing some ground to a new protégé of the DPM, a brilliant Singaporean economist lured back from Harvard.

The DPM himself had had his own disappointments. He was still not Prime Minister as everyone had expected. MTC had gone into a period of deep mourning after the death of his beloved wife, then bounced back, as energetic as ever, to take control. He had succeeded finally in destroying V. S. Ponnusamy, who had vowed that he would take up his cause at the United Nations and who was last heard to be in quiet meditation in an ashram in India.

Ben had heard that Vincent had ended his liaison with Fiona Goh, and had started dating another woman, a lawyer, then broke up with her too. He could not have cared less about Vincent's affairs; neither was he bothered by an elderly woman, presumably Vincent's mother, who peeped at him from behind a screen for the entire duration of his visit.

'Where's Xiang Min?' said Ben, and was disappointed when Vincent told him that the boy, now seven, was spending the school vacation with cousins in London. Xiang Min was the only reason Ben had accepted the invitation to 2-B Rochester Park. Vincent showed him a recent picture of the boy: he had grown tall and strikingly handsome, and had his mother's large, pensive eyes. Vincent said proudly that he was in the gifted children's programme at school. It would be too much, thought Ben, to expect a little boy to keep his mother's memory active over two years, even though they had loved each other so much. In a year or two his recollections, including that of the traumatic day of meeting in the National Singapore Kindergarten, would have vanished.

'Did you know,' Vincent said, 'that Yin Ling's mother has passed away? In fact, just a month ago. The cancer was very painful at the end. I made arrangements for her to go into the Singapore Hospice, as she had requested.' Kwan was involved in some business in Indonesia and doing fairly well, by all accounts.

Ben walked out of 2-B Rochester Park, wishing he had never stepped into it.

Once he and Yin Ling had stood together joyfully before Ah Heng Cheh's ashes at the Buan Lok Thong Temple. Now he looked at the urn without any feeling. Ah Heng Cheh seemed to be in some distant void that made remembrance irrelevant.

Her god, though, remained alive and worth visiting, if only because he had promised to make the journey to China with Yin Ling. Sometimes in his dreams at night, Ben made the journey, sitting beside her in the plane, holding her close, pulling the blanket over her, reaching for her under it.

One afternoon, just before he had left for Singapore, he had walked into the woods near his ranch in Idaho and felled three trees, one after the other. He hacked and hacked with ferocious energy until he was exhausted and lay on the ground. Since the dead could hear, he looked up into the sky and shouted, 'It's not fair, you leaving me like this!' Then he fell asleep, and if the dead heard and chose to answer in dreams, whether during the day or night, he might have seen the loved face, and heard the loved voice once more. But he woke up having seen and heard nothing.

In late 1994, Ben Gallagher made arrangements to fly to China to visit Ah Heng Cheh's god in the temple where Yin Ling had placed him, hoping to see all the places she had mentioned in her letter which he carried in his wallet. He visited them all, saw with his own eyes, touched with his own hands all the objects she had seen and touched, including the rough, wooden altar that Ah Heng Cheh's god, still in his robe of gold, shared with several fellow gods. He remembered clearly that Yin Ling had altered the robe to make a better fit for the funny little god with the round belly, and had shown the completed garment to him proudly, holding it against her own chest and laughing. He stood for a long time looking at it, then fingering it lovingly, until an old man, presumably a keeper in the temple, came up and shook a disapproving forefinger at him.

In 1995, Ben Gallagher, still restless and unhappy, decided to visit the island closest to where the plane had crashed. Pulau Merbok, hardly inhabited, was accessible by boat from the small seaside village of Ikan Mas on the east coast of Malaysia. On the way, he decided to stop in Singapore to see Xiang Min, whose large pensive eyes brought an ache of recogniton and longing to his heart. To his surprise and delight, the boy remembered a great deal about his mother, and asked a lot of questions, wanting to know more.

Vincent looked happier. He was engaged to be married to a Miss Priscilla Hoon, an executive in a finance company, who had been introduced to him by a cousin of his mother. He actually appeared pleased to see Ben and even took him and Xiang Min out for dinner.

The first visit to Pulau Merbok was wrenching. Ben stood on the beach, gazed out to sea for a long time and wept. He made up his mind to return to the spot on each anniversary, determined to invest the tragedy with love. He would carry the sorrow in his heart for the rest of his life, but it would always be touched by the grace of hallowed and tender memory.

To his delight, in 1997 Xiang Min asked to be allowed to make the anniversary visit to Pulau Merbok with him. Vincent had reservations about safety and hygiene on a remote, barely habitable island, but the boy's eagerness bore down his resistance. And so Ben and Xiang Min went together, full of excitement and joy at being able, for the first time, to honour and cherish together the memory of one they had loved so much.

Vincent, relieved when his son returned safely, wanted to know all about the trip. 'Tell Mummy and me,' he said, with Priscilla by his side, for they had recently married.

Xiang Min gave a vivid description of the windswept, isolated island and of the boat ride to reach it, choosing, in the wisdom of his ten years, to omit any reference to the private ceremony that he and Ben had conducted together, especially that part when Ben had stood on the edge of the beach with Xiang Min pressed close to his side and shouted, into the roar of wind and water, the words of a poem Yin Ling had written.

Vincent said, biting his lip, 'Son, that was a dangerous journey to make. You said the waves hitting your boat were how high?' Then he wrote to Ben to tell him not to ask the boy to go on any more trips to Pulau Merbok. So in 1998 Ben went alone. On his way back to the States, he stopped in Singapore to see Xiang Min and tell him about the trip, aware that this visit, too, would be the last one allowed by Vincent and Priscilla.

'Please understand,' said Vincent in his letter, 'that there is no point in all this. The past is the past; let the boy grow up unburdened by it. My wife and I hope you will understand and no longer contact our son.'

Ben threw Vincent's letter away. He would grow old, not burdened by the past but comforted and strengthened by it.